CHAPTER THIRTEEN
A NOVEL

Maria A. Palace

This is a work of fiction. Names, characters, places, and incidents are products of the author's imagination or are used fictitiously and are not to be construed as real. Any resemblance to actual events, locations, organizations, or persons, living or dead, is entirely coincidental.

World Castle Publishing, LLC
Pensacola, Florida
Copyright © Maria A. Palace 2021
Paperback ISBN: 9781953271891
eBook ISBN: 9781953271907
First Edition World Castle Publishing, LLC, April 12, 2021
http://www.worldcastlepublishing.com
Licensing Notes
Cover: Karen Fuller
Editor: Maxine Bringenberg

For my mother, who has long since passed,
and still continues to inspire me.

"All that we are is a result of what we have thought."
Buddha

APRIL 13, 1936
MORGANVILLE, PENNSYLVANIA

In the darkest hours before the dawn, in the sleepy town of Morganville, the well-known Brewer mansion sits atop a wooded knoll illuminated in shimmering streaks of lightning. As the full moon orchestrates the gale with its spellbinding light, the mansion bows to an aura of incandescent flames. The heavens are quick to reciprocate with thunderous applause, enticing a torrential rain. The fire subsides, and the grand Victorian is spared, all but for the imprint smoldering in the heart of the parlor, from a torch whose flame can never be extinguished.

Chapter One
April 13, 1999
Ithaca, New York

A blanket of low-lying clouds rippled through the sky, and a steady drizzle overtook the streets. Katy sat in the passenger seat of her boyfriend's '84 Dodge with her head resting against the window, fixated on the raindrops pulsating against the glass.

Mark flipped his wipers on, creating a sediment-layered rainbow across the windshield, the chatter of split rubber blades ricocheting back and forth, propelling Katy deeper into a meditative state.

"I need new wipers," said Mark. "I can't remember the last time I replaced them." He glanced over at Katy. "Are you okay?"

Katy let out an exasperated sigh. "Sorry, I was just thinking about the rain. Why does it always have to rain on my birthday?"

"Well, for starters, you were born in April. And then there's the matter of the *day* that you were born...."

Katy watched him grin with those irresistible dimples indenting the centers of his cheeks and flashed him a playful smile before giving him a light whack on the shoulder.

"So how disappointed was your mom when you told her you couldn't make it home this weekend?"

"You know my mom. She said she had already made plans to throw me a big party, and now she has to scrap those plans—but not to worry, because she's going to throw me a big summer bash instead. Then she had to remind me, once again, how she wished I had picked a college closer to home. I guess that's the downside of being an only child—you tend to become the center of their universe. It's a good thing she has her photography and charity work to keep her busy. I explained that this was a hectic time for me. Our junior year at Ithaca State is almost over, and finals will be coming up soon. Which reminds me, when are you leaving for your student mission to South America again?"

"Not till the end of June."

Katy stopped to take a breath, then exhaled. "I'm going to miss you," she said, pinching his cheek, "and not just because of your boyish good looks."

"Don't worry, I'll only be gone for two months. Besides, you'll be busy with your internship at the *Ithaca Journal*."

"Hopefully, it'll turn into full-time after I graduate. Look out, Barbara Walters, there's a new girl in town, and her name is Katy Barton!"

Mark pulled into The Asylum parking lot and began combing the aisles, trying to find an empty space. The bar was a popular hang-out for the campus crowd and was always packed—especially on Thursdays because it was karaoke night.

He caught sight of someone leaving at the far end of the lot and sped up to claim the spot. Katy lifted the door handle to get out of the car when he suddenly grabbed her by the shoulder. "Wait! Before we go in, I want to give you your birthday present." He reached into his pocket and pulled out a small, blue velvet box and handed it up to her.

Katy hesitated for a moment, her sparkling blue eyes locked into his ardent gaze. Then slowly, she lifted the lid to find a golden locket in the shape of a heart. It was ornately engraved with flowering vines encapsulating two intertwined hearts. Her right palm quavered over her mouth. "Oh Mark, it's beautiful! It looks like an heirloom. Where on earth did you get it?"

"I found it in this little antique shop just outside of Morganville. The lady who sold it to me said it was real vintage Victorian, dating back to the late 1800s. Look inside!"

Katy carefully unlatched the locket and opened it up to find an inscription:

Forever In My Heart, MS.

"You had it engraved!"

Mark blushed. "Actually, no. It was already like that when I bought it. Can you believe it?"

"Can you help me put it on?" asked Katy, spinning around and lifting her strawberry blonde tresses. He clasped the pendant around her neck, after which she turned to give him a very long and heartfelt, "Thank you."

A good twenty minutes went by before Mark said, as he was tucking in his shirt, "We'd better get going. They're probably wondering what happened to us."

Katy pulled down her visor to check her reflection in the cracked makeup mirror and applied a fresh coat of red lipstick to her already crimson lips. Then she pulled her rain jacket up over her head, and the two of them made a mad dash toward the entrance of the bar.

When they walked through the door, they were immediately attacked by a blast of multi-colored lights synchronizing to the beat of loud music. Mark and Katy began to weave their way through the crowd trying to locate their friends when Katy's roommate spotted them beneath a floodlight of band-related posters.

"We've been waiting for you guys. What took you so long?" asked Laurie.

"Oh, you know...," swooned Katy, pulling out her pendant for her roommate to see. "Look what Mark gave me."

"Very nice," said Laurie, moving her glance over to Mark to give him a "Now I know what took you so long" look. "Follow me," she said, leading them to the table where the rest of their friends were waiting. Katy was removing her wet jacket to place it on the back of her chair when she was met by a waitress carrying a small, white frosted cake, topped with twenty-one brightly burning candles.

"Happy Birthday, Katy!" her friends shouted in harmony.

"Awe, thanks, you guys, you remembered."

"How could we forget your twenty-first birthday? You are now of official drinking age!" said Laurie. "Now make a wish and blow out the candles!"

Katy closed her eyes tightly, clutching the pendant around

her neck, and made a wish. Then she took a super deep breath and let out a long, lingering blow. She reopened her eyes to find that thirteen candles continued to burn unabashedly. She puffed at them a few more times, and still, they refused to die out. "What are these, trick candles?" she squealed. Mark walked over to help her, and together they were finally able to extinguish the flames.

As her friends clapped and cheered, the waitress came back with a round of tequila shots, which Laurie had previously ordered. "Can I see the birthday girl's ID?" asked the waitress.

Katy pulled her driver's license out of her purse and proudly handed it up for her to see. Then she leaned over with a smirk on her face and whispered into Laurie's ear, "Now, I can finally throw out that fake ID." The waitress pretended not to hear and walked away, leaving the group to clink their glasses together and simultaneously down their shots in a single gulp.

"What did you wish for?" asked Mark.

"I'll never tell, but I'm gonna put in a song request right now, and that will be your clue!" Katy jumped down from her highboy and ran toward the stage, where she handed the DJ a slip of paper. By the time she returned to the table, she was met with a second tequila shot, although the rest of the gang had switched to beer.

Mark looked at her with adoring eyes. "Cheers to you, babe! May all your dreams come true — and I hope they include me."

Katy slammed her empty shot glass against the table and immediately lifted it back up, waving it at the waitress who was at the next table taking orders. "Another shooter!" she barked. "After all, it *is* my birthday. Oh, and this time, follow it up with a Lite Beer chaser — a girl's gotta watch her figure, ya know!"

"Whoa, slow down, birthday girl," said Mark. "You need to be upright for your performance, remember? So what song did you pick?"

Katy hiccupped. "You'll see."

Laurie rolled her eyes. "I bet I know what it's going to be — she's only been singing it every night since school started."

"Shushshsh, don't tell," insisted Katy, holding her index

finger up to her nose.

"So, how are your classes going, Katy?" asked her friend, Candace. "I know you're majoring in journalism, but did you ever decide on a minor?"

"Yeah—psychology. I figured it might come in handy when I become a reporter. Like maybe it'll help me understand what motivates people to do the sh-t they do."

All of a sudden, the DJ called out, "Katy B., come on up!"

Like a current of electricity, Katy jumped out of her chair and raced up the steps toward the stage. She grabbed the mic out of the DJ's hand and clenched it between her two fists. "I'm dedicating this song to my boyfriend, Mark, sitting right over there," she announced, proudly pointing him out to the crowd. Mark casually slumped down in his seat in an effort to camouflage his embarrassment.

"I'm going to be singing '*I Will Always Love You*,' by Whitney Houston." Katy clutched the mic between her two fists and slowly raised it to her lips. She started out soft and low, then gradually raised her voice until it reached its maximum decibel.

"I'll always love youuuuuu. That's right, Mark—you!"

The 5'9" long-legged beauty illuminated the stage in her cropped T-shirt and jeans, belting out the lyrics with her emotions radiating through every pore of her body.

"She's fearless," commented Laurie. "I've never gotten up the nerve to sing in front of a crowd."

"Well, she *is* an Aries," Mark pointed out. "You know that's a fire sign."

"They also love to be the center of attention," added Candace. "Isn't that how you guys met?"

"Yeah, in our freshman year in high school. The school was hosting a fundraising event that included a talent show competition. I first noticed her when she got up on stage and sang that Blondie song. You know, the one that goes, 'One way, or another, I'm gonna find you and then I'm gonna get you.' Besides her looks, it was her confidence that drew me in. She didn't just sing it. She really got into it. After the show, I was intent on getting *her*, and so I started following her around."

"Looks like you followed her all the way to Ithaca State," interrupted his buddy, Drew.

Mark laughed, turning a little red, and took a slug of his beer before continuing with his story. "So while I was following her around, I started singing to her, 'You know I'm gonna get you.' All of a sudden, she spun around and looked me straight in the eyes with this fiery gaze that could've melted steel and threatened that if I didn't stop following her, I would live to regret it. That's when I said to her, 'I'll take my chances.' And the rest is history."

"Sounds like you're a glutton for punishment," snickered Drew.

As Katy was about to hit her final chord, an eruption of cheers and applause spewed from the crowd, culminating in a long, boisterous whistle from Mark. After a succession of bows, she ran back to the table and plopped back into her seat, exhausted from her emotionally charged performance. With a smile of satisfaction, she turned toward Mark and leaned over until she was an inch from his face. "Do you know why I love you so much? Because of how much you love me!"

Before he could say anything, she grabbed his chin and planted a big wet one on his lips, then jumped to her feet and held up her shot glass, screeching at the top of her lungs. "Cheeeeers to Mark! I want the whole world to know how much I love him!" She then proceeded to pound her third shot of tequila, chasing it down with a couple of slugs of Lite Beer.

It wasn't long before she was back up on stage singing to the tune of Prince's, "1999."

By the time she got back to her seat, people were slowly filtering out of the bar. She tried calling the waitress over for another beer. "I'm parched from all that singingingggg...," she sputtered.

That's when Laurie decided to intervene. "You are SOOO drunk. We gotta get you back to the dorm before lights out. Don't you have a class tomorrow?"

"Isss notttt tillll tennnnn."

Mark stood up from his chair. "I'll take her back to the

dorm. Do you need a ride?"

"No thanks, I'm gonna bum a ride with Candace and the others. We're going to stop at Taco Bell. Want us to bring you back anything?"

"No, thanks. I *do* have an early class tomorrow."

"Okay then," said Laurie, turning a crooked smile. "Make sure you get her all tucked in."

"Will do," said Mark, propping her arm up around his neck to lead her out of the bar. "Now, let's get you home, Katy."

"Buuutt, I donn wanna go home. I wanna party like it's 1999!" she stammered.

"You've done enough partying for 1999."

They stepped outside into the misty darkness, and Mark lifted his face, relieved that the rain had let up because it was probably going to be a long walk across the parking lot.

When they got to the car, he opened the door and was helping Katy ease into her seat when she blurted out, "Waaaaait, where's my purse? I furrrrgot my purse!"

"Don't worry, I've got it right here in my left hand," he reassured her, lifting it up for her to see.

He drove her back to the college dorm, holding her upright while he led her up the steps and through the hallway. No sooner did they walk into her room than Katy plopped down on the bed, landing on her stomach with a beam of contentment plastered across her face. He pulled the covers up over her, then gave her a gentle kiss on the forehead and whispered in her ear, "And I, I will always love you, Katy Barton."

~*~

At the crack of dawn, the shrill echo of the telephone hearkened Katy out of a deep comatose sleep. Her half-open lids wandered across the room to the bunk where her roommate Laurie lay, seemingly unfazed by the unnerving sound. Then she twisted her neck toward the nightstand to observe the glowing digits on her alarm clock. *Who the hell is calling me this early in the morning?* Still reeling from a hangover, she yanked her pillow up over her head and tried to diffuse the sound, but the phone kept ringing. There was only one way to make it stop. She rolled over onto her side to answer it, holding the receiver in one hand and cupping the side of her throbbing head with the other. With her lips pressed against the mouthpiece, she stumbled out a faint, "Hello, who is this?"

"It's your father," said the voice on the other end. His speech was low and cracking and almost indiscernible. "I don't know how to break this to you, Katy Bear." He hadn't called her that in years. "Your mother has passed away."

CHAPTER TWO

Staring out from the tinted window in the back seat, the funeral procession looked like a black and white photograph where all the color had been stripped. Katy felt as though she were drowning in a sea of grey, unable to come to grips with her mother's death. "How could Mom just die of a heart attack? She was so happy and full of energy."

Harold Barton stood tall and resolute while helping her out of the black sedan. "We can never know why these things happen, so we convince ourselves that there is a greater cause that is not under our control."

Katy knew the depth of her father's love for her mother and that stone façade could crumble at any moment, so his words did little to reassure her.

Her knees weak and trembling, Mr. Barton took his daughter's arm and led her into The Good Shepherd Episcopal Church. The pews were overflowing from the huge outpouring of mourners who showed up for the funeral. Harold and Marilyn Barton were well known for their outstanding contributions to the town of Morganville. He was a financially successful banker, and his wife donated much of her time doing charity work.

The Reverend David Sykes presided. His eulogy prevailed upon the fact that "Marilyn Adele Barton lived each day to its fullest. She appreciated beauty in all its forms and saw in others what they didn't see in themselves. She was a woman whose zest for life and loving spirit spread to everyone she knew. She was loved by many, and many will miss her as their own."

He could not have said it any better. That's exactly who she was, thought Katy. She sat there, fixated upon her mother's casket at the base of the altar, while her dark eyeliner bled until it formed a thick sable ring around her bloodshot eyes. The reverend directed everyone to stand in prayer. She dabbed her eyes and nose with her disintegrating tissue and pulled herself up, holding onto the pew in front of her. Just as she raised her head to pray out loud, she was overcome with an overwhelming sensation, like a repressed dream. It felt as though she had stood in this very spot before, grieving her mother's death. It lasted through the entirety of the prayer and didn't subside until everyone had reseated themselves and her father was tugging at her coat for her to sit back down.

After the funeral, everyone returned to the Barton home for the wake, including Reverend Sykes. One after another, people she knew and people she didn't know stopped to pay their respects and offer their condolences. "If there is anything we can do, please don't hesitate to call us," offered longtime-friends Blake and Johanna Lankershim, who lived down the street from the Bartons. Another lady put her arms around Katy and tried to console her. "Your mom lived her life on earth as an angel, and now she'll be watching over you from Heaven."

She couldn't hold it together any longer. She slipped out of the living room to hide out in her old bedroom. As soon as the door shut behind her, she fell face-first onto her satiny pink bedspread, knocking several of her stuffed animals onto the floor. Her favorite one, Fluffy, with its cock-eyed whiskers and yellow eyes, was still wedged between two pillows. She had named it after her own cat that had died. She pulled Fluffy free and squeezed him as hard as she could, then burst into a cascade of tears. Her lacey pillow sham had become completely saturated when she sat up and wiped her eyes. Katy moved to the edge of the bed to survey the room and reminisce about her happy childhood when she stopped to pick up the framed photograph sitting on her nightstand. It was a picture of her and her mom sitting on the dock at Twin Lakes.

Her mom loved to take pictures and carried her prized 35-millimeter camera with her almost everywhere she went. She would constantly remind Katy to be aware of the natural beauty surrounding her. Whenever something caught her mom's eye, she would pull out her camera to snap a photo, be it a magnificent sunset, a shadowy lake before a storm, or a tiny chipmunk nibbling on an acorn. "You must preserve the moment, so you can bask in its glory forever," she would say.

"But what if you miss your chance?" Katy once asked her. "What if the rainbow disappears before you get a chance to take a picture of it?"

"Then it will be lost; not forever, mind you, but it may take a long time before another opportunity comes along."

Mr. Barton spent most of his time behind a desk, but when he could, he would break away to the peaceful serenity of the lake where fishing became his steady source of mental distraction. Katy's mom loved to go too, especially in the fall, when she could "capture" the full beauty of the season. On that particular day the picture was taken, Katy's dad hadn't caught anything worth keeping and was tying his small fishing boat up to the dock.

"Oh, please take our picture from there!" begged his wife, Marilyn. "The trees have reached their maximum peak of color and will provide such a lovely backdrop. We must seize the moment!" she insisted, walking over to hand her husband the camera.

"You know I'm not adept at using this thing," he reminded her.

"Don't worry, I've already set the aperture for you. All you have to do is point and shoot."

"The lovely backdrop has nothing over the two beautiful ladies adorning the dock," he stalled as he fumbled with the camera, trying to get the picture just right. "Okay now, smile."

Katy sat on the edge of her bed, clutching the photo in one hand while gently running her fingers over her mom's image with her other when she was startled by a few quick knocks on the door. She set the frame back down on the nightstand, wiped the tears from her cheeks, and cleared her throat before exerting a muted, "Come in."

The door opened ever so slowly to reveal her boyfriend Mark standing there. "I thought I might find you here," he said, walking over to sit down next to her on the bed.

"I just needed to be by myself for awhile."

"I know," he said, comforting her with a lingering embrace. He noticed the picture lying flat on the nightstand and leaned over to pick it up. "That's a nice picture of you and your mom. You both look so happy."

"We were," said Katy, breaking into tears again. "I'm going to miss her so much. How can I go back to school? I'll never be able to concentrate on my studies, and finals are coming up. I don't know how I'll be able to handle it."

Mark grabbed her by the shoulders and looked directly into her eyes. "I know you, Katy—you can do anything you put your mind to. Your inner strength is what makes you a survivor."

Katy looked down and shook her head back and forth. "I don't know, Mark."

"You just need to take some time off. I'm sure your professors will understand, and I'll be there by your side to help you through it." He raised her chin with his two fingers. "You know your mother would not want you to give up."

Katy took a deep breath. "You're right."

~*~

Two weeks had passed, and Mr. Barton was loading up the car to bring Katy back to school. "Are you sure you're ready to go back?"

"I'm sure, Dad. Maybe it will help get her off my mind—not that I want to get her out of my mind."

"I know, honey, I know," said her father, stopping to give her a hug.

"I'll be right back," said Katy.

She wanted to take one last stroll along the perimeter of the stately colonial-style home she'd grown up in. The white picket fence stretching along the expansive property set it apart from the other homes in this affluent yet more rural part of town. As her eyes focused on the majestic oak commanding the front yard, her mind took her back to the time when she was around the age of six. She was playing hide-and-seek with her mother and was hiding behind the massive tree. When her mother found her, she picked her up and swung her around, only to lay her back down on the thick green grass and tickle her until she begged for mercy.

Katy stood there with a dazed smile on her face, recapturing the moment, until she was interrupted by the sound of her father's voice calling, "Come on, Kate, we have to get going if we're going to beat the traffic."

CHAPTER THREE

Katy didn't return home after finals. Instead, she continued taking classes throughout the summer semester. She found that the harder she worked, the easier it was to suppress her grief.

When Mark returned from South America, he and Katy rented a small apartment off campus. Before they knew it, Thanksgiving was just around the corner, and Katy finally felt that she was emotionally ready to go home. "I haven't seen my father since he drove me back to school after the funeral. Besides, I'm ready for a break. I can't believe I have a psych class tomorrow—the day before Thanksgiving!"

"Traffic will be terrible on Wednesday, and it's going to take about five and a half hours to get there, so we should probably leave later in the evening," suggested Mark.

After class on Wednesday, Katy finished packing her things, and by ten that night, they decided they had better hit the road. She did a quick once-over at the open suitcase on her bed, then popped the lid down and zipped it shut. Mark was already packed and loaded, so she locked the door behind her and lugged her bag down the iron steps from their second-story apartment. As she rolled her suitcase through the dimly lit parking lot, she could see Mark shining his flashlight underneath the hood of his car.

"What's wrong?" she yelled out.

"I think I might have an oil leak. I should probably get it checked when we get back," he yelled back, slamming the hood down. Katy climbed into the passenger's seat while Mark grabbed her luggage and walked over to the rear of the car, where he lifted the hatchback and threw it in. When he sat down in the driver's seat, she was still fiddling with her seat buckle.

"You also need new seatbelts," she pronounced forcefully.

"I know, I know," answered Mark, inserting the key into the ignition. "What I *need* is a new car, but this one's going to have to do — at least until graduation."

"Wait a minute," shouted Katy. "I forgot my purse!"

"Not again," grumbled Mark, shifting the car back into park.

In a huff, she tugged at her belt until it unlatched, then ran back up the stairs to the apartment. She opened the door and surveyed the room until she spotted it sitting on the chair next to her desk, on top of her textbook, *Modern Psychology*. She grabbed it by the strap and barreled back down the staircase.

"That was a close one — I can't forget my pills!" exclaimed Katy, throwing the handbag over the folded-down seat behind her. Once again, she made the attempt to buckle her seatbelt. When they had reached the main road, she was still fidgeting with it. "Oh my God!" she fumed, trying to force it into the slot. "What's wrong with this thing?"

"Relax, Katy, it can't be that hard," said Mark, starting to get annoyed.

A few more minutes passed when Katy finally let out an exasperated breath, "Okay...(click). I got it!"

When they were well on their way, she tried to relax, but all she could think about was walking through the door of her girlhood home and not having her mother there to greet her. Even though she was looking forward to seeing her father, it was sure to be bittersweet. "Thanksgiving won't be the same without my mother," she lamented. "But I need to be there for my dad. I'm going to make the whole dinner myself. I've got it all planned out."

"Hey, you know I can help. I can make some mean mashed potatoes," Mark burst in, trying to lighten the mood.

Katy yawned. "I'm so tired. I had that dumb psychology class today. The instructor is so boring, I practically fell asleep during his lecture." She rested her head against the passenger window with her fingers twisting the heart on the locket around her neck back and forth until she eventually dozed off.

Katy had been asleep for several hours when the sound of heavy rain pounding against the windshield awakened her. Her eyes opened up about halfway. "How long has it been raining?" she asked groggily.

"For over an hour now, but don't worry, we're almost there. We're going to take a shortcut. I know a back road that will save us at least half an hour," said Mark, abruptly turning the wheel to make a sharp right onto a muddy, crater-laden road.

Katy's eyes were fully open now and fixated on the windshield wipers cantankerously jetting back and forth at max speed. "Aren't you going a little fast?" she said nervously.

Mark patted her on the knee. "Don't worry, you know I grew up around here. I know this area like the back of my hand."

"Well, since we're almost there, I'm going to get my purse out of the back and put it up front with me. I want to make sure I don't leave it in the car when we get to the house."

She undid her seatbelt and leaned over the back of her seat, extending her arms out to grab her purse, then turned back around and set it on her lap. "There!" she announced, yanking at the seatbelt multiple times to try and refasten it around her waist. "Why is this so difficult?" she wailed, concentrating on the buckle in her lap. "I can never get it to stay in the groove."

Mark turned his head and looked down at her belt to see if there was anything he could do to help. When he glanced back up at his front windshield, he let out a screeching, "Oh Shi.i.i.i.i.i.i...!" swerving the steering wheel sharply to the left. In a matter of seconds, the car went careening off the road with the driver's side of the vehicle violently sideswiping a row of trees, until it struck a huge protruding elm almost head-on, causing it to come to a final rest. Katy hadn't even had time to look up when her head flew forward, smashing into the dashboard.

~*~

Early the next morning, she regained consciousness, only to find herself lying in a hospital bed with a bandage around her forehead. Her father, looking very weary, was seated at her side. "What happened?" she mumbled, still in a daze.

"You were in a bad accident, sweetheart."

With a look of confusion, she stared down at the white sheet covering her body, trying to conceptualize what her father just told her.

"Do you remember any of it?" he asked.

Her memory remained foggy as she tried her hardest to recall the events that took place. "All I remember is Mark deciding to take a shortcut home. We were driving down a dark road, and it started to rain really hard...." Katy stopped mid-sentence. "Where is he? Where is Mark?"

There was a moment of silence. Her father lowered his voice, and in a somber tone, he uttered, "I'm sorry, Katy Bear. Mark didn't make it."

"What do you mean, he didn't make it? No, no, that can't be!" she screamed, trying to get up from her bed.

Her father grabbed her arms to hold her down. "The man who saved you told the hospital attendant that he wasn't able to pull the driver out of the car before it went up in flames."

"Flames, what flames? Who is this person? I want to talk to him!" she demanded.

"I don't know," replied her father. "He dropped you off in the hospital emergency around three in the morning, telling the attendants you were in a car accident and advised them to call the police. The check-in nurse said she ran out to the parking lot to get more information from him, but he was nowhere to be seen. He had just disappeared."

"Maybe we'll be able to find him," insisted Katy. "*Someone* in the hospital must remember what he looked like!"

"They described him to be in his mid-to-late twenties, maybe early thirties, but they didn't get a good look at him because the cowboy hat he was wearing was partially covering his eyes."

Katy stared at her father blankly, her eye sockets like white tea cups that had been emptied of hope.

"Thank goodness he had the foresight to bring your purse, so the hospital staff was able to identify you. I came to the hospital as soon as they called me."

Katy buried her face deep in the palms of her hands and broke down weeping, then slid her fingers down around her neck. "My locket!" she yelled, "Where's my necklace?"

"It's okay, Katy," reassured her father. "The nurse told me she removed it when they were examining you. She put it safely away in your purse."

Katy fell back against the bed, stunned and silent, trying to assimilate all that had happened.

A short time afterward, the doctor came into the room and asked Mr. Barton to step outside in the waiting room while he examined Katy. The doctor expressed his deepest sympathy for the loss of her boyfriend but told her she was lucky to be alive. "Thanks to the actions of a good Samaritan."

"You'll need to stay an extra day for observation because you suffered a pretty bad concussion. Other than a few stitches on your forehead, which will probably leave a scar, you'll be all right," he explained. "And rest assured, your baby will be perfectly fine too."

CHAPTER FOUR
AUGUST 13, 2005
MORGANVILLE, PENNSYLVANIA

What am I doing here, in this cave, this tunnel? The smoke is so thick I can't breathe. I have to start running. It's so dark, I can barely see. I'm stumbling. It's so hot. Flames are erupting all around me. I have to get out of here, but how? It seems never-ending. Wait, off in the distance, I see a light. Maybe that will lead me to safety! Keep running, keep running, you'll get there. The light is growing bigger, wider. It's so bright now, I have to shield my eyes. Hang in there, Katy. You're almost there. Wait, stop! What's this?

Katy lunged forward in her bed, coughing, choking, and covered in sweat, as if she had run a marathon. She crossed her arms tightly around her waist as she tried to catch her breath. Her sheet and blanket were on the floor, twisted in a knot at the edge of her bed. Her eyes turned toward her nightstand where her locket lay resting in front of her alarm clock, its glowing digits reflecting in her pupils: 2:38 a.m. She'd been having this recurring nightmare ever since Mark passed away.

She tried to fall back asleep, but after several hours of tossing and turning, she figured she might as well get up. Luckily, it was Saturday, and she didn't have to go into work. She took a hot shower, got dressed, then went into the kitchen to make a pot of coffee. While waiting for her coffee to brew, she separated the sheer white panels hanging over the kitchen window and observed the sun making a feeble attempt to show its face. After a few cups of coffee, her mind and body were revitalized, so she decided to take advantage of the morning by taking a leisurely stroll through Longley Park.

By the time she arrived at the park, the sky had resumed its overcast outlook. The weatherman had predicted rain, but not until later that afternoon. She was hoping he was right — she hated the rain.

She hadn't been back to Longley Park since high school. In the summer, the park was cloaked in green, brimming with a wide assortment of trees, but it wouldn't be long before the autumn winds scattered the dried foliage, transforming it into a sea of brown. Walking along the perimeter of the man-made pond brought back a wave of memories. She remembered spending many a weekend there with her mother when she was a child. Even though there were signs posted all around the lake prohibiting the feeding of the ducks, her mother had always brought along a small bag of stale bread crumbs to toss to them.

As Katy meandered along the asphalt path, she spotted her favorite tree just up ahead, an enormous willow that had been around long before the park ever was. She started to make her way toward it, but before crossing the path, she took a quick glance to her right and noticed a woman in grey sweats fast approaching. She stopped at the edge of the trail to make room for the jogger to pass. As the young woman with thick black hair tied in a scrunchy ran by, Katy did a second take. She'd recognize those dark freckles over that pale complexion anywhere.

"Janice?" she yelled out.

The jogger stopped abruptly and turned around. "Oh my God, Katy! Is that really you? Imagine running into you here, at Longley Park!"

"Hi, Janice! How've you been?"

"Oh, you know, same ol', same ol,'" Janice answered flippantly.

"And what does that mean?"

"It means I'm still single and, you know, still dating the same ol' shmucks."

Katy laughed. "Yeah, you never were very good at pickin' em'."

"Um, the problem is I allow them to pick me," retorted Janice.

"So are you working?" continued Katy.

"I'm working for the Department of Transportation—been there for seven years now. I feel like I run the joint!" Janice pulled out a business card from her pants pocket. "Here's my card," she said, handing it to Katy.

"You happen to have a card on you?"

"Hey, you never know who you might run into jogging, you know what I mean? Look, I ran into you, didn't I? But enough about me, what about you? It's been so long! I haven't seen you since the funeral. What are you doing here, visiting?"

"I live here now," responded Katy. "I moved back in the early spring. I can't believe how much it's changed. It's not the small town it used to be."

"Yeah, they're extending the freeway. Morganville will no longer be a speck on the map. So what made you decide to come back to your hometown?"

"Well, after I got my degree, I worked at the local newspaper in Ithaca for a while, then I landed this job here, working for PTTV out of Pittsburgh, as a reporter for the *Morganville News*."

"Wait a minute—you gave up a job in New York to come back here?"

"I was just writing for the local newspaper there. My goal was to land a job at a news station. When my dad told me there was an opening at PTTV, I jumped at the chance. I know Morganville isn't much, but after everything that happened…. It was like something was calling me back here. I don't know. Maybe I'm just trying to find myself again."

"That's great, but why haven't you called? We used to be best friends! I haven't lived at home for a while, but my parents could've gotten a hold of me."

"Well, we're still getting settled. We just moved into a townhouse on 21st Street, so I wouldn't be too far from the city."

"Wait, *we*?" asked Janice, with eyebrows raised.

Katy gave a yell out to a little girl off in the distance, who was busy chasing ducks by the pond. "Be careful, Lilly, don't get too close to the water. Come here. I want you to meet someone!"

For a moment, Janice looked confused, then let out a gasp,

"Oh my God — you have a daughter!"

"Yes," said Katy, with a hint of melancholy. "She's Mark's."

"I had no idea!"

"Well, it came as a bit of a shock to me too," admitted Katy. "I didn't learn about it until after the accident."

"So, how did you do it? Janice asked, immediately getting red in the face and rephrasing the question. "I mean, how did you manage to finish school with a baby and all?"

"I have to admit, it wasn't easy, but I did what I had to do. Of course, I couldn't have done it without the help of my wonderful father. That's another reason why I chose to come back. I missed him dearly, and I wanted his granddaughter to be closer to him."

"If you don't mind my asking, how were you able to deal with it emotionally? I mean, coping with the loss of your mother, and then Mark?"

"Well, let's just say I had a hefty dose of therapy," confessed Katy. "It's an ongoing process. I still have trouble sleeping due to recurring nightmares. My therapist in New York gave me a referral to see someone here in town, but I've been putting it off." Katy cut her conversation short when Lilly ran up to her, wrapping her arms around her mother's leg. "This is Lilly," she said proudly.

Janice looked down at the beautiful, golden-haired little girl. She truly was the spitting image of her mother. "Well, hello, Lilly. My name is Janice."

"Say hello, Lilly," instructed her mother. "Janice is a very old friend of mine. We have known each other since middle school."

"Hello," Lilly responded shyly.

"You're so big!" remarked Janice.

Lilly, who could never contain her shyness for more than a minute, suddenly perked up. "I'm five years old."

"She's tall for her age," Katy broke in. "Takes after her dad."

"Um, you're not exactly short either," Janice replied

sarcastically.

"I'm starting kindergarten on Monday."

Janice looked over at Katy. "Where are you sending her?"

"I've got her enrolled at the Morganville Christian Academy. They have an all-day kindergarten program there. Besides, that's where I went to school."

Janice turned to Lilly again. "Oh, you're going to *love* kindergarten!" she emphasized loudly. Just then, she felt a raindrop on her arm and looked up at the slate-colored clouds moving in. "Oh-oh, it looks like it's about to rain, and I promised my folks I would stop in for a mid-morning breakfast. Sorry, but I have to get going." Janice stooped down to shake Lilly's hand. "It was very nice meeting you, Lilly." Just as she started to jog away, she turned back around and yelled, "And let's get together real soon, Katy—I mean it!"

"I'll call you," Katy shouted back, pulling Janice's card out from her pocket and waving it up in the air.

"Oh, and good luck with the new job!" hollered Janice as she sprinted off.

It started to sprinkle harder, so Katy pulled the hood of Lilly's powder-blue rain jacket up over her head. "We'd better get going too," she said, grabbing her daughter by the hand. "But first, I want to show you something."

Lilly did her best to keep up with her mom, following her across the path toward the great weeping willow. Just before they reached the enormous tree, Lilly let go of her mother's hand and darted to go stand underneath it. She leaned her back up against it with her arms curved up over her head and yelled, "Look, Mommy, it's a giant umbrella!"

Katy ran over to join her. "This is a very special tree," she told her daughter.

"Why?" asked Lilly.

"Look!" Katy lifted her up and pointed to some initials carved into its asperous trunk. "It says, KB ♡ MS."

"What does that mean?"

Katy's eyes teared up, and her voice cracked. "It means Katy Barton loves Mark Stevens—that was your father."

Lilly, who was still in her arms facing the tree, twisted her waist around to pull the heart-shaped pendant out from her mother's shirt collar. "Is that who gave you this heart necklace?"

"Yes it is, baby, yes it is."

Lilly took her small hand and wiped a tear from her mother's cheek, then hugged her neck.

Katy ran her fingers over the blackened letters. "We carved our initials in this tree when we were in high school."

"Are they going to be there forever, Mommy?"

"Yes, baby, forever and ever."

CHAPTER FIVE

Katy climbed into bed, hoping for a reprieve from her nightly torment, only to be hearkened once more by the glaring digits on her nightstand boring a hole through the pitch blackness of the night. She scooted herself out of bed and picked the blanket up off the floor, then staggered over to the kitchen. She poured herself a drink from the faucet and stared out the window into the shadowy darkness. *Where are all the stars tonight? Mother used to say that stars are the symbol of hope, the light that can help us find our way in times of darkness. Where are they when you need them?* She set her empty glass in the sink and made her way back to her bedroom. Then she slipped back into bed, praying for just a little more rest before having to get up for work.

She barely had time to fall back asleep before she was rocked awake by her radio alarm, with Celine Dion blasting "My Heart Will Go On." Katy lay there, numb from hopelessness, absorbing each and every word. *I don't know if my heart can go on without you, Mark.*

Her eyes were welled up with tears when her daughter came running into her room and jumped up on her bed. "Wake up, Mommy. I have to go to school today, remember?"

"Oh, yeah, I guess it's Monday," Katy muttered, wiping the pools from her eyes.

"Why are you crying? Don't you like this song?"

"No, honey, I love this song," she sniffled, twisting around to hit the *off* button on the radio.

"Then why are you crying?"

Katy sat up and tried to pull herself together for her daughter's sake. "I'm crying because today is your first full day of school, and I'm thinking about how much I'm going to miss you!"

"Don't worry, Mommy, I won't be gone *all* the day. Besides, you'll have work to keep you busy."

"You're right, honey. You are so mature for your age!" Katy lifted herself out of bed. "Now, let's get you ready for school."

While Lilly was at the kitchen table eating her cereal, Katy made herself an extra-strong pot of coffee. She always brewed a full carafe so she could have a cup before she left the house and enough to fill her thermos to take with her in the car.

The sun was smiling brightly on this special morning, amplifying Lilly's excitement. Katy parked her car in the school parking lot and took her skipping daughter by the hand to walk her to her classroom. As they wandered through the school building looking for Room 15A, Katy noticed they were being shadowed by another woman and young girl. Katy turned to ask which room they were looking for, and it happened to be 15A. The woman was tall and attractive, with short auburn hair, and her little girl looked like she could easily have been a contestant in a child beauty pageant. The perfectly placed pink bow in her hair served only to highlight her frilly dress and matching anklets.

Katy removed her sunglasses and stretched out her hand. "Hi, I'm Katy, and this is my daughter, Lilly. Sorry about the dark circles—I didn't get much sleep last night."

"Burning the midnight oil?" asked the young woman.

"Um, you could say that."

"You know, you look really familiar. Have we met before?"

"I don't think so, but you may have seen me on TV."

"Of course—Katy, Katy Barton. You're that news reporter from PTTV! Nice to meet you. I'm Sue Blakeford, and this is my daughter, Meghan."

Meghan started out a little bashful, partly hiding behind her mother. Lilly, on the other hand, had already emerged from her cocoon and broken away from her mother's grip. "I like your hair," she said, stroking Megan's long, sable tresses.

"Thanks," said Meghan. "I like yours too."

Lilly grabbed Meghan's hand. "Come on," she said, leading her new friend down the hall, skipping in unison.

"She's so friendly," remarked Sue.

"I don't know who she takes after," laughed Katy, knowing full well she had behaved the exact same way at her age.

When the two moms arrived at Room 15A, they motioned for their girls to come back from the far end of the corridor. Just inside the doorway stood a grey-haired woman, with wire-rimmed glasses hanging from a chain around her neck.

"I'm Mrs. Randolph, the kindergarten teacher. And who are these two lovely young ladies?" Katy and Sue introduced themselves and their daughters. "Well, you two are off to a good start," expressed Mrs. Randolph, observing the little girls giggling, hand-in-hand. She then pointed to the tiny desks in the classroom, situated in rows of two. "Now, why don't you two go find a desk and sit down?"

After a set of tearful goodbyes from their moms, the girls wasted no time running in and picking out two seats right next to each other in the middle of the room. "Love, you!" a teary eyed Katy called out one more time. "Sorry," she told Sue. "I'm even more emotional than usual when I don't get enough sleep."

The two moms hit it off as well as their girls, and they continued their conversation well into the parking lot. Sue handed Katy her business card. "I work part-time at the Reeves Art Gallery downtown, but I can pretty much make my own hours. Give me a call, and maybe we can set up a play date for later on this week."

Katy got into her car and gulped the last drop of coffee from her thermos before making the thirty-minute drive to the news station. As soon as she arrived, she headed straight for the break room to get herself one more cup of coffee before settling down at her desk. On her way, she spotted her coworkers, Vicky and Jack, at the far end of the hallway. Jack had been co-anchoring the early evening news for several years now, and Vicky had started working for PTTV as a reporter for the Morganville Division a year before Katy. When Katy hired on, Vicky was sent to assist her counterpart in Pittsburgh, while Katy took over for Morganville.

The two of them were standing face-to-face just outside the copy room. Vicky, petite and pretty with her streaked, platinum, pixie-cut, was leaning with her back against the wall; and Jack, with his conspicuously bleached, thickly moussed blond hair, had his right arm stretched over her head with his palm pressed against the partition. As Katy got closer, she could hear Vicky putting on that louder-than-necessary, phony laughter for Jack, who had that usual pompous grin plastered on his face. Lucky for Katy, the break room was halfway from where they were standing, so she was able to duck in there quickly without being noticed.

There wasn't much coffee left, but just enough to get her through lunch. She poured the dark, gritty liquid into her cup, then propped herself up against the counter, taking slow, deliberate sips in the hope that Jack and Vicky would be gone by the time she had finished it. Unable to choke down that final drop, she dumped it into the sink and took a quick peek around the corner to make sure the coast was clear. *Yes! They're gone!*

She barely had time to settle down in her chair and turn on her computer before her boss and managing editor, Mr. Bruckman, stopped in front of her cubicle. His sleeves were rolled up as usual, as if he were buried in paperwork and had to swim out. "You don't look so great," he was quick to remark.

She wanted to come back with, *You don't look so great yourself.* He looked much older than his fifty years. His hairline was receding, he was at least thirty pounds overweight, and he had a croupy cough that would come and go. She'd caught him smoking cigarettes in the parking lot out near the garbage bins on more than one occasion, even though he insisted he had quit. Word had it he had been divorced for some time, which wasn't hard to fathom because he always looked like he was in need of a shave and wore the same unpressed beige shirt every day. Underneath that rough exterior, though, Katy saw him as the big old teddy bear that he was and considered him more of a father figure than a boss.

"Did you party a little too much over the weekend?" he asked.

"No, it's not that. I haven't been sleeping very well lately."

"Why don't you go see a doctor? Maybe he can prescribe you some sleeping pills."

"That's a good idea," responded Katy, not wanting to mention she had been seeing a therapist for years and had already tried that.

"By the way, how are you coming with that story on the local animal shelter?"

"I'm scheduled to interview Vera Gibbons, who runs the shelter, tomorrow morning."

"Good, good. I need to have it for tomorrow's early evening news. Can you get it on my desk by noon?"

"No problem," said Katy. *Provided I can get up in time.*

Chapter Six

There they were again—those illuminated numbers, 2:38 a.m., flashing deep into Katy's retinas. *I can't keep living like this,* she mumbled, wiping the beads of moisture from her brow. At six, she was startled awake once more, only this time by an obnoxious auto loan commercial blasting from her radio alarm. As she rolled over to hit the OFF button, she willed herself up and began digging through her nightstand. There it was, resting in its rightful place—underneath the small photo album containing pictures of her and Mark. It was the referral card she had gotten from Dr. Mittinger, her former therapist in New York. She looked at the name on the card.

Brian Fleming, PsyaD, L.P., CCHT

It was too early to call for an appointment, so she stuffed the card into her purse, figuring she'd do it when she got to the office.

After boiling her usual full pot of coffee, she realized she was running late again, so she hurried over to Lilly's bedroom and rolled her daughter's shoulder from side to side. "Wake up, sleepyhead," she said, with as much enthusiasm as she could muster.

Lilly turned over and let out a big yawn.

"Time to get ready for school, baby."

"Can I have pancakes for breakfast, Mommy?"

"I'm sorry, honey, I have a morning interview I need to get to. You're going to have to have cereal again. How 'bout I make pancakes for you this weekend?"

"Promise?"

"Promise. Now go brush your teeth. We're running late."

"Yay," yelled Lilly, jumping out of bed.

Katy smiled languidly as she watched her daughter race to the bathroom, thinking of how lucky she was to have such an agreeable child.

She dropped her daughter off at school just as the final bell rang, then drove directly to the Morganville Animal Shelter. By the time she got there, her cameraman was already there unloading his van. She pulled up into the empty spot right next to his and got out of her car. "Good morning, Dan."

"Morning. You look like hell."

"Well, that's a fine 'how-do-you-do,'" pounced back Katy. "Do I really look that bad?"

"Let's just say you might want to touch up those puffy, dark circles under your eyes before you get in front of the camera."

Katy gave him a dirty look, then pulled out the small compact mirror from her strappy purse hanging around her neck. She took a close look at herself, breathing out a low-pitched, "Ugh!"

"I can lighten up the image a little, but I can't perform miracles," smirked Dan.

"Okay, okay, do what you have to do. But in the meantime, I have to go in and prep Ms. Gibbons."

Before entering the one-story cinder-block building, she could already hear the echoes of thundering barks reverberating from the inside. When she pulled open the door to the front office, it triggered a bell chime, alerting the staff that someone had come in. She looked around and saw stacks of empty boxes, half-opened bags of pet food, and a variety of near-empty supplies. As she stood at the front counter waiting for someone to assist her, she couldn't help but notice on the other side of the counter was an enormous, free-standing relic of a copy machine, and right next to that was a small cart with a Mr. Coffee sitting on top. The pot had about an inch of mud-like coffee simmering at the bottom, which smelled as if it had been brewing for days. At the opposite end of the room, she spotted a young lady sitting behind a metal Steelcase desk, staring into an old IBM computer that looked like an early prototype. Katy figured the girl must not have heard the chimes over the loud barking coming from behind the office door. Either that, or she didn't want to be bothered.

She cleared her throat and exerted a very loud, "Hello! Excuse me! Is Vera Gibbons here?"

The girl, who appeared to be barely in her teens, cocked her head at Katy and answered in a muted tone, "No, she's in the back feeding the animals."

"My name is Katy Barton. I'm supposed to meet her here this morning to conduct an interview."

The girl slowly began inching her chair out, responding in a long, heavy, drawn out breath. "I'll go tell her you're here."

"No, that's okay," said Katy. "I'll go find her myself. I'd like to see the whole shelter, if I may."

"Whatever," said the girl, easing her seat back into place.

Katy stepped through the heavy metal door and began her trek down the austere concrete hallway. Surprisingly enough, this was her first time in an animal shelter, so she hadn't been prepared for the effect it would have on her. The hallway was centered between two endless rows of metal bars separating the dogs — *like jail cells*, she thought. As she walked along the corridor absorbing their dismal spirit, she was overcome with pity at the number of homeless and orphaned dogs of every size and every color. Some looked scared, some looked brazen, but they were all looking at her with those same sad, wanting eyes, barking in unison, as if they were begging her to please take them home.

As she neared the end of the hallway, stacks of smaller cages came into view, and crouched down next to them on the dank cement floor was a woman wearing jeans and a black apron. She appeared to be feeding the animals from a bucket of food sitting next to her. When she noticed Katy, she turned her wrist to glance at her watch and immediately stood up. As Katy approached, the slender woman with the long grey ponytail wiped her hands on the sides of her apron and said, "You must be Miss Barton."

"And you must be Vera Gibbons," replied Katy, leaning forward to shake her hand.

"I'm sorry, I lost track of time — so many animals to take

care of, you know."

"It's quite all right. We still have a little time to prep before the interview."

"Let me take off my apron. I'm done feeding the cats. We keep them at the rear of the shelter because the sweet things are so much less needy than the dogs."

Katy peeked into the crates and noticed one particular charcoal-colored feline cowering quietly into a ball in the corner of her cage. She poked her finger into the crate. "Here, kitty, kitty," she squeaked. The cat lifted its head for just a second and gazed at her with its dejected colorless eyes before dropping its head back down into its inky black coat. "I do have a soft spot for cats," sighed Katy. "I used to have one when I was a little girl."

"The black ones are the hardest to place because of the stigma of bad luck associated with them, I suppose. You know, contrary to popular belief, animals with dark fur and skin are not unlucky at all. The melanin in their deep coloration is actually known to boost their lifespan. That might be the reason why they are said to have nine lives. *'For three he plays, for three he strays and for the last three, he stays.'* They thrive on human companionship. Perhaps you'd like to adopt her?"

"I'd love to, but I'm just not ready to commit right now. Maybe next year," Katy said, with true remorse trickling in her voice.

The camera interview got underway as news reporter Katy Barton raised the primary issue that had brought her here today. "Ms. Gibbons, is there any way the shelter can survive with its lack of funding from the town of Morganville?"

"I don't think so," answered Ms. Gibbons, "unless the community gets involved. We are having a fundraiser this Saturday. There will be refreshments and balloons for the kids, and our volunteers will be here to accept any donation, large or small. In addition, we will be prepared to take applications for immediate, on-the-spot, pet adoptions."

"Thank you, Ms. Gibbons," commented Katy, who then turned to look directly into the camera. "So there you have it. Come down and bring your family and friends from ten to three this Saturday. This is a very worthwhile cause. There are too many homeless pets that need your help. If you can't make it to the fundraiser, you can send a check directly to the Morganville Shelter and save these poor unwanted animals from being euthanized. This is Katy Barton reporting for PTTV in Morganville." On that final note, Katy bent over to pet a large shaggy mutt sitting at the base of her feet. "Back to you...."

"And it's a wrap," closed Dan.

They returned to the television station, and Katy put her purse in her desk drawer and was about to start working on her edit when she remembered there was something she needed to do first. She took her purse back out of the drawer and removed the referral card from Dr. Mittinger. Then she held it up in her hand and took a deep breath. *It's now or never*, she thought, pressing the corresponding numbers on her desk phone keypad.

"Friday afternoon sounds great," said Katy, ending her call. Just as she was hanging up the receiver, she happened to glance over her partition and caught sight of Mr. Bruckman making his way toward her cubicle. *It sure would be nice if I had an office where I could have some privacy*, she thought, slumping down into her chair.

It didn't surprise her when he stopped directly in front of her desk. "So, how did the interview go?"

"Great," said Katy, straightening her posture. "I was just about to start working on the edit."

"Good, good. Oh, and don't forget, the story needs to be sent over to the *Herald* in plenty of time for the advertisement of the fundraiser."

It just so happened that Katy's duties as a reporter for PTTV Morganville included working in tandem with the Morganville Newspaper, *The Morganville Herald*, writing corresponding articles for the news stories she covered. "I know, Mr. Bruckman. I'm on it." He had just turned around to return to his office when she stopped him. "Hey, uh, Mr. Bruckman, do you mind if I take some time off Friday afternoon? I'm going to the doctor...um...to get that sleeping pill prescription you suggested."

"Sure, no problem. But don't forget, you've got another

interview Monday morning at the Flamingo Trailer Park to interview those hoarders. It's at nine. You think you can be on time for that?"

Dan must have said something to him — that nark! "Don't worry, boss, I'll be there 'bright-eyed and bushy-tailed!'"

CHAPTER SEVEN

Katy entered the unassuming brown brick building with an innate feeling of trepidation. *Ready or not, here I come,* she thought, as her shaky finger pressed the elevator button to the fourth floor. The doors opened up to a long narrow hallway, which she followed until she reached the last suite on the right. The brass inscription on the door told her she was at the right place.

BRIAN LLOYD FLEMING, PsyaD
LICENSED PSYCHOANALYST — CERTIFIED CLINICAL
HYPNOTHERAPIST

Before opening the door, she took a deep long breath. *I hope this Dr. Fleming is all he's cracked up to be,* she chuckled to herself, trying to relieve her angst. All those sessions with Dr. Mittinger back in New York had helped her cope with the day-to-day stress of bringing up a baby while going to school and working, but they hadn't done much to help her combat her grief.

"The doctor will be with you momentarily," said the receptionist.

Katy was the only person in the tiny waiting area. She sat down on one of the four chairs, next to the artificial ficus in the corner, and looked around the room. The walls were bare, except for a news article with an out-of-focus, black-and-white photo of the doctor (she guessed) mounted in a cheap frame. Just as she stood up to go read the article, Dr. Fleming opened the door to his office.

Her first impression of him was that he looked extremely

intelligent, like a college professor or a Nobel prize winner. He was the opposite of Dr. Mittinger, who was stumpy and clumsy. Dr. Fleming was very distinguished looking. He was at least 6' 4" in height, and his hair was a rich combination of salt and pepper. His face was long and thin, but the small round, wire-rimmed glasses teetering on the base of his nose balanced it out. Katy did think it funny, however, that he wore a short white smock over his brown corduroy pants as if he were going to perform some kind of surgical procedure.

"Come on in, Kate. I'm Dr. Fleming," he said, extending his right arm for a handshake. Tucked under his left elbow was an expanding manila folder. "Why don't you have a seat while I finish looking over your file?" He sat down at his desk and removed the papers from the folder.

While he was busy perusing the file, Katy did a quick scan of his office. It was twice the size of Dr. Mittinger's office. Two entire walls were lined with floor-to-ceiling shelves, each packed tightly with thick, hard-bound books. Above his desk hung two diplomas, one for a Doctor of Psychoanalysis Degree and another for a Masters Degree in Transpersonal Studies from the University of Virginia. There were also half-a-dozen licenses and certificates, including a membership award for the Society for Psychical Research (SPR).

The first thing that popped into her head was, *Oh great, how much is this going to cost me? It's a good thing my insurance plan covers mental health.* Katy had to comment. "I have to say, Doctor, I'm very impressed with your credentials. And I thought you were just a psychologist who dabbled in hypnotism," she added, with a hint of sarcasm in her voice.

Dr. Fleming smiled modestly. "Well, the reason I do what I do is rooted to my primary persuasion—that being parapsychological studies."

Katy wasn't sure what that meant, so she didn't respond. Instead, she continued to scrutinize her surroundings, trying to figure out exactly what it was this doctor was into.

The furniture was what you'd expect of a shrink's office—a green leather sofa next to a brown leather, high-back chair separated by a small table with a stand-up lamp on it. There was only one piece of artwork on the wall, which conspicuously stood out from everything else. Katy was immediately taken in by it. It seemed to provide a calming effect and the reassurance that she was in the right place.

It was an oversized oil painting bound in a beautifully carved gold-leaf frame. The portraiture was that of a young woman in a cerulean blue gown, lying on a purple chaise in the middle of a grassy green meadow. The waif-like maiden's wide eyes are calmly fixated on a splattering of twinkling yellow stars against a blackened cobalt sky, while a host of cherubs are floating above her, sprinkling shimmering dewdrops upon her face.

Taped underneath the frame was a white label with the painter's name and its title: *Awaken Your Dreams*.

"I just received your file from your former therapist in New York yesterday. The file refers to you both as Kate *and* Katy. Which do you prefer?"

Katy was still lost in the painting. "Sorry. Uh, what?"

Dr. Fleming looked up at the painting, then back at Katy. "Dr. Mittinger's file, it refers to you both as Kate and Katy. Which do you prefer?"

"Oh. Uh, it doesn't matter. I go by both."

"So what made you decide to come and see me — Kate?"

"Well, for starters, you came highly recommended. Dr. Mittinger told me he was very familiar with your casework and that he had attended several of your lectures."

Dr. Fleming looked up at the ceiling for a moment. "Yes, I seem to recall meeting Dr. Mittinger after a presentation I gave at the University of Pennsylvania. That was about ten years ago. In any case, Kate, after reviewing your case, I think you've come to the right place."

"I've never been to a 'hypno'-therapist before. I have to be honest with you, I've procrastinated coming here because I really don't believe in hypnotism."

"Why?" asked the doctor.

"I just don't believe people can be induced into a hypnotic sleep that quickly — especially me."

"You'd be surprised."

"Even if it is possible, I don't think it can help, much less prove anything."

"Then why are you here?"

"Well, I've been having trouble sleeping ever since my boyfriend died. I've had this recurring dream that I'm walking through a tunnel surrounded in flames, and I wake up in a sweat, coughing and barely able to catch my breath. It scares the heck out of me because it feels so real. The worst part is that it always occurs at the exact same time: Two-thirty-eight. Needless to say, afterwards, I have a hard time getting back to sleep, and I wake up feeling terrible. It's interfering with my work."

Dr. Fleming was still seated across from Katy, quietly taking notes as she continued.

"Dr. Mittinger said I was suffering from depression because I was still going through the grieving process."

Dr. Fleming flipped back to Dr. Mittinger's notes. "So your boyfriend — *Mark*, was it?"

"Yes."

"Died in November 1999?"

"Yes. It was the day before Thanksgiving. We were going to my house — "

Dr. Fleming interrupted. "And you've been having these nightmares ever since then?"

"Yes, and they haven't let up."

"How often would you say you have these dreams?"

"Four or five times a week."

"So for over five years now, you've been having these recurring nightmares."

"Yes. I mean, I still miss him dearly, but shouldn't I be over 'the grieving process' by now?"

"Not necessarily. Depression is oftentimes repressed. The roots of grief can go much deeper than the obvious. There can be many underlying factors."

"So what can I do about it?" Katy asked impatiently.

"You may not believe in hypnosis, but if you are open to it, hypnosis can unlock your soul and release the tragedies and regrets of the past, including those in former lives."

"Former lives? You mean like reincarnation?"

"Yes."

"I learned a little about that in my psychology courses, but I have a hard time believing in reincarnation. To be frank, Doc... tor Fleming, it sounds like a lot of bunk."

"You must keep an open mind. In other words, 'don't knock it till you try it.'"

Katy was silent for a moment, contemplating the idea. "I have a five-year-old daughter, and I need to get on with my life."

"Oh, is she Mark's?" asked the doctor, making a note.

"Yes," answered Katy. Then she took in a deep breath and exhaled. "Oh, what the heck, I guess I'll give it a try. What've I got to lose?"

"Very good then. But before I start, I need to have your permission to record you, but only while you are under hypnosis."

"Why do you need to record me?"

"It will help you because you may not remember all that is revealed, and it will help me capture every minute detail, so I can evaluate it more thoroughly afterwards."

Katy agreed half-heartedly, at which time Dr. Fleming walked over to the sole window lighting the room and pulled shut the heavy, floor-length drape. The funeral-like atmosphere only heightened her anxiety when he instructed her to lie down on the sofa while he positioned his recorder on the small table between them. He turned the table lamp on to its dimmest setting and sat down in the leather armchair with a pad and pen on his lap.

The next thing he did was to explain how, through a process of guided relaxation, he was going to put her in a state of mind of increased suggestibility. "Through intense concentration and focused attention, you should achieve a heightened state of awareness, called a 'trance.' Are you ready?"

Despite Katy's skepticism, her mind proved to be easily susceptible, and it didn't take long for her to fall into a deep trance.

"Now I want you to share with me all that you see playing

out before you," instructed the doctor.

Her mind instantly took her to the passenger's seat of Mark's old Dodge Colt on that Thanksgiving Eve in November 1999. Katy began to verbally share what she was seeing.

"Mark is driving. It's been raining for a while, but now it's begun to rain really hard, so he decides to take a shortcut. It's really dark. All I see is a thick wall of trees on either side of the road. It's a dirt road. I can tell because it's uneven and full of potholes, and I can hear the mud flapping all around us. He's going too fast. I tell him to slow down, but he doesn't...." There is a pause.

"Oh no! There's a massive buck standing in the middle of the road! He's frozen—I can see his yellow eyes staring blindly into our headlights. Mark panics. He makes a sharp turn to the left with his steering wheel to avoid hitting the deer, which causes him to swerve off to the side of the road and onto the gravel shoulder. His side of the car is getting pummeled by trees!"

The doctor noticed Kate becoming visibly shaken in her stance but encouraged her to keep going.

"The car has come to an abrupt stop. We've hit a really big tree almost head-on! The front-left side of the vehicle is crushed, and the hood has popped open. The engine is smoking." Katy paused again, her lips quivering. "Mark's head has smacked down so violently against the steering wheel, I don't know if he is dead or alive."

Dr. Fleming sensed Katy's growing distress, but again, prodded her to continue.

"My head has hit the dashboard. I think I might be unconscious. I can see gasoline fluid leaking from the gas tank, and black smoke is billowing from the rear of the automobile."

Katy seemed to want to stop, but once again, Dr. Fleming persuaded her to go on.

"Suddenly, out of nowhere, a black truck drives by. It's come to a stop a few car lengths ahead of us. A man dressed in jeans and a cowboy hat is getting out of the truck and is walking toward our vehicle. The rain has let up a bit. It's so dark, I can't make out his face. All I can see is the glare from the headlights against the sprinkling rain. He's walking over to the driver's door and yanks on it a couple of times. He's finally got it open. Mark is lying unconscious with his head resting sideways against the steering wheel. He's covered in blood, and his left leg looks mangled. The stranger is trying to pull him out, but Mark's legs are stuck beneath the compressed dashboard. He's unable to remove him from the car.

"Now he's running over to the passenger's side of the car, where I'm sitting. He's able to open my door right away and is pulling me out. I see him carrying me over to his truck with my long purse strap dangling around my neck. He's laying me down, very gently, on his passenger's seat, reclining it just a bit. Now I see him running back to the car as if he's going to make another attempt to get Mark out."

Katy stops before letting out a loud cry.

"NOOO! It's too late...the car has burst into flames! The man is just standing there, rigid, watching the flames spewing out like hot lava from a volcano. I see him turn around and walk back to the truck. His head is pointed low to the ground."

Katy was whimpering and visibly grieving. In order to maintain a relaxed state, Dr. Fleming instructed her to take a deep breath and resume a steady breathing. Once she had done so, he told her to keep concentrating on the revelation playing out in her head. Her posture began to soften, and she resumed speaking.

"We're in the truck driving now, me and the stranger. I see myself half-sitting, half-lying in the front passenger's seat. My head is tilted to one side, and blood is trickling from my forehead. He must be taking me to the hospital. While I'm lying there, something strange is happening to me. It's like I'm dreaming, only it's more fluid. I can't explain it. It's like I'm looking through my subconscious mind's eye—*at myself*. I see myself in a dark tunnel trying to find my way out. There's a light off in the distance. I can feel its warmth, its radiance. I feel drawn to it, so I start running toward it, faster, faster. I've almost reached it...."

Another pause.

"There's another light, a much dimmer beam, coming into

focus. It seems to be projecting from the opposite direction. The two lights are beginning to intersect. My transparent body has come to a dead stop. I don't know which light to follow."

The doctor interjected at this point. "Which one do you choose, Kate?"

Katy looked as though she were staring into an abyss while Dr. Fleming waited for her response. "I don't know," she uttered. A few more seconds went by, and she continued.

"I'm back in the truck again and pulling up to the emergency entrance of the hospital. The stranger has run in for help. Several people have rushed out to lay me on a wheeled bed and are rolling me into the hospital. I can hear the stranger's low voice telling the nurse behind the desk to call for the police and to send out an ambulance. The nurse is leaving the reception room, but when she returns, he's no longer there. I see her running out into the parking lot to look for him, but there is no sign of him. She's scratching her head as if he has vanished into thin air."

At this juncture, Katy appeared to be in a catatonic-like state. She was expressionless and not moving, so Dr. Fleming made the decision to snap her out of her hypnotic trance. Slowly she came to, at which time she began to sob unrelentingly. "It was so real like I was reliving my nightmare. Only this time, I uncovered the missing pieces!"

Dr. Fleming turned off his recorder and handed Katy a box of tissues while he tried to calm her down. Once she regained her composure, he had her sit up so he could cast some light on one pertinent observation which had not been previously made evident.

"Along with a copy of your records from Dr. Mittinger, I also got a copy of the police report." He held it up for her to see. "It appears that the clock on the dashboard of the ravaged vehicle was found miraculously intact. The time had stopped, but it was still readable. Are you aware of what was written on the report as being the time of the accident, based on the clock on the dashboard?"

"I never actually read the police report, but the nurses told me I was dropped off at the hospital around three-thirty in the morning."

Dr. Fleming said nothing but peered keenly over his bifocals into Katy's eyes. She looked back at him with dilated pupils, and in the form of a question, she softly spelled out, "Two...thirty...eight...?"

"That's correct."

Suddenly, Katy felt as though a burden had been lifted off her shoulders.

When the session was over, and she was getting ready to leave, Dr. Fleming remarked, "I think we've made considerable progress here today. Would you like to schedule your next appointment now?"

"I don't think I need to make another appointment," she replied. "I think I've learned all I need to know."

Dr. Fleming raised his eyebrows in surprise. "Are you sure?"

"I'm sure."

Chapter Eight

That evening, Katy went to bed, confident that she wouldn't have another nightmare. To her despair, she was aroused once again by those omnipresent flames burning in her core. In a semi-somnambulant haze, she rose from her bed and followed the short, dark hallway to the kitchen, stopping in front of the sink to pour herself a glass of water. *I don't get it,* she murmured to herself. *I thought I was cured.* As she stood in front of the window sipping her water and wondering what to do next, she gazed out into the night sky. It had come alive in a sea of twinkling stars. They appeared to be winking at her as if they had some sort of secret she wasn't privy to. And then it struck her.

Maybe it wasn't about facing her *subconscious* past—maybe she needed to face her *conscious* past. Ever since she returned to Morganville, there was something she had been putting off. Something she wanted to do, needed to do, but had not been ready to face—until now. Perhaps it was just the thing that could provide the closure she needed.

~*~

"I'm hungry," cried Lilly, tugging on her mother's blanket.

Katy looked at her clock—it was already nine. "Did you just wake up, baby?"

"No, I've been up for a long time playing with my dolls, but now I'm hungry," whined Lilly.

Katy gathered up all her energy and got out of bed. While she was putting on her robe, she remembered a promise she had made. "Hey, do you know what day it is?

Lilly put her index finger over her pursed lips and stopped to think.

"It's Saturday!" Katy proclaimed enthusiastically. "And do you remember what I promised to make you this weekend?"

"Pancakes!" squealed Lilly at the top of her lungs.

"That's right!"

"Can I help?"

"You bet you can!"

After breakfast, Lilly went back to playing in her room while Katy cleaned up the mess left in the kitchen — compliments of her little helper. She got herself dressed then went into Lilly's room, where she found her daughter jumping up and down on the bed, as she often did.

"Come on, Lilly," she said, trying to grab her. "Let's get you out of those pajamas and into some clothes. Today we're going someplace special."

"Where, where?" Lilly asked excitedly.

"You'll see."

Katy did not want to have to drive all the way into the city, so she was hoping the small, family-run florist in Morganville was still in business. It had been six years since she'd been there. After pulling into one of the two designated spaces out front, she was relieved to find the sign on the door read OPEN. As she and Lilly stepped inside, a small bell rang, and they were immediately greeted by a middle-aged woman who Katy didn't recognize.

"Do you need any help?" asked the woman.

Katy walked over to the refrigerated enclosure to peruse the colorful assortment of flowers. "I think I'd like two of those bouquets," she said, pointing through the glass encasement. "I like the pink and white carnations with the green roses. I've never seen green roses before."

"Green is the color of life, abundant growth, and constant renewal of life and energy. The green rose signifies the constant rejuvenation of spirit," explained the saleswoman.

"I didn't know that. I guess I picked the right ones then."

"Can I get you anything else?" asked the woman as she rang up the transaction.

"No thank you," replied Katy. "By the way, does Gladys still work here?"

"She comes in every once in a while," said the woman. "She hasn't been able to move around very well since she developed that rheumatoid arthritis."

"I'm sorry to hear that. What about her husband, Pete?"

"Oh, he passed away last spring. His brother, Paul, has taken over the business. He's not in right now, but he should be back in an hour if you want to come back later."

Katy was saddened by the news and reminded of how much can change in just a matter of a few years. "That's all right. I have to get going."

By mid-afternoon, they were about to enter one of the oldest landmarks in Morganville: Holy Trinity Cemetery. The moment she drove through those massive, concrete pillars supporting the corroded cast-iron archway, Katy was overcome with emotion but held it in as best as she could for the sake of her daughter. She drove around for a few minutes trying to recall where to park until she finally just picked a spot and hoped for the best.

Before getting out of the car, she grabbed both bouquets in one hand and a milk bottle she had filled with water prior to leaving the house in the other. "Come on, Lilly," she instructed. "Follow me."

After trekking between markers and monuments through the withering grass for a good fifteen minutes, a breathless Lilly finally asked, "What is this place, Mommy?"

"This is where people come to rest."

"I don't see anybody resting."

"That's because they're invisible."

Lilly appeared to be in deep thought while scouting the cemetery grounds. "Can they see us?"

"Absolutely," answered Katy, wishing that were true.

At long last, she spotted it at the far end of the cemetery. They came upon the ebony-colored monument that was imprinted with the words: *Rest in Peace Our Dear Son, Mark Stevens (Nov. 17, 1977 – Nov. 25, 1999)*. Katy placed one bunch of flowers in the special vase provided and filled it with half the water from her milk jug. She stood there facing the stone, caressing the heart-shaped pendant around her neck while tears trickled down her face.

"Why are you crying, Mommy?"

She wiped the droplets from her cheeks. "This is where your daddy is resting."

"I can't see him. Is he invisible?"

"Yes, Lilly, he is, and he's looking at you right now with a big, proud smile on his face."

Lilly walked over and stretched her arms across the commanding marker in an attempt to hug it, then her mom bent down and did the same. Katy stood up to face the headstone once again, then gently held up her palm to blow him a kiss. "I'll always love you, Mark," she whispered. Katy turned back toward her daughter. "Now, there's one more person we have to visit," she said, grabbing Lilly's hand.

"Who is it?"

"Someone else who loves you very much."

"I bet I can find 'em," declared Lilly, breaking loose from her mother's grip and running off. Katy was doing her best to catch up to her daughter while scanning the names on all the monuments she passed. She couldn't remember the exact spot where her mother was buried.

Lilly, who had been dashing from gravestone to gravestone, came to a sudden stop in front of a massive headstone off in the distance. Katy watched from afar as her daughter plopped down on her knees in front of it. When she caught up to her, she was kneeling in front of the headstone with her little body bent forward, circling the engraving on it with her tiny fingers.

"Lilly, what are you doing? Get up!" shouted Katy.

"But I like the picture on this one."

Katy stepped forward to take a closer look and immediately recognized the prominent heart etched into the granite in the center of the monument. Stamped in the middle of the heart were the words: *Forever Captured in our Hearts, Our Beloved, Marilyn Adele Barton (January 3, 1953 – April 14, 1999).*

She lifted her hand to cover her gaping mouth. "Oh my God, Lilly! You found it!"

"I did?"

"This is your grandmother's resting place—Grandma Barton! But, how did you...?"

"I heard her calling me!" stated Lilly, with an accomplished smile on her face.

Katy looked at her daughter, then looked at the headstone, then looked at her daughter again in disbelief.

"Can I put the flowers in the vase, Mommy?"

She watched as her daughter carefully tucked the flowers into the pre-positioned vase, then Katy poured the remaining water into it. She stood there somberly for a few minutes until she broke down crying. Then she raised her head up to the heavens and shouted, "Why must the people I love be taken from me? If there's a reason for everything, God, then I want to know what it is because it makes no sense to me!" She sniffled and looked back down to her side to remove a tissue from her pocket. As she was blowing her nose and wiping away her tears, it dawned on her that her daughter had probably witnessed her outburst. Concerned that she had, Katy turned around immediately, but Lilly was no longer by her side.

She looked all around until she saw that her daughter had once again wandered off to another gravesite near the edge of the cemetery. "Come on, Lilly!" she hollered, "We have to go now. There's no one here left to visit." Lilly turned to look at her mother and got up, and started running toward her. All of a sudden, Katy's vision began to blur, and she was overcome by a hallucination of some sort.

She saw what appeared to be an open coffin lying on the gravesite that Lilly was running from. Standing over the coffin was the ethereal image of a woman, completely dressed in black and her face shrouded by a large brimmed hat and dark veil. Her arm was extended outward, and dangling from her finger was a gold pendant. She tipped her finger and allowed the chain to slide off into the casket. Katy continued to watch as the pendant was falling...falling...in slow motion.

Lilly grabbed her mother's hand, and Katy was joggled out of her illusion.

As the two of them began to make their way toward the

car, Katy slowly turned her head to look back at the gravesite.
The woman in black was still there, only this time, the coffin was
gone, and she was laying a bouquet of white lilies on the grave.
There was something so familiar about the woman that Katy
could not stop staring.

"Whatcha lookin' at, Mommy?"

Katy's gaze turned to her daughter's angelic face. "Oh,
nothing, honey, I thought I recognized that lady over there, that's
all."

"What lady?" asked Lilly, stretching her neck back around
to see.

Katy pointed her finger toward the gravesite. "That one
over there..." But she was gone.

"I can't see her," said Lilly. "Maybe she's invisible."

Chapter Nine

She was late again. Katy rushed into the news station Monday morning with her sunglasses on, crouching along the open maze of partitions, hoping her boss wouldn't see her. As she was snaking her way to her cubicle, she came just two inches from hitting Martha's belly head-on. Martha was Jack's co-anchor for the evening news.

"Whoa," said Martha, stroking her belly. "What's your hurry?"

Katy stood upright and removed her sunglasses. "I've got to get my notes before I head out for my interview. Oh, by the way, Martha, congratulations—I heard you're expecting!" Katy had heard the news from Vicky. She thought Martha was starting to look a little big but hadn't wanted to say anything to her until she knew for sure—she'd made that mistake before.

"Yeah," said Martha, patting her tummy again. "Kid number three."

"So, how far along are you?"

"Almost four months now."

"Well, you hide it very well," lied Katy. "Sorry, but I have to get going. I'm late for an assignment." *Where is that file?* Katy huffed, tearing her desk apart.

As luck would have it, Mr. Bruckman happened to be walking by and saw her squatted down in front of her open file drawer. He lifted his arm to look at his watch. "What are you doing here? You were supposed to be at the trailer park by nine!"

"I know, I know. I forgot my notes and my directions," Katy answered, frantically tossing papers around.

"It's the Flamingo Trailer Park—lot number 361—off

Flamingo Road!" he yelled in an aggravated tone.

Katy raised the file up in the air and giggled nervously. "Aahh, here it is—right where I left it." She jumped up and stuffed it into her valise and started making her way toward the door, with Bruckman following closely behind.

"You know, Kate, if you wanna get ahead in this company, you'd better start taking your job a little more seriously."

Katy came to a sudden stop and slowly turned around. She knew Bruckman's bark was bigger than his bite, so she had no problem telling him how she really felt. "Maybe I'm late because my subconscious is trying to tell me I shouldn't be wasting my time doing *trashy* stories about packrats."

Bruckman's eyebrows raised at least an inch. "What's that supposed to mean?"

"Every once in a while, I'd like to report some real *hard* news instead of this trivial human interest crap."

"If you don't like it, I'm sure I can find someone else who does."

Katy didn't want to lose her job, and she couldn't take back what she said, so she was quick to correct her tone. "I mean, it would be nice if every now and then I could do a story with a little more substance."

"You realize you're a reporter for the town of Morganville? Not a whole lot of *hard news* happens in Morganville."

Katy didn't respond.

"Look," Mr. Bruckman continued. "I know you're good at your job—you've proven that. But you haven't been here that long, and there's something called 'seniority.'"

Katy looked at her boss, this time with a little humility in her eyes, "You're absolutely right." Then, with half a smile on her face and a hint of mockery in her voice, she added, "Well, I'd better get going. I need to dig up some dirt before someone else scoops it up."

"That's very funny," retorted Bruckman, with a half-cocked smirk and a gleam in his eye. He wouldn't think of firing her. He liked her spunk.

When Katy pulled up to the trailer park, her cameraman

Dan was already there, leaning against his van. "Bout time you got here."

"I know, I know—sorry I'm late. Let me gather up some statements from some witnesses, and then we can set up for our live presentation."

Once she gained access into the park, she noticed a handsome young fireman standing near the entrance. He was speaking to an older gentleman, who was obviously the health inspector, judging by the Department of Health and Human Resources insignia on his cap.

What is it about that uniform that makes firefighters look so damned hot? she thought, biting her lower lip. She could tell he noticed her too by the way he casually lifted his head and followed her gait with his eyes. She made sure to correct her posture as she strutted by with all her confidence, all the while doing her best to eavesdrop on their conversation. His commanding voice resonated loud and clear to her ears.

"Well, I've conducted my survey, and besides the obvious unsanitary conditions, the place is a fire hazard. If they don't clean it up within two weeks, they'll have to be evicted."

Katy turned around and strode back toward the two men, hoping to get some information and see if they would agree to do an interview. "Excuse me, gentlemen, for butting in, but I'm Katy Barton from PTTV, and I was wondering if I could have a few words with you regarding the hoarding situation going on in trailer 361?"

The fireman abruptly stopped talking to the inspector and gave Katy the once over, from her head to her feet and back up again, stopping short of her neckline where her heart pendant was hanging over her blouse. "Excuse me, miss," he said rudely. "But we're in the middle of a conversation here."

Katy was taken aback by the manner in which he spoke to her. No one, other than her boss, ever spoke to *her* like that. "I'm sorry, but it'll just take a moment of your time."

He continued to look at her with those deep dark eyes and articulated in an even harsher tone. "Look, Miss...PTTV. I don't have time for that. I've got to get back to the fire station."

"Maybe I can just get a written statement from you before you go?" she persisted.

He took a few steps toward her until he was no more than two inches from her face and raised his voice indignantly. "If you want a statement, you'll have to come down to the Morganville Fire Station." Then he shot her a calculating smile and stormed off in the other direction.

Katy turned a few shades of red and spun around toward the inspector, who had an empathetic look on his face. "Do you have a moment?"

After speaking with the inspector, who did agree to an interview, she marched over to trailer #361 to talk to the hoarder in question. She stepped over the splintered, slatted stairway, being careful not to scuff her patent leather heels, and gave a few hard knocks against the paint-chipped door. The occupant came to the door, only to hold it slightly ajar. That was just enough to almost cause Katy to heave from the horrid stench emanating from inside the trailer. It also provided her with a brief peek through the entryway, proof that the home was beyond cluttered and more than likely vermin infested as well.

The alleged hoarder answering the door was a woman, probably in her fifties, wearing a tattered house robe. It became clear she was in no mood to cooperate. After curtly answering one or two questions, she practically slammed the door in Katy's face, so Katy proceeded over to the trailer next door. The neighbor lady was a lot more agreeable since she was the one who had "anonymously" alerted the health inspector's office as to the existing situation.

Dan had positioned his TV camera directly in front of the hoarder's trailer, and Katy was almost ready to conduct her live interview with the neighbor and health inspector at her side. She stood in front of the camera, patted down the sides of her suit jacket and tight skirt, and adjusted her mic. Just as she was about to motion to Dan that she was ready, that obnoxious fireman paraded over, grabbed the health inspector by the arm, and pulled him a few steps away.

"I forgot to inform you...," she heard him say, to which

the inspector pulled out a notepad from his pocket and began scribbling some notes. The two of them stood directly in front of Katy, immersed in their own private conversation, completely oblivious to the fact that she was getting ready to go on air.

"EXCUSE ME!" she blurted out in the fireman's direction. "But I need my inspector back!"

The fireman gave Katy a ruthless look. "Maybe I'm not done with *your* inspector!"

"Oh, I'm sorry," said the inspector, taking a few steps back to his designated spot.

"I don't know if you realize it, but do you see that camera right there?" Katy pointed, "We were just about to go on air, and you're blocking me. I'm going to have to ask you to MOVE! Besides, don't you have to be getting back to the station?"

The fireman got right up in Katy's face again with his overpowering glare. "Oh yeah, Miss PT—TV. I think *MY* job here is a little more important than yours, and I *WAS* just leaving, so perhaps *YOU* should move out of *MY* way!"

"I'm not moving!" defied Kate, standing tall and holding her head up high, all the while trying not to melt from his devilish good looks.

"Then I'll report you to your station manager," he retorted.

"And I'm going to report you to...your...uhh, chief, or captain, or...whatever! What's your name?"

"It's Michael—Michael Stratton! Would you like me to spell that out for you? S...T...R...A...T...T—"

"Don't bother, I've got it forever ingrained in my brain!" shouted Katy, poking her finger repetitiously against the side of her head.

At that, the firefighter acquiesced. "Fine, I'm moving!"

In a huff, Katy touched up her hair, yanked on the cord of her microphone, and proceeded with her news story and two interviews, finally ending with, "This is Katy Barton with PTTV in Morganville, signing off."

Still rattled, she yanked the sounding device from her ear and untangled the transmitting wires from around her leg in an angry fit, practically tripping over them with her high heels.

"He's got a lot of nerve. Who does he think he is?" she fumed at her cameraman. "I get stuck doing these lousy stories, AND I have to put up with this bullsh...t!"

"Well, at least you don't have to lug this heavy equipment around everywhere you go," said Dan.

"Yeah, but you knew what you were getting yourself into when you took your job. I thought the job of a reporter would command more respect. I didn't think I would have to put up with this kind of belligerence from people like him."

"I guess I'm just your humble servant," quipped Dan. "I don't want to completely burst your bubble, but didn't you tell me you had some sort of degree in psychology to help you deal with people like this?"

"Yeah, I did, and I learned the only thing that motivates that type of guy is arrogance and self-entitlement. I think I dealt with him exactly how he wanted to be dealt with. In the end, people like that get what they deserve."

After the two of them arrived back at the news station, Katy was on her way to the edit room when she heard Bruckman call out from his office, "So how did it go?"

She backtracked a few steps, stopping in front of his open door. "It was all right—except for this annoying fireman who got all up in my face and tried to prevent me from doing my job."

"Oh?"

"Don't worry about it. I handled it."

"Okay, um...," said Mr. Bruckman, clearing his throat. "Well then, your next assignment, 'should you decide to accept it,' is to schedule an interview with Mr. and Mrs. Greely at the Morganville General Store. It's a family-run business handed down for over eighty years, and now they're being forced to close up shop. The building is going to be torn down because of the new highway extension, which is gonna be running through there."

"I'll gladly accept it," Katy responded, with extra verve and fortitude, hoping to appease him after their earlier confrontation that morning, all the while thinking to herself, *As long as I don't run into that cocky fireman again.*

Chapter Ten

Katy rolled up into the empty spot next to Dan's van and put her car in park. He had both doors open and was unloading his equipment.

"Wow, you're actually on time—with a minute to spare," he said, with that grimace she had come to despise. He pointed to the Greelys, who were standing under the covered wood-plank porch of the general store. "They're waiting for you."

Katy grabbed her notebook and hurried over to meet with them. The interview wasn't set to air for half-an-hour, so she had plenty of time to prep them.

"Why, I haven't seen you since you were about yay high," said Mr. Greely, motioning with his hand.

"It *has* been a long time," agreed Katy. "I'll go over a few things with you, then as soon as my cameraman has his equipment all set up, we can get started."

Once they were all properly positioned in front of the store, she gave Dan the go ahead, and he started his countdown. "And five...four...three—"

"Oh wait!" burst in Mr. Greely, "I almost forgot—I have to run in and get somethin'." He scuttled back into the store, and when he came out, he was holding a large black-and-white photograph in his hand.

"What's that?" asked Katy.

"Oh, just a special photograph I'd like our viewin' audience to see."

Katy laughed out loud in her head. *Viewing audience? Sounds like he's been practicing for his fifteen minutes of fame.*

When they were all re-situated, Katy once again gave Dan

the okay to resume his countdown. "Five…four…three…two…one…and we're live."

"This is Katy Barton with PTTV, and I'm standing here in front of the Morganville General Store. The store has been scheduled to be demolished by the end of the month because of the new Highway 46 extension the state plans to run directly through the Greely's property. The extension project is scheduled for completion by the middle of next year."

Katy went on to introduce George and Helen Greely, who were standing on each side of her, staring nervously into the camera.

"Mr. and Mrs. Greely, I understand your store has been a staple here in Morganville for over eighty years."

"That's right," replied Mr. Greely, bowing to the microphone while making sure to keep his eyes pointed directly into the camera. "The property used to belong to my granddaddy, then he passed it along to my ma and pa. They put up the store and run it till they got too old to take care of it. That's when me and my wife, Helen here, took it over."

Helen didn't say a word. Her lips were pressed tightly together while she stood there, rigid as an ironing board in her plain cotton dress, with her hands clenched in front of her.

Katy continued. "The building itself looks pretty old. Just how old is it?"

"Well, it used to be an old horse barn. I think it was built in the late 1800s," responded Mr. Greely.

"My, that is old," said Katy, trying to inject a little enthusiasm into an otherwise boring interview. "And what did your father do before he opened the store?"

"He used to work in the coal mines, just like his daddy did before him until he got tired of doin' that. He thought it'd be a good idea to have a general store in these here parts. It was a real inconvenience for people to have to travel all the way into the city every time they needed somethin'. Morgan Brewer thought it'd be a good idea too. Well, if it weren't for Mr. Brewer, who lent my daddy the money to convert that 'ol stable, this store would a never been built."

Katy's ears perked up. "That's very interesting. And what is this you have in your hand?"

Mr. Greely held up the photo for the camera to zoom in on it. "I brought this here picture out. We keep it hangin' over by the cash register — you know, in commemoration."

"Would you mind telling 'the viewing audience' who these people are in the picture, Mr. Greely?"

"It's a picture of Ma and Pa...," he pointed them out in the photograph, "...standin' next to Mr. and Mrs. Brewer and their daughter — I believe her name was Evelyn. She was about eighteen or so when this photo was taken. Real beautiful girl she was...." Mr. Greely paused for a moment to look up at Katy. "In fact, she looked an awful lot like you, Miss Kate." He looked at the picture again and then back up at Katy. Then, Mrs. Greely bent over to examine the photo, lifting her head back up to look at Katy.

The young reporter could feel herself turning flush from embarrassment as the Greelys simultaneously turned their heads to gape at her with their mouths hanging open. They each had that dumbfounded expression on their face while she stood between them in an awkward moment of silence.

Mr. Greely finally shook his head back and forth. "Hmm, uncanny resemblance." Then he continued, "But she ain't been seen around here since she supposedly went off to college — that was decades ago."

After a few more questions, Katy ended the interview by thanking each of them. As she and Dan began packing up their equipment, Dan had to comment, "That was weird."

"Yeah, tell me about it," said Katy. "You know, it's a shame they have to demolish the old general store. I remember stopping here as a kid whenever we went to the lake. My father would stop here to buy bait for his fish, and my mother and I would pick out snacks for the trip. There was always a hat stand near the entrance of the store with an assortment of hats on display, and one day, there was one particular hat that stood out from all the rest. As soon as I saw it, I had to have it. It was a straw hat with a bright yellow ribbon and purple and yellow plastic flowers on the side. I begged my mother to buy it for me. As luck would have it, I lost it on the boat that day when a gust of wind came and blew it off my head. It flew out toward the other side of the lake until it was out of sight. I was so upset. My father trolled all around the lake, trying to find it, but we never did. We even stopped back at the general store on the way home to see if they had another one like it, but they didn't. Since no other hat would do, I pouted all the way home.

"The next day, I was still sulking over that hat. I did my best to make my mother feel guilty for leaving me home with the nanny while she went off to do charity work—like her charity work was more important than me! It must have worked because when she came back, she had this cute little furry white kitten in her arms—a consolation gift, I suppose. Well, it worked because I quickly forgot about the hat."

Dan forced out a laugh. "Wow! It sounds to me like you were a spoiled little brat."

Chapter Eleven

Katy couldn't stop thinking about the way the Greelys had looked at her during their interview. She tucked Lilly into bed and walked over to her bedroom closet, where she kept her three large photo albums. She plopped down on the floor, with her back against the bed and her legs crossed, and began thumbing through them one-by-one. The first album was dedicated strictly to Lilly, from the day she was born to the present, and the second album contained mostly pictures of herself when she was younger. As she filtered through the second album, she stumbled across a picture of her and her dad in front of the general store. There she was, wearing, of all things, the long-lost hat with the yellow ribbon and plastic flowers. An aura of melancholy swept over her. She had forgotten all about that picture. Her mother must have wanted to "capture the moment" before they set off for their fishing trip.

She flipped through a few more pages and came across the photograph she was looking for — her high school graduation picture. Katy studied it for a moment. She really hadn't changed much since then. Her blonde hair had since darkened and used to hang midway down her back. When she entered the working world, she opted for a more professional cut, styling her shoulder-length curls in a way to gently frame her face. She looked more mature, too, perhaps due to the tiny wrinkles that had formed around the corners of her mouth and eyes.

She set the book on the floor atop the other one and moved on to the third album, the one that held a hodge-podge of old family photos. She flipped through the yellowing pages rather quickly until one photo, in particular, caught her eye. It was black-and-white and slightly faded. Even though it was taken from a distance, it was clear enough to distinguish that it was her father standing in front of the Morganville Bank. She couldn't help but let out a ripple of laughter. He was wearing that notoriously awful pinstriped suit her mother had hated because she said it made him look like a gangster. As she studied the photo, she thought about what Mr. Greely had told her about Morgan Brewer helping to finance the store. She had heard that the Brewer name was somehow synonymous with the town of Morganville, but she really didn't know much more than that. It suddenly occurred to her that it might be a good idea to do some research on Mr. Brewer, as well as the Brewer family history. It might make for a good follow-up story to the demolition of the general store, and who knows, maybe provide a little more "substance" to an otherwise boring news story.

The next morning she decided to make a quick stop at the Morganville Public Library to see what she could dig up before heading into work. As she strolled along the quaint cobblestone path leading to the front entrance, she tried to recall the last time she had been there. She must have been too young or too consumed with boys to appreciate its classic, traditional architecture. When she stepped onto the elongated concrete stairs leading to the massive double-glass doors, she noticed something else she had never paid attention to before. It was a bronze commemorative plaque with the outline of a man's bust. Inscribed beneath the image were the words,

In commemoration of Morgan Randolph Brewer, benefactor and founder of the Morganville Public Library on this, September 3, 1920.

This Morgan Brewer must have been pretty important in this town, she thought, entering the building. She wasn't sure where to start looking, so she asked the librarian, who looked as though she'd been there from the day they broke ground, where she might find a book delineating the history of Morganville. Katy bit her lip impatiently as she followed the creaky librarian plod her way through the maze of towering shelves at the speed of a banana slug. When she finally arrived at her destination, she pointed to several books on one of the taller shelves.

"This one is probably the most concise," she stated, doing her feeble best to wedge out the oversized text. "There are also old newspaper articles dating back to the early 1800s on microfilm if you'd like to examine those."

"Thank you," said Katy, taking the bulky volume into her hands, "I think this will do for now."

The large hardbound manual was full of early black-and-white photo reproductions and illustrations. It outlined how Morgan Randolph Brewer, the only son of an English immigrant, settled in the town that later became known as Morganville. He grew to become a well-known businessman who made his fortune in the large coal mining industry in the surrounding area. He had gone into business with his old friend, Milton S. Shilby, who he had known from their younger days when they worked in the coal mines together. Mr. Brewer was an admired philanthropist who did much for the town of Morganville, including dedicating the library and other local business establishments. In the early 1900s, he commissioned several architects to design a magnificent custom Victorian estate to be built on the outskirts of town. It became recognized near and far as The Brewer Mansion.

Katy rifled through the pages, getting completely immersed in Morganville's fascinating history. She couldn't believe this was all new to her. She decided she had better go sit down to study it more closely and started making her way toward the reading tables in the mid-section of the library. With her face still buried in her book, she completely failed to notice the young man standing in her path. He had just grabbed a book from one of the higher shelves when she literally ran right into him, knocking his book to the floor.

"Excuse me!" she blurted out, bending over to pick it up. The two of them shared a glance for a brief second while she handed him his book.

No sooner had she turned her focus back into reading than all of a sudden, she was startled by the rough feel of his hand grabbing her arm.

"Hey, aren't you that reporter from the trailer park doing the hoarder story?"

That voice sounded really familiar. She raised her eyes to take a second look at his face and realized who he was. "Why, excuse me again," she sounded off sarcastically, trying to recall his name. "I didn't recognize you without your helmet on. Aren't you that rude, obnoxious fireman who was going to report me?" Before he had a chance to respond, his name suddenly came to her. "Well, fancy meeting you here, Mike—uh, Michael!"

"Why, fancy meeting you here too," he responded. "What was *your* name again?"

"If you don't remember, why should I tell you? So you can report me?"

"Look," said Michael, "I take my job very seriously, as I'm sure you do. I'll tell you what, let's forget that whole 'run-in' at the trailer park ever happened and start fresh with a clean slate, okay?"

He then offered his hand in truce. Katy hesitated for a moment, but damned, if he wasn't so good looking. She reciprocated with a weak handshake, only to follow it up with a surrendering smile.

"My name is Michael Stratton, but you can call me Mike. And you are?"

"My name is Katy Barton, or you can call me Kate, or Katy, or whatever you like—I go by both. So, did you find the book you were looking for?"

"Oh, yeah," he answered, patting the manual between his hands. "I was looking for a book on collapsing fire hazards. And what are you reading there that had you so engrossed?"

Katy lifted the heavy volume up slightly. "This is a book about the history of Morganville. I was doing some research for a possible story."

"It looks like we *both* take our jobs seriously."

At least fifteen minutes of light, flirty banter went by before Mike suggested, "After we've finished with our research, maybe you'd like to have some lunch? I mean, it's almost noon, and you do like to eat, right?"

"I do like to eat," said Katy, realizing how silly that sounded. "I mean, um…sure."

"Great! Then let's meet at the Boar's Head Diner across the street at say, one o'clock?"

"It's a date!" said Katy a little too enthusiastically, then blushed with embarrassment because it sounded like she was presuming it was a date.

When they met outside the diner, Mike was quite the gentleman, rushing to open the door for her. When the hostess led them to their booth, he noticed crumbs on the seat and wiped them off with his hand before she sat down. She was impressed. Most guys she met lacked any amount of chivalry. *This guy's pretty "old-school,"* she thought to herself.

Katy was famished. She hadn't eaten anything all morning, as usual. While she was examining the menu, she could feel Mike's unwavering stare from across the booth. *I hope he can't hear my stomach growling*, she thought, feeling herself start to blush again. "So much to choose from," she blurted out, trying to relieve her awkwardness.

All of a sudden, he pulled the menu out of her hold, grabbed both her hands into his, and looked directly into her eyes, "I'm sorry if I'm staring, but you're so beautiful! Your eyes are like two burning flames smoldering in a sea of blue."

"Wow, that's quite a line. I've never heard that one before."

"I'd like to know what's in that ocean. What long buried passion are you hiding?"

Katy could feel the blood rushing to her head again. "Nothing that I know of," she responded nervously, assuming her face was red as a beet by now.

"Then tell me about yourself, 'Miss Katy.' What's a nice city girl like you doing in a small town like Morganville?"

"What makes you think I'm a 'Miss?'"

"If you weren't, I don't think you would have agreed to have lunch with me."

"Okay, you're right about that. And what makes you think I'm a city girl?"

"Because there's a certain air of refinement about you."

"Well, I'm originally from here in Morganville. My father used to run the Morganville Bank, but he's since retired. I haven't been around for a while, though. I attended Ithaca State, where I earned my degree in journalism. After that, I continued living and working in Ithaca for a couple of years, but realized I missed my hometown, so I came back. I got this job as a reporter for the local news station, and here I am."

Mike continued to gaze into her eyes as though he were examining her inside and out, making her increasingly uncomfortable.

"So what about you, Mike—what's your story?"

"I don't have much of a story. I grew up in Pittsburgh, went to school in Pittsburgh."

"And how did you end up in Morganville?"

"There was an opening at the Morganville Fire Department. I liked the small town atmosphere, the close-knit community."

"So, how long have you been here?"

"I've been with the Morganville Fire Department for almost six years now."

"There can't be a lot of fires in Morganville," joked Katy.

"We also provide back-up for other fire departments in and around the Pittsburgh area, as well as offer assistance to other states during catastrophic events, such as wildfires. So we have plenty to keep us busy."

Katy felt bad for making the comment she did, but Mike continued to talk.

"My long term goal, though, is to retire on a ranch, with a little land and some horses."

"I love horses," said Katy, letting out a bashful smile.

He squeezed her hands tighter. "So, what's this assignment you're working on?"

Katy filled him in on the recent interview she had with the Greelys and how the city was going to bulldoze the general store because of the freeway expansion project. "Apparently, Morgan Brewer helped finance the store, so I was trying to uncover a little history on him."

"I've heard stories around the fire department that there

was a fire at the Brewer mansion a long time ago. Luckily, Mother Nature provided a helping hand in putting it out. It was the family gardener, however, who was credited for extinguishing the fire inside before it overtook the whole house. I don't know the details, but apparently, someone died in the fire."

Katy raised her eyebrows in interest. "Really?"

The conversation continued to flow easily throughout lunch, so much so that she couldn't help but tell him, "You're so easy to talk to. I feel like I've known you my whole life."

Mike stared into her eyes and smiled. "Me too."

After they finished their lunch, he was quick to pick up the check, then walked her to her car. For a couple of seconds, the two of them stood there facing each other in awkward silence until he clasped one of her hands between his. "I'd really like to see you again, Miss Katy."

She could feel her heart begin to flutter but vacillated. "I think you should know something first...I have a five year old daughter."

With no hesitation and an enigmatic twinkle in his eye, he responded, "I love children."

Katy lowered her head, then raised her chin ever so slowly to reveal a diminutive grin. "Yes, I would *very much* like to see you again."

Chapter Twelve

The first dismissal bell rang at Morganville Christian Academy, releasing a wave of tiny bodies. Katy sat in the pickup line in front of the school, sandwiched between a line of cars that extended halfway down the street. While waiting for her daughter to surface, her mind wandered back to that coincidental meeting with Mike at the library. Then, the way he held her hands and looked at her during lunch. As flattering as it was, it had left her with an uneasy feeling. Maybe she shouldn't have been so quick to agree to a second date.

Her thoughts were quickly grounded by a repetitive smacking noise against the window and the squeaky little muffled voice that followed. She turned her head to observe her daughter trying to get her attention while attempting to open the car door. Katy pressed the unlock button and ran out of the car to help her in.

"Didn't you see me?" whined Lilly.

"I'm sorry, honey. I guess my mind was in the clouds. So how was school today?"

"It was good, except Mrs. Randolph is kinda mean."

"Oh?"

"She said I shouldn't make things up."

"What do you mean? Like what kinds of things?"

"I don't know!"

"Hmm, I'll have to ask her about that the next time I see her."

"And then she made me and Meghan sit at different desks so we wouldn't talk so much."

"Well, you *do* need to concentrate on your schoolwork,

honey."

"Can Meghan come over when we get home? Can she, can she, Mommy? Please!"

"All right, all right. I'll call her mom when we get home."

Just as Katy began rolling up the driveway of their first floor townhome, Lilly belted out a halting screech, "Look out, Mommy! There's a cat!" Katy slammed on her brakes just short of the little black cat who was about to cross in front of them. Lilly wasted no time unbuckling her seat belt and jumped out of the vehicle. "Here, kitty, kitty," she squealed. The little cat cautiously meandered over to her, meowing and rubbing up against her ankles. It was not much bigger than a kitten, with soft black fur and copper colored eyes. "He's sooo cute," cooed Lilly, bending down to pet him as he purred and continued to rub against her leg. "He likes me! Mommy, can we keep him? Please, please!"

"He *is* cute. But he probably belongs to someone," said Katy.

"But he's not wearing a collar."

"That's very perceptive of you, honey."

"I think he's hungry. Can we give him some milk?"

"He is sweet," said Katy, bending down to scratch his little head. "He kinda reminds me of the cat I used to have when I was a little girl, except that he was white."

"What happened to him?"

"He went to kitty heaven." Katy smiled poignantly, standing back up. "I'll tell you what—we'll put up some flyers around the neighborhood, and if no one claims him, we can keep him. The last thing I want to do is see him get locked up in a shelter."

Lilly jumped up and down, shrieking with joy, and enveloped the little stray in her arms. "You're going to belong to me!" she told him. "I'm going to name you…um, um…*Tandy!*"

"Tandy? How did you come up with that name?"

"I don't know," shrugged Lilly with an impish grin on her face. "It just popped in my head. I can't wait to show Meghan my new kitty!"

Chapter Fourteen

Mike wasted no time—he called Katy the very next day. "Are you busy Friday night?" he asked.

Katy still hadn't made up her mind about him. She thought about the way he acted at their first encounter at the trailer park. He came off as callous and arrogant. But when they had lunch at the diner yesterday, he was the complete opposite—respectful and gallant. She perceived his arrogance differently now. She identified it as showing strength in character—someone in command, someone you could depend on. She liked that. And never mind his looks! Being that he was a firefighter, he was in great physical shape. He was tall, dark, and handsome, and those deep, dark, mysterious eyes made him almost impossible to resist.

But there was something else holding her back. Mark's death had left her extremely guarded. How could she fall head-over-heels with someone when there was always that risk of losing them?

"Hold on, let me check my calendar," she responded, even though she very well knew she was free.

"How would you like to go bowling? Some of my buddies from the fire station are going to be there, and I'd love for you to meet them."

She thought about it for a minute. *It's not like we're going on a romantic getaway. It's just bowling, as friends. Besides, I need the exercise.* "Sure, that sounds fun."

"So, I'll pick you up at six?"

"Sounds great."

At a quarter of six, the doorbell rang. It was Mike. "I'm

ready," she told him, leaving him to stand at the door. "I just have to grab my jacket."

He took a few steps in and looked around. "This is a nice place. How long have you been living here?"

"Just since March—thanks."

"So where's your daughter...uh...." He couldn't recall if Katy had mentioned her name.

"Lilly is with her grandpa. She loves going over there. That's part of the reason why I moved back, so she could be closer to him."

~*~

When they arrived at the bowling alley, they were warmly greeted by a group of Mike's friends. After a round of introductions, one of the guys said to her, "We've heard a lot about you."

How could they have heard a lot about me? thought Katy. *I just met him on Tuesday.* She looked over at Mike with a quizzical look on her face, and this time *he* blushed.

They were all putting on their "clown shoes," as Katy liked to refer to them when she noticed that another one of Mike's friends had his eyes fixed on her. He finally got up from his seat and walked over to her. "Excuse me," he said, "but you look really familiar."

Katy thought she had seen him before, but she couldn't quite place him. "Um, what was your name again?"

"I'm Ted Burns. Weren't you Mark Stevens's girlfriend?"

A lump formed in her throat as she choked out a reluctant, "Yes." Mike, who was seated nearby putting his shoes on, overheard the remark and was paying close attention to the conversation.

"I used to be good friends with Mark," explained Ted. "You probably don't remember me because I didn't go to Christian Academy. I went to a different school."

Katy remained silent.

"I'm really sorry about the accident."

Katy felt as though she were about to cry. "Me too," she said, trying her best to hold back the tears.

Ted continued. "Mark had told me all about you. I was at his funeral, but when I went to express my condolences, I couldn't find you."

"I seem to recall your face, but I remember very little about the funeral. I was still in shock, and my state of mind was in a complete blur."

Mike walked over to where Katy was standing, trying to pretend like he hadn't heard anything, even though he had ingested every word. "What do you say we get this game started?" he announced.

The mood was lightened, and everyone had a good time, including Katy, after her spirit had rebounded. After bowling ended, some of the guys were going to a local tavern to hang out and asked the two of them if they wanted to join. Katy was up for it, but before she could answer, Mike told his friends he had to get her home early. She just looked at him, then whispered in his ear, "I don't need to pick Lilly up until tomorrow morning."

"If you don't mind, I'd like you and me to go out for a drink by ourselves, maybe somewhere quiet, where we can talk."

"Sure," she shrugged. "That sounds nice."

They arrived at the dimly-lit bar and were seated at a small table off in the corner. "How's this?" he asked, pulling the chair out for her.

"This is fine, thank you."

After a brief moment of idle chit-chat, Mike changed the tune of their conversation and brought up the discussion she and Ted had had earlier at the bowling alley. Katy took a deep breath, but before she could start, the waitress came by to take their drink orders. Mike ordered a beer, but Katy decided she was going to need something a little stronger if she was going to be spilling her guts out. "I'll have a vodka tonic, please, with a twist."

The next hour was filled with Katy recounting the tragic misfortune of her mother's untimely death and the horrific accident resulting in the death of her one true love, Mark, ultimately revealing that Lilly was his child.

Mike reacted sympathetically. "Wow. That's a lot to handle in such a short period of time." All the while, his eyes were fixated on the pendant resting over her baby-blue cashmere sweater. "Was that from him?" he asked, motioning to it with his eyes.

Katy reached up and squeezed the locket gently in her hand. "Yes," she blushed. "How did you know?"

"Lucky guess."

"Yeah. Um, there's something else you should probably know," began Katy.

Mike was all ears as if he couldn't imagine what she could possibly have to add to this unfortunate series of events.

"After Mark's death, I began having this recurring nightmare, so I started seeing a therapist. I'm still seeing one — actually, he's a hypnotherapist. I've been having these visions too. I don't know. Maybe I'm crazy."

Mike reached across the table and squeezed her hands together in his again. "You went through a lot — you're not crazy. The heart you wear around your neck should remind you of that."

At the end of the evening, Mike walked Katy up to her door. She inserted her key into the keyhole, and just as she turned back around to say goodnight, he boldly wrapped his arms around her to bestow a long, lingering kiss. After finally bidding each other goodnight, he turned to walk toward his car, but midway, he swiveled back around with a look of indecisiveness on his face. "You know, I don't have to be at the station for my next shift until tomorrow afternoon. Would it be all right if I took you to breakfast?"

Katy took a hard gulp. She had not "been" with anyone since Mark. "I don't know...," she held back. "I have to pick my daughter up in the morning."

"Maybe you can call your father and tell him you'll pick her up a little later."

Again, Katy wavered. This was barely their second date. She was not ready to take that next step.

"Great! Then I'll pick you up tomorrow morning at eight, sharp."

Wow, she thought, relieved. *He truly is an old-fashioned guy.*

At exactly eight, he showed up in a black crew-cab pick-up. Katy was surprised. "You have a car *and* a truck?"

"Yeah," he responded. "Every guy needs a truck. You never know when it'll come in handy."

He ran over to open the door for her, but it became evident that Katy was going to have a hard time climbing up into the truck in her sexy tight jeans and sling-back heels. Immediately he scooped her up into his arms and placed her on the seat. For a few fleeting seconds, a strange feeling came over her, literally giving her goosebumps. And then something caught her eye. Resting on the back seat of his truck was a black Stetson hat.

When they had reached the outskirts of town, Mike took Old Grange Road until it forked into two narrow dirt trails, at which time he veered toward the left and followed it until they arrived at their destination. Nestled along the left side of the road were two adjoining log cabins. Each cabin had its own hand-carved shingle hanging from a rusty chain above the door. The first sign read, *Gilroy's House of Maple,* and the second one simply read, *Antiques.*

"How did you hear of this place?" asked Katy.

"How have you *not* heard of Gilroy's? It's been here forever. Best flapjacks in the state — they even make their own syrup! The Gilroys passed away decades ago, and the business was passed on to their two daughters, Milly and Maude. Milly and her husband ran the restaurant while Maude ran the antique store. When Milly's husband passed, her boys helped her keep the restaurant going. Milly still does all the cooking herself."

Mike parked his truck in the loose gravel lot next to the creek running along the backside of the cabins. He helped Katy out of the vehicle and held her hand as they meandered their way over to the restaurant. The bubbling surge of icy cold water from the rushing creek rippled through her ears, sending her adrift once more.

"Are you all right?" asked Mike, noticing the distracted look on her face. Apparently, he had been talking, and she hadn't heard a word he said.

"You know, it's weird, but since I've been back home, I've

been having these strange déjà vu moments."

"Well, you *are* from here. Maybe your mind is bringing back long-lost memories from your childhood — or maybe you were just *meant* to be back."

The dining room had limited seating, but there was only one other couple having breakfast when they walked in. A lumberjack of a man in his mid-forties, wearing a plaid shirt, grabbed two single-page menus and led them to a wobbly table in front of a large picture window. The knotty pine decor rendered the cabin even more rustic with its lack of proper lighting, but the fact that it overlooked the creek made it strangely romantic. The restaurant may have been unsophisticated, but Mike was right about the food. The homemade sausage and pancakes smothered in real maple syrup were the best Katy had ever tasted. When they had finished eating, Katy pushed back her chair and patted her tummy. She had eaten more than she should have, and her tight jeans had stretched themselves to the limit. Maybe it was the food, or maybe it was the ambiance, but she hadn't felt this satisfied in a long time.

While Mike was busy paying the bill, Katy thought she'd wander next door to take a peek inside the antique store. She stepped through the clanging door to find an eclectic mix of baubles, trinkets, clothing, and furniture, from ordinary junk to seemingly invaluable artifacts. As she was passing a glass encasement of jewelry, she noticed a woman in a colorful caftan sitting behind the counter. She had jet black hair pulled high up on her head and held together with gold and silver rhinestone-studded hair combs.

The woman immediately got up from her stool. "Can I help you find something, sweetheart?"

"No thank you, I'm just looking," said Katy. "Are you Maude?"

"Guilty," replied the woman, repositioning one of her hair combs.

Katy bent down to more closely examine the large assortment of jewels and trinkets beneath the glass. "You certainly have some unique pieces here."

"I can unlock the case if you like."

"That's all right. Although, I do love that ring right there with the beautiful pink stone," said Katy, pointing.

"You've got good taste. That one there is my most expensive piece. That pink stone is a 20.00 carat Morganite."

"Really, a Morganite? I've never heard of a Morganite stone before."

"I know, ain't it fitting? It's encrusted with real diamonds, and the band is 18 kt rose gold. It looks like it might be your size. You wanna try it on?"

"I'd love to, but I'm sure I can't afford it. If you don't mind my asking, where do you find these one-of-a-kind pieces?"

"Oh, here and there," said Maude. "Sometimes people fall on hard luck and are forced to pawn even their most precious belongings. Way back, when I was just a girl, old man Watters, we used to call him, would come in the first of every month. He was a gravedigger at the Morganville Cemetery—I'm sure that don't pay much. He'd bring in small Bibles, fancy cigarette cases, watches, the like, but mostly jewelry. We never asked no questions. He finally left town when he was accused of grave robbin'. Ain't seen him since—of course, that was eons ago."

Katy surreptitiously lifted her hand against her pendant to make sure it was safely secured beneath her jacket. Just then, she heard the clanger from the door. "There you are," called Mike, finding his way through the clutter.

"Are you sure you don't wanna try anything on? I've got some less expensive rings over here—maybe get your boyfriend to buy you one," winked the woman.

"No thanks," said Katy, feeling herself turning red with Mike standing there and making a quick turn to leave.

The two of them took their time strolling back to the truck, admiring the view and breathing in the crisp morning air. Mike had just begun to pull the door open for her when he stopped short, opening it just a crack. "Before I take you home, I'd like to take you somewhere."

"But I promised my father I would pick Lilly up by—"

"Don't worry," he interrupted. "I'll have you back by

noon. I'd really like to show you something."

"All right," Katy said reluctantly. She couldn't imagine what he could possibly have to show her. After driving for over half-an-hour, her curiosity got the best of her. "Okay, where are we going?"

"You'll see, we're almost there."

You'll see? she thought. Her curiosity became replaced by anxiety. Where was he taking her, and why? What did she really know about him? For all she knew, he could be a serial rapist, or murderer, or both. Here they were in the middle of nowhere, surrounded only by pastures and farmland. No one would ever find her body out here. *I can't think like that*, she kept telling herself, trying hard to calm her fears.

Finally, he stopped his truck at the edge of a vast golden meadow, completely unencumbered except for two massive trees that looked as if they had been there since the beginning of time, with their far-reaching branches posing as ancestral guardians of the virgin landscape.

"Here we are!" he announced, jumping out of the vehicle toward her door. Maybe it was the openness of the valley that prompted the wind to bluster so angrily because he had to hold Katy's door open with all his strength to keep it from blowing shut. He held her hand while she scooted out of the vehicle and led her out a few feet, where he stopped to stare out into the open field.

Katy's tall, thin frame reeled in the current while the forceful breeze blew her amber tresses in circles, emulating the lofty golden grasses swaying amidst the sun's incandescent rays.

"What is this place?" she yelled, trying to sweep the hair off her face.

"This will be mine one day," Mike yelled out over the bellowing breeze.

As Katy looked out on the horizon, the sun beat down on her with the warmth of a radiant furnace, and for one split second, she was struck with another déjà vu moment. This time, however, it was followed by something else. While gazing out into the open field, her eyes began to reveal an image gradually coming into focus. She couldn't be sure if what she was seeing was real or if it was some sort of mirage.

Two horses were galloping toward her. A man dressed in black, with a black cowboy hat, was riding a black mare, and a woman in white with a white cowboy hat was on a white horse. The nearer they got, the clearer the images became. The horses were running side by side but then slowed down to a trot until they stopped just a few yards from where Katy was standing. The couple, whose faces were shadowed beneath their cowboy hats, reached out to hold each other's hand. They sat motionless upon their horses as the blazing sun continued to glare down upon them. As Katy cupped her hands over her eyes and squinted to get a clearer view, the figures slowly transformed into fine sculptures of sand. But then the image took an ominous turn. A cyclone rose up and whirled around them like a giant dust devil until it disintegrated, leaving nothing in its path but two mounds of powder.

Katy let out a partial scream, and Mike turned around to see what was wrong. She just stood there transfixed, unable to move. He grabbed her by the shoulders, trying to coax her back to reality. The illusion disappeared, and Katy gradually regained her composure.

"What's the matter, Kate? You look like you just saw a ghost!"

"I'm okay, it's nothing—it must have been sunspots."

Mike just looked at her curiously.

Not wanting to say anything more about it, she quickly changed the subject. "Now, why are we here?"

Mike answered in an apologetic tone, "I just wanted to show you this spectacular spot. Remember when I told you my goal was to own a ranch someday? This is it. This is the place I had in mind. What do you think?" He let out a nervous laugh. It was obvious he was thinking this might not have been such a good idea after all.

That would explain the cowboy hat, thought Katy. Still, she wasn't sure why he had felt the need to bring her here so early on in their relationship. Nevertheless, with her arms still shaking, she reached them up around his neck to give him a grateful kiss. "It's beautiful, Mike!"

He smiled sheepishly. "I was hoping you'd like it. Well, we'd better get you back home so you can pick up your little girl."

Chapter Fifteen

Lilly was sitting at the kitchen table eating her lunch and coloring on a piece of white construction paper when Katy walked in. She immediately dropped her crayon down on the table and shouted, "Look, Mommy, Grandpa made me a grilled cheese sandwich, and Merriweather is helping me eat it!"

Katy's old ragdoll was hunched over in the chair next to Lilly. "How did you know my doll's name?"

"Grandpa told me. He said Grandma thought of that name when she bought it for you because the doll's dress had a picture of a sun with a smiley face on it."

Katy leaned over to give her daughter a hug while at the same time pretending to sneak a taste of her sandwich. "Mmm, that looks good. Can I have a bite?"

"Hey, get your own," squealed Lilly, moving her sandwich away from her mom's mouth. "It's only for me and Merriweather."

Katy straightened back up and looked at her father. "When did you learn how to cook, Dad?"

"A man's gotta eat, you know. Want me to make you one?"

"No thanks, I already ate," said Katy, looking at her daughter's stick-figure portrait. "What are you drawing there, Lilly?"

"It's a picture of me in bed holding a kitty."

"You mean Tandy?"

"No, silly, Tandy's at home! I slept with your kitty last night—you know, the white one."

"Oh, you mean my stuffed cat, Fluffy."

"Yeah, Fluffy." Lilly re-examined her drawing. "Oops,

I forgot something." She took a dark crayon and drew a large square around the smaller square that was meant to be the bed. "Now it's picture-perfect," she said with a big grin on her face.

Katy gave her daughter a strange look, wondering where she had heard that. She hadn't heard those words in a long time — maybe her dad said something to Lilly. "Well, that's a very nice picture. Now finish your sandwich and go gather up your things while I help Grandpa clean up. We have to get going so Grandpa can get some rest. I'm sure you kept him quite busy."

Lilly collected her picture and crayons, grabbed Merriweather by the arm, and ran into the bedroom while Katy stayed in the kitchen to help her dad clear the table.

"So, how was your date last night?" he asked.

"Good," Katy said humbly.

"Do you plan on seeing him again?"

"Prrrrrobably," she answered, dragging the word out and ending with a reticent smile.

"Well, I'm looking forward to meeting him."

Katy remained quiet while she filled the sink with water, not wanting to give away too much too soon. When she was finished with the dishes, she excused herself to go see how Lilly was progressing. She walked into her old bedroom to find her daughter sitting on the floor, having an animated conversation with Merriweather. "Lilly, you haven't packed anything!"

"Yes, I did!" Lilly answered defiantly, pointing to her little pink Cinderella suitcase on the floor.

Katy looked at the open suitcase. Randomly tossed inside were her shirt, her pajama bottoms, one sock, her toothbrush, and the picture she had drawn. "Here, I'll help you," she said, as she began picking up the rest of her daughter's clothes off the floor.

While she was folding them up and placing them neatly into the suitcase, Lilly climbed up on the bed and started jumping up and down. "I like spending time with Grandpa and sleeping in your old bed with all your dolls and stuffed animals."

"I'm glad, baby. Grandpa loves you very much."

Lilly stopped jumping for a moment to pick up Katy's old stuffed cat. "Can I take Fluffy home with me?" she asked, stroking its disheveled white fur. "So Tandy has a friend to keep him company when I'm not home."

"Are you sure you don't want one of my other stuffed animals?" asked Katy. "He's pretty worn — he looks more scruffy than he does fluffy."

Lilly started laughing and began jumping on the bed again, with Fluffy under one arm.

"You know, Fluffy was my favorite stuffed animal when I was little. I named him after my real one — the one that's in kitty heaven now.

"Is that where grandma lives?"

Katy smiled. "Yes, that's where grandma lives." Then she resumed packing and looked at the doll with the smiley-face dress lying on the floor. "You can bring Merriweather home too, if you like."

"No, she has to stay here and keep Grandma company when she visits," stated Lilly, very matter-of-factly. Katy gave her daughter, who was still jumping up and down, a strange look, when Lilly blurted out, "I saw Grandma last night."

Katy stopped folding the pants that were in her hands and froze. "What?"

"I saw Grandma when I went to sleep last night, and she talked to me."

"Honey, I'm sure it was just a dream."

"No Mommy, she was standing right there," said Lilly, pointing to the front of the bed. "She was smiling, and then she said I was 'picture-perfect.'"

Katy could feel the hair on her arms standing on end. "I'm sure it was just a dream," she repeated, as if trying to convince herself. Then she began to toss the rest of her daughter's things into the suitcase, without bothering to fold them, as fast as she could. "We have to go."

When they returned to the kitchen to say goodbye to her father, Katy turned to him and asked, "By the way, Dad, do you still have Mom's old camera — you know, the Canon 35 millimeter?"

"Yes, of course, I do. Do you want it?"

"I don't know, maybe."

"Well, let's go look. After your mother died, I put it up in your bedroom closet and haven't touched it since. You know I was never good at using that thing—your mother was the expert." Katy followed him back to her room, with Lilly following closely behind. He opened up the white slatted closet door and began scanning the shelves. "Hmm, that's strange. I thought I put it up there on that top shelf."

Lilly squeezed herself between their legs and pointed downward. "There it is!" Katy and her father turned their eyes to the floor, where it was laying in clear sight.

"That's strange," said Mr. Barton. "I'm sure I set it up there on that top shelf. Hmm, I guess it must have fallen. I hope it still works."

Katy bent over and picked it up to examine it. She stared at the camera for a moment then looked back down on the floor. "The lens cover is off. Maybe it came off when it fell. Other than that, it looks all right. Why don't you hang onto it a little bit longer, Dad? Maybe I'll get it next time I'm here."

Chapter Sixteen

Katy finally made good on her promise to call her old friend, Janice. They made plans to meet for lunch at the Bluebird Cafe on Monday, which was halfway between PTTV and the DOT, where Janice worked. She hurried to clear off her desk and was just about to leave when Mr. Bruckman approached her.

"You wanna come into my office for a minute, Kate?"

Oh great, this can't be good, she thought, glancing at her watch. "Of course," she responded, trying to remain upbeat while she followed him to his office. His office was at the far end of the hallway, visible through a clear Plexiglas wall. It wasn't fancy, but at least he had an office. He even had a window where he could look out—even if the view was the parking lot—which would explain how he always seemed to know exactly when she came in.

As Katy entered the room, he shut the door behind her and walked around his expansive wraparound desk. He grabbed the edge of its dark veneer, which was barely visible beneath the pile of news stories waiting to be reviewed, and dropped down into his worn and faded leather chair. "Have a seat, will ya?" he said, motioning his hand over to the chair facing him.

Katy sat down, her posture erect.

"How long have you been here—about seven months now?"

"Yes sir," she answered enthusiastically.

"I've been very happy with your work, Kate. You've been doing a really swell job. You're pretty easy to get along with, and *most* of your coworkers like you," he grinned.

Ha, ha, thought Katy.

"So, starting next week, I'm giving you a ten percent raise."

What Katy wanted to say was, *Ten percent! That's it?* Instead, she chose to project an artificial smile and respond with, "Thank you very much, Mr. Bruckman. I appreciate it."

"I just want to make sure you're happy. We would hate to lose you."

"Yes sir, I'm quite happy—except for one little thing."

Bruckman raised his eyebrows. "What's that?"

"I don't mean any disrespect, but as I've mentioned to you before, I wish I could do a story with a little more substance. I don't know, maybe something with some historical value."

"What about the Morganville General Store? Didn't that have historical value?"

"Yes, yes it did. In fact, that's exactly what prompted me to want to do something more. I grew up here. I feel a close connection to this town, and since I've been back, that feeling has grown even stronger."

"Well, I don't know how much 'substance' this next assignment holds, but it does have some historical value, and you could definitely tie it in with the demolition of the general store."

Katy was all ears.

"I don't know if you've heard of the old Brewer mansion?"

"Yes, I've heard of it. In fact, I started doing a little research into Morgan Brewer, and I found him to be quite fascinating. I was surprised to learn how much he's done for this town."

"Yeah, well, the mansion is located just inside the periphery of Morganville. The Department of Transportation wants to bulldoze it—same as the general store—to pave the way for the new Route 46 extension set to run through there. Several city and state officials have tried to get ol' Miss Brewer to sign off on the property, but she'll have nothing to do with it. She refuses to let them in the house, and her phone has apparently been disconnected. I'd like you to go out there and try to get an interview with her."

"What a shame they have to bulldoze it," said Katy. "So, what's the story with Miss Brewer?"

"When Morgan Brewer died back in '61, he left everything

to her. She was his sole heir—no other living relatives. She never married and is a bit of a recluse. No one, other than her housekeeper, has seen or talked to her in years—at least no one from around here. It may take you a few tries, but I'm sure with your tenacity, you'll find a way to get her to open up. I'd like to air the story before the demolition date."

"Which is?"

"We don't have one yet, so you've got some time to prepare. But I'm sure it won't be long from now, seeing as the store has already been set to be demolished by the end of the month."

"Don't worry, Mr. Bruckman. If anyone can get to Miss Brewer, it's me."

Bruckman pushed aside a small stack of paperwork on his desk and leaned in toward her, and in a hushed tone said, "You know, Kate, the lead anchor, Martha, is going to be going on maternity leave in a few months. If you keep doing a good job, it could lead to a semi-promotion, as a fill-in co-anchor."

Katy felt uplifted, her voice spiking. "I won't let you down, sir!"

She jumped up and pushed her chair back in when Bruckman added, "By the way, how are those sleeping pills working?"

"Uh, they're helping—a little."

~*~

Katy jumped into her car and raced over to the Bluebird Cafe to meet her friend. When she walked in the door, she immediately spotted Janice, with her thick mane of naturally-curly black hair, sitting in a middle booth, sipping on a tall glass of Coke. "I'm so sorry I'm late, but my boss called me into his office just as I was getting ready to leave—"

"It's okay," interrupted Janice. "It gave me time to figure out what I want. You know how I can never make up my mind."

Just then, the waitress came by to take their order. "Have you decided?"

"No, but I have narrowed it down," said Janice, still eyeing the menu.

"In the meantime, I'll have a Sprite, please," said Katy.

Janice took another sip from her straw then folded her elbows on the table. "I'm glad we were finally able to get together. So what've you been up to since we ran into each other at Longley Park?"

"Well, I met this guy —" began Katy.

"Hold on!" Janice barged in. "I want all the sordid details."

"His name is Mike, and —"

Just then, the waitress came by again with her Sprite. "I'll be back in a minute to take your orders."

Katy pressed her lips together until she had gone, then proceeded to fill Janice in on how they met and what a gentleman he turned out to be.

"So when are you going to see him again?"

"I don't know. Because he's a fireman, he works weird hours. He'll work for a few days and then be off for a few days. He suggested we catch a play at the Pittsburgh Playhouse sometime during the week." Katy stopped to take a sip of her Sprite.

"Oh yeah, what's playing?" asked Janice

"I think, *Our Town* — you know, by Thornton Wilder."

"Isn't that the one where everyone has boring lives, and then they die?"

"No! It's much more than that — I read the play in school. It's about appreciating every moment of your life because it goes by so fast."

"Sounds like a barrel of fun," Janice smirked sarcastically. "Still, most of the guys I know wouldn't be caught dead going to a play. They'd rather be camped out on the couch watching sports on the boob tube."

Katy took a long, heavy breath. "I just don't know if I'm ready for him to meet Lilly."

"Why? Are you worried she won't like him? How could she not? He sounds like the perfect guy." Janice paused to gulp down the rest of her Coke.

"It's not that — it's me. I'm just not sure I'm ready."

"You've had over five years, Katy. How long do you need?"

Katy swished the ice around the bottom of her glass with her straw. "I guess you're right."

The waitress came back to take their orders, and when she left, Janice resumed the conversation. "So, how is it that you're always landing such great guys, and I'm out there meeting all these losers?"

"Don't worry, Janice, the right guy will come along for you, too. Maybe you're trying too hard."

Janice gave Katy a designing look. "Or maybe, I'm not trying hard enough...."

Katy didn't say anything—she'd seen that look before.

Chapter Seventeen

Punctual as usual, thought Katy, hurrying over to answer the door. There he stood with a big grin on his face, holding a beautiful bouquet of autumn lilies in vibrant shades of red, yellow, and orange.

"How beautiful! You shouldn't have!"

"Lilies—in honor of your daughter," said Mike, entering the living room.

A subdued chuckle filtered out of Katy's throat. "Let me put these in water."

Mike looked around the room as he followed her into the kitchen. "So, where's Lilly?"

"Oh, I dropped her off at my dad's."

"When am I going to get to meet her?" he asked, with a hint of acrimony in his voice. "Uh, soon," said Katy, trying to diffuse the topic while she bent down to get a vase from one of the lower kitchen cabinets. She filled the vase halfway with water, arranged the flowers haphazardly, and set them on the kitchen table. Finally, she swiped her palms together and said, "Okay, I'm all ready. I just need to get my coat."

Mike followed her back into the front room without saying a word, clearly disappointed that Lilly wasn't there, and helped her with her coat.

"What time does the play start?" asked Katy.

"It doesn't start until eight, so I thought we could stop and get something to eat first. How does pizza sound? I know this great little trattoria – they've got the best pizza in town."

"Sounds great."

The ride into the city was mostly subdued, with Katy

doing most of the talking. When they walked into the restaurant, it appeared that Mike had gotten over his disappointment of not meeting Lilly when he requested they be in a cozy booth in the corner, then wasted no time ordering a bottle of Chianti.

While they were waiting for their pizza to be cooked in the wood-fired brick oven, Mike raised his stemmed glass and looked into Katy's eyes. "Cheers."

"Cheers," echoed Katy, taking a small sip of her wine.

Mike's glass was still up in the air when he added, "Here's to meeting your daughter — *soon*."

And here we go again, thought Katy, smiling impishly, then taking a much larger gulp. "Mmm, it sure smells good in here. How do you know all these good places to eat?"

Mike looked at Katy as if to say, "I know what you're doing — changing the subject." Then he responded, "Well, when you live alone, you tend to eat out a lot."

"Speaking of that, I don't even know where you live!"

"I live here, in Morganville."

"I know, but where exactly?" pressed Katy, wondering why it was taking him so long to answer the question.

"Where else, but the beautiful Morgan-Villa Apartments down on Newcastle Road — about a mile west of the Morganville Christian Academy. Isn't that where you went to school?

"Uh, yes, it is."

"Doesn't your daughter go there too?"

Katy took another drink from her glass. She couldn't remember telling him that. "Um, yeah — it's a private K through twelve school."

"Which brings me to ask the question again — why haven't I met her yet?"

Katy was really starting to get annoyed. Why was he forcing the issue so much? "I...I just want to be sure, that's all."

"Of what? My intentions?"

"No, it's not that. I know your intentions are honorable. I'm just, um...I guess I'm just afraid."

"Afraid of what?"

"I've lost two very important people in my life, and I'm

afraid of it happening again. I don't want to put my daughter through the same pain I went through of losing someone she loves."

Mike did that thing again, where he reached across the table to grab Katy's hands in his, inevitably causing her heart to flutter. "I understand," he said. "But, you can't be afraid of the future, Kate. You have to *believe* that everything will turn out as it was meant to be. You must live in the present. Everything happens for a reason."

Hmm, now where had she heard that before? Oh yeah, that's what her dad tried to tell her at her mother's funeral.

After arriving at the playhouse, they found their seats, and Mike held Katy's hand throughout most of the performance. When the final curtain came down, and the lights were switched back on, Mike noticed the droplets pooling in the corners of Katy's eyes. She never was good at keeping her emotions in check, much less hiding them.

"You're so sensitive," he said, wiping away a rogue tear with his finger.

Katy tried to make humor of it. "Yeah, my mother used to say I would cry 'at the drop of a hat,'" she sniffled.

They exited the intimate little theatre and walked silently, hand-in-hand, under the illusory path of the streetlights. Eventually, Mike broke the silence. "Let me ask you a question, Katy."

Katy turned to look at him. "Yeah?"

"If you could relive your life, would you?"

"Not if I knew all the pain I'd have to endure."

"Even if it held the promise of a new beginning?"

Katy did not respond but kept walking as she tried to absorb what he was alluding to. After a few minutes of quiet contemplation, she finally said, "Okay, the next weekend you have off, I promise you can come over and meet Lilly."

Chapter Eighteen

Mike was so excited about finally getting to meet Lilly that he made sure to get the next weekend off. There was a fair in town at the Old Mill grounds, so he proposed they all go.

When the doorbell rang early on Sunday morning, Katy peered through the peephole to see who it was. She still had a towel wrapped around her head. It was Mike.

She opened the door and looked at her watch. "Weren't you supposed to here at ten?"

Mike blushed. "Sorry, I guess I was overly anxious to meet Lilly."

"Well, come in and sit down. You're going to have to wait a while. We're still in the process of getting ready."

As soon as Mike stepped inside, Lilly ran into the room with her pajama's still on. At first, he just stared at her and seemed to be studying her face. Then he knelt down and stretched out his arm to shake her hand. "Why hello, Lilly, my name is Mike. I am so happy to *finally* be meeting you."

Lilly extended her hand shyly. "You don't look like a fireman," she remarked.

Mike glanced up at Katy, then back at Lilly, and laughed. "That's because I'm not wearing my helmet."

~*~

By the time they arrived at the fair, Mike had already built up a friendly rapport with Lilly, and it was obvious she took an immediate liking to him as well.

"Hey, let's go try and squirt the ducks!" he yelled, grabbing her by the hand. Katy couldn't help but smile as she watched them run off toward the water gun booth. "We won!" shouted

Mike, and with an enthusiastic grin on his face, he handed Lilly the prize — a small purple bear with a red heart on its chest. Lilly grabbed it out of his hands immediately and held it close to her chest.

"Say thank you," reminded Katy.

"Thank you," Lilly articulated in her most demure voice.

Katy looked at Mike. "You're a natural with children."

Mike swelled with pride. "I guess I'm just a kid at heart."

"Look, farm animals!" squealed Lilly, making a mad dash toward the baby goats with her bear clutched under her arm. Mike and Katy took off after her, doing their best to keep up. After petting each and every animal in the petting zoo, Lilly rubbed her stomach, complaining she was hungry, so they stopped at one of the vendor booths to grab some lunch.

"Can I have a corndog and some lemonade?" she asked.

"Of course you may," Mike jumped in, getting his wallet out.

After wandering around a bit, they were able to secure a picnic table in a somewhat shaded area. Lilly took a big gulp of her lemonade and a few bites of her corndog, then looked up at Mike. "Do you like being a fireman?"

"Yes, I do. I love being a fireman."

"But don't you get scared when it's a really big fire?"

"I never have time to be afraid. When I'm putting out a fire, all I can think of is saving the people and their houses."

"What about the animals?"

"Animals too," he smiled. "Hey, maybe one day you can come out with your mom and visit the fire station, if you like.

"Yeah, I'd like that!" she shouted, jumping up and down. "Can we, Mommy, can we?"

"Sure," said Katy.

Mike excused himself to use the public restroom. On the way, he passed a souvenir stand with a display wall featuring a variety of hats in all colors and sizes. When he returned, he had something concealed behind his back.

"Look what I found!" he said, pulling his arm out from behind his back to reveal a shiny red plastic helmet. Lilly's face beamed with sheer delight as he placed it on her head. It was a little loose, so she reached up with her little hands, grabbing onto the sides to keep it from falling off. "Now, you'll be prepared when you come to visit me at the station."

"You're spoiling her," said Katy, taking note of that victorious smile emphasizing his chiseled jawline.

After a full day of fun and amusement rides, Lilly was exhausted. She was barely able to finish her cotton candy, let alone make it to the car at the far end of the parking lot, so Mike picked her up and carried her while staying several strides ahead of Katy. Katy couldn't help but marvel at him from behind. *Besides the fact that he has a great ass, he'll make a great dad someday.*

Lilly fell asleep the minute her head hit the seat, with her purple Care Bear folded tightly between her arms.

Katy stroked Mike's arm as he drove. "Lilly and I had a wonderful time today. Thank you."

"It was *my* pleasure — really."

Chapter Nineteen

Monday morning arrived after another sleepless night. Katy had to fight with Lilly, who insisted on wearing her new red helmet to school. By the time she got to work, she was already exhausted. As the workday was winding down and she had finished everything on her to-do list, Katy noticed she still had half-an-hour to spare before having to leave to pick up her daughter. She took a quick peek over her cubicle, then pushed her keyboard aside and, using her arms as a cushion, laid her head on her desk.

"I'm coming, I'm coming. Hold on," mumbled Katy, who was immersed in dreamland and believed there was someone knocking at her front door.

"Wake up, Katy, wake up!" yelled an obstinate voice.

Katy snapped to, realizing the knocking she heard was coming from Vicky knocking on her partition wall.

"How much beauty sleep do you need?" said Vicky sarcastically.

"I don't know — what time is it?" asked Katy, still groggy. Before Vicky could answer, Katy looked up at the round industrial-sized black and white clock on the wall. "Oh my God, I have to go!" She jumped out of her chair and pulled her purse out of her drawer.

As she was leaving, Vicky called out to her, "It's a good thing I caught you instead of Bruckman." Finishing her sentence in an inaudible whisper, "Of course, I'll make sure he finds out about it."

By the time Katy pulled up to the Morganville Christian Academy, there weren't many cars left in line. Most of the children had already been picked up. Lilly and Meghan were sitting on the front steps of the school with their pink backpacks haphazardly strewn around them. They were so absorbed in their own little world, laughing and waving their Barbie dolls in the air, that they didn't even notice Katy's car drive up. She jumped out of the vehicle and grabbed their backpacks. "I'm sorry I'm late, sweetie. I forgot Meghan was coming home with you today," she said as she opened the door to the back seat to help them in.

"It's okay," said Lilly. "Meghan brought her Barbie dolls, and we were pretending they were Cinderellas."

"But they didn't need a carriage to go to the dance, 'cause they can fly," added Meghan.

"Oh, that's nice," remarked Katy, starting the engine and pulling away from the curb.

"Me and Meghan are both going to be Cinderellas for Halloween!" Lilly shouted excitedly.

"Yeah!" chimed in Meghan.

"I can't believe it's almost Halloween," said Katy. "I wonder if your costume still fits from last year."

"Can Meghan come over to our house and go trick-or-treating with me?"

Katy could see the anticipation in her daughter's eyes from her rearview mirror. "Of course, she can. So how was school today?"

"BORING!" yelled Lilly. "Except for when we had a fire drill. I told you, you should have let me wear my fireman's hat!"

"We all had to go outside, and Mrs. Randolph wouldn't even let us get our jackets, and it was really cold out!" complained Meghan, pouting her lips and wrinkling her tawny brows.

"Mrs. Randolph is a mean old witch!" blasted Lilly, folding her arms across her chest. "She grabbed my arm really hard."

"What? That's terrible," exclaimed Katy. "Why would she do that?"

"I don't know," replied Lilly, dropping her voice impishly.

"I'm going to have to talk to her about that."

As the three of them were walking to the front door of their townhome, they could see Tandy's dark shadow pacing nervously on the sill behind the semi-sheer curtains. The minute Katy unlocked the front door, he jumped off the window ledge and headed straight for Lilly, who immediately dropped her schoolbag to give him a big squeeze. "I love you, Tandy!" she bellowed in his ear as he licked her face with his raspy tongue. "I'm so glad nobody came to get you. You're going to be my kitty forever and ever!"

"Okay, girls, now you run along and play while I get dinner ready."

"Come on, Meghan, let's go to my room and play with our Barbies!" The two of them ran into Lilly's bedroom, with Tandy tagging closely behind.

About an hour later, Katy returned to her daughter's room to let the girls know it was time to eat. When she walked into the bedroom, she noticed that the throw rug under the dollhouse was sopping wet. "What happened here?" she asked sternly, pointing to the rug.

Lilly, with Ken doll in hand, pointed him to the Barbie car, which was leaning against the dollhouse upside down. Katy also observed two sets of Barbie feet sticking out from underneath the car. "We were pretending the Barbies crashed into the house, and then the house caught on fire."

"It's a good thing Ken is a fireman, 'cause he put out the fire just in time with this bucket of water," explained Meghan, raising an empty Dixie cup.

"Except he could only save one of the Barbies," added Lilly, squeezing her lips and lowering her head while lifting her gaze until they met her mother's eyes.

Katy got a puzzled look on her face, then shook her head back and forth. "Okay, girls, let's clean this up before we go into the kitchen and eat."

She walked over to the bathroom to get a towel. There she found Lilly's fire helmet laying upside down on the bathroom floor. It had been partially filled with water, and crouched down next to it was Tandy, lapping it up as if he didn't expect to be drinking again for days.

Chapter Twenty

Katy jerked forward, gasping for air, while the glowing digits on her bedside clock flashed 2:38 a.m. Her top sheet was tangled around one leg, and her fleece blanket was dangling on the floor. She wanted to scream out loud but held back for fear she'd wake her young daughter in the next room. Instead, she covered her face with her hands and cried softly. *My God, I thought I resolved this problem! Maybe I do need to go back to Dr. Fleming.* She got up to rearrange the sheet and gathered up her blanket. Then she fell back into bed, tossing and turning and staring at the ceiling for at least two hours until she finally dozed off. No sooner had she fallen asleep than she felt a slight tug on her blanket.

"Wake up, Mommy, wake up!" squeaked a little high-pitched voice.

Katy turned over to look at her clock radio. "Oh no, I've overslept again!" she bellowed, frantically jumping out of bed. "I must have turned off the alarm, thinking I hit the snooze button."

Lilly pulled on her mom's pajamas to get her attention. Katy looked down to see her daughter put her hands on her waist and proudly turn her body back and forth. "Look, Mommy, I dressed myself." Her socks didn't match, and her button-down cotton dress was on backwards, but other than that, she had done a pretty good job.

"Lilly, you are so grown up. I don't know what I'd do without you!"

"Will you make me breakfast, Mommy?"

"I'm sorry, honey. I don't have time. Pop Tarts will have to do again."

It was a blustery autumn morning, just as the weatherman had predicted. When they walked out to the car, the wind blew so hard Katy had to use all her strength to pull the door open. Lilly let out a tinkle of laughter while she tried to hold her dress down to keep it from blowing up in her face.

"I think pants might have been a better idea today, Lilly, but it's too late to go back in and change."

The last bell was ringing when she pulled up to the Morganville Christian Academy. She rushed to unbuckle her daughter's seatbelt and helped her out of the backseat. "Bye, sweetie, I love you! Oh, and here—don't forget your lunchbox!" she shouted, reaching back into the car to get it.

Katy had hoped to get an earlier start this morning because she had planned on driving out to the Brewer mansion. She wanted to get a feel for where it was located and to get a general assessment of how the property was going to interfere with the intended highway route. She was also hoping to get a chance to speak with Miss Brewer.

After exiting the main road, she pulled over to the shoulder to check her map to figure out the fastest way to get there. *Let's see, if I make a quick turn onto Route 20 and keep going for 6.2 miles....* Once she thought she had it figured out, she started up her engine and proceeded along until the paved road ended. According to the map, the shortest way was to make a sharp right-hand turn just up ahead, which she did. At that point, the black asphalt turned into a narrower dirt road, dredged with potholes. As her car sputtered and slid along the scattered rocks, an eerie feeling began to loom over her. She felt as though she had been down this trail before. In fact, it looked a lot like the road where the accident happened on the night Mark took that ominous shortcut home.

Suddenly, she was hit with another déjà vu moment. Her mind flashed back to that rainy night—to the moment that buck was standing in the middle of the road. The moment fleeted by, but when her psyche boomeranged back to full cognizance, there really *was* an actual deer standing in the middle of the road— *again*! The only difference was that this was a doe instead of a buck. Immediately Katy slammed on her brakes, causing her rear tires to skate back and forth over the loose gravel until her car came to a screeching halt—just in time to avoid the collision. The doe just stood there, gazing nonchalantly at Katy through the dusty windshield, when out from the thicket appeared a small spotted fawn. When it caught up to its mother, the doe pranced off, with her fawn following closely behind.

In an exhaustive state of relief, Katy dropped her head in the middle of the steering wheel and exploded into tears. She sat in the middle of the roadway for at least ten minutes until she finally took a long deep breath and broke out into a guttural laugh of remission that ended with her shouting at the top of her lungs, "There are way too many deer around here!"

It dawned on her that she had better get moving, lest some unsuspecting vehicle crash into her from behind. Luckily, this was a desolate road with very little traffic. *Okay, Katy, get a grip,* she thought, pulling down her visor mirror to wipe the smudged mascara from her eyes. She then shifted the car into drive and continued along the road until it changed back to a never-ending, winding asphalt road. *Where the heck is this place? I can understand why they want to extend a highway through here!*

Just when she was beginning to think she might have taken a wrong turn, the road finally straightened out to become a serene, powdery trail lined with towering trees arching up over the middle, creating a virtual canopy where only scattered shafts of sunlight were permitted to filter in.

As Katy reached the end of the domed trail, the distinctive Victorian perched atop a ridge spotlighted by the sun's shimmering rays suddenly came into view. Goosebumps erupted from her skin as a weird sense of familiarity crept through her bones. She felt as though she were about to enter another realm as she continued forth, completely disregarding the No Trespassing sign.

The powdery trail proved to be an ingress to an elongated driveway sloping upward toward the mansion. Katy parked her car at the base of the incline, but wanting to get a better scope of the area, she got out of the car and began making her ascent by foot. As she drew nearer, the encroaching oaks and pines began to intervene upon the welcoming sun's façade to produce a collage of foreboding shadows.

She had almost reached the top when she stopped to take in a closer view. It appeared as though the house had been neglected for a countless number of years, but even in its weathered state, it exuded an aura of stately countenance. What caught her eye was the massive oak commanding the front lawn. Hanging on one of the lower branches was a swing made of heavy rope, with a thick wooden slat at its base. As Katy fixated upon the tree, she was struck with a strange sensation, rendering her into an almost dreamlike state.

A vision appeared before her, that of a little girl running in and out of the trees, her small hand gripping the rim of her straw hat to keep it from falling off her head. Katy could hear the young girl laughing and yelling, "You can't catch me!" A woman appeared, running closely behind, the bun pulled loosely atop her head of jet black hair unraveling. Their bodies were diffused from the transcending glow of the midday sun shining through the barren trees. A brisk current suddenly caused the girl's dress to billow while a whirlwind of fallen leaves fluttered endlessly in circles around her. Darting through the mounds of dry foliage, she made her way toward the swing. She pulled the ropes toward her and positioned herself carefully on the wooden seat. "Push me, Mommy, push me!" she shouted. The mother caught up to her, thrusting her palms forward in a series of gentle nudges. Once again, Katy heard the little girl, whose smile was as big as the ocean, yelling, "Faster, Mommy, faster!"

The woman continued to push harder and harder until the swing was propelled to its limit, causing a burst of wind to flow up into the little girl's hat. The hat went flying off her head, up, up into the air, high into the trees. "Oh no!" the little girl shouted as she watched its yellow ribbon and colorful flowers being ripped from its center and trail off into the distance as the vision slowly faded.

Katy, who was frozen in her tracks, barely had time to return to reality before she was instantly beset with another vision.

A cruel wind was blowing again, only this time, instead of leaves, it was blowing sheaths of gossamer flurries against a crowd of people bundled in dark overcoats, huddled before a casket that was about to be placed in the ground. In the center front row stood that same little girl, barely recognizable now due to the somber guise that had overtaken her previous carefree demeanor. A man who appeared to be her father stood next to her, squeezing her little hand tightly as the casket was lowered into the ground. Gradually, this vision too faded to black.

No sooner had Katy's hallucination vanished than she was approached by a short, rotund woman, startling her back into the present. She was wearing thick, flesh-colored stockings and a full apron over a paisley dress, which did little to differentiate her waistline. Her streaked grey hair was pulled tightly into a neat little bun atop her head, which made her round face look even rounder.

"May I help ya, miss?" yelled the woman. Then she repeated herself, louder this time, "I SAID, MAY I HELP YA, MISS?"

Katy squeezed her eyes shut and shook her head while she tried to regain clarity. "Yes, umm…are you Miss Brewer?"

"No, I'm not," replied the woman. "I'm Mrs. Flaherty, the housekeeper. And who might *you* be?"

Katy cleared her throat, a little embarrassed. "Um, my name is Katy — Katy Barton. I'm a reporter for PTTV — "

Before she could finish her sentence, Mrs. Flaherty cut her off. "Miss Brewer is not acceptin' any guests. Didn't ya see the No Trespassin' sign when you were drivin' in?"

"Uh, no," lied Katy. "I was hoping to make an appointment with Miss Brewer to discuss the highway that's going to be constructed through this property."

"There'll be no such highway runnin' through here, miss — not if Miss Brewer can help it."

"But I was hoping to just talk to her about it."

"No appointments, no visitors, and that's final! Now you run along, miss!"

Katy started back down the driveway toward her car, turning her head back around, only to see Mrs. Flaherty's eyes fixed on her as she was leaving. As she maneuvered her car back toward the trail, she took a quick glance in her rearview mirror to observe the old woman still keeping a watchful eye over her. As Katy proceeded to drive to the news station, she felt a little disappointed but far from discouraged.

It was a good thing Mr. Bruckman was out for the afternoon because she was having a hard time concentrating on her work. Those visions, or flashbacks, or whatever they were, back at the mansion, kept resurfacing. She felt like she was losing her mind. She had to call Dr. Fleming right away, even though she did feel a little silly calling him when she told him she wouldn't be needing his services anymore.

"I'd like to see him as soon as possible," Katy told the receptionist.

"Can you hold for a moment while I check with the doctor?"

Barely a moment went by before Dr. Fleming picked up the phone. "Why hello, Kate. I thought you were done with hypnotherapy."

Katy gulped in embarrassment. "I thought I was too."

"Well, lucky for you, I just had a cancellation today if you'd like to come in at one o'clock."

"Perfect," said Katy. "That'll leave me enough time to pick up my daughter after the appointment."

Chapter Twenty-One

In the corner of the room, obscured by the artificial ficus, Katy sat on the edge of her chair, tapping her feet restlessly. Her eyes were fixed on the round-faced clock hanging on the wall, absorbing every tick, tock. Just as the clock was about to strike one, a young man dressed in jeans, with a blank look on his face, stumbled out of the doctor's office. A few minutes later, the receptionist's phone buzzed. "You can go in now," she announced.

"So tell me, Kate, what brings you back here?" asked Dr. Fleming.

"Well, I'm still having the same recurring nightmare—but there's more. Ever since I moved back to Morganville, I started having these strange déjà vu moments. And lately, I've been having these 'visions,' that I can't even begin to explain."

"Why don't you try."

"Um...okay, where do I begin?"

"Why don't you begin with your first vision?"

"That would be at the cemetery. It happened after our last appointment. I went there with my daughter, thinking if I got some closure, I wouldn't keep having those recurring dreams. Needless to say, it didn't help. While I was there, I saw this apparition of a woman standing atop a gravesite, dropping a pendant into an open casket."

"What did she look like?"

"She was dressed all in black and was wearing a large brimmed hat with a dark veil completely covering her face."

"Did your daughter see her?"

"No. I mean, I don't think so."

"Anything else?"

"Yes. I went on a date recently—my first real date since Mark's death, actually. We—my date and I—drove out to an open field, where I had another 'vision'—or maybe it was a mirage, I don't know. But I was looking out into the horizon and saw these two horses being ridden by a man and a woman, galloping toward me. The sun was glaring, and I couldn't see their faces. They stopped just yards from where I was standing. That's when they turned into these sand-like sculptures. All of a sudden, the wind started blowing all around them, like a cyclone, until it fizzled out. All that was left were two small mounds of sand."

There was no clear reaction on the doctor's face as he was busy taking notes.

"There's more," said Katy.

The doctor adjusted his bifocals and looked up. "Go on."

Katy went on to explain how she almost hit that deer on her way to the Brewer mansion. "I'm almost certain it was on the same road where my accident with Mark took place. I thought I was about to relive it all over again. It literally left me shaking."

Dr. Fleming did not comment but quietly continued to take notes.

"The moment I crossed that property line, I got this eerie feeling, and while I was there, I had these two visions." First, she told him about the little girl on the swing, following up with the second one, where that same little girl was standing before a casket being laid into the ground. "Tell me, Doctor, am I going crazy?"

The corners of the doctor's mouth curved up slightly, suggesting the hint of a smile. "Well, I wouldn't jump to that conclusion just yet."

"Then why is this happening to me? Why am I having these visions?"

"It's hard to say right now. Have you ever been to the Brewer mansion any time prior to today?"

"No, but I *feel* as though I have."

"Have you ever met any member of the Brewer family?"

"No." A curious look came over Katy's face. "At least, I

don't think so."

"I think I need to put you under hypnosis again."

Katy looked at him apprehensively.

"Are you prepared for it, mentally?"

"No," she quavered. "But if you truly believe it will help, I guess I have no other choice but to trust you."

"Then let us proceed."

Dr. Fleming turned on his recorder and instructed her to lie down and relax while he induced her into a trance-like state. When she appeared to be completely under, he told her to go back in time to the mansion. "Are you there yet?"

A minute or two passed until Katy answered, "Yes, I'm there."

The doctor proceeded. "Now, I want you to go back to the little girl you saw playing in front of the mansion. Do you see her?"

"Yes, I see her."

"What is she doing?"

"She's running. A woman is chasing her, and now, she's pushing her on the swing."

"Why do you think that's important?"

"I'm not sure."

"Then how does that make you feel?" asked Dr. Fleming.

"It reminds me of when I was her age, and my mother would chase me around the yard in much the same way. I felt how that little girl must have felt—loved."

"And that is a good thing," emphasized the doctor.

"Yes, it was." A passive smile came to rest on Katy's face.

"What is happening now?" continued Dr. Fleming.

"The little girl has lost her hat. A big gust of wind has blown it right off her head. It's blowing higher and higher up into the trees—I can't see it anymore."

"How do you think she feels?"

"Sad," replied Katy.

"Why?"

"Because she lost her hat."

"But it's just a hat," pointed out the doctor.

Katy's forehead wrinkled, and her eyes tightened as if she were confused.

"Maybe it's symbolic," said the doctor. "She has lost something that was very near and dear to her." A few minutes of silence went by before Dr. Fleming continued. "Now, what do you see?"

Katy's facial expression changed again, and her voice took on a much more somber tone. "I'm entering the mansion now to an upstairs bedroom. The room looks stark. All the curtains are drawn. I see that same woman, the one pushing the little girl on the swing. She's lying in a bed covered in white linens, except for the yellow, saturated pillow beneath her ruffled hair. A damp towel is laying across her forehead. Her face is wet from sweat, and her eyes are sunken in a puddle of dark circles. She looks very ill."

Katy is clearly becoming uneasy, her body shifting back and forth, but Dr. Fleming prods her to go on.

"There are two men standing next to her bed. One of them must be a doctor. His sleeves are rolled up, and he has a stethoscope hanging over his vest. He's talking to the other man. There is profound sadness in the man's eyes as if his world is about to come to an end. I can hear the doctor now. He's explaining how the flu she had been suffering from has turned to pneumonia, and the prognosis looks very dim."

Katy seems to shift her attention. "Wait....there's a loud banging on the door. On the other side of the bedroom door, I see the little girl—the one on the swing. Her tiny fists are pounding with all their might. I can hear her crying and screaming, 'Father, please, let me in! I want to see my mother!' Her father is opening the door. He's bending down and grabbing her arms before she can run into the room. 'You must not go in there. Your mother is very sick and needs a great deal of rest.'"

Tears are welling up in Katy's eyes while she is relating this to Dr. Fleming.

"It's okay, Kate, you need to resolve this. What do you see next?"

Katy's vision suddenly takes another turn.

"I see the little girl again. She's standing in the cemetery next to her father. They are watching the casket being lowered into the ground. The little girl's face has turned to stone—she looks stripped of all emotion. Her father is holding her hand and looking down at her. 'You have to be strong, my little one.'"

At this point, Katy began to weep inconsolably, so Dr. Fleming decided it was time to release her from her hypnotic state.

"It's okay, Kate, it's okay. I am going to count up from one to five. At the count of five, I am going to snap my fingers, and you'll be back in my office again, where you started from. One...two...deep cleansing breath...three...four...you are re-entering my office...five.... (snap, snap). You're back now, Kate."

Gradually Katy came to, and Dr. Fleming turned off his recorder. "It was so painful," she said tearfully. "I felt like I was that little girl. Why am I witnessing this?"

Dr. Fleming flipped back his notes. "You know you suffered a similar loss with your own mother's death, the only difference being, other than the cause, your age. Perhaps there is some kind of parallel connection between you and that little girl. I think we need to delve deeper."

"But I'm afraid to delve deeper!" cried Katy.

"If we don't, you may never understand why you are having these visions. It's likely that they will continue to haunt you until the root of their significance has been brought to light."

~*~

By the time Katy pulled up in front of the school, her daughter was already outside waiting for her. On the drive home, Lilly was quick to observe that her mom was unusually quiet. Her mind was still lying on the doctor's couch.

"What's the matter, Mommy? You look sad. You didn't even ask me how school was today."

Katy lingered for a moment before answering the question. "I was just thinking about something I lost a long time ago."

"What?" asked Lilly.

"A hat," said Katy.

"Was it your favorite hat?"

"Yes, it was, Lilly — it was my favorite hat."

"Can't you go to the store and buy another one?"

"I could, but it wouldn't be the same."

"Why does it have to be the same?"

"Because some things, Lilly, can't be replaced."

"But maybe you might like the new one better."

Katy looked at her five-year-old daughter through her rearview mirror, pearls of wisdom radiating from her innocent face. "So, how was school today?"

Chapter Twenty-Two

After a thorough search on her computer came up with nothing, Katy pulled out an old phone book that had been sitting in the bottom of her file cabinet for who knows how long. She began running her finger through the pages. *Brewer...Brewer... Evelyn...no...Brewer...Morgan – yes!* There was still a listing under Morgan Brewer's name, but when she tried calling the number, all she got was a recording saying it had been disconnected. Not to be defeated, Katy decided to pay Miss Brewer another visit. *Only this time, I'm not going to let old Mrs. Flaherty get in the way.*

So she drove back to the mansion, but instead of stopping halfway up the drive, she followed the inclining path all the way to the top of the ridge. She parked her car next to a row of neglected bushes and got out to inspect the grounds. The bushes appeared to have been at one time a border for an extensive flower garden. It was barely recognizable now. Saplings that had erupted from the dry, cracked soil had fought hard for survival, their withered remnants molded into the ground like rare fossils. Walking along the crackling hedge, an imaginary picture came to mind of what must have once been a magnificent display of efflorescence. As she stopped to breathe-in its beauty, the image in her mind took on a tangible quality in the form of another hallucination.

A young woman appeared in the flourishing garden, which had come alive in a rainbow of vibrant color. Her fair complexion was protected by a wide-brimmed straw hat, allowing a cascade of sun-kissed locks to caress her shoulders. The afternoon sun was casting a hazy glow over her flowing chiffon dress, making her appear almost angelic. As she was bending over to cut the flowering stems with her shears, Katy heard a bittersweet melody ascending from her lips, one that rang familiar to her ears. Suddenly, out of nowhere, a man in a black Stetson hat snuck up behind her, catching her by surprise, causing her to drop her shears. As she rose back up, he got down on one knee and took her hands into his. He appeared to be proposing because the woman lifted her hands to her mouth and vigorously began to shake her head up and down. The beaming young man jumped back up to lock her in an embrace. In the surrender of a kiss, her head slowly bent backward while her hat gently...gently...floated to the ground.

Katy's vision slowly faded, only to be followed by another. She saw what looked like the same young woman. However, this time she was not standing in the middle of a luxurious, sun-drenched garden but in a vast withering field of grey markers cambering to an overcast sky. She was standing before a gravestone in a dark trench coat, her face obscured by the dark veil draping over the brim of her black hat. Somber clouds closed in to produce a cold and steady rain, but the woman appeared unfazed as she languidly bent down to place a bouquet of white lilies on the grave. Slowly she stood back up, her gaze reverent upon the lilies that had become engorged by the very water that had given them life. She wiped a tear from her cheek and gently blew a kiss upon the grave. As she turned to leave, this vision too slowly faded.

Katy shuddered her head back and forth, recalling the ethereal image of the woman she saw in the cemetery. It was the same image. She slowly pulled herself together, trying to refocus on what she came here to do — to speak to Miss Brewer.

She made her way toward the mansion's huge portico, where her gape rose from the faded mahogany door and sediment-layered mosaic stained-glass to the depressed turrets and loose festoon shingles. The magnificent three-story Victorian had suffered the scourge of age and neglect, but its timeless beauty transcended its forlorn façade. *It's a monument to an era of affluence and pride. How could anyone think of demolishing it?* she asked herself.

Katy approached the front entrance slowly, intimidated

by its massive formalness. Carefully she lifted her finger to press the doorbell imbedded in a corroded brass plate to the right of the door. After pushing it once, twice, three times, she wondered if it even worked since she wasn't able to hear any ringing or buzzing echoing from within. Level to her shoulders were two heavy brass knockers, also tarnished in varying shades of black and green. She took one into her fist and knocked it against the door as hard as she could several times over. Again, no response. She was not about to give up that easily.

She stepped off the porch and followed the path toward the back of the manor, looking for another entryway. There had to be someone in this great big house, although every window she passed seemed to have the shades drawn. As she was walking, she looked to her left and noticed what appeared to have been a vegetable garden overwrought by the intrusion of weeds, having assumed the same fate as the flower garden. To the far left of that stood a small cabin which might have been a gardener's quarters—which would make sense, considering the amount of gardening that would have to be done in order to maintain such an enormous property. The driveway came to an end just straight ahead, with a centuries old carriage house set before a backdrop of brown rambling vines. When she turned the corner, she spotted an enormous, run-down stable off in the distance, surrounded by broken wood horse fencing, and not surprisingly, no horses.

Katy began walking along the rear of the mansion when there it was: a narrow door with a broken screen, barely hanging from its rusty hinges. Hoping to find it unlocked, she pulled open the screen and tried turning the doorknob. The knob turned, but the door appeared to be jammed. With the side of her upper arm, she gave it a few hard shoves, and to her thrill, it opened.

She stepped inside a dark, musty-smelling room with a tiny window at the edge of the ceiling that provided just enough light to reveal a pantry of sorts. She began to tiptoe her way through the room, trying her best not to bump into anything, while her eyes adjusted to the darkness. On one side of her were countless shelves lined with dusty jars of preserved foods—relics from the desolate garden, no doubt. On the opposite side was a large assortment of candles in all shapes and sizes.

Katy noticed an open door just ahead and started to walk toward it, cringing along the way. The dusty wooden floorboards creaked so loudly, surely anyone in the vicinity would have been alerted to an intruder's presence. Nonetheless, she exited through the open door to follow a long corridor running alongside a massive winding staircase. Ultimately, she found herself standing in front of a magnificent stone fireplace in a grand, oval-shaped drawing room. The unsettling squeal of the floorboards was overtaken by the repetitious tick-tock of the antique arrows on the face of the mahogany clock in the center of the mantel.

All the shades were pulled, rendering the room quite dim, except for the effect created by a single beautifully-crafted, stained-glass window strategically angled at the base of the cathedral ceiling. It was positioned directly in line with the afternoon sun, allowing a kaleidoscope of light to radiate throughout the room. Katy's senses were ignited by the majestic aura embossing the antique furnishings and paintings on the walls.

The one thing that stood out as the focal point of the room was the opulent, elongated chaise, upholstered in a bright, flowery print. Katy walked over to the chaise and, in a slow, deliberate motion, spun her body around, absorbing the room in all its grandeur. The clock on the mantel began to chime, signaling the top of the hour, and when it stopped, she discerned another sound—a faint humming sound, which seemed to be coming from the far left corner of the room. Katy turned her head to observe the silhouette of an old woman sitting at a gothic-style desk facing the wall. With pen in hand and her head down low, she appeared to be writing under the visual aid of one dimly lit candle. Katy listened intently, trying to decipher the melody. It was the same song she'd heard the young woman in the garden humming in her vision.

The old woman calmly swiveled around in her chair and looked directly at Katy. "I've been waiting for you," she announced in a profound and succinct voice.

Katy strained to get a good look at her through the

darkened room until a runaway ray of bright yellow light streamed like a bolt of lightning through the mosaic window overhead, completely illuminating the old woman's face. Katy put her palm to her forehead, squinting to diffuse the glare on the woman's face, but the only thing she could see was the mirrored transparency of her own reflection.

"The eyes are the windows to the soul," cracked the old woman, her voice resonating a strange aura as if Katy had met her before.

Chapter Twenty-Three

"Are you Evelyn Brewer?"

"Yes," replied the old woman, setting her notebook down and slowly making her way toward the chaise. Sitting next to the chaise was a small table with a tiffany lamp on top. She tugged on one of its two gold chains and turned it on. "I'm sorry about the lighting. I'm accustomed to using candles. Not only do they cast light on the written word, but they illuminate my mind in a way that artificial light cannot."

"What are you writing, if you don't mind my asking?"

"It's my memoir. I'm drawing nearer to my final chapter, where everything shall unfold as it was meant to be."

Katy cleared her throat. "I should introduce myself. I'm Katy, Katy Barton—"

"My mother's name was Katherine," interrupted the old woman.

"I'm sorry I had to sneak in the back door, but I rang the doorbell and tried knocking at the front door, and there was no answer," explained Katy. "And what do you mean you've been waiting for me?"

"Our doorbell hasn't worked for years, and my housekeeper, Ruby, informed me that you were here the other day. I suspected you'd be back. Why don't you have a seat?"

Katy sat down in one of the two armchairs across from Miss Brewer, who had already positioned herself in the middle of the chaise. In that moment, a short, stout lady in a full apron entered the room.

"Pardin' me, Miss Brewer. I didn't hear the young lady come in or I woulda' barnished her."

Katy recognized that accent immediately. It was the same woman who'd caught her trespassing the first time she set foot on the property.

"It's quite all right, Ruby. Miss Barton is our guest. Perhaps you could offer her some tea."

Ruby bowed her head. "Excuse me, Miss Brewer." Then she turned to look at Katy. "Would ya like some tea 'n crumpets, miss?"

"No thank you," replied Katy.

"I'd like some more, if you don't mind," inserted Miss Brewer. "The pot on my desk is almost drained." Miss Brewer watched Ruby with fondness in her eyes as she walked over to gather up the empty teacup and pot. "Mrs. Flaherty is more than just a housekeeper—she's been endowed with many talents. She has been with me for forty-three years now. We met when I was studying abroad in England. After my father passed, I was wrought with loneliness, so I got back in touch with her and made her an offer she couldn't refuse. It wasn't hard to convince her since she already had family living in this part of the country. I don't know what I would have done without her. She's bridged the gap to my existence."

Katy released a sympathetic smile. "Um, I noticed your pantry on the way in. It looks like you once had a bountiful garden."

"Yes, I did. Unfortunately, Ivan, my gardener, passed away eight years ago. He had been the family gardener from the time I was a little girl. With no one around to care for it, the garden has run dry. No matter, though. I have enough preserved to last me the rest of my days."

Katy moved her eyes around the room. "This is a lovely sitting area."

"It's called a parlor. This room holds very special memories for me," said Miss Brewer, scanning the perimeters herself. "Good fortune kept it from being totally destroyed in the fire."

"I heard about the fire," expressed Katy, with empathy in her voice.

"It's still fresh in my mind like it was yesterday. Most of

the furniture has since been replaced, including this chaise," she said, patting the cushion. "It's always been my favorite place to sit. The floral print reminds me of the beautiful flower garden that once occupied the grounds." Miss Brewer took a sip of her tea. "The fire took a great deal from me, but the memories have been spared."

Just then, Mrs. Flaherty walked back into the room with some freshly brewed tea and two teacups and set them down on the elongated coffee table between them. "I've brought an extra cup in case ya change your mind, miss."

"Thank you," said Katy, who was busy taking in the rest of the room. She spotted an antique phonograph with a wide-mouthed brass bell horn sitting on top of a hutch against the wall and pointed to it. "Does that still work?"

"As a matter of fact, it does," said Miss Brewer, with a gleam in her eye.

Katy then got up and walked over to the other side of the room to admire the grand piano. "It's beautiful," she said, running her flat palm along its smooth ebony surface.

"It's a vintage 1912 Steinway," replied Miss Brewer.

"Do you play?"

"A little. My mother was the real piano player. She played beautifully. The piano suffered some minor damage in the fire. My father had it restored, but it's been a very long time since I laid my hands on those keys. My true passion was singing. When I was a little girl, my mother would play the piano while I sang along. My father was so proud. Whenever we had dinner parties at the house, we would gather in here after the meal, where he insisted that we entertain the guests with our music. We were quite the duo, my mother and I."

Katy cleared her throat as she turned to go sit back down. "Well, I guess you know the reason why I'm here. I've been asked to interview you regarding the state's plan to extend the freeway, which would allow alternate routes to cut into several properties in the area."

"Yes," replied Miss Brewer. "It's a shame the Morganville General Store will be gone for good. Our families have been friends dating back many, many years."

"Then you know," continued Katy, "that your home has been marked for demolition as well."

"Yes, I am aware. The government authorities have come up with creative ways to serve me the legal documents necessary to take my property away from me. This, in part, is the reason I must keep my shades drawn at all times. This house is a testimonial to my father's dedication and love for this town. He came from nothing to become a pillar of society. Morganville is indebted to my father. Without him, there would be no Morganville. I am his sole heir, with no living relatives and nowhere else to go. Mark my word, I shall never leave."

"I think it would help your cause if you would agree to a live interview, so people can appreciate your position and connect with you."

"No, I will not agree to that. I demand that my privacy be respected."

Katy's expression turned solemn and contemplative. She felt empathy for the old woman—besides, it would be a shame to destroy this beautiful estate. She was suddenly struck with an idea. "I completely understand, Miss Brewer, and I promise to do my best to help you retain your property. I'm going to go back to my boss and convince him to allow me to take this story in another direction."

Miss Brewer smiled. "I like you, Miss Barton. You possess the same resourcefulness and perseverance that I adhere to."

"Why, thank you, Miss Brewer. By the way, you can call me Kate...or Katy, or whatever you prefer."

"And you may call me Evelyn."

"May I come back again?"

"Yes, yes, you may. And next time, you have permission to enter through the front door." Evelyn got up from the chaise. "Here, let me see you out."

Evelyn led her out of the parlor and into a circular foyer at the front entrance. In the center was a single-pedestal, hand-crafted table with an expensive-looking blue and white vase on top, and on the surrounding wall hung three large portraits. Katy had to stop and admire them, one by one, while Evelyn stood behind her.

"Thankfully, these paintings survived the fire. That was my father, and that was my mother," said Evelyn, pointing. "They were both fairly young then. They were painted shortly after my father had the house built."

Katy gulped. The lighting in the room was diffused, but there was no doubt, these were the same people she had envisioned the first time she set foot on the property. This was the woman in the jet black chignon, pushing her little girl, and he was the man at her bedside while she lay dying.

And then Katy walked up to the third portrait. "Is this a painting of you?"

"Yes, it is," replied Evelyn, taking a few steps forward until she was standing right next to her. "That one was commissioned much later when I was around the age of seventeen."

Katy looked at the painting and then at Miss Brewer. Even though the years had befallen her, her striking features had not diminished—those high cheekbones and soulful blue eyes. "It's beautiful," she uttered, but when she turned back to the painting to study it more closely, she had to squint from disbelief. Maybe it was the light bouncing off the glass indentations in the domed ceiling that was playing tricks on her, but it drew an uncanny resemblance to her own high school picture. As she continued to stare at it, she noticed something else that literally rendered her speechless. Resting around the young Evelyn's neckline was a heart-shaped pendant that looked identical to the one she had received from Mark. Evelyn tilted her head in Katy's direction as if trying to get a read on her expression. Katy surreptitiously raised her hand to clutch the locket around her neck. *It's just a painting*, she repeated to herself, *a bizarre coincidence, that's all.*

Chapter Twenty-Four

Katy slammed on her brakes and had to back up a little. She was so energized from her visit with the eccentric recluse that she'd almost run the stop sign. She couldn't wait to tell Mr. Bruckman her idea for the Brewer story. When she peeked into his office, he wasn't there, and his desk never looked cleaner. She wandered around the news station looking for him when she happened to pass her coworker, Vicky's, desk.

"Hey, Vicky, do you know where Bruckman is?"

"He's out. He won't be back until the end of next week."

Katy raised her eyebrows in surprise and asked if he was on vacation, although if he were going on vacation, he surely would have told her.

"He flew to New York. I guess he's meeting with the big heads from our parent station and another big network regarding a buyout and a possible merger with our sister station in Johnstown."

"How did you find out about that? He never mentioned anything to me about it."

"I got the inside scoop from Jack about a month ago that there was probably going to be a big shake up around here. You might want to step up your game and start showing up on time if we're going to be competing with the Johnstown team—they're pretty slick over there. Better yet, you might wanna start thinking about a 'Plan B'—if you know what I mean."

Katy could feel the blood rushing to her head. Was the whole office talking about her behind her back? She stood silent, contemplating for a moment, worried about whether or not she *should* do a different take on the Brewer story. What if her boss wanted her to stick with the prescribed format so as not to cause any conflicts for the station? Now she wasn't sure what to do.

"So, how's that Brewer story going?"

Katy shrugged her shoulders. "Oh, uh, it's going fine."

"I wouldn't spend too much time on it. Bruckman's just got you filling up empty space in the newscast for an insignificant little town where nothing ever happens."

Katy could feel the fumes seething from her ears—her blood had hit the boiling point. Who did Vicky think she was anyway? Vicky had started out covering the news for Morganville the same as Katy. After Katy was hired, Vicky was sent to assist her counterpart in Pittsburgh. It wasn't like she took over the whole territory. "So what about you, Vicky? What's your 'Plan B?'"

"Me, I've got my eye on that anchor job. Word is, Martha will probably be leaving. Jack says I've got nothing to worry about. I'm good as gold," she said smugly. "Now, if you'll excuse me, I have to go and make some copies." Vicky gathered up the papers from her outbox, patted them down hard against the desk, and turned to walk away.

"Well, I've got to get going too," Katy yelled after her. "Uh, thanks for the info...Vicky."

Feeling demoralized, Katy plodded back to her workspace, trying to decide what to do. *Oh, what the heck, what've I got to lose — except maybe my job. I'm going to go with my instincts on this, for better or for worse.* She picked up the desk phone and punched in the numbers to Mr. Bruckman's cell phone. There was no answer, so she left him a message.

"Hello, Mr. Bruckman, this is Katy...you know, Barton? I've been to the Brewer mansion and met with Miss Brewer like you asked. Our meeting went really well, even though I couldn't get her to agree to a live interview. But don't worry! I think we formed an instant bond, and I'd like to take this story a step further in a different direction. I'll talk to you more about it when you get back into the office next week."

Chapter Twenty-Five

Beep…beep…beep…beep…. Katy rolled over to turn off her alarm and forced herself out of bed. She usually didn't set it for a Saturday morning, but this was going to be a special day. Mike had the weekend off, and she had invited him for dinner at her place. He had immediately said yes, even though she warned him in advance that she wasn't a very good cook.

She'd been having trouble getting to sleep ever since her conversation with Vicky, worrying about her job. This, compounded by the lack of sleep from her recurring nightmares, made for a muddled state of mind. In any case, she was determined to get an early start making her special marinara sauce for the spaghetti and meatballs she'd be preparing later.

After a hot shower and a couple of cups of strong coffee, she felt regenerated. Lilly was begging to help, so she enlisted her with the task of retrieving supplies.

"I'm glad Mike's coming over," said Lilly, handing her mother a wooden spoon. "I like him. He's fun."

"I like him too," smiled Katy, "very much."

After mincing some garlic and chopping the onion, she poured some olive oil in a pot and turned on the stove. When the oil was hot enough, she dumped in the vegetables and began to sauté them until she became distracted by the ringing of the telephone. She hurried over to the other side of the kitchen to answer the phone mounted on the wall. It was her boss, Mr. Bruckman, who she hadn't heard from all week.

"I just got notice that Miss Brewer has been served with eviction papers this morning under the law of eminent domain. She's being ordered off the property by the end of the month so that demolition on her house can begin. We've gotta get the ball rolling on this story, Kate. You've got to get back over there and convince her to do that interview!"

"They can't do that!" Katy screamed into the mouthpiece. "Didn't you get my message that I want to take this story in a different direction?"

"Yeah, I got the message. What exactly do you mean by 'a different direction?'"

"I'll explain it to you on Monday, right after I go to the Department of Transportation and find out what this eviction bullsh...t is all about!"

"Look, Kate—" her boss started out until she interrupted him.

"I'm sorry, Mr. Bruckman, I have to go." No sooner had she slammed the phone down in frustration than her attention was diverted by the piercing sound of the smoke detector.

"Mommy, Mommy," screamed Lilly, yanking on her shirt and pointing to the pot on the stove.

Katy pushed her daughter aside. "Get out of the kitchen!" she yelled, coughing from the wave of smoke that had settled overhead.

Katy ran over to turn off the burner. The vegetables were scorched, and black smoke was billowing from the pot. In a panic, she removed the pot from the stovetop and threw it into the sink, then turned on the faucet, leaving the charred remains to smolder in the hot liquid.

"Whew, that was a close one! Thank goodness it didn't catch on fire," she said out loud, waving her hands in the air to try and move the smoke around.

The smoke detector was still blaring, so she turned on the exhaust fan above the stove. She then ran over to the window above the kitchen sink, where the cauldron was still seething, to try and lift it open. The window was jammed, as usual, and Katy's nervous frustration was building. She climbed up onto the counter and yanked the window up with all her might, knocking the screen out in the process.

Lilly ran back into the kitchen just as Katy jumped off

the counter. "No, honey, don't come in here yet. It's still too smoky." The shrill vibration of the alarm would not let up, so she accompanied her daughter back into the living room while she set out to open additional windows throughout the house.

"Wait, where's Tandy?" asked Lilly as she began calling his name. "Come here, Tandy! Don't be scared, it's all right. Tandy, where are you?" Lilly took off running through the house, searching for him. "Mommy, Mommy, I can't find him. He's gone!"

"Oh honey, he must be around here somewhere. He probably got scared from the noise and is hiding in a closet or a corner somewhere."

Together they searched the whole house but could not find him anywhere. Katy went back into the kitchen. "Oh no!" she said aloud, not realizing Lilly was standing right behind her, "The cat must have freaked out and jumped out the kitchen window."

Lilly immediately burst into tears and started screaming, "Oh no! Tandy — we have to find him!"

"Okay, maybe if we hurry, he may still be close by," said Katy, grabbing their sweaters and making sure to lock the front door.

First, they scoured the entire perimeter outside the townhouse, and then they walked up and down several blocks. After more than an hour of searching, there still was no sign of Tandy. "We have to go back home now, Lilly," Katy said with regret.

Lilly began to wail, "We'll never find him!"

"I'll tell you what. When we get back home, we'll make a bunch of flyers with Tandy's picture on them, and tomorrow you and I will put them up all around the neighborhood. On Monday, I'll go down to the animal shelter and leave a flyer with them, as well — just in case someone drops him off there." Katy grabbed her daughter's hand, and the two of them made their way back home — dejected but hopeful.

By the time they returned home, Katy was bushed, and the house was freezing from all the windows having been left open, but before she went around to each room to shut them, she needed to make a call.

"Hello, Mike, I'm afraid dinner's going to be a little later than planned."

~*~

Mike showed up with a bottle of wine and a gift for Lilly.

"What is it?" she asked.

"Go ahead and open it."

Lilly tore it open to find a book whose cover had a picture of a cat on a pole wearing a fire hat. Her eyes opened as wide as her mouth.

"It's about a cat named Pickles, who's adopted by a local firehouse. He gets to ride on the fire truck and learns how to become a fire cat, putting out fires and rescuing people."

Katy looked at him appreciatively. "Where on earth did you find that?"

"I stopped at a bookstore before I came over. I wanted to get Lilly something to maybe cheer her up, and the book just jumped out at me."

At the end of the evening, Lilly fell asleep with the book under her arm, and Katy and Mike snuggled up on the couch with their wine.

"Why did you say you were a bad cook?" asked Mike. "Dinner was great."

"I guess I haven't had much practice. In the past, I was always burdened with school, work, and a small child, so I opted for quick or ready-made meals. I never really had a whole lot of time to experiment with food or try new recipes."

As the two of them chatted the evening away, Katy's feelings for Mike were growing ever deeper. There was so much she wanted to share with him—her visions and her sessions with Dr. Fleming—but she held back for fear he'd think less of her.

Mike suddenly put his glass down on the table in front of them and removed hers from her hand. Then he leaned in for a series of long, sensual kisses, rendering Katy limp in his arms. She admired his respect for her by not pushing the boundary for complete intimacy, but she longed for it.

Chapter Twenty-Six

On Monday morning, after dropping her daughter off at school, Katy drove straight to the animal shelter. Vera Gibbons, the shelter's director, was in the front office when Katy walked in and immediately recognized her from their interview. "Have you changed your mind about adopting a cat?"

"No, I'm sorry. We've lost our cat, Tandy, and I'm here to leave you with a copy of a flyer if that's all right. That's a picture of him on it."

Ms. Gibbons examined the picture. "Hmm, a black cat with those lucent, copper-colored eyes is not common. I'll be happy to post the flyer up on our bulletin board."

"Please call me if you get a cat that looks anything like him," implored Katy. "My daughter is heartbroken—and so am I."

"It's amazing how animals can quickly become a fixed member of the family," related Ms. Gibbons. "They fill us with an unconditional love that transcends human emotion."

There was one other important mission that needed to be undertaken that morning. After leaving the shelter, Katy drove to the Department of Transportation to try and find out what steps she could take in order to put a halt to the demolition of the Brewer mansion. After taking a number and waiting for half-an-hour to speak to someone, she was exasperated to find out that she had to take another number in order to speak to someone else who "might" be able to answer her questions. Another half-hour went by before she got up from her rigid chair and walked over to the reception clerk to find out how much longer it would be. While she was waiting for an answer from the woman behind the

counter, a familiar face stepped out from one of the back rooms —
her old friend Janice.

"Hey, Janice," yelled Katy. "I forgot you worked here!"

Janice walked over to where her friend was standing.
"Yeah, what are you doing here? Business or personal?"

"Actually, a little of both," answered Katy, who went on
to explain the Brewer situation to her.

Janice lowered her voice and motioned Katy over to the
door she had just walked out of. "I'll tell you what, come into my
office, and I'll see what I can do."

"Oh my gosh, thank you! I was afraid I'd be waiting here
all morning." Katy followed her back to her office, and Janice sat
at her desk while Katy had a seat in front of her. "Look at you,
your own office! Must be nice. I'm surrounded in a sea of cubicles
with barely half a partition to hide behind."

"Community college, baby!" Janice asserted loudly.

"So where do I begin?" asked Katy.

"The first thing you need to do is to get a lawyer to get a
restraining order to stop the demolition of the house. You need to
do that as soon as possible. Then, a motion has to be filed to halt
or delay the freeway construction project."

"But where do I find a lawyer who could take on this type
of litigation?"

Janice leaned in closer to Katy, and in a hushed tone, said,
"I'm not supposed to share this type of information, so you didn't
hear it from me, okay? But I know a lawyer who's an expert in
this sort of thing."

"Really? That's awesome!" exclaimed Katy. "The only
problem is that I need to run it by my boss first."

Janice raised an eyebrow at her friend.

"But, *I'm sure* I can convince him to see it my way!" Katy
jumped up from her chair. "I have to get back to the office—I've
got some persuading to do!"

"Aren't you forgetting something?" said Janice, handing
her the lawyer's card. "His name is Doherty, John Doherty."

"Thanks, Janice, I owe you."

"By the way, are you still seeing that fireman?"

"Yeah, why?"

"Just wondering."

~*~

Katy drove back to the station, excited and hopeful that Mr. Bruckman would, in fact, see things her way. She didn't even stop at her desk to remove her jacket but proceeded directly to her boss's door. As she neared his office, she could see him through the clear partition examining his watch with an irritated look on his face, as if he had been waiting impatiently for her all morning. She gave a quick knock on his open door to let him know she was about to enter and started talking the minute she walked in.

"Mr. Bruckman, I'm sorry I couldn't explain everything to you over the phone, but I didn't expect you to be gone for a whole week." She paused for a breath. "By the way, is there something I should know?"

"Don't worry about it, I'll fill you in later. But it's nothing that concerns you. So tell me, what's going on with the Brewer story?"

Without bothering to sit down, she explained everything that had transpired between her and Miss Brewer. When she was done, she leaned forward with her hands on his desk to face him directly. "I don't just want to do an interview exploiting her for the victim she is in this situation. She's old and all alone in that big house — except for her housekeeper, and from what I gathered, she has no one to help her fight for her rights. I want to do more than cover an unjust demolition due to a freeway expansion like I did with the Greelys. I want to *help* Evelyn."

Mr. Bruckman leaned back in his chair as if he were slightly taken aback by her audacious behavior. "Oh, so now you're on a first-name basis with her?"

"I want to take the story in another direction. I'd like to bring the Brewer mansion's history back to the forefront." Katy stopped and suddenly got this look on her face as if a light bulb just clicked on in her head. "You know, Mr. Bruckman, if we can save the house from getting demolished, perhaps it could be preserved — as a historical landmark!"

"Katy, this was supposed to be a simple interview with a reclusive old woman who refuses to move, and now it's turned into a personal crusade for you!"

"Please, Mr. Bruckman!" At this point, Katy was merely ad-libbing, throwing whatever she could out there to get her boss to bite. "If we can make this happen, not only will it benefit Miss Brewer, but the spotlight will also be on *you* and *our news station* for making a difference for the community of Morganville!"

Mr. Bruckman suddenly got a twinkle in his eyes. "Getting the house preserved as a historical landmark is *actually* a good idea," he conceded. His elbows were resting on his desk while he tapped his fingers together, pondering the suggestion. After a minute or so, he brought his hands up to his nose and announced, "Okay, Kate. I'm willing to back you up financially on behalf of the news station. You know, I'm personal friends with Jim Elders, the Mayor of Morganville, and I think he would agree. I'm gonna talk to him and see if he can help us out, politically as well as financially — maybe get this matter moving a little quicker. In the meantime, why don't you go ahead and make that appointment with that lawyer, Mr. — uh, what's his name?"

"John Doherty," Katy responded enthusiastically.

"In addition to filing an injunction or whatever, to stop the demolition of the house, and a motion to delay the construction, have him get started right away on whatever steps need to be taken in getting the house preserved as a historical landmark."

"I will, I will. Thank you so much, Mr. Bruckman!" Katy expressed gratefully, almost to the point of bowing, then she raised her fist up in the air. "I won't let you down, you'll see! The Brewer mansion will go down in history! PTTV will go down in history!"

"Yeah, yeah, now go on, get outa here," Bruckman ended, with a crooked smile on his face.

Katy literally ran back to her desk to make the call to John Doherty. "I need an appointment to see him right away," she said adamantly to the person answering the phone. After being put on hold for what seemed like an eternity, Mr. Doherty got on the line, whereby she explained the situation to him as quickly and thoroughly as possible.

"I can see you tomorrow afternoon," he told her. "But first, I need you to obtain as much background information on Morgan Brewer as you can and bring it with you to the appointment. We can't just nominate a property as a landmark, we need to have the proper documentation to back it up, and Miss Brewer will have to sign a petition, as well as some other pertinent documents. In addition, I'm going to need you to get to work on getting as many people involved as you can in obtaining the necessary amount of signatures required for the petition. We'll discuss it in more detail when you come into my office."

Chapter Twenty-Seven

The next morning, Katy headed back to the library to continue her research before her afternoon meeting with John Doherty. As she filtered through the archives of the *Morganville Gazette* microfilms, she was astonished at what she uncovered. There was a series of articles dating back from the late 1800s relating to the Brewers, some with fuzzy black-and-white pictures, and some even making the front page. The more Katy read, the more she became infatuated with the Brewer family history.

February 7, 1918. Founded by investor and entrepreneur, Morgan Brewer, The First Bank of Morganville opens its doors to the public for the first time.

Katy was surprised to read this. *Hmm, I didn't know Morgan Brewer founded the bank run by my father.*

September 3, 1920. A dedication ceremony is held at The Morganville Library, where its illustrious benefactor, Morgan Randolph Brewer, cuts the ceremonial yellow ribbon.

There was a picture of Morgan Brewer surrounded by a group of people, cutting the yellow ribbon.

December 16, 1923. Katherine Brewer, wife of Morgan Randolph Brewer, dies from pneumonia brought on by complications from the flu after the peak of the nation-wide flu epidemic. In addition to her husband, she leaves behind her only daughter, Evelyn Katherine, age six.

April 2, 1936. Morgan Brewer is proud to announce the engagement of his daughter, Evelyn Katherine Brewer, to Marcus Allen Shilby, son of Milton S. Shilby, Morgan Brewer's long-time friend and business partner.

There was a headshot of a younger Evelyn Brewer and her very handsome fiancé, Marcus, wearing a black Stetson hat.

April 13, 1936. The Brewer mansion suffers a debilitating fire. Sadly, Marcus Allen Shilby, the son of Morgan Brewer's business partner, perished in the fire.

Katy's mouth dropped open. It was Evelyn's fiancé, Marcus, who died in the fire!

December 14, 1961. The entire town of Morganville grieves the death of Morgan Randolph Brewer, who has died of a progressive lung disease he battled over the course of many years. Mr. Brewer, who never remarried after the death of his beloved wife, Katherine, has no surviving heirs other than his only daughter, Evelyn, who is slated to inherit his entire estate.

Katy spent most of the morning at the library taking notes and making photocopies of pertinent information when she finally looked at her watch. She realized she had better get going if she wanted to make it in time for her lawyer's appointment, so she quickly gathered up her papers and stuffed them into her briefcase. She hurriedly made her way through the maze of tables and chairs with her briefcase in one hand while attempting to slip on her jacket with the other. She had managed to filter one arm into its sleeve and haphazardly twisted her body around, trying to find the other sleeve. Preoccupied with her sleeve, she didn't notice that someone carrying a stack of books had just walked through the front entrance, causing her to collide straight-on with that person. An avalanche of books tumbled to the ground, and papers went flying out of Katy's briefcase—which in her haste she had forgotten to latch—and scattered all over the floor.

"Oh dear, let me help ya with that," exclaimed a voice she was sure she'd heard before.

"That's all right," said Katy. "I can get it. I was in a hurry for an appointment." While she was on the floor collecting her materials, she glanced up to see a plump old woman with a tight little knot on the top of her head, stooping down to help her. "Why hello, Mrs. Flaherty, remember me?"

"Why, yes, aren't you that reporter—Miss Barton?"

"Yup, that's me."

"Well, fancy meetin' ya here."

"Likewise," responded Katy. "Do you come to the library often?" she added, for lack of anything better to say.

"Actually, I do," replied Mrs. Flaherty. "It's one of the weekly errands I run for Miss Brewer. She does a lot of readin', and I was just returnin' and renewin' some books for her."

Katy couldn't help but glance at the titles of the books that were laying on the floor: *Reincarnation and the Law of Karma; Letters on Occult Meditation; The Spirit World Unmasked.*

"My," said Katy, trying not to sound too judgmental. "Miss Brewer seems to enjoy reading about the afterlife."

"We've both had a fascination with theology and mediumship and that sorta' thing for a long time. In fact, that's what drew us together back in England so many years ago. Of course, her vision is not what it used to be—all those years readin' and writin' under candlelight—so oftentimes, she has me read aloud to her. She says I'm good at facilitatin' the melodramatics."

Katy looked at her watch. "I'm sorry, but I have to get going. I'm already running late. Nice running into you, Mrs. Flaherty."

"Likewise, my dear. Miss Brewer will be interested in knowin' we ran into each other."

"Oh, and tell her I'll be by to see her soon—with good news!"

"Oh, I will. God knows we don't be needin' anymore bad news."

On her way out, Katy couldn't get those book titles out of her mind. *I wonder why Evelyn is so interested in the afterlife?* she thought. *It must just be because she's old.*

Meeting John Doherty for the first time caught Katy a little by surprise. He was not the stereotypical lawyerly-type she had expected to meet, like the ones you see on TV, with their slick haircuts and perfectly pressed suits. He was probably in his mid-forties and somewhat attractive, but his disheveled hair was clearly in need of a haircut. His shirt was haphazardly tucked into his trousers, and the top two buttons of his shirt were unbuttoned, with his tie hanging loose around his neck.

Except for the wall of law texts behind his desk, his office looked as disorganized as he did. There were large accordion files stacked up all along the floor and on his desk. "Sorry about the mess," he said, moving a stack from his desk to the floor.

Because of his "nutty professor" persona, Katy was a little worried about his overall competency. However, once she sat down and he explained the whole legal process that would be taking place and how he was going to be handling it, her mind was put at ease.

After the attorney had had some time to review the documentation Katy brought in, he was very pleased. "I don't foresee any problem getting this matter pushed through very rapidly. There is every reason why the Brewer mansion should be preserved. There is so much history here," he emphasized, fanning the copies out on his desk.

The two of them spent a good deal of time going through the paperwork and sorting through the details, so much so that Katy lost track of the hours. When she finally looked at her watch, she let out a shriek. "Oh my gosh, the time has flown by! I'm sorry, Mr. Doherty, but I have to run. I have to go and pick my daughter up at school. I'm already late." Katy scooped up copies of the documents she had signed and stuffed them in her briefcase, as well as several for Mr. Bruckman to sign on behalf of the station, which included the formal retainer.

"That's all right, I'll be in touch," said Mr. Doherty. "As soon as I get this petition drawn up, I'll let you know, and we'll take it from there."

~*~

By the time she arrived at her daughter's school, there were just a few cars left in the parking lot, and Lilly was not sitting on the front steps like she usually did. Katy parked her car and went inside, praying that her daughter was in her classroom. The classroom door was open, and Mrs. Randolph was sitting at her desk, marking some papers. Lilly was seated at her own little desk in the middle of the room, busily writing in her workbook. Katy gave a quick knock as she entered the room. Mrs. Randolph peered at her over her spectacles before dropping them down from their silver chain, revealing a scowling frown.

Lily looked up and jumped out of her chair, and ran over to her mother. "Mommy, Mommy, I thought you forgot about me!" she cried, wrapping her arms around her mom's legs.

Katy bent over to give her daughter a hug. "I would never forget about you, baby!"

At that point, Mrs. Randolph had gotten up from her desk and marched over to meet Katy face-to-face. "You know, you really should make it a priority to pick Lilly up on time," she said authoritatively. "If you cannot be on time to pick your daughter up from school, perhaps you should find someone else who can do it for you."

Katy felt embarrassed and ashamed, just as the teacher was making her out to feel. She was also growing a little defensive due to Mrs. Randolph's tone. "I'm sorry, but I was involved in an important work-related assignment, and I completely lost track of time. I'm not married, Mrs. Randolph, so I am the predominant person Lilly has to depend on."

"Children whose parents don't care enough to pick them up when they're supposed to grow up to have abandonment issues. You might want to keep that in mind, *Miss* Barton."

Not only did Mrs. Randolph know how to make Katy feel like the worst mother in the world, but she also made her feel like a disobedient child. "I promise, Mrs. Randolph, I'll never be this late again."

"Don't promise me — promise your young daughter, Lilly,

here."

Katy took her daughter's hand and proceeded to walk out of the classroom, with her head lowered down in shame.

While they were walking out to the parking lot, Lilly pulled a note out from her backpack and began waving it in the air. "I almost forgot, Mommy! I got this note for parent-teacher conferences. I don't have to go to school that day. Yay!"

That's just great. I can't wait to see Mrs. Randolph again. "Let me see that," she said, grabbing the note from Lilly's hand to check the date. "Hmm, I think that's the week your grandpa will be in Syracuse visiting his brother. I guess I'm going to have to find another sitter for you that day."

Chapter Twenty-Eight

The spot where Tandy would always curl up with Lilly at night was empty, and Katy had just finished reading *The Fire Cat*, the book Mike had given her the day their cat went missing.

"I can't sleep. I miss Tandy!" cried Lilly.

"I know, honey, me too. I bet I know what will help you fall asleep."

Katy walked over to the small white bookcase against the wall, jam-packed with children's books, and pulled out *Good Night Moon*. It was the first bedtime story she had ever read to Lilly and soon became her favorite. So much so that it turned into a nightly ritual. Katy had read it so many times, she knew it by heart.

By the time she whispered those last three words, "Goodnight noises everywhere," Lilly was fast asleep, her features softened by "the old woman whispering, hush." Katy gave her a light kiss on the forehead and got up, and placed the chunky book back on the bookshelf.

She walked into the living room and plopped down on the sofa, brushing her hand over the empty spot where Tandy would cozy up next to her. Mike had just gotten off his shift and was on his way over. She grabbed the remote off the coffee table and turned on the TV. The nightly news was on, but her mind was elsewhere, particularly on her meeting with John Doherty and her confrontation with Lilly's teacher. She stared at the screen, barely paying attention to the news being reported. Several wildfires in California were spreading out of control, and out-of-state crews were being called in to help contain them.

When the doorbell rang. Katy turned off the TV and went

to answer the door. The last time she had seen Mike was the day she almost started a fire in her kitchen, and Tandy jumped out the window.

"I can't stay long," said Mike, entering the living room and giving her a loving embrace. "I just wanted to see you before I leave tomorrow morning."

"Where are you going?"

"Me and some of the other guys in the precinct are being dispatched to California to help put out the wildfires."

Katy's face took on a worried look. "How long will you be gone?"

"I don't know."

She was quiet for a moment. "Would you like a drink?"

"I'll have a beer if you've got one."

Katy went into the kitchen to see if she had any. There was one can of Bud Lite in the corner of the fridge. She came back with the can and a mug, set them down on the coffee table, and scooted up next to him on the couch.

Mike poured the beer into his glass. "So what have you been up to since I last saw you?"

"You know how I told you I was assigned to do a story on the demolition of the Brewer mansion due to the highway expansion?"

Mike took a swig of his beer. "Yeah."

"Well, I finally met with Miss Brewer, the old woman who lives there."

He put his beer down and turned to look at her.

"I felt sorry for her, all alone in that big, old house, just her and her housekeeper. I got this sudden urge to help her. Then, I had an idea: Why not try to save the mansion from being demolished? So I went down to the DOT and talked to my friend there, who gave me a referral to a lawyer.... "

Mike just listened as she kept on talking.

"When I met with the lawyer, he told me I needed to obtain as much information as I could regarding the estate's history. So I went to the Morganville Library to do some research. Remember when you told me that someone supposedly died in the mansion fire in 1936? Well, do you know what I found out? It was Miss Brewer's fiancé who died in that fire!"

Mike got a strange look on his face and gulped down the rest of his beer. "That's really interesting, but I've really got to get going."

Katy walked him to the door and wrapped her arms up around his neck. "Be careful...I'm going to miss you."

"I'll call you as soon as I get back."

Katy lingered by the open door as she watched Mike pull out of the driveway. When he was out of sight, she shut the door, turned out the lights and got ready for bed. Then she sat on the edge of her mattress and unclasped the pendant around her neck, laying it down in the same place she did every night, between her phone and her alarm clock. Laying her head on her pillow, she pulled the blanket up over her chin and prayed for Mike's safe return, and that she would not wake up to another nightmare.

Chapter Twenty-Nine

Katy stopped by the office to tie up some loose ends before heading back out to the Brewer estate. She couldn't wait to tell Evelyn about her meeting with John Doherty and their plan to get the Brewer mansion designated as a historical landmark. She was sitting at her desk checking her messages when Vicky stopped by.

"Hi, Katy. I've noticed you've been making an effort to come in on time lately," she said sarcastically.

Katy forced a half smile without looking up at her. "Uh, yeah, so what's up?"

"You seem to have been working pretty hard on that Brewer story. Why are you so hell-bent on saving that decrepit old mansion?"

Katy still didn't look up. "I think it's a worthwhile cause."

"I don't know what you think is in it for you, but you're just spinning your wheels. You know you can't beat the system. That old house is going to get bulldozed one way or another."

Katy stood up from her chair and walked around her desk to go stand directly in front of Vicky. "We'll see about that," she said, looking her straight in the eyes. Then she turned around and walked back to her chair, pulled up her computer screen, and began pounding the keys of her keyboard with raging intensity until Vicky was well out of sight.

~*~

As usual, it took a few hard knocks before Mrs. Flaherty came to the front door and invited her in. "Nice seein' ya again, miss."

"Nice seeing you too, Miss Flaherty. Is Miss Brewer in?"

"She's in the library. Would ya like ta follow me?"

"Sure," said Katy, surprised to hear she wasn't in the parlor. She followed Mrs. Flaherty down the shadowy, parquet-patterned hallway, passing a grand dining room surrounded in fine tapestries and baroque sconces cradling taupe-colored candles and a table that stretched far enough to seat at least twenty people.

Mrs. Flaherty waved Katy through a dark, French-paneled door. Katy's mouth opened in awe as she marveled at the ceiling, which must have reached the highest peak of the house. The walls were encased in infinite volumes that would entice any scholar, with a moving step ladder to allow access to the highest shelves. A multihued Persian rug covered most of the room, which was scattered with maroon leather couches and chairs and ornate tables and credenzas. There were but two stand-up tiffany lamps in the entire room that provided a mellow-hued ambiance, while off in the corner in a winged high back chair sat Miss Brewer. And next to her was a small table with, of course, a lit candle on top.

Miss Brewer set her book on her lap and lowered her reading glasses to the end of her nose to look upward. "Why hello, Kate. Won't you come join me?"

"Hello, Miss Brewer."

"Evelyn, remember?"

"I mean.... Yes....hello, Evelyn. This room is amazing," remarked Katy, walking toward her and glancing at the title of the book on her lap. It was one of the books Ruby had dropped on the floor in the library the other day: *The Spirit World Unmasked*. "What are you reading there?" Katy asked coyly.

"Oh, just something I had Ruby renew for me from the library. I hadn't quite finished it. My reading is getting a little slow these days. I tire easily, and my vision isn't all that it once was. So, I understand you ran into her — Ruby — at the Morganville library."

"Yes, I did, but I don't understand why you would need to get books from an outside library when you must have enough literature here to provide you with a lifetime of reading," said

Katy, with her eyes moving up and down and across the shelves.

"There is a vast universe of knowledge out there. One can never be too enlightened."

Katy casually nodded as she wandered toward the bookcases. With her head bent to the side, she sauntered along, randomly perusing the titles, until she stopped in front of one of the shelves. There was a whole set of properly alphabetized Sherlock Holmes titles. Katy pulled one out and held it flatly in her hand, reading the title out loud. *"The Adventures of Sherlock Holmes* – I love all the Sherlock Holmes novels."

Evelyn stood up from her chair and ambled over to where she was standing. "Did you know that before Sir Arthur Conan Doyle began to publish his Sherlock Holmes series, he had published many short stories in the 1880s reflecting his interest in Spiritualism?"

"No, I didn't."

"He was particularly interested in the afterlife and conducted psychic research with the help of mediums." Evelyn pulled out one of the books and opened it up. "In 1926, he wrote *The History of Spiritualism* — his most noteworthy accomplishment — wherein he traces Spiritualism and its related phenomena."

"Hmm," muttered Katy, admiring the antique bound volume opened up in Evelyn's hand. "Mrs. Flaherty mentioned that you and she both shared an interest in the afterlife."

"Yes, we do. We also believe you can channel the souls of the departed."

"You mean, like through a medium?"

Evelyn cracked a smile. "Yes, like through a medium."

"I don't mean to discredit your beliefs, but I think mediums are nothing but extortionists who try to take advantage of the vulnerable."

"It's true. Some are. But there have been many famous mediums throughout the course of history. Have you heard of Lenora Piper?"

"No."

"She was born in the mid 1800s and is considered to be the greatest American medium of all time. The British Society for Psychical Research employed private detectives to investigate her to prove that she was a fraud, but all they could do was confirm her genuineness." Katy silently bit her lip, obviously not convinced, so Evelyn changed the subject. "So what, might I ask, brings you here today?"

"Oh, I almost forgot. I wanted to tell you that I spoke with my boss about the possibility of getting the Brewer mansion preserved as a historical landmark. If we can do that, the government authorities cannot have it demolished. I hope you don't think this was presumptuous of me, but I've already met with a lawyer — a Mr. John Doherty — to discuss what needs to be done to move ahead with this matter."

"Presumptuous? I live by your presumptuousness, Kate."

CHAPTER THIRTY

Katy curled up on the couch under a warm fuzzy blanket and clicked on the remote to watch the evening news. The California wildfires were still the top news story. Images of the fire spreading over the densely forested mountainside flashed on the screen. The background lit up with an explosion of fireworks consuming the dusky skyline as the reporter was airing the story.

"The fire, which was thought to be under control, is being fueled by severe and shifting winds. Several firefighters became trapped in a combustion of flames, and we are sorry to report that two of them have perished in the inferno. They were said to be a back-up crew from out of state. Unfortunately, we are unable to release their names until their families have been notified."

A knot began to form in Katy's stomach. A week had gone by, and she had yet to hear from Mike. Surely, it couldn't be. She tossed the blanket to the floor and ran into the kitchen. Mike's cell phone number was taped up next to her wall phone mount. She punched in the number and took a long, hard breath. After several rings, there was still no answer. The recording came on, and at the tone, she left a message. "Mike, it's Katy. I just heard the news and wanted to make sure you were all right. Please call me as soon as you get a chance...." CLICK.

The rest of the week went by, and she still hadn't heard back from him. She had trouble concentrating at work—he was all she could think of. What if he was one of the men who died in the fire? The thought of losing him in a combustion of flames, the way she had lost Mark, was more than she could fathom.

On Friday, she had just stepped out of the news station when a sharp pain ran through her chest. She could feel a panic attack coming on. Her heart began to beat faster and faster as she tried to catch her breath. She barely made it to her car. Lightheaded and weak in the knees, she fumbled with her keys, trying to get the door open. When she did, she fell into the driver's seat, clutching the steering wheel rigidly between her fists. Her head dropped to the center, and a floodgate of tears came rushing out. She sat there slumped over the wheel in the parking lot until she was finally able to pull herself together enough to go pick up her daughter.

The evening passed with Katy merely going through the motions. She tucked Lilly in and got ready for bed. Then the phone rang. It was well past her father's bedtime, so it couldn't be him—unless it was an emergency—and it couldn't be her boss. He wouldn't be calling her this late. Her pupils expanded to the size of nickels as the phone on her nightstand vibrated a second time. *God, don't let it be the fire chief or anyone else with news of the unthinkable.* She had all but abandoned her faith since her mother and Mark had died, but this time, she raised her face to the ceiling and made the sign of the cross. It rang one more time before she gathered up enough nerve to answer it.

"Hello?" she said faintly.

"It's me, Mike."

"Thank you, God!" she exclaimed before he could say anything else. I was afraid I'd lost you for good!"

"Don't ever be afraid, Katy. I'd never let that happen," Mike said emphatically.

When can I see you?" she jumped in.

"I just got back today, and I'm pretty tired—but I've got the weekend off. Why don't you come over to my place on Friday? We can order a pizza and watch a movie or something."

Friday afternoon, Katy dropped Lilly off at her father's house, letting him know she'd pick her up the next morning in case she got home too late. Then she went back home to shower and change before heading out to Mike's apartment. She was so jittery with anticipation she kept smearing her mascara while she was getting ready. As she was walking out the door, she had a quick afterthought and rushed back in to grab a movie from her small video collection.

Oddly enough, this was the first time she had ever been to his place and had to drive around the apartment complex for a while until she located his unit and found a place to park. She climbed up the wooden steps to the second-story apartment and stood outside his door for a few minutes, with her purse hanging over her shoulder and movie in her hand, while she tried to calm her nerves. Then she took a deep breath and pressed the doorbell buzzer. Not a second later, Mike opened the door. One look into his smoldering eyes, and she jumped into his arms, the VHS tape dropping to the floor. Not a word was exchanged as they remained locked in each other's embrace. The electricity running through their bodies took on a tangibility of its own, steering them directly to the bedroom, where their long repressed passion was finally consummated.

After their pizza was delivered, they sat down on the two barstools facing the kitchen counter and proceeded to devour half of it. "I can't believe how hungry I was," said Katy, holding her stomach.

Mike smiled and poured her a glass of wine. "So, how's your Brewer project going?"

"It's going great. I've already started circulating the petitions to get the mansion designated as a National Historic Landmark."

"Have you been back to see Ev...Miss Brewer?"

"Yeah."

"And what does she think about it?"

"She seems to be on board with it. It's hard to tell with her sometimes—she's kind of strange. She talks a lot about the afterlife and mediums and weird things like that. I think maybe she's just bored, or lonely or something."

Mike put on a deft smile and changed the subject. "What do you say we make some popcorn and camp out on the sofa?"

They settled into Mike's worn-out sofa with a big bowl of popcorn between them when he reached over and picked up the VHS tape stuck between the cushions. "So, what's this movie you brought?"

"Have you ever seen *Somewhere in Time*?"

"I don't think so, but it sounds familiar."

"It's one of my all-time favorite movies. It's about a young man who travels back in time to find the love of his life."

"I can relate to that," said Mike, moving in closer to light a subtle kiss upon her lips.

"What do you mean, you can relate to that?"

"I mean, I would gladly travel back in time if it meant I could be with you." Katy gushed while Mike put the movie in. As the story came to an end, tears were trickling down her cheeks. Mike set down the bowl of popcorn and went to grab a tissue to dab her watery mascara. "Hey, they'll be together in the end," he said, referring to the movie.

Katy popped a few more kernels of popcorn into her mouth. "I guess I'm just a hopeless romantic," she blubbered, as Mike proceeded to absorb every essence of salt from her reddened lips.

Katy broke away for a moment and pulled herself together. "Have you ever been in love, Mike?"

At first, he didn't say anything, then made a joke, laughing, "I don't know—maybe in a past life."

Katy gave him a light whack on the shoulder. "No, seriously, Mike, have you ever been in love before?"

Gently he raised her chin with his forefingers and gazed into her aqueous blue eyes. "You're the one I love, here and now."

She wiped her eyes, put her arms around his neck, and smothered herself into his gorgeous jawline.

The next morning, Katy opened her eyes just as the sun was coming up. She did not have a recurring dream that night. She was lying next to him, feeling more refreshed than she had felt in a long time.

Mike rolled over and pressed his lips against her naked shoulder. "Kate, I want us to be in a committed relationship."

As she wrapped herself around him, the words spilled out of her mouth with untainted conviction. "I do too."

Chapter Thirty-One

Halloween conveniently arrived on a Saturday this year. Katy volunteered to take the girls trick-or-treating in her neighborhood, which worked out well for Meghan's mom because the Reeves Art Gallery was hosting a Halloween soiree exhibiting the works of an up-and-coming artist. Sue had described his paintings as dark and esoteric, which made Halloween the perfect time to showcase his work.

Katy looked at the half-eaten piece of toast and scrambled eggs that had barely been touched on Lilly's plate. "Come and finish your breakfast!" she yelled out from the kitchen.

Lilly was in the living room with her hands and face pressed up against the big picture window. "But Meghan will be here soon!"

"She won't be here till noon, Lilly. That's three hours from now!"

"I'm not hungry. I just wanna put my costume on!"

Katy threw the kitchen towel down on the table and led Lilly to her bedroom to help her on with her Cinderella costume. "All right, keep still," she insisted, trying to get her arms up into the sleeves. "This is probably the last time you'll be wearing this. I don't think it'll fit you next year."

"Maybe we'll find Tandy when we're out trick-or-treating."

"Maybe," sighed Katy, examining the creased cardboard crown from last year. Many of the plastic gemstones she had meticulously hot-glued on its facade had fallen off, leaving a woeful trail of pock-marks. No sooner had she placed the crown on Lilly's head than her little princess scampered over to the full length mirror hanging over her closet door. As she stood there examining herself, her smile quickly turned into a frown.

"Something's wrong," she pouted, crossing her arms together.

"I know, I know, your crown is missing some sparkle."

"That's not it!" shouted Lilly.

Katy stood behind her daughter, looking into the mirror's reflection, and thought for a minute. "Oh, wait, you're missing your wand! I never finished making it after your old one from last year broke. I've already got the stick. We just need to cut a piece of cardboard into the shape of a star and hot-glue it to the stick. We'll spread some Elmer's glue on the star, and then you can sprinkle it with glitter. Come on, we can do it right now!"

Lilly squeezed her lips together and wrinkled her nose while she continued to study her reflection. "It's not that," she insisted, tossing her crown to the floor and pulling open the closet door.

Katy threw her hands down in frustration. "What, then?"

She came out of the closet wearing her red fireman's helmet, then ran over to grab Fluffy off her bed. "That's what's missing," she said, grinning with satisfaction.

"Oh my God, Lilly, you are obsessed with that helmet! Cinderella doesn't wear a helmet, she wears a crown."

"No!" stormed Lilly, stomping her foot down. "I'm a Cinderella that saves lost kitties!"

"Is that why you're holding Fluffy?"

"No, silly, Fluffy's not lost. But if Tandy sees me carrying him, he'll recognize him and know it's me." Lilly paused, pursing her lips together and lifting her finger to her chin. "I better bring my magic wand too—just in case."

"How are you going to carry all that while you're trick-or-treating: a wand, a stuffed cat, and a bag of candy?"

"I guess *you* can carry the wand in case I need it."

"But I'm going to be carrying some other things," responded Katy.

"Like what?"

"Well, I'm going to be carrying a clipboard with lots of

papers on it."

"Why?"

"Because I'm going to be asking people to sign them."

"Why?"

"Never mind, it's something for work."

"Then why can't you do it at work?"

"Ugh...!" Katy sounded out in frustration. Just then, the doorbell rang. Meghan had arrived — not a minute too soon.

Lilly made a mad dash for the front door and let out a scream, "She's here!"

"Thanks again," Sue reiterated. "I have to go in early and help set up for the party. Are you sure you don't mind Megan staying overnight?"

"Not at all. Let me know how the party goes."

Katy glued the star on the wand, and the girls took turns sprinkling glitter on it while the majority left a nice, slippery glean on the floor. While it was drying, they ran off to play, and Katy hurried to clean up the mess. She wanted to get an early start because she had promised to take them to the fire station first. She fed them a bowl of Spaghetti-O's, helped them collect their things, and by four o'clock, they were suited up and ready to go. Katy packed her two little Cinderellas — one wearing a crown and the other a helmet — into the back seat of the car with their little jackets, their empty candy sacks, their magic wands, and of course, a stuffed cat named Fluffy. She buckled them in, and off they went.

Mike had to work that day, but the station was handing out candy, so he had told her to bring the girls by. He took one look at Lilly when she got out of the car and couldn't help but laugh out loud. "There's my firefighting Cinderella," he said, picking her up and swinging her around. "I'm glad you're going to be helping me tonight!"

Lilly giggled with delight while Katy stood by, observing the smitten look on her daughter's face.

As he was helping the girls up into the fire truck, Katy asked if he wouldn't mind keeping an eye on them while she circulated her petition around the fire station to have the Brewer mansion preserved as a National Landmark.

"Why don't you leave them with me? I'll make sure and get them signed. You need to get out there and start circulating them in your neighborhood."

"Oh, Mike, I'm so lucky to have you. You've been so supportive of my efforts to save the mansion."

"How could I not? You were born for this."

Katy smiled humbly and hung out a while longer before she told the girls it was time to go. From the sounds of their laughter, it was clear they weren't ready to leave.

"Okay, Cinderellas, it's time to go help Mom circulate petitions."

"And get more candy!" they squealed.

"And get more candy!" he repeated, at which point, he stooped down and tossed some extra treats into their bags.

When he got back up, Katy was standing in front of him. He put his hands around her waist and gave her a kiss. "Just make sure you're back by midnight, or you'll all turn into pumpkins."

Before this evening had arrived, Katy had already begun circulating petitions, recruiting as many people as she could to help. Her friend Sue had even brought a stack of them to the Halloween soiree.

It didn't hurt that Katy was well liked and well recognized in her neighborhood. Many people answered their door, asking, "Aren't you that reporter on TV?" which always caused her to blush. If she wasn't identified from her news reporting, she was recognized as the pretty young mother tacking missing cat posters all around town with her daughter. She was also very good at convincing people that the preservation of the mansion would be a major asset for the town of Morganville. And, thanks to her boss, she was able to inform her neighbors that the mayor, Jim Elders—who happened to be up for reelection next year—had taken a major interest in the matter and was offering his full support for the cause. Needless to say, Katy had no problem obtaining all the signatures she needed.

CHAPTER THIRTY-TWO

The pieces were falling perfectly into place, and Katy's vision was unfolding precisely as she had hoped, thanks to the overwhelming support from her boss, Mayor Elders, and the excellent work by attorney John Doherty. The demolition of the estate had been halted, and the Brewer mansion was nominated for an (NHL) National Historic Landmark Designation with the State of Pennsylvania. In addition, the highway expansion project was successfully delayed, pending the mansion's designation as a historical landmark. The only deterrent was that they were still waiting to hear from the Landmarks Committee, and that whole process could take anywhere from two to five years. Katy had planned on paying Miss Brewer a visit to update her on all the progress that had been made immediately after her dreaded parent-teacher conference with Mrs. Randolph.

"The conference itself shouldn't last for more than half-an-hour, but I have to go on a work assignment afterward, so I probably won't be back for several hours," Katy explained to her babysitter, Darla.

Darla put her hand up over her mouth, "Oh no, I forgot to tell you—my mother made a doctor's appointment for this afternoon. She doesn't drive, and I'm the only one who can take her. I'm sorry, but I'm going to have to leave right after your conference."

"Shoot," said Katy. "Then I guess I'm just going to have to bring Lilly with me after I get back from the conference."

Katy entered the classroom to find Lilly's teacher seated at a large round table in the far corner of the room. Mrs. Randolph did not stand up or come over to greet her but simply watched her from the top of her glasses as she moved toward her. "Nice to see you again, Miss Barton. Won't you have a seat?" she said curtly, pointing to the child-size chair across the table from her.

Katy squeezed herself into the tiny chair while Mrs. Randolph, who was seated in an adult seat, looked down upon her. "I'd like to start out by telling you that Lilly is a very bright child and is doing a good job all around. She is very outgoing and gets along with all the other children in the class. *However*, she can be overbearing toward the other students and oftentimes makes some outlandish assertions."

Katy looked puzzled. "What do you mean by 'outlandish?'"

"Well, for one, she said that her father died in a fire. Is that true?"

Katy wrinkled her forehead, taking on a concerned look. She had never told Lilly how her father died. Maybe Katy's dad told her, but she had specifically asked him a long time ago not to say anything to Lilly. She wanted to be the one to tell her — when the time was right. "Yes, it's true," she answered.

Mrs. Randolph held an unwavering glare upon Katy, then continued. "A short while ago, we had a fire drill. All the students were asked to line up in single file before we headed out of the classroom. Lilly refused to leave her seat. She said she wanted to stay and help put out the fire. I told her that was the job of the firemen. When she still refused to budge, I had no choice but to grab her by the arm. That's when she said it didn't matter if she died."

Katy was speechless.

"Miss Barton, children Lilly's age do not have a clear understanding of death, and therefore it should be approached to them as delicately as possible. Her father's death clearly has had an impact on her. Have you thought of bringing her to a child psychologist?"

"I guess it never occurred to me."

Mrs. Randolph proceeded to lay out some of Lilly's schoolwork, as well as some of her artwork, across the table. "As you can see, she seems to be developing at an average pace." Mrs. Randolph kept a close watch on Katy as she inspected each item until one drawing in particular caught her eye.

"What is this?" she asked, picking up the picture.

"The children were recently instructed to draw and color a picture of themselves at home with their family members."

Katy examined the colorful drawing with the slightly embellished stick figures. She presumed all the figures were female because they were all wearing triangular skirts. The littlest figure had long yellow hair and a hat on her head. She was standing between and holding hands with two other stick figures, who also had hats on their heads. Off to the side was a little black stick figure with four legs, pointy ears, and black whiskers. They were all standing on patches of green grass with little white flowers between them and a yellow sun shining above them. On the opposite side of the paper, she had drawn a brown house with red crayon streaks shooting out the top, and above it was a gray cloud with dots raining down on it.

Mrs. Randolph resumed speaking. "I asked Lilly who the two women were in the picture, and she told me they were her two mommies." The teacher looked up at Katy. "Does she have a stepmother?"

"No," answered Katy, looking totally perplexed.

"Perhaps it's her grandmother?"

"Her grandmother passed away a long time ago—before she was born, so she never actually knew her." Katy's mind wandered back to the cemetery when Lilly found her grandmother's headstone among the hundreds of gravesites, and then the time she spent the night at her grandfather's house and told her she had "spoken" to her grandmother. Maybe it *was* meant to be a picture of her grandmother.

"What about the house beneath the cloud?" pointed out Mrs. Randolph. "It looks like it's on fire. Lilly seems to have a propensity towards fire. Wouldn't you say?"

Katy could feel herself getting flush. "I don't know. My boyfriend is a fireman. Maybe that has something to do with it."

Mrs. Randolph gave her another one of those stern, questioning looks.

"But we do have a cat!" Katy blurted out. "I mean, we *did*

have a cat...until it...." She decided to stop there since the cat had jumped out the window during what could have easily become a fire.

Mrs. Randolph tightened her lips, and the lines on her forehead became more imbedded. "If you don't want to bring your daughter to a psychologist, perhaps you might want to have a talk with her. Children's imaginations run deep. They are often used as an outlet to express their fears."

Oh great, thought Katy. *Now I have two shrinks.*

~*~

On the drive home, Katy reflected back on everything Mrs. Randolph had told her — and then there was that bizarre picture that Lilly had drawn. She thought about the advice she had given her, to take her daughter to a shrink. *I think she's making a big deal out of nothing,* Katy kept telling herself. *It's just a five-year-old child's imagination — nothing more, nothing less.*

The moment she opened the front door, Darla jumped up from the couch with her coat in her hand as though she had been counting the minutes for her return.

"I'm sorry, Darla, I guess that took a little longer than I expected."

"Lilly is just finishing her lunch," said Darla, rushing to get her arms through her coat sleeves. Katy was in a hurry as well, so as soon as she paid her, she shut the door behind her and hollered over to her daughter, who was still in the kitchen. "Come on, baby, we have to go!"

Lilly ran into the living room, wiping the milk moustache off her face. "Where are we going, Mommy?"

"I told you I had to take care of some work-related business. Now let's put your jacket on. It's cold outside."

Katy rushed her daughter out to the car and buckled her into the back seat.

"Are we going to your work?"

"No, honey, somewhere else."

"Where?"

"We're going to someone's house."

"Who?"

"I have to see a very old woman to give her some good news."

"Can't you just call her on the telephone?"

"Her phone doesn't work! Okay, Lilly, enough with the questions. Don't you want to know how my conference with Mrs. Randolph went?"

"Yeah, what did she say about me?" Lilly asked excitedly.

"I'm very proud of you, Lilly. Your teacher said you are doing very well in school." In the meantime, Katy was trying to figure out how she was going to approach the other concerning matters that Mrs. Randolph had brought up. She wanted to make sure and pose her questions as delicately as possible so as not to upset her little girl. "First of all, Lilly, how did you know your father died in a fire?"

"I dreamt it."

"What?" said Katy, startled. "You never told me that."

"I might of forgot."

Katy checked her daughter's expression through her rearview mirror, trying to figure out how to respond to that. The only revealing thing about it was that there was nothing revealing about it. A few minutes of silence went by while Katy tried to come up with the right thing to say next.

"Do you know how much I love you, Lilly?"

"How much?"

"I love you more than anything in the whole, wide world. So why did you tell Mrs. Randolph that it didn't matter if you died when your school had a fire drill? You mustn't think like that! Don't you know how much I would miss you if anything ever happened to you?" Lilly didn't respond.

Katy waited a few more minutes before bringing up the subject of the picture. "Mrs. Randolph showed me some of your artwork. There was one picture that I'm *kinda* curious about."

"Which one?"

"The one where you are walking with two mommies?"

"Oh, that one."

"Who is the other mommy? Is it Meghan's mom, Mrs. Blakeford?"

"No."

"Is it Mike?"

"No, silly," giggled Lilly. "Mike is a man!"

"Okay, I give up."

"It's another mommy."

"O...kay...," Katy annunciated slowly. "Does that *other* mommy live in the big brown house in the sky?"

"Yeah!" Lilly sounded surprised her mom had figured it out.

"But why is the house on fire?"

"I don't know, it just is! Now *you* stop asking *me* questions!"

Katy breathed in a deep sigh and held her breath. Perhaps she should just leave well enough alone.

Chapter Thirty-Three

Once they came upon the long and winding asphalt road, Lilly became unusually quiet. *Maybe I asked her too many questions*, Katy worried, observing her daughter through her rearview mirror again. Lilly was lifting her head up and stretching her neck from left to right, taking in everything around her. Something must have captured her attention because a glaze came over her, as though she were transfixed by what she was seeing. Little did Katy know that her little girl was having a vision of her own.

As Lilly stared out the window from her rear passenger seat, she perceived the image of a straw hat blowing in the wind. She watched as the hat rose higher and higher into the trees until it was out of sight. When she looked back down, she saw the shadowy image of a cat weaving through the green and brown thicket.

Lilly lowered her chin and curled her tiny fingers into fists, and began rubbing her eyes. "I saw him, Mommy, I saw Tandy!"

"What? That can't be, baby. We're too far away. You must have imagined it."

"No, Mommy, I saw him!"

"It was probably a fox or maybe a baby deer."

"No, Mommy, it was Tandy!"

When Katy was halfway up the gravel driveway, Lilly spread her palms up against the glass and leaned in with her face to get a good look out the window. "That's the house, Mommy!" she squealed, pointing to the mansion. "That's the house in my picture!"

Katy shook her head in disbelief. She tried to reconcile Lilly's implausible declaration by making a joke of it. "Do you wish you lived in a big house like that? Because I don't think we'll ever be able to afford it."

"Look, there's the swing!" shouted Lilly.

Okay, now how did Lilly know there was a swing? That must be a case of wishful thinking.

When Katy pulled up near the front of the house, Lilly unbuckled her seatbelt herself, pushed the door open, and jumped out of the car. She then ran directly toward the front steps leading to the porch, with Katy sprinting after her.

"Can I knock?" Lilly asked excitedly.

"Sure," said her mom, trying to catch her breath while lifting her up so she could reach the knockers.

Lilly bit her lower lip as she took one of the large, weighty handles between her two fists, and with a fierce look of determination on her face, smacked it as hard as she could against the wood several times until Mrs. Flaherty came to the door.

"Come on in, miss," she said, holding the door open just long enough to allow some sunlight to enter the room. "And who might this be?"

"This is my daughter—"

But before Katy had time to finish her introduction, Lilly ran straight over to Miss Brewer, who had slowly begun to make her way into the foyer. Lilly stopped just short of the old woman and raised her head to look directly into her shadowy face. "Do you remember me?"

"Of course I do," beamed Evelyn. "Your name is Lilly."

"How do you know her name?" asked Katy, who had caught up to her and was standing behind her.

Evelyn vacillated for a second before shrugging off the question. "Oh, you must have mentioned it when you were here last."

That's odd, thought Katy. *I don't remember ever mentioning it to her.*

Evelyn's attention was firmly fixed on Lilly. "You know, I used to have a magnificent flower garden filled with all sorts of beautiful flowers, but my favorite was always the lily." She stooped down until she had reached eye level with the child and lifted her small chin upward, stroking her hair and caressing her cheek. "You have long, golden hair as I did when I was your age."

"Then how come your hair is all grey now?"

"Lilly, that's not polite," shushed Katy, looking a little embarrassed.

"Sadly, time has turned it to ash, from whence we came," responded the old woman.

Lilly looked around the room contemplatively, when out of her mouth came a most unlikely question. "Is Tandy here?"

"Lilly, Tandy couldn't possibly be here. It's too far from home!" burst in her mother.

"But I saw him! He was running this way!"

Katy was becoming visibly unnerved, so Evelyn quickly interjected. "I once had a cat. He was as black as the coal mine where my father found him during one of his inspections. His eyes were as bright as the full moon rising on the day he brought him home. He was the best present my father could ever have given me. He took the place of someone I had lost very early in my childhood."

"What happened to him?" asked Lilly.

"He disappeared during a fire a long time ago."

"Maybe he'll come back," Lilly reassured her. "Maybe he's lost, like Tandy."

"Yes, cats are said to have nine lives," sighed Evelyn. "I'm sure one day, he'll find his way home."

"Can I go play on the swing?" asked Lilly, abruptly changing the subject.

"Of course you may," replied Evelyn, looking a bit bewildered and amused.

Mrs. Flaherty held open the heavy front door and watched Lilly as she bolted out toward the swing.

Katy couldn't hold it in anymore. "Evelyn, the reason I'm here is I have some excellent news for you. Can we sit down?"

"Of course, my dear," replied Evelyn, leading her into the dimly lit parlor.

"I don't know if you've heard, but I've been very busy the last few weeks. Our lawyer has been successful in stopping the demolition of your home and delaying the construction of the highway expansion through your property." Katy stopped to take a breath. "So you won't have to vacate the premises, at least not anytime soon!"

"That is good news since I wasn't planning on leaving," retorted Evelyn.

"And there's more! I did some necessary research into your father's past. With everything he did for this town, your home has all the viability of being considered a historical landmark. We've already nominated it for an NHL—that is, a National Historic Landmark designation—with the State of Pennsylvania. We've obtained more than the required signatures in our petition, so right now, we're just waiting to hear from the Landmarks Committee. The only downside is that the whole process could take anywhere from two to five years. I still need your official approval, though. I have a few papers here that I'm going to need for you to sign."

Evelyn appeared to be overwhelmed by all the news, lowering her chin and looking toward the doorway.

"Is something wrong?" asked Katy.

The old woman breathed out a slow and calculated response. "No dear, everything is just as it was meant to be. I will gladly sign the papers."

Katy bid Evelyn goodbye as Mrs. Flaherty shut the door behind her. "Come on, Lilly, we have to go now," she yelled over to her daughter, who was bent down on the ground in front of the swing. "What are you doing?"

Lilly got up and ran over to her mother. "Look what I found!" she exclaimed, pulling some objects out of her pocket. She cupped her two hands together to display a pinecone, a shiny black quartz-like rock, and a small, faded, yellow and purple plastic flower. As Katy stared at the flower in her daughter's hands, her heart missed a beat.

On the way home, she looked at her daughter through the rearview mirror. "How about we stop at the animal shelter on the way home to see if Tandy showed up?"

CHAPTER THIRTY-FOUR

"She's finally asleep," said Katy, tiptoeing out of Lilly's bedroom to join Mike on the couch. "We stopped at the animal shelter yesterday to see if by chance Tandy was there, but he wasn't. I'm sure they would have called me if he was. I told Lilly we could adopt another cat, but she started crying, 'I only want Tandy!'"

"You need to relax," said Mike, scooting over to the far end of the couch. "Why don't you lie down?" he said, patting the top of his thigh. Katy stretched herself out and laid her head on his lap. He caressed her cheek, admiring her alabaster skin. Then he ran his fingers through her tousled locks and noticed something that, strangely enough, he hadn't seen before. Up in the left-hand corner of her forehead was a scar about the size of a postage stamp. "When did you get this?" he asked, gently outlining it with his finger. "I've never noticed it before."

"That's because I do a good job of concealing it with my hair," smiled Katy. "It's been there since the automobile accident. It's where my head hit the dashboard. I call it my 'Lilly scar' because that was also the day I found out I was pregnant. *And*, it's in the shape of an 'L' — for Lilly."

Mike leaned over and kissed it, then began to rub her shoulders. "You feel tense."

Their relationship had grown to the point where Katy felt she could safely confide in him. "I need to talk to you," she said, sitting up abruptly.

Mike looked as though he was fearful of what she might say.

She started out by telling him about the parent-teacher

conference. "I just don't know what to make of Lilly's comments to Mrs. Randolph during the fire drill—and then there was that picture she drew!"

At first, Mike didn't say anything, as if he were searching for an explanation. "I wouldn't worry," he finally reassured her. "All kids have vivid imaginations. I'm sure you did too when you were little."

Next, she went on to tell him how strangely Lilly acted on her way to the mansion. "She said she saw Tandy running through the woods."

"Maybe she *did* see a cat running in the woods. It's not impossible."

"Yeah, but she even asked Miss Brewer if *she* had seen Tandy."

"That's not a stretch—kids have no sense of distance."

"Oh my God, Mike, you have an answer for everything!"

Mike shrugged his shoulders while a smug grin formed over his jaw.

Katy continued. "But it's the way she acted around Miss Brewer like she'd known her for years. I don't know, Mike, I can't help feeling there's something 'not right' about it all. Maybe I *should* take her to see a psychologist like Mrs. Randolph suggested."

"Why would you want to put her through that? It wouldn't prove anything. It might even make things worse and cause her to act out even more."

Katy thought about it. "You're right. I need to make another appointment with Dr. Fleming anyway. Maybe he can give me some insight into children's minds."

Mike took Katy into his arms. "I think you're getting all worked up over nothing."

"You keep me sane, Mike. I don't know what I'd do without you."

~*~

Katy sat in Dr. Fleming's waiting room, nervously rap-tap-tapping her fingertips against the side table. She had been anxiously looking forward to this appointment because this time, it wasn't just about her. It involved her daughter.

A woman in an expensive suit and heavy make-up stepped out of his office, and a few minutes later, the doctor opened his door. "Come on in, Kate, and have a seat." He sat down and opened the manila folder on his desk. "It's been a while since I've seen you. You seemed a little reluctant to come back after our last session."

"Yes, well, I've been really busy. But it's not so much about me this time. It's about my daughter, Lilly." Katy went on to tell him all about her daughter's comments at school and the picture she drew. She told him how Lilly thought she saw their missing cat, Tandy, running through the woods and how strangely she had acted toward Miss Brewer. "She even asked Miss Brewer if she remembered her—and if she had seen Tandy. I'm worried about her, Doctor. What could it all mean?"

For a while, Dr. Fleming said nothing except to scribble a series of notes on his notepad.

"What are you writing?"

Dr. Fleming put his pen down. "Have you heard of Dr. Ian Stevenson?"

"No."

"He is a famous psychiatrist, albeit a bit controversial to many. He is internationally known for his research into reincarnation, particularly with regard to children. He travelled extensively, investigating three thousand cases of children around the world who claimed to remember past lives. He believed that children are more susceptible to remembering past lives and that memories, emotional trauma, and even physical injuries in the form of birthmarks can be transferred from one life to another. He has published many books on the subject, including *Where Reincarnation and Biology Intersect*."

Katy wrinkled her forehead. "I'm not sure I buy into that."

"Tom Shroder, a *Washington Post* journalist, who accompanied Dr. Stevenson during some of his fieldwork, was a skeptic at first but grew to become a staunch believer. He later corroborated the doctor's research by writing a book himself, entitled *Old Souls: The Scientific Proof for Past Lives*. You should read it if you get a chance."

"So you're saying that Lilly may have a past life recollection of the Brewer house, and perhaps Evelyn herself?"

"I'm saying it's not out of the question. I think you should bring Lilly in to see me."

"Oh no, that *is* out of the question," Katy said adamantly. "I am *not* going to subject my five-year-old daughter to hypnotherapy."

"Then I think *you* need to undergo more hypnosis. It may help clear up some of these unanswered questions."

Chapter Thirty-Five

Dr. Fleming drew the blinds, and the room immediately took on a somber tone. Katy lay on the couch with her palms squeezed tightly together. "Are you sure you're ready?" asked the doctor as he sat down in the chair beside her.

"Yes," she answered unconvincingly. "I need to find out what's going on in my daughter's head."

"All right then, let us proceed." Dr. Fleming turned on his recording device and instructed Katy to clear her mind of all burdening thoughts, after which he began to institute a series of verbal suggestions.

Slowly, Katy succumbed, then fell into a deep subconscious state. A vivid scape burgeoned to the surface of her mind.

Before her appeared a charcoal sky, highlighted by sinister clouds swirling past a moon that had reached its maximum stage of luminosity. Rising to the forefront was a grand Victorian manor, whose ominous façade was defined by the tempestuous horizon, illuminating it in a silver halo.

"Kate, I want you to share with me everything you are seeing," prompted the doctor.

"I see the Brewer mansion," she said out loud as her mind's eye moved her to the inside of the house. "I see a magnificent grand parlor. The room is very dimly lit, with only a couple of candles. One is on a desk in the far corner of the room, and one is in the middle of the room, on a low table in front of a flowery chaise. There's a young woman lying on the chaise. She appears to be sleeping. It's hard to tell because her face is in the shadows. There's a book, or maybe a journal of some sort on her lap."

A smile appeared on Katy's face, followed by a warm

chuckle.

"A cat jumped up on the chaise, and she's opening her eyes. I can hear her talking. 'You startled me, Tandy—I must have dozed off.' She's stroking his black fur, slowly, gently, over his head and the rest of his body. A young man just walked into the room. He's leaning over the back of the lounge and is giving her a gentle kiss on the forehead."

Katy appeared to be savoring the moment, the way she was moving her head from side to side.

"Go on," said the doctor.

"He's very handsome. He has dark hair and dark, piercing eyes. He's telling her something. 'It's getting late. Aren't you tired after a full day of riding, my darling?'

"The woman is patting the cushion with her hand. 'I never tire when I'm with you, Marcus. Come, sit with me a little longer.'

"'My dear fiancée, as much as I'd love to spend the whole night here beside you, out of respect for your father, I shall retreat to the gardener's quarters, which I will gladly share with your humble servant, Ivan. Besides, we have a big day ahead of us tomorrow.'

"'What is it?'

"'I cannot tell you, it's a surprise. Now get some sleep, my lovely.'

"He's leaning over to kiss her again, this time longer and more passionately, on the lips. He's getting up to leave the room now, and I can hear her calling out to him, 'I love you, Marcus—more than life itself!' He's turned around with a lingering smile on his face and looks hesitant to leave. Now he's walking out the front door. Someone else is walking into the room—a young, black woman in an apron and servant's cap. She's got a worried look on her face. I hear her talking to the young woman on the chaise. 'There's a storm about to brew, miss. I've shut all the windows in the house except for the one next to your writing desk. Would you like me to go shut it for you?'

"'No, thank you, Molly, I'll get it myself when I go upstairs to bed.'

"The servant notices the empty cup and teapot sitting next

to the candle on the table in front of the chaise. 'Can I get you anything before I retire for the night? Would you like some more tea?'

"'No thank you, I believe I've had my fill of tea.'

"'Then have a good evening, miss.'

"'Thank you, Molly, you too.' The woman set her book on the table. She's whispering to her cat. 'Come, Tandy, it's late. We'd better go upstairs.' She's picking up the candle on the table in front of her, and I see her making her way toward a tall, winding staircase, with the little black cat following her every footstep. She's speaking again in a low, loving voice. 'Oh Tandy, you are like my shadow.' She's at the top of the stairs now and is walking down a long hallway until she has reached the last door on the left. The woman is turning the knob very slowly and opens the door to her bedroom. She's walking over to her bedside table and placing the candle on it. She's blowing it out as she's falling into bed. I can see the little silhouette of the cat jumping up on her bed as she's beginning to doze off. 'I didn't realize how tired I was, Tandy....'"

Katy lay silently for a while as if she, too, were sleeping.

"Go on, Kate," prodded Dr. Fleming. "Can you see or hear anything else?"

Katy wriggled her body for a bit, then continued.

"There's a storm setting in. I hear thunder and lightning and the harsh sound of the wind as if it's battering everything in its path. I'm back in the parlor now. The room is completely dark, except for the blurred light of the smoldering candle that was left on the desk. There's a tall, narrow window right next to the desk. Its thin lace curtains have begun to billow. She forgot to shut the window. It was left open just a crack, but the velocity of the wind has reignited the spark. The flame is leaping high and low like it's performing a ballet recital. A huge gust has just blown one side of the curtain into the candle. It's being consumed, almost immediately, from deep red to brown. It's disintegrating before my very eyes. Embers are billowing everywhere."

For a moment, Katy said nothing and then recommenced.

"The fire is spreading. Shards of trajectory flames are

rising up toward the beams in the ceiling. They're glowing like kindling in a nighttime campfire."

She winced but went on.

"I'm back upstairs now. The cat is yowling and jumping wildly across the bed. The woman is waking up. I can hear her coughing. Her room is full of smoke. The cat has jumped to the floor and is scratching frantically at the door. There are plumes of smoke creeping up underneath it. The woman is walking over to the door with her hand cupped over her mouth. I see her opening the door and the cat making a mad rush out of there, disappearing into the hallway. Smoke and burning debris have filled the corridor. She's stumbling out of the room, gasping and choking, through the dark hallway. She's trying to feel her way toward the banister. She's made it to the top of the stairway. I see her making a blind attempt to position her foot onto that first step—she missed. I see her falling, tumbling down the staircase. She's lying motionless, face down, at the bottom of the stairs."

There was another pause as Katy lie frozen on the couch. Shortly, she resumed.

"I hear the ticking of a clock. It's getting louder...louder.... It's so loud!"

Katy lifted her arms and pressed the palms of her hands against her ears as if the noise were deafening.

"It's coming from the fireplace mantle, but there's so much smoke, I can barely read the numbers on the face—wait, they're coming into view. Oh, God—it's 2:38 a.m.!"

Tears began to stream down Katy's cheeks, for which Dr. Fleming allowed her some respite—until another image emerged, and she continued with her revelation.

"There's a tiny cottage across the property. The cabin is in pitch darkness except for intermittent flashes of lightning, amplifying every surface throughout the inside. I can hear the shutters banging against the shingles. There's a man inside. The noise must have awakened him because he's getting out of bed. There is a huge lightning strike, and I'm getting a fleeting view of his face. His skin looks weathered and brown, probably damaged from the sun. He must be the gardener. He's going into the kitchen. I see him standing in front of the kitchen sink, pouring himself a glass of water and looking out the window. It appears he notices something. Flames are billowing high above the rafters from one corner of the main house. I see him running over to a sofa, where another man is sleeping. He's shaking him awake. 'Wake up, Marcus, wake up!' Marcus has jumped up from the couch and is running over to the kitchen window to look out. I can hear him yelling, 'Ivan, you run to the back entrance of the house where the servants, Molly and Elsa's, rooms are. They may still be asleep. You must alert them and get them out of the house. I'll run into the front of the house for Evelyn!'"

Katy's feet became restless, as though she were running herself.

"Now I see Marcus standing at the front door of the mansion, fidgeting to pull out a key from his pocket. He's unlocking the front door and entering the foyer. The room has been overtaken by thick fumes, and he's shielding his eyes. He's calling her name, 'Evelyn, Evelyn!' With his arm stretched in front of his face, he's able to make his way toward the staircase. There, at the base of the stairway, he finds her—Evelyn, lying on the floor, unmoving. He's turning her over and sees that her forehead is bleeding. He's looking up and sees that the flames have almost reached the beam above the staircase. I see him picking her up and carrying her outside. He seems to have reached a safe distance from the house and is laying her on the lawn near the flower garden. I see him feeling for a pulse and gently shaking her. 'Evelyn, Evelyn, speak to me!' She appears to be unconscious. 'You mustn't die, Evelyn, please don't die!' He's now giving her mouth-to-mouth resuscitation."

Katy was breathing heavier and started to gasp, only to carry on with her imagery.

"She's coming to! She's wheezing and gasping for air! Her lips are moving. She's trying to speak but is struggling for her breath. Her voice is very faint, but she's able to force out a few words. 'Tandy...where is my Tandy?'

"Marcus is turning his head to look around. 'I don't see him. He must still be in there.' Evelyn is crying, 'Oh darling, you have to find him!'

"The young man appears to be hesitating. 'I know how much you love him. Don't move. I'll be right back.'

"Marcus is running back to the house. The two maids, Molly and Elsa, have joined Evelyn on the lawn and have taken over tending to her. The rain is coming down in buckets now, and Ivan has run over to the shed. He's hooking up some kind of hosepipe. It looks very big and heavy. He's dragging it over to the mansion.

"I see Marcus again, standing in the parlor at the bottom of the stairs. I think he sees the cat because he's bending down and calling his name, 'Tandy, Tandy, come here, boy!' His eyes are moving to the top of the staircase, where a burning beam has become engulfed in flames. It's breaking away from the ceiling.... Nooooo!"

Tears were pooling in Katy's eyes as she fell into a state of bereavement. Dr. Fleming allowed her to undergo a limited period of grieving before coaching her back to full cognizance but no sooner than he did, her vision faded, and another scene materialized in her brain.

"I'm having another vision now. I see the same young woman, Evelyn. She's just waking up. The room is stark, white. She's in a hospital bed. There is a bandage wrapped around her head. A man has entered the room wearing a white smock—he looks like a doctor. He's walking over to the side of her bed with a very solemn look on his face. He's taking her hand into his and is about to say something to her. I'm having a hard time making out his words."

"Concentrate, Kate," encouraged Dr. Fleming.

"He's speaking very softy. Wait... I hear him now. He is saying, 'I'm sorry, Evelyn. I hate to have to tell you this. I don't know if you knew you were pregnant, but unfortunately, you suffered a miscarriage.'"

At this juncture, Katy began to sob profusely, and Dr. Fleming decided it was time to bring her out of her subconscious state. Gradually she began to ease out of her rigid posture, finally slumping into a level of total exhaustion. Dr. Fleming was busy scribbling away in his notepad while she lay there. When she appeared to regain full awareness, she sat up abruptly and burst out, "I saw it! I saw it all—how the whole fire happened and how Marcus died trying to save Evelyn's cat, Tandy. My God, his name was Tandy!'"

"It's all right, Kate, calm down," said the doctor, setting down his notepad and turning off his recorder.

"And Evelyn—Evelyn suffered a miscarriage!" Katy fell silent, her mind weighing heavy when she glanced up at the doctor with a stumped look on her face. "But what does that have to do with me?"

Dr. Fleming was quiet for a moment, then lowered his eyeglasses to look directly into her eyes. "Given the strange way your daughter has been acting and what has just transpired here, it's quite possible that your Lilly is the reincarnate of Evelyn's deceased child."

Katy looked at Dr. Fleming, stunned, her eyes wide and her mouth open, as if she had just realized she'd been pushed off a cliff. But before he could say anything else, they were interrupted by the beeping of his telephone.

The doctor looked at his watch and picked up the receiver. It was his receptionist informing him of his next appointment. "I'm sorry, Kate, but our time is up, and my next patient is here. We'll have to probe this more deeply at a later session."

CHAPTER THIRTY-SIX

Katy lumbered out of the doctor's office with puffy red eyes and more questions than she'd had going in. *Calm down*, she told herself, trying to regain her equanimity. *You have to pick up Lilly, and you can't let her see you like this.*

Katy parked in front of the school, waiting for her daughter to come bolting out of the building's large double doors. Lilly soon appeared, with Mrs. Randolph hovering very noticeably behind her. Katy lifted her hand to give the teacher a wave but received nothing more than a probationary look in exchange.

While Katy was getting her daughter situated in the backseat, she noticed that she too wasn't her usual perky self. "So, how was school today, honey?"

"Okay," murmured Lilly, staring blankly out the window.

A good ten minutes of silence went by when Katy determined she needed to say something. "You know, Lilly, it doesn't matter how many mommies you have, as long as I'm your favorite." Katy looked in her rearview mirror for a reaction. What she saw was Lilly's contemplative expression come to life with a full-size grin.

After parking her car in the front driveway, Katy and her daughter walked up the two cement steps to their door. She inserted her key into the keyhole and found the door to be unlocked. "Hmm, that's strange. I could swear I locked the door when we left this morning," she said aloud. She was about to push the door open but then hesitated. "Wait, Lilly," she said, holding her daughter back with her arm. "Stand by the door and let me go in first—just in case." She didn't want to frighten her little girl by telling her that there was a possibility that someone could have broken into the house.

Katy tiptoed into the living room and heard a rumbling in the kitchen. In a panic, she grabbed an umbrella from the stand in the hallway and held it up over her head, ready to use it as a weapon. Her heart began thumping out of control when she perceived the shadow of a man about to come around the corner. All of a sudden, the man yelled, "SURPRISE!" Katy let out an ear-piercing scream just as she was about to clobber Mike over the head with the umbrella.

"Oh my God, you scared me to death!" she huffed, dropping the umbrella down to the floor and lifting her hand to her heart.

In the meantime, Lilly ran in. "Mommy, Mommy, are you okay?"

"I'm fine. It's just Mike," she said, still trying to catch her breath. Then she turned to Mike. "How did you get in?"

"I thought you would have been home by now. When I didn't see your car in the driveway, I figured you had parked it in the garage. I tried knocking a few times, then noticed that the front door was unlocked."

Katy looked confused. "I could have sworn I locked it this morning. I don't remember a lot of things, but I always remember to lock the door."

"I'm sorry I scared you," said Mike, going in for an embrace. "I wanted to surprise you by coming over and cooking a special dinner for you and Lilly. I was in the kitchen preparing it when you walked in."

Katy inhaled, then let out a deep breath. "It smells good. What are you making?"

"I am making an English pot roast with green beans and a Caesar's salad. And for dessert, brownies `a la mode."

"I love brownies!" jumped in Lilly. "But what's...ah...la... mode?"

"They're brownies with ice cream on top."

"Yummm!"

"I went to the market this morning to pick up the ingredients. I also got a loaf of French bread and a nice bottle of

Burgundy — it'll go well with the pot roast."

"It sounds wonderful," said Katy. "Only next time, you might want to give me a heads-up. I thought you were a thief. "Look," she said, holding out her arm. "I'm still shaking!"

"I promise. I really didn't mean to scare you."

"It's okay. I'm glad you're here! I've had a rough afternoon with Dr. Fleming. That might be the real reason why I'm still shaking. I'll tell you about it later. In the meantime, you might want to crack open that bottle of wine."

When they were all done eating, Katy got up to clear the table, and Mike insisted on helping with the dishes.

"You've done enough," said Katy. "By the way, that meal was fabulous! How did you get to be such a good cook?"

"We have a big kitchen at the fire station, and we take turns cooking in shifts, so I've had a lot of practice."

"You're too good to be true," said Katy, landing him a firm kiss on the lips.

When it was time for Lilly to go to bed, she begged Mike to tell her a bedtime story. He was really good at making up bedtime stories on the fly, and Lilly loved hearing his unique and entertaining tales.

"How 'bout I tell you the story about the little girl who didn't know she was a princess?"

Lilly's eyes lit up. "Yeah, yeah, tell me that one!"

Not surprisingly, he ended the story with, "And the little princess of Morganville lived happily ever after in her castle on the hill." Lilly insisted on hearing what happened after that, but Mike promised he'd have a sequel for her the next time he came over.

He and Katy had finally settled comfortably down on the couch when she asked, "How do you come up with these creative fairytales on the spot?"

"I don't know. I think Lilly just brings out the best in me."

"Well, it seems Dr. Fleming brings out the worst in me," exclaimed Katy. Mike might think her crazy, but she believed he loved her unconditionally, and she couldn't hold it in any longer. So she proceeded to tell him all about her earlier session with

Dr. Fleming and everything she had seen while she was under hypnosis. She told him how the Brewer mansion had caught on fire and how Evelyn tripped and fell down the staircase. "And the accident happened at exactly the same time as my accident—at 2:38 a.m.!" Then she went on to explain how Evelyn's fiancé had perished in the fire—not from trying to save Evelyn, but from trying to save her cat. "And the cat's named was *Tandy*!" Lastly, she told him that when Evelyn was in the hospital, the doctor told her that she had been pregnant and lost her baby.

Throughout her rant, Mike never said a word. He just had this far-off look on his face, as though he were processing it somehow.

"I know I'm throwing a lot at you right now, but what do you think about everything I've told you?"

It took him a while to respond, and when he did, he looked at her like he hadn't heard a word she said. "What?"

"I said, what do you make of all this, Mike?"

Finally, he said, "I think you have a very vivid imagination, Kate. Now we know where Lilly gets it—the fruit doesn't fall far from the tree, you know," he added jokingly.

Katy gave him a hard slug in the biceps. "Don't make fun of me, Mike! It was so real, like I was watching a movie of Evelyn's life play out before me."

He turned and put his hands on her shoulders. "I think you need to get some rest, Kate. You've been working way too hard on this Brewer story. It's starting to affect you mentally."

"But wait!" she burst in. "I left out the most important part. At the end of the session, Dr. Fleming introduced the notion that Lilly could be the reincarnation of Evelyn's deceased child! Can you believe that?" When he didn't answer, she jumped up from the couch and started pacing back and forth with an untamed look in her eyes. "Why must I continue to be haunted by Evelyn Brewer's past? I feel like something is missing, something that would connect all the pieces together. I've got to get this resolved, Mike, or I'll go crazy!"

Mike stood up and grabbed a hold of Katy's shoulders again, only firmer this time. "This has gone too far. I'm worried about you, Kate. I think all this hypnotherapy is what's making you crazy."

Katy looked at him like she was about to start crying.

"Look, Katy, I didn't mean to mock you. Whatever you think you've seen is in the past. You mustn't dwell on it. The future is all that matters."

Puddles settled into Katy's lower lids, and she found herself caving under his hypnotic gaze. "But I'm afraid. What if it's some sort of omen?"

"You mustn't be afraid, Kate. All you need to know is that I'm here for you. I love you, and nothing can change that." He continued to hold her shoulders tightly while a visible lump descended down his throat. "Will you marry me, Katy Barton?"

His words penetrated her soul, sealing the hypnotic spell she was under. Throwing all caution to the wind, she released a resounding, "Yes, yes, I will!" Then she wrapped her arms around his neck and molded herself into his hot, smoldering lips.

Mike became immediately pumped at the prospect of their permanent union. "I want to celebrate!" he said. "I've got the whole Veteran's Day weekend off. Let's drive to Atlantic City! We can leave Thursday and come back on Sunday."

"That's two days from now. Besides, isn't it a little cold to be going to Atlantic City in November?"

"We can hole up in a hotel, maybe hit up a few casinos and walk along the boardwalk. We'll have each other to keep us warm."

"Will there be anything even open along the boardwalk?"

"I'm sure a few restaurants and souvenir vendors will remain open."

"I don't know — what about Lilly?"

"I think we need some time alone. Couldn't she stay with your dad? You said you wanted her to spend more time with her grandfather."

"You're right. She'd love that. But...it's such short notice. I don't know if I'll be able to take time off from work."

"Katy, you've earned it — a few days won't make any difference. Besides, it'll do you good to get away and clear your mind of all this *crap* Dr. Fleming's been feeding you."

Chapter Thirty-Seven

"Are you all packed, baby? Grandpa will be here soon," Katy yelled out while frantically thrashing her clothes about.

"Yeesss, Mom!" Lilly shouted from her bedroom. "Come look."

Katy lifted her head up from underneath her bed and sped to her daughter's room. She gave the inside of Lilly's suitcase a quick once-over and zipped it shut. "Good girl. Now go finish your peanut butter and jelly toast. I have to finish packing myself." She then scurried into the bathroom and started digging through the hamper. *Where is my necklace? I hope I didn't lose it!* It had become a nightly ritual. Every evening before bed, she would take it off and set it on her nightstand. Every now and then, she'd forget to put it on in the morning, but it would always be sitting on her nightstand when she got home.

When she first noticed it missing, she had gone into work and checked every nook and cranny of her office. She called Dr. Fleming's receptionist, Marjorie, to see if it was there. It could have slipped off her neck during her last session. She even called the library, in the rare instance someone might have turned it into the lost and found, all to no avail. There was one more place that she hadn't checked — the Brewer mansion.

Lilly swallowed the last drop of milk from her cup as the doorbell rang. "I'll get it!" she shouted, running for the door with a thick white mustache on her upper lip. "Grandpa!"

"Come over here, Princess. Come give your grandpa a big hug!" Lilly jumped into his welcoming arms, awarding him her biggest hug ever.

"Guess what, Grandpa?"

"What?"

"I don't have to go to school till Monday."

"I know that, Lilly. That's why I've got something special planned for us this weekend."

Katy rushed into the front room. "Thanks, Dad. I really appreciate you doing this."

"It's no problem. You know I love spending time with my favorite granddaughter!"

"What are we gonna do, Grandpa?"

"I'm going to take you fishing over at Twin Lakes. That was your mom's favorite place to go when she was a little girl."

Lilly's eyes lit up like rockets. "Are you gonna teach me how to fish, Grandpa?"

"I sure am!"

"Isn't it a little cold to be fishing in November, Dad?" interrupted Katy.

"I won't be taking the boat out. We'll just be fishing from the shoreline. Besides, the weatherman predicted a couple of days of mild weather — an Indian summer! But don't you worry, I'll make sure and have Lilly bundled up real good."

"Yay!" yelled Lilly, who was running in circles, then suddenly stopped and scrunched up her face. "What if Tandy comes back and nobody's here?"

Katy dropped down and looked into her daughter's bright blue eyes. "Don't worry, Lilly, Tandy can fend for himself, like he did before we found him. If he comes back, I'm sure he'll wait for you to come home. Now let's go make sure we pack a warm jacket and hat. We'd better throw in your mittens and boots, too." Katy grabbed her hand, and the two of them went back to Lilly's room to add the extra items to the suitcase.

Lilly and her grandpa were headed out the door when she tugged on his sleeve, "You said it was a *twin* lake, Grandpa — which twin are we going to?"

Mr. Barton laughed. "You'll see when we get there."

Katy went out on the porch to wave goodbye as the car pulled out onto the street. The air was crisp, but the sun shone bright, promising a good weekend. She had just turned to go back into the house when she heard a car pull into the driveway. *I wonder if they forgot something.* She turned back around to see that it was Mike. He jumped out of his car, revved up and ready to go.

"Are you ready?" he called out.

"I just have to get my bags out of the bedroom," said Katy.

"It's almost a nine-hour drive, and I'd like to get there before sunset."

When they were well on their way, Mike kept looking over at Katy, who seemed unusually pensive and staring out her passenger window. "Is something wrong?" he asked. "I thought you'd be a little more excited."

"I'm just upset because I can't find my locket—the one that Mark gave me. I've looked everywhere for it."

"Maybe it fell off at work," said Mike.

"I checked."

"Maybe Lilly has it."

"I already asked her, even though I know she would never have taken it. She knows how much it means to me."

"Don't worry, it'll probably turn up when you least expect it."

Katy let out a long sigh. "I hope so."

"So, how did your father react to the news?"

"What news?"

"What news? The news of our engagement, of course!"

"Oh, um...I haven't exactly told him yet."

"Why not? Are you afraid he won't approve of me?"

"I'm sure he'll approve of you. I'd just like for both of us to be there when we tell him."

They arrived in Atlantic City and were checking into the casino hotel when Katy said, "You know, I've never gambled before. I'm afraid of losing."

"It's all in the power of manifestation. You have to *picture* yourself a winner."

Katy thought about her lost pendant. Maybe she could manifest that back to her.

"Are you a gambling man, Mike?" she asked.

"I've been known to dabble a bit," he smirked.

Katy gave him a slanted look before dropping the subject as they rode the elevator up to their 20th-floor suite. And when she stepped inside the beautifully appointed sitting room, she quickly forgot all about her lost pendant. "Oh my gosh, Mike, did you hit the jackpot or something?"

"Not yet," he replied, unleashing a devilish grin.

Sitting on the mirrored coffee table in front of the sofa was a glass vase with a dozen red roses and an ice bucket with a bottle of Dom Perignon and two crystal flutes. She turned to give Mike a heartfelt look, then dropped her bags to the floor and rushed toward the balcony, where she slid open the double glass door and stepped outside. As she stood there, leaning against the railing and gazing out into the open sea, Mike walked out to join her with the two flutes in hand, which he had already filled with champagne.

"Oh Mike," she swooned. "The view is breathtaking!"

"You're worth it," he said, handing her a glass and moving in closer to shield her from the frosty wind. Then he raised his glass up to hers. "To us."

Maybe it was the champagne, or maybe it was the resplendent moonlight penetrating the room, but Katy's euphoria was not interrupted with a recurring nightmare. Her body clock did, however, wake her up at the crack of dawn, just in time to catch the sunrise. She was able to wake Mike long enough to share the magnificent hues emanating through the glass balcony doors until the colors faded into the horizon, after which they quickly settled back to sleep.

"Wake up, Sleeping Beauty," Mike whispered into Katy's ear.

Katy lazily rolled over to face him. "After I fell back to sleep, I had the most vivid dream."

Mike paid careful attention while she went on.

"I dreamt I was pregnant with Lilly again. It was so real. It felt as though my abdomen was rising up and down, and I could hear her breathing inside of me."

Mike laid his hand over her belly. "Did it scare you?"

"No—it was beautiful."

Mike leaned over and kissed her navel.

Katy's façade took on a glow of gratification as she turned and looked up at the ceiling. "What time is it, anyway?"

"It's almost noon. Why don't we get dressed and walk along the boardwalk and find somewhere to grab some breakfast—I mean, lunch," he chuckled.

"That sounds great," she murmured, slowly dragging herself out of bed.

The two of them strolled along the boardwalk in the gusty wind. Katy, clutching her coat tightly with one hand while holding Mike's arm with the other, was busy admiring the majestic waves crashing along the shore. The cresting surf reflected deep into her blue eyes, suggesting her inner thoughts to be as profound as the sea. She took in a deep breath. "Aahh, I love the smell of the fresh, salty ocean air. I want to breathe it all in and clear my mind of all negative thoughts."

"What negative thoughts?" asked Mike.

"You know—fearing the unknown, that the worst could happen at any time."

"Then go ahead, Katy, breathe it all in. That's why we're here, to rid you of all those negative thoughts and fears."

"That's what I love about you," said Katy, her lips quivering from the cold. "You're fearless. I guess that's why you became a fireman."

Mike smiled and didn't say anything.

Katy closed her eyes, breathing in the wind against her face. "The power of the ocean is so mysterious."

"It's not that mysterious," said Mike. "The gravitational pull of the moon and sun affect the tide of the ocean."

"It's a good thing there won't be a full moon tonight because I heard that there are more accidents and more people go insane during a full moon because of that gravitational pull," laughed Katy.

"I don't know about that," said Mike. "But statistically, there are more crimes committed during a full moon because it provides more illumination for the criminals."

"You are so logical," she said, her lips quivering slightly from the cold. "You tend to view things as either black or white. I, on the other hand, am emotionally driven."

Mike looked up, squinting into the vividness of the blue horizon. "I'm more emotionally driven than you know."

Shivering, Katy wrapped herself tightly in Mike's arm, and their exchange came to a halt when they came upon a little Mexican restaurant.

"How's this?" he asked.

"Perfect. Maybe a margarita will help warm me up."

After a hot and spicy lunch and a couple of margaritas, they were both sufficiently warmed to begin their leisurely stroll back to the hotel.

The carnival rides had been closed down for the season, but the roar of the wind heightened the mood of the imaginary sights and sounds of the midway pier, as well as adding to the amusement of the curious vendor shops that remained open along the way. As they wandered past a row of dingy, blue-sided buildings, they came upon a thin woman in a red bandana and brightly-colored, wool shawl. She was standing against the wall of one of the tiny storefronts with her arms crossed against her waist, clutching her wrap tightly. Displayed in the large, wood-framed window behind her was a deteriorated cardboard sign that read:

Fortune Teller — $25.

An invisible cloak of uneasiness immediately fell upon Katy as she walked by. She could feel the gypsy woman's cold penetrating stare following her with her piercing dark eyes. "You vant your fortune?" yelled out the woman in a Hungarian accent. "I give you for twenty dollar."

"No, I'm good," answered Katy, forcing a smile.

"No, you are *NOT* good — you must know the truth!" the woman yelled back.

Katy's smile turned to chagrin.

"Never mind her," said Mike. "She's just trying to drum up some business."

The gypsy woman ran up behind Katy and began to follow

her. "Things are not vat they appear to be," she proclaimed loudly. Katy started walking faster, trying to break away from her, but the woman continued to follow at a more rapid rate. "A voman, an older voman—she vonts your life!"

That's when Mike turned around abruptly to face the gypsy, "Look, back off and leave us alone!" he yelled, looking as though he were about to deck her.

The gypsy woman stopped in her tracks and uttered these final words. "You vill see—in time, you vill see."

They finally lost sight of her, but Katy was visibly shaken and upset. Mike tried his best to reassure her by making light of the situation. "Don't worry, I'm not going to leave you for an older woman."

Katy knew she would be getting home late Sunday evening, so she had planned on picking Lilly up the following morning and taking her to school. When she and Mike were almost home, they were hungry, so they decided to stop at the Golden Buddha to get some carry-out Chinese food. By the time they were done eating, it was pretty late, and Mike was exhausted from the long drive. He had a long four-day shift ahead of him in the morning, so he decided to go back to his apartment and get some sleep.

Katy walked him to the door, where he leaned in for a kiss. "Thank you," she said, tenderly, "for a wonderful weekend."

"Believe me, it was *my* pleasure."

It was a good thing he left because she was exhausted too. *All I want to do is sleep,* she thought to herself, crawling into her warm, cozy bed. Unfortunately, try as she might, she could not get to sleep. She kept tossing and turning from the sharp stinging pains in her stomach. *I shouldn't have eaten that spicy Kung Pao Chicken so late in the evening. What was I thinking?* She got up and popped a couple of antacids in her mouth, then washed them down with a drink of water. Once she laid back down, she still couldn't get to sleep. But this time, it wasn't due to heartburn. It was because she couldn't stop thinking about what that gypsy said to her on the boardwalk. "An older woman wants your life!"

Katy lay in bed wracking her brain. *Who would want my life? It couldn't be Janice. We've been best friends since middle school.*

Of course, she is a little older than me by a few months. And she's never tried to hide the fact that she has always been jealous of me — ever since I won that singing competition back in high school.

Eventually, Katy fell asleep.

CHAPTER THIRTY-EIGHT

Katy reached up to hit the snooze button one more time on her alarm before she realized it was Monday morning, and she had to go pick Lilly up at her dad's and take her to school. By the time she arrived, Lilly was all dressed and packed and ready to go. "Grandpa made me oatmeal with raisins and cinnamon, Mommy!" she boasted.

Katy leaned over to kiss her Dad. "Thanks so much, Dad, you're the best!" Then she leaned over to give her daughter a big hug. "I missed you so much!"

"I caught a fish!" Lilly blurted out proudly. "But it was too little, so Grandpa said I had to throw it back in the water so it would have time to grow bigger, and we could come back and catch it next year."

"That's wonderful, honey. You can tell me more about your weekend in the car. We have to get going, or you'll be late for school."

After dropping her daughter off at school, Katy drove into work, still groggy from her lack of sleep. She hadn't had time to brew her usual pot of coffee at home, so as soon as she walked into the news station, she headed straight for the break room. Mr. Bruckman had just filled his mug and was walking out the door when she ran into him.

"How was your weekend in Atlantic City?"

"It was w-o-n-d-e-r-f-u-l."

"It must have been—you don't look like you got much sleep," he said, with a mischievous grin on his face.

Katy blushed. "It's not that. We had late night Chinese carryout, and it must have disagreed with me."

"Suuure," he replied sarcastically. "So, how's that Brewer story coming?"

"I'm almost done writing it. I just want to run it by Miss Brewer and hopefully, this time, convince her to do the live interview."

"Good. Let me know when it's ready to go. The *Herald's* been asking for it."

Just as Bruckman was turning to leave, Katy stopped him. "Wait a minute — so what's going on with the station? You said you'd fill me in when you got back. I'm not going to lose my job, am I?"

"Oh yeah, about that — there'll be some big changes coming. We're going to be taken over by a new parent company, and we'll be merging with our sister station, WJPTV, in Johnstown. Nothing *you* have to worry about, though, Kate. You're not going to lose your job — I've got you under my wing." At that, he gave her a wink and proceeded out to the hallway.

Katy felt better, but there was something else that was weighing on her mind. She poured herself a full mug of coffee, went back to her desk, and picked up the phone to make a call. "Hi, Janice, how's it going?" she asked nonchalantly.

"Great, everything's great," Janice responded in her usual brash tone. "So, how was your romantic getaway?"

"Magical. I didn't tell you before, but Mike proposed to me."

"What? Get out! It's like you just met him. Don't you think you should get to know him a little better before putting that final nail in the coffin?"

"Well, when it's right, it just feels right. So, anything new happening on the freeway project that I should know about?"

"No, the project is on hold pending notification from SHPO."

"From what?"

"You know, The State Historic Preservation Office."

"Oh, yeah, yeah."

"So when are we gonna get together again? I think you owe me a lunch. After all, I did set you up with a great lawyer, didn't I?"

"Um, yeah, you did do that."

Janice broke in again. "Wait a minute! I've been dating this guy — well, technically, we've only been on two dates — but anyway, why don't we get together for dinner, like a double date? You know, you and Mike and me and my date…what's his name."

"Um, sure," Katy agreed half-heartedly. "I'll call you."

"Promise?"

"I promise, but I have to go now and pay Miss Brewer another visit. Talk to you soon."

~*~

When Katy arrived at the Brewer estate, she was surprised to be greeted by Mrs. Flaherty after just one knock on the door. "Come in, Miss Barton."

"Nice seeing you again, Mrs. Flaherty."

"Miss Brewer is in the parlor. Follow me."

Of course, she is, thought Katy, holding back a smile while she followed Ruby into that splendid room, rendered obscure by the pulled shades and candlelight. Evelyn was seated on the flowery chaise with a fountain pen in her hand and her black leather-bound journal in her lap. "Why hello, Kate," she said, setting them down on the table in front of her. "I was just going to have some tea — would you like some? I have a freshly brewed pot sitting right here."

"No, thank you. I've had enough caffeine this morning," she responded, rubbing her stomach in circles.

"So what brings you here today, my dear? I hope it's not bad news."

"Oh no. On the contrary, I'm here because I wanted to give you an update on what's been happening. Everything is moving along smoothly. Mayor Elders is lending his full support. He's very excited about having a historical landmark here in Morganville. I plan to run a full-page article in the *Morganville Herald* as a tribute to the Brewer family, as well as outlining the town's efforts to have the mansion preserved as a historical landmark. I intend on running the story in this Sunday's newspaper, and if it's all right with you...." Katy slowed her speech, being careful to pose her request as delicately as possible. "I would like to do a live interview with you in front of your home on Saturday morning before the story is released in the Sunday paper."

By the look on Evelyn's face, Katy knew what her answer was going to be.

"I think it's admirable that you're doing the story, but I'm sorry, I cannot agree to a live interview."

Katy's frustration was clearly pronounced by the wrinkles that formed on her forehead. "I'm very disappointed to hear that, Evelyn, but I will respect your wishes. However, would you allow me to do a live news story in front of the mansion without you in it?"

Before Evelyn had time to answer, a strange look came over her face, and she reached her hand up over her heart as her body began to slump over.

"Oh my God!" shouted Katy, grabbing ahold of her and calling for Mrs. Flaherty. Ruby rushed in. "Mercy, Miss Brewer, shall I rush inta' town and get the doctor?"

"That'll take too long," jumped in Katy. "You can use my cell phone."

"It's okay, Ruby, I'll be all right....you know this has happened before," gasped Evelyn, holding her throat and trying to catch her breath. "Sometimes my heart beats so fast, it feels like it's going to jump out of my bosom."

"It sounds like heart palpitations. My mother died of a heart attack—you need to see a doctor," insisted Katy, leaning Miss Brewer back up against some pillows.

"She shouldn't be drinkin' so much tea. That's what I keep tellin' her," Ruby spouted off.

And then Evelyn forced out the words, "One mustn't worry about that which is inevitable."

"It doesn't *have* to be inevitable if you see a doctor," Katy said forcibly.

"Don't worry about me, Kate. I'm an old woman. My time is limited. It is the young soul that will need nurturing."

Katy offered Evelyn another pillow to help make her more

comfortable and continued to sit with her. While the old woman was regaining her strength, Katy couldn't help but think about her own mother's sudden death and how much she missed her. The holidays were especially difficult. That's when she realized that Thanksgiving was only two weeks away.

"I was just wondering, Evelyn, Thanksgiving is coming up, and if you don't have any plans, I'd like to invite you to my home — well, actually, my father's home — for Thanksgiving dinner."

"That's very kind of you, dear, but I'm really not comfortable around strangers."

"But I hate to think of you all alone in this big house — "

"I'll be fine. I'm quite used to it. Besides, I have Ruby here to keep me company." Evelyn looked over at Ruby with a beguiling smile on her face. "Her magnetic personality could 'wake the dead,' so to speak."

Katy glanced over at Ruby, who in turn gave Evelyn the evil eye before tramping out of the room.

~*~

Katy never re-asked Evelyn whether or not she could do her live news story in front of the mansion. Instead, she took a bold move by just showing up early Saturday morning with her cameraman. She positioned herself about three-quarters up the driveway to allow for a nice view of the estate, being mindful not to intrude too closely into Miss Brewer's personal sphere.

Then Dan began his countdown. "5, 4, 3, 2, 1...and we're live."

"Hello, this is Katy Barton for PTTV News here in Morganville. I'm standing here in front of the well-known Brewer mansion, which had been scheduled to be demolished to make way for the new Highway Extension 46. As many of you already know, a petition was circulated by PTTV, the mayor, and the whole community of Morganville, on behalf of Miss Brewer and the Brewer family estate, to halt the demolition and reroute the freeway in order to allow for the preservation of the mansion and to have it designated as a National Historical Landmark. You'll be able to read the whole story in a special front-page section of tomorrow's weekend edition of the *Morganville Herald*."

"And that's a wrap," said Dan, shutting off his camera. Then, he and Katy packed up their equipment and climbed into the PTTV news van without as much as a breath of life erupting from the confines of the residence in their periphery.

Chapter Thirty-Nine

There it was, in full display, on a huge billboard just off the freeway: SAVE THE BREWER MANSION, printed in big, bold letters, with an enlarged picture of the estate. Katy could barely hold back her pride when she passed it, even though she had to credit her friend Sue. She had been instrumental when it came to finding the perfect artist to render the beautiful depiction and for getting the Reeves Gallery to generously donate the funds for the billboard.

Katy left work early on Monday to check up on Evelyn after her "episode" and to bring her a copy of the Morganville newspaper. She followed Ruby into the parlor to find Evelyn sluggishly making her way from her candle-lit desk toward the chaise.

"Why hello, Kate. Come, sit down. I didn't expect you back so soon, inasmuch as you were just here on Saturday."

"You look better."

"Yes, I feel much better—for now."

Katy sat on the edge of the chair, facing the chaise without removing her coat. She felt a little uncomfortable after doing a live presentation in front of the Brewer estate without Evelyn's express permission. Hoping to appease her, she stretched her arm out to hand her a rolled-up copy of the newspaper. Clearing her throat, she began, "I came by to bring you a copy of the weekend paper so you could read the article on the front page." And without waiting for a response, added, "The newspapers were all sold out by noon!"

"Thank you, but Ruby procured a copy for me yesterday morning. I had her read it to me. The small newspaper print is hard on the eyes when you get to be my age."

"So what do you think? I mean, about the article."

Evelyn bit her lower lip as if she was trying to suppress her disapproval and dodged the question by saying, "Mrs. Flaherty mentioned running into you at the library again the other day."

"Why, yes. I was there doing research on the Brewer family history. I needed specific information for our application to The Historical Landmark Commission. Did you know that they have newspaper articles dating back to the 1800s? That's where I gathered the facts for my article." Katy broke for a moment, then softened her voice to divulge as gently as she could, "That's when I found out that your fiancé, Marcus, died in the fire."

"I don't think it was appropriate for you to bring up the details of the fire, particularly where Marcus was concerned."

"I simply stated that he was your fiancé and that he died in the fire—nothing more. It's no secret that there was a fire here in 1936 and that he perished in that fire. It made the front page news in what was then the *Morganville Gazette*." Katy tried to get Evelyn to understand her rationale. "The article I wrote is what's called a 'human interest story.' It was supposed to make people empathize with you and *want* to be on your side. I did it to help our cause to save the mansion. I thought you'd understand."

"What you don't understand is that Marcus was the love of my life. I gave up a music scholarship at Oberlin to be with him. We were to be wed the month after he died." Evelyn forced a chuckle. "He was a cowboy at heart. He had scoped out a piece of land not far from here where he was planning to build a ranch. We already had the horses. My father had lost interest in them after my mother passed. Our plan was to live here with my father until the ranch was completed.

"After Marcus died, I could have gone on to Oberlin, but I had lost my *joy de vivre*. Music was no longer important to me. What I sought was spiritual guidance to help me cope with the tragedy I had suffered. So I left for the United Kingdom to study theology, which spawned my attraction to Eastern and Indian religions. From there, I traveled to China and Southeast Asia, ultimately spending most of my time in India and Tibet." Evelyn took an extended breath. "Unfortunately, I was forced to return home to the news of my father's chronic lung condition. I helped care for him and stayed by his side until his death in 1961. By then, I was forty-four years old."

A knot began to form in Katy's stomach from her overwhelming sense of guilt for treading where she probably should not have. Maybe steering the discussion toward religion was a good idea. "So, you studied Buddhism and Hinduism?"

"Yes, among others."

"Aren't they all pretty much the same? I mean, they all believe in reincarnation, right?"

"They do have similarities but differ in various aspects. For instance, Buddhists and Hindus believe that there is a certain 'waiting' period before one's soul can reincarnate, whereas the Jains believe that reincarnation can happen *instantly*. And Taoists use the term 'transmigration' instead of 'reincarnation.' Zhuang Zhou, who was one of China's most significant early interpreters of Daoism—now known as Taoism—said: 'Birth is not a beginning; death is not an end. There is existence without limitation; there is continuity without a starting-point. Existence without limitation is Space. Continuity without a starting point is Time. There is birth, there is death, there is issuing forth, there is entering in. That through which one passes in and out without seeing its form, that is the Portal of God.'"

Katy quietly pondered Evelyn's quote. "So, which of these religions do you believe in?"

"I abide by *all* of them. Religion is all-encompassing. I don't think anyone should be restricted to any singular doctrine of ideology."

"Hmm," muttered Katy, for lack of a better response.

"As you may have witnessed from your 'chance' meetings with Mrs. Flaherty at the library, I continue to study the teachings of re-embodiment in all its forms. Have you heard of Animism?"

"No."

"It started among the primitive people who imagined spirits or souls as vapors or shadows transferring life from one body to another. They believed that souls could pass, not only between human beings, but into plants, animals, and inanimate objects as well." Evelyn paused, surveying Katy's expression. "Do you believe, Kate?"

"Believe in what, exactly?"

"Do you believe that a soul can take over another soul?"

Katy couldn't help feeling as though she had been put on the spot. "I don't know," she answered dubiously.

"I don't suppose you've read, *The Tibetan Book of the Dead*?"

"Uh, no. I've never even heard of it."

"According to the Chikhai Bardo, when death is imminent, you are faced with a choice of whether to follow the bright light or the dim light. At the time of the fire, Marcus found me lying at the bottom of the stairs — I was on the verge of dying."

In that very second, the prismatic light from the mosaic window overhead radiated over Evelyn's face, enlivening her features in an intimidating mystical way.

Katy, who had been growing increasingly uncomfortable from their conversation, became spooked and turned her wrist to look at her watch. "Oh, my goodness, I have to get going, or I'll be late picking Lilly up at school." She jumped up from her chair. "Don't worry, I'll let myself out," she said, as she hurriedly made her way toward the foyer.

Evelyn likewise stood up, attempting to follow her. Just as Katy was about to step through the doorway, Evelyn yelled out to her. "The dimmer light, Kate. I chose to follow the dimmer light."

As Katy was driving, she couldn't stop obsessing over Evelyn's last words. "I chose to follow the dimmer light." What could she have meant by that? Then something resurfaced from the back of her mind from the very first time she had undergone hypnosis, reliving the car accident. While she was in the truck being driven to the hospital, she remembered seeing her transparent body walking through the dark tunnel and being confronted with two lights. First, the radiant one and then the dimmer one. The next thing she knew, her earthly body was in the hospital.

Which choice did I make?

CHAPTER FORTY

The evening of the "big date" had arrived. Lilly ran to the door to greet Mike with a colossal hug. "Look, Darla's here!" she shouted, grabbing him by the hand to lead him into the kitchen. "She's making me dinner."

Darla was busy cutting up some lettuce when he walked in. "Hi," she said timidly, avoiding eye contact.

"Hi, Darla, whatcha makin?" asked Mike, extending his neck over her shoulder.

Before she had a chance to respond, Lilly jumped in. "Darla likes salad, but she's making me hot dogs and French fries—the kind you put in the oven."

"Mmm, that sounds great! I think I'd rather eat here than go out." he declared with a wide grin on his face, causing Darla to blush.

Katy walked into the kitchen. "Okay, I'm ready. I told Janice we'd meet them there around quarter-to-six." Mike raced out in front of her to open the door. She smiled appreciatively. She still couldn't get over what a gentleman he was.

"I'm sorry I won't be able to spend Thanksgiving with you and your family. You know I have to work the whole weekend."

"I know, Mike, it's okay. Sometimes our jobs have to take precedence. Speaking of precedence, let me tell you about my visit with Evelyn earlier this afternoon."

"Why did you go over there? Did you need to have her sign some more papers?"

"No, I wanted to check up on her after the 'episode' I told you about. Also, I wanted to bring her a copy of the Morganville paper, so she could read my article."

"So how is she?"

"She seemed all right, only a little more tired than usual. But while I was there, she started telling me how she'd been studying Buddhism and Hinduism and all this other stuff. She asked me if I've ever read *The Tibetan Book of the Dead*! Apparently, it teaches you that when you die, you are faced with a choice of whether to follow a bright light or a dim light. Then she said she chose the dimmer light. Why would she tell me that?"

"I think you should stop going over there."

"I don't know, maybe you're right. But I feel like there's some kind of connection between us, something I can't explain." Katy pressed her lips together tightly, and after a brief period of contemplation, she decided to confide in him even further. "There's something I never told you before. I mean, I've mentioned it, but not in great detail."

Mike turned his head to observe Katy's expression.

"Remember when I told you about my recurring nightmare that always happens at the exact same time? Well, there's more to it than that."

Mike took his eyes off the road once again to look at her.

"I told you that in my nightmare, I'm walking through a dark tunnel surrounded by fire and smoke, and I see a bright light, and then I wake up. What I didn't tell you was that the first time Dr. Fleming put me under hypnosis, I relived the automobile accident. I actually saw myself in my unconscious state. I saw myself in that same tunnel, and as I'm moving toward the bright light, another light, a dimmer one, comes into focus and intersects with my path. I am suddenly faced with a decision of whether to follow the bright light or the dimmer light."

Without saying anything, Mike removed his right hand from the wheel and stretched his arm out to grab Katy's hand. "Do you remember what happened next?"

"I don't know. The next thing I saw was my body being wheeled into the hospital." A few minutes of silence went by when Katy spread her eyes wide. "That's it, Mike!" she burst forth. "That's the link — the invisible thread that's holding Evelyn and I together! I have to go back to Dr. Fleming!"

"What makes you think Dr. Fleming can help? He might make things worse."

"How can he make things worse? He has enabled me to see things I otherwise could never have even begun to conceptualize."

"He could be putting things into your head that shouldn't be there. Your destiny has been decided, Kate — you cannot allow him to alter your course."

Katy said nothing, confused. *What do you mean 'my destiny has been decided?'*

Mike squeezed her hand and leaned over to give her a kiss on the forehead. "So what's this guy's name, Janice's boyfriend-of-the-month?"

~*~

They arrived at the restaurant to find Janice and her date seated at the far end of the bar. Janice yelled out an excited, "Hi!" as they walked over to greet them and jumped up from her stool to give Katy a hug.

From Katy's own personal observation, Janice had lowered her standards significantly. Her date had clearly failed to conceal a bald spot on his head with a bad comb-over and a paunch revealed itself beneath his shirt. "We got here a little early, so we're already on our second drink," said Janice, eyeing Mike with a seductive smile. "It's so nice to finally meet you, Mike. I've heard *so* much about you." Then she bent over to whisper in Katy's ear, "I must say, you definitely have a type."

Katy was watching for Mike's reaction. This was the first time she had seen *him* blush.

"I hope it's all good," he responded, sounding a little embarrassed.

"So far so good," said Janice, as if she were intimating at something.

"Aren't you going to introduce us?" interrupted her date, who had been silently and awkwardly standing there until now.

"Oh, sorry! This is Ben. Ben, this is my *best friend* from junior high, Katy, and her boyfriend, Mike. Or is it Michael?" she asked, inadvertently twitching her eye, although Katy perceived it as a wink.

"Um, you can call me Mike," he answered sheepishly.

Katy was surprised Janice still referred to her as "her best friend." They had been close at one time, but that had changed in high school when Janice tried to sabotage her relationship with Mark.

"So where's this ring?" asked Janice, examining Katy's ring finger.

Katy looked embarrassed, so Mike intercepted. "I'm waiting to get her something extra special."

Janice rolled her eyes slightly.

Katy felt sorry for Janice's boyfriend, who pretty much sat there like a bump on a log, pretending to enjoy the evening, while Janice flirted with Mike all through dinner. It soon became clear that Mike rather enjoyed the attention. At the end of the evening, as they were walking out the door, Janice made it a point to say, "We've *got* to do this again real soon."

It didn't take long after Mike opened the car door for Katy for her to begin venting. "Did you hear that? *'We've got to do this again real soon.'* I wasn't born yesterday!"

"What's wrong with that?" he asked innocently.

"Oh, don't plead ignorance with me! Janice was all over you, and you *loved* the attention."

"I did not. I was just trying to be nice to your friend."

"You didn't exactly go out of your way to be nice to...uh... what's his name."

"You mean Ben?" snorted Mike.

"Yeah, Ben. From now on, I'm going to have to keep a close eye on Janice. I don't want her trying to lasso you away from me." *Like she tried with Mark.*

"I'm not 'lassoed' that easily. Besides, that's just her personality." You could tell he was beginning to enjoy that jealous part of Katy he had not seen before. "Maybe the next time you see Dr. Fleming, you can find out if Janice stole your boyfriend in a previous life."

Katy gave him a light slug on the shoulder, followed by a sarcastic comment. "Maybe I'll find out which light I *should* have followed!"

Chapter Forty-One

"This is my first Thanksgiving ever at Grandpa's," Lilly said excitedly from the back seat of the car.

"That's right, baby," said her mom, looking back on the night she and Mark were headed there for Thanksgiving but never made it. For a long time, she couldn't bear to go back there. While she was in New York, she always came up with one excuse or another: too preoccupied with school, too far to drive with a baby, can't take time off from work. So her father had always gone up to see her during the holidays. Now that she was back in Morganville, there could be no more excuses.

When they pulled up to the house, her father came outside to greet them. Lilly helped by carrying a bag of buns while Katy carried in the turkey she had prepared earlier that morning. The only thing left to do was to pop it in the oven for three to four hours.

"Look, Grandpa, I brought the buns!"

"Why, yes you did, Lilly. Why don't you go set those on the dining room table while I help your mother get the rest of the things out of the car?"

Katy was already in the kitchen preheating the oven when he brought in the mashed potatoes and cranberry dressing. "Thanks for making the salad, Dad."

"No problem. Your Aunt Hildi is bringing the green beans and the pumpkin pie. Oh, and I hope you don't mind, I invited Johanna Lankershim over too. Do you remember her?"

The last time she had seen her and Mr. Lankershim was at her mother's funeral. "Of course, I do. They live in the big grey house with the black eves down the road. How are their sons,

Charlie and Marty? I remember I used to have a crush on Marty back in middle school."

"Well, their boys have done very well for themselves. Charlie is a doctor, and the younger one, Marty, became a lawyer like his dad. They've both since moved out of state, though. Her husband, Blake, passed away three years ago. You know, they used to be our best friends—me and your mom, that is. Now Johanna is all alone in that big house, so I thought I'd invite her over."

"That was nice of you, Dad."

"So when do I get to meet this elusive boyfriend of yours?"

"Dad, I told you he's a fireman and works full days at a time. I promise, you'll meet him *soon*."

"The important thing is that Lilly likes him."

"Lilly *loves* him."

"Yes, she's told me," said Mr. Barton. "She said he's funny and that he's a really good cook."

Katy laughed and headed into the dining room to set the table. Lilly had already thrown off her coat and ran into Katy's old room to play with her dolls and stuffed animals. "Lilly, I told you, you don't just throw your coat on the floor!" she yelled after her, picking it up and walking over to the hall closet to hang it up.

The turkey had just about one more hour to go when the doorbell rang. It was her dad's brother, Hank, and his wife, Hildi. It had been a long time since Katy had seen them. The last time was when her father came up to spend Thanksgiving with her in Ithaca. Lilly was only two then. Uncle Hank and Aunt Hildi had made the drive from their home in Syracuse, which was only about an hour away, and they all celebrated by feasting alongside a host of other patrons at the local restaurant in the hotel where her father was staying.

As soon as they walked in the door, Aunt Hildi set the casserole dish she was carrying on the dining room table and walked over to Katy to give her a warm embrace. "It's been so long, my dear. Look at you, you are as beautiful as ever!" exclaimed Hildi, giving her a European kiss on each cheek. "Now, where is that precocious child of yours your father is always bragging about?"

"Lilly!" Katy gave a shout, and Lilly ran out of the bedroom with Merriweather under her arm. "Meet your Uncle Hank and Aunt Hildi. You probably don't remember them because the last time we were together, you were only two years old."

Lilly let out a meek, "Hi," while she held on to her mom's legs.

"Let me give you a hug, dear," said Aunt Hildi, extending her arms out to Lilly as she attempted to bend down in her oversized coat. Hildi was a tall, robust woman of Nordic descent and intimidating to any small child, so Lilly moved forward with caution as she prepared herself for a suffocating hug. With childlike cunningness, she was able to squirm out quickly by pulling her doll through her aunt's encroaching hook.

"Look, Aunt Hildi, this doll used to be my mom's when she was little."

"Oh, she's lovely, like you," said Hildi, smoothing the doll's hair, then moving her hand over to Lilly's head to caress her hair in the same way.

This provided the perfect opportunity for Lilly to maneuver herself out of her aunt's reach. "Sorry, I have to go. Merriweather is still in her pajamas. I have to go put her smiley face dress on so she'll look nice for Thanksgiving dinner." Then she took off running.

"Yes, Thanksgiving dinner. That reminds me," said Hildi. "Hank, why don't you go get the pumpkin pie out of the car while I go put this green bean casserole in the refrigerator?"

A short while later, the doorbell rang again, and Johanna Lankershim showed up with a platter of homemade pastries. "Mmm, those smell as delicious as they look," said Mr. Barton, smiling deliriously. Katy couldn't help but notice a gleam in her dad's eyes as he bent over to inhale their sweet, fresh aroma.

Just as everyone was about to sit down for their Thanksgiving feast, Mr. Barton showed up at the table with his wife's old 35 mm camera in his hands. "We've got to 'capture this moment,'" he announced. Upon hearing those words, Katy immediately became teary eyed.

Lilly grinned from ear to ear. "Capture the moment," she repeated, "like what Grandma says." Katy gave Lilly a curious look, wondering where she had heard that before, as she wiped the beads from her eyes.

"I want to get a picture of everyone sitting at the table with this beautiful turkey and all the delicious fixins around it," declared Mr. Barton. "Now smile," he said, fumbling with the camera. Katy could see the frustration building on her father's forehead as he attempted to "capture the moment." It was apparent that he still hadn't figured out how it worked. "These fancy cameras are way too complicated," he grumbled, trying to get it to focus.

Katy decided it was time for her to jump in, so she got up from her seat and walked over to the head of the table next to where her dad was standing. "Here, let me help you, Dad. I took a photography class as part of my journalism curriculum. I'll show you how it works."

"You know what, Kate, why don't *you* take the pictures? You're better at it, and that way, we know they'll turn out right."

Katy took multiple pictures of the turkey and "the fixins," and everyone at the table.

"Come here, Johanna," called Mr. Barton. "Get in the picture with me." Katy pressed the CLICK button as they tilted their heads closely together, flashing big moon-pie smiles.

Finally, the meal began with everyone holding hands as Mr. Barton said grace. Afterwards, he held up a glass of wine and made a toast. "To family and friends, without which, we are none."

The conversation flowed merrily until Mrs. Lankershim brought up the newspaper article in the *Morganville Herald*. "That was a truly interesting article you wrote about the Brewer mansion, Katy. It certainly put many of the rumors to rest. After Mrs. Brewer died (making the sign of the cross), God rest her soul, Mr. Brewer shipped his daughter, Evelyn, off to boarding school in England. She would come home and spend summers at the mansion, only to be raised by the nanny and the housekeeper.

You know, I actually met Evelyn very briefly when she was a young lady before that horrible fire occurred. She was as pretty as you, Katy. I don't know how you did it—that is, get her to open up to you. Most people haven't seen her in years, let alone have a face-to-face conversation with her."

Then Mr. Barton chimed in. "I never met Evelyn, but I did have the opportunity to meet her father, Morgan Brewer, on one occasion, just before he fell ill."

"Did you meet him at the bank, Dad?" Katy asked, eager for more details.

"No, it was at a fundraiser your mother and I were involved with. As much as he did for the town of Morganville, he never did business with the Morganville Bank, even though he founded it. I heard that some of his holdings were with the Bank of Pittsburgh but that the majority of his investments were locked in foreign reserves."

"So, who's ready for dessert?" interrupted Mrs. Lankershim, scooting herself up from her seat.

At the end of the evening, Uncle Hank and Aunt Hildi had said their goodbyes and Katy's dad was helping Johanna on with her coat. Lilly had fallen asleep on Katy's old bed, and Katy was in the kitchen washing dishes. She was a little surprised when she overheard Mrs. Lankershim speaking to her father.

"See you on Tuesday for Bridge Club. Oh, and don't forget, Friday is lasagna night at the Community Center, and it's our turn to bring the wine." When she left, Mr. Barton entered the room and asked Katy if he could help by drying the dishes. "Sure," replied Katy, followed by a minute of silence. "So, you and Mrs. Lankershim appear to have gotten pretty *close*."

"Well, Katy, you know it's been quite a few years since your mother passed, and when you were gone, it got pretty lonely around here. After Johanna's husband Blake died, we were like two lost ships in the night looking for an empty dock. I don't think your mother would mind, Kate. She and Johanna were best friends."

"It's okay, Dad. I'm just surprised you never said anything before."

"I just didn't know how you'd take it, Katy Bear."

Then it struck her. She was just like her father—keeping secrets and waiting for the perfect opportunity to reveal them. "I've got something to tell you too, Dad. Mike and I are engaged. I was just waiting for the right time to tell you."

"I guess this turned out to be the right time for both of us," said Mr. Barton, turning to give his daughter a hug. "I'm so happy for you, Kate."

By the time she had cleaned everything up, she was exhausted. Since Lilly was fast asleep in her bed, she decided to grab a blanket and pillow and crash on the couch. The next morning she packed up the car, and as she and Lilly were getting ready to leave, her father asked if she could take the film from her mom's camera in to be developed.

"I hope I can find a place that still develops film, Dad. Everything is starting to go digital now."

"I hope so too. Just make sure you have them make duplicates of all the pictures. Say, Katy, why don't you take the camera too? You know how to use it better than I do. Besides, your mother would have wanted you to have it."

Chapter Forty-Two

Dr. Fleming held the door for Katy as she walked into his office. "It's been a while, Kate, have a seat."

"I tried to get in to see you earlier, but Marjorie said you were booked."

The doctor walked over to his desk and sat down. "So, how've you been?" he asked, peering up from his bifocals.

"Pretty good."

"Are you still having recurring nightmares?"

"Yes, but not quite as often as before."

"How often would you say they happen?"

"About two or three times a week."

"And are they exactly the same as before?"

"Yes, I'm walking through a dark tunnel surrounded by smoke and flames, when off in the distance, I see a light. The closer I get to it, the larger and brighter it becomes. Then, just before I reach it, a dimmer light intersects with my path—and I wake up. Why does it end this way? When will it stop?"

Dr. Fleming put his pen down and looked directly at his patient. "I don't know, Kate. Perhaps once you have accepted your fate."

"What do you mean, once I've accepted my fate? I've given birth to Mark's child, and I've moved on with my life—what more is there to accept?"

Dr. Fleming didn't respond.

Katy continued. "There's something else I need to speak to you about. I recently met with Miss Brewer—"

"Yes, I read your article. It was very interesting. There was a lot I didn't know about the Brewer's family history."

"Yeah, well, Miss Brewer is a very interesting person, to say the least. Did you know she studied psychology in England?"

"I did not know that."

"She met a woman named Ruby Flaherty while she was there and convinced her to come to the States. I guess she came out after Miss Brewer's father died, and she's been living at the mansion with her as her housekeeper ever since."

"That's a long time."

"Yeah. But I get the feeling Mrs. Flaherty is more than just her housekeeper."

"Well, after that much time together, I imagine the two of them must have become very close."

Katy continued her rambling. "When I ran into Mrs. Flaherty at the Morganville Library, she had checked out a bunch of books on reincarnation and the spirit world. She told me that she sometimes reads to Miss Brewer because she's good at 'facilitating the melodramatics.' What's that supposed to mean?"

"It could mean a lot of things," said the doctor.

"Well, it seems Miss Brewer is obsessed with reincarnation. She spent a lot of time in India and Tibet, studying religions like Buddhism, Hinduism, Jainism, and even something called 'Animism.'"

The doctor's curiosity seemed to pique. "Really?"

"She asked me if I had ever read *The Tibetan Book of the Dead*. She told me that when you die, you are faced with a choice — to follow the bright light or a dimmer light. Do you have any idea what she could be talking about?"

"I *have* read *The Tibetan Book of the Dead,* and yes, I do know what she is talking about."

"Then please, enlighten me because all that talk is starting to freak me out."

Dr. Fleming got up from his desk and began pacing the room while he spoke. "I'll try and lay this out as plainly as possible. The *Tibetan Book of the Dead* reveals the teachings of attaining birth on a higher plane, the ultimate goal being Nirvana. At the moment of death, one experiences the ultimate *ego* death or the illusion of self. All of one's conscious self, which in reality is a manifestation of the subconscious self, ceases to be, and one is alone with the subconscious self — the clear light. Most people, not having prepared themselves for this moment of death, lose consciousness at this point and thereby fail to recognize the clear light. Those who have prepared, and recognize the clear light as themselves, become the clear light and are liberated from the cycle of birth and rebirth, or Nirvana. Those who fail to recognize the primary clear light are relegated to at least one more lifetime."

Dr. Fleming paused to look at Katy. "Are you following so far?"

Katy had a blank look on her face. "I think so."

Dr. Fleming continued. "From the moment one fails to recognize the light, the subconscious begins to manifest itself again in duality and ego. Once the subconscious begins manifesting itself again, one is separated from the subconscious and becomes the manifestation. From this point on, one's purpose is to attain rebirth in the state that will be most conducive to one's liberation for the next time around. The intermediate state into which the ego enters an earthly body after leaving the astral body is what theosophists call Devachan. The soul is in a type of limbo. Devachan is the idealized continuation of the terrestrial life just left behind, a period of retributive adjustment and a reward for unmerited suffering experienced. Any person who has experienced instances of unselfish love in his or her life will enjoy some time in Devachan."

"So, how long does Devachan last?" asked Katy.

"It depends. The depth and duration of it will be different according to the spirituality of the person. However, Devachan is not necessarily a 'spiritual' state. It still belongs to the sphere of the 'personal ego.' It is a state of intense selfishness, during which an ego reaps the reward of his unselfishness on earth. He or she is completely engrossed in the bliss of all his personal earthly affections, preferences, and thoughts and gathers in the fruit of his meritorious actions. It can last for what we know to be lifetimes, or it can be immediate, but once the subconscious self begins to re-manifest itself into the conscious self, then rebirth is imminent."

Katy sat there quietly, trying to absorb what the doctor just said and remembering what Evelyn had told her. "Then, why would Miss Brewer choose the dimmer light?"

"Because she knew if she did, her rebirth would be imminent."

"But why would she be telling *me* this?"

"It's obvious that she trusts you. Perhaps she feels a spiritual connection to you."

"I don't know, Doctor. I feel like she's trying to tell me something else."

Just then, Dr. Fleming's phone began to beep. "If you'll excuse me, I have to get this. "Mm...hmm... Mm...hmm," he murmured, then hung up the receiver. "I'm sorry, but apparently, I have a patient with an emergency. We're going to have to continue this discussion at our next session."

Once again, Katy left Dr. Fleming's office feeling empty from the lack of resolve. Since the appointment was cut short, she had plenty of time to stop at the drugstore and pick up the film she had brought in for developing before picking up Lilly. She was anxious to see how the Thanksgiving pictures turned out, and maybe looking at them would brighten her mood.

After paying the clerk, she jumped into the car and immediately tore into the envelope. As she thumbed through the photos, one by one, a reminiscent glow shined upon her face, and for a brief moment, she forgot all about Miss Brewer and all that reincarnation mumbo jumbo Dr. Fleming had filled her with. There was her turkey, which she had beautifully plated, as the centerpiece of the dining room table. She felt pretty proud of herself—it had turned out quite well for an amateur. There was Uncle Hank, holding up his wineglass for a toast, already looking a tad bit toasted himself from his pre-dinner Manhattan. There was Aunt Hildi, with a whole turkey leg clenched in her fist and a mouth full of teeth showing, ready to gnaw off a sizeable chunk. There was Lilly, grinning from ear to ear, with an equal combination of pumpkin pie and whipped cream smeared all over the lower part of her face. And there was her dad and Johanna Lankershim, revealing themselves as the true lovebirds they were.

As Katy turned up the last photo in the pile, her lips parted, and her eyes expanded to the size of silver dollars. There, in her hand, was a picture she knew full well she hadn't taken herself. It was a snapshot of Lilly sitting up in Katy's old bed holding her stuffed cat, Fluffy. In the photo, Lilly's close-mouthed, mile-high turned-up smile looked as though she was trying to keep from laughing. And up in the right-hand corner, just above her head, was a strange spot of bright light, slightly diffused, yet shimmering—like an orb. Katy shoved the picture back into the envelope as quickly as she could, while chills ran up and down her spine.

Chapter Forty-Three

The days had become significantly colder since Thanksgiving. Katy was admiring the frost-mantled trees from her passenger window as Mike's truck rambled down the broad gravel road. "They look so reverent—I mean, the trees," she said. "Like they're preparing for their spiritual retreat."

"Well, in a way, they are," said Mike.

"It's up here, on your right."

Mike turned just past a white picket fence and followed a long circular drive, which ultimately led him to an impressively large, white colonial with black shutters. "What a great house," he said, parking directly in front of the entrance. "So this is where you grew up?"

"Yup, this is it. In some ways, it feels like I never left." They stepped out into the icy air and began following the walkway leading to the front door. "You look nervous," said Katy, scratching Mike's neck.

"How can I *not* be nervous? I'm about to ask your father's permission for his daughter's hand in marriage. Does he have any clue?"

"Actually, he does. I told him about our engagement on Thanksgiving. He's looking forward to meeting you."

"You never told me that," he said, surprised, then suddenly turning back around. "I forgot the wine."

Mr. Barton, who'd been eagerly awaiting their arrival, opened the door before they even had the chance to ring the doorbell. "Come on in, you two."

"Dad, this is Mike. Mike, this is my father." The two of them exchanged handshakes.

"So this is the young man my daughter's been raving about. Looks like you finally got a weekend off," said Katy's dad sarcastically. "So, where's my little granddaughter?"

"She's at a friend's house," said Katy. "We dropped her off on the way here."

Mike handed Mr. Barton the bottle of wine. "I hope you like Sauvignon Blanc."

"We thought it would be a nice light wine for the middle of the afternoon," added Katy.

Mr. Barton led them into the front room. "Let me take your coats."

"It's okay, Dad, I'll hang them up," said Katy.

"Then why don't you have a seat on the couch, and I'll go and uncork the wine?"

Mike sunk down into the overstuffed Victorian-style sofa. Katy noticed his jitters hadn't subsided. "Relax, Mike. I'll be right back," she said as she headed into the kitchen to join her dad. "Hey Dad, do you have any cheese and crackers or something I can throw together so we're not just drinking on an empty stomach?"

"Sure, honey. I've got gouda and white cheddar in the fridge, and there are some crackers in the pantry. Make yourself at home — after all, this *is still* your home."

"I know, Dad," she said, leaning over to give him a kiss on the cheek. Mr. Barton popped the cork, and Katy grabbed three tall-stemmed glasses and followed him back into the living room. She set the wine goblets down on the beveled, glass-top coffee table, and Mr. Barton poured the wine. Then he held up his glass.

"Here's to finally meeting you, Mike."

Katy took a swig of her wine and promptly excused herself. "I'm going to go into the kitchen to put together a few hors d'oeuvres." As she was about to leave the room, she tilted her head at Mike and gave him the "go-ahead" with her eyes.

While in the kitchen, Katy prolonged the task of cutting and arranging the cheese and crackers for as long as possible while doing her best to listen in on their conversation. Mike's hardy voice resonated clear as he outlined his personal history for her father, which included where he lived, where he grew up, how he liked being a fireman and, last but not least, what his plans were for the future. Katy let out a chuckle. *Dad is really grilling him.*

As the chatter subsided, Katy felt it was safe to walk back into the room with her tray of snacks. It appeared that all went well because they were standing up facing each other, and her dad was patting Mike on the back.

Mr. Barton turned to his daughter. "Well, Katy, I believe congratulations are in order." He raised his glass once more. "You both have my blessing." Katy hugged her dad, and a more laid-back conversation ensued.

As they were getting ready to leave, Mike excused himself to go to the restroom. He didn't really need to use the restroom. He stood in front of the mirror for a few minutes, examining himself closely, and released a deep sigh of relief. *It's over. I did it! Why was I so nervous? It's not like I've never done this before.*

Katy carried the empty glasses and tray into the kitchen, and Mr. Barton followed her with the empty bottle of wine. "I don't know why it took you so long to bring him around, Katy. Mike seems like a wonderful guy, and I think he'll make a good husband and father to you and Lilly."

"It wasn't him. I knew you'd like him. It was me. I put it off because I wasn't ready emotionally. After Mark died, I was afraid to fall in love again."

"You mustn't live in fear, Katy. Not only did your mother believe you should 'capture the moment' with a picture, but she also believed that 'you should capture the moment with your heart.'"

Katy gave her father a big hug and kiss. "Thanks, Dad. Which reminds me, I have your duplicate photos from Thanksgiving, but I left them in my purse in the truck. I'll be right back." She ran out to get them, but there was one picture she had purposely taken out—the picture of Lilly in her bed. That one was safely tucked away in her nightstand at home.

While they were looking over the pictures and reminiscing about the wonderful time that was had by everyone, Katy thought she'd bring something up in a roundabout way. "Dad, are you *sure* you never used Mom's camera before this Thanksgiving?"

"Oh no, Katy Bear. After your mother died, I couldn't get myself to use it. It was *her* special camera. That's why I put it up on the closet shelf in your old room, so I wouldn't be reminded of...well, you know. This Thanksgiving was the first time I felt it would be okay to take it out — in her honor — because it was the first time we were celebrating Thanksgiving all together in this house."

Chapter Forty-Four

It looked like a scene from a Thomas Kinkade painting. The cultural district in downtown Pittsburgh was aglow with multi-colored lights while a scattering of flurries danced through the night air. Unfortunately, this didn't do much to put Katy in a festive mood for the office Christmas party. Mike was unable to accompany her because he had to work, but it was just as well since she regarded these parties as nothing more than a work obligation anyway.

PTTV had been holding their annual Christmas party at the old Beaumont Hotel for the past five years. It was built in the early 19th century, but its architectural integrity had been well preserved, still boasting its original Edwardian brick façade Katy pulled her car up to the front curb and turned off the engine. A valet helped her out of her vehicle, and she handed him her keys, while a doorman, dressed in mid-century coat and tails and a top hat, was at the ready, holding the door open for her.

Katy walked in with her head held high, ready to put her best foot forward, although she hated the politics of office parties. This was where people were expected to maintain a professional demeanor while they networked and mingled under the influence of one-too-many cocktails. There would be plenty of important people here this evening from surrounding news stations. This included their sister station, WJPTV, with whom they were rumored to be merging. Some people from local government offices were also expected to be in attendance.

She made her way over to the coat check and removed her coat when she suddenly realized that her brand-new, form-fitting dress had ridden up to the top of her thighs. In a flush of embarrassment, she glanced back and forth to see if anyone in the vicinity had noticed, then quickly straightened it out as inconspicuously as possible. As she was ambling her way through the overflowing grand lobby, she stopped to admire the beautifully sculptured mahogany bar with its giant backdrop of chamfered mirrors framed in mosaic tiles.

In that moment, a waiter in white gloves came by with a tray of tall stemmed glasses. "Would you care for a glass of champagne, miss?"

"Why yes, thank you," she replied, glad that he came by as soon as he did with a drink to calm her nerves. While she was standing there sipping her champagne, she noticed Mr. Bruckman waving her down from the center of the crowded room. She maneuvered her way through the assemblage of bodies, holding her clutch purse against the front of her dress with one hand to try and keep it from riding up and balancing her drink with the other hand, trying not to spill it.

To Katy's surprise, Bruckman had cleaned up pretty well. There was no sign of bristly stubble on his face, and he was wearing what looked like a brand new charcoal-grey suit and a festive red tie. Of course, in his left hand was his drink of choice — gin. You could tell it wasn't his first one of the evening either because his bushy eyebrows were doing little to overshadow his reddened nose.

"Kate, I'd like you to meet Jim Elders, our mayor."

"Pleased to meet you," said Katy, shaking his hand. This was the first time she had actually met him. He looked a lot older in person than he did on TV.

"The pleasure is all mine," replied the mayor, tilting his head as if he were about to kiss her hand. She couldn't help but feel uncomfortable with that smitten-boy look on his face and his eyes grazing along her modestly-scooped neckline. "Mr. Bruckman tells me you are the instigator for halting the freeway project and the inspiration for the preservation of the Brewer mansion. I think it's very admirable of you to have initiated the plan. You should be very proud of yourself."

"Why, thank you," replied Katy. "Of course, I couldn't

have done it without the help of Mr. Bruckman and the whole PTTV family. Not to mention *you*, Mr. Mayor, and the rest of our caring Morganville community."

Mayor Elders smiled appreciatively at her modesty. "Please, call me Jim." Then he held up his glass of what looked and smelled like a scotch on the rocks, "Here's to you, Miss Barton."

"Please, call me Katy."

"Okay, Katy," said the mayor, who stopped to take a big glug from his glass and continued talking. "You know, my father was a friend of Morgan Brewer. In fact, Mr. Brewer had plans to run for mayor of Morganville himself until he took ill with that black lung disease. All those years working in the coal mines when he was a young man finally got the best of him."

At that point, Mr. Bruckman butted in, grabbing the mayor's arm. "Excuse me, Kate. Jim, I want you to come and meet...," and moved him away in another direction.

Katy was left standing there with a half-empty glass in her hand when another waiter came by with a tray of hors d'oeuvres. It suddenly hit her how hungry she was. She hadn't eaten anything all day except for a doughnut she had picked up on the way to work that morning. She snatched up two hors d'oeuvres from his tray, even though she wasn't sure what they were, and stuffed them into her napkin. She popped one in her mouth, barely finishing it before shoving the next one in.

She was standing there looking like a hamster with hoarded cheeks when she spotted Martha, the evening news anchor, coming toward her. She had to hand it to Martha, she always looked camera ready, even for a woman in her last month of pregnancy. Her artificially colored red hair only spotlighted her flawless skin, which was perfectly accentuated with makeup that looked like it had just been professionally applied.

Martha stopped directly in front of her. "Are you enjoying that?" she asked in a cheeky tone. Maybe she was trying to be funny, but Katy wasn't laughing.

"Yes, as a matter of fact, I am," she gulped, attempting to swallow more than she had chewed. "I haven't eaten anything since breakfast. You look like you're about ready to pop."

"I certainly am. I just hope it doesn't happen here," Martha laughed, rubbing her belly.

"Maybe you'll have a New Year's baby! If you do, Dan and I will be in your hospital room to get the first shots."

"Yeah, well, you'd better give me a heads-up so I can get my makeup done and be anchor ready," Martha said jokingly, although Katy knew she wasn't kidding.

"So when is your last day—I mean, before you go on maternity leave?"

"I'll be gone all of January and February and back to work on March 1st. I asked for an extended maternity leave because this is my third kid, and I don't know how Nick, my husband, is going to be able to handle the whole brood while I'm at work. I mean, it's been great that he's been able to do it so far, but I think he's getting a little tired of being 'Mr. Mom.'"

"So he's looking for a job—um, outside the house?" Katy asked, trying to phrase her question with political correctness.

"Yeah, he's got a few prospects, but they're out of state, so I don't know how that's going to pan out." Martha moved in closer. "So Katy, I understand Bruckman's been grooming you to fill in for me while I'm on maternity leave."

Katy was hesitant to answer, unsure as to Martha's feelings about it. "Um, I don't know, maybe."

"Of course, you'll be co-anchoring with Jack."

"Of course."

Katy took a final gulp of her champagne while Martha continued. "You know, Vicky started at the station a year before you, at the same level as you. Jack had referred her to Mr. Bruckman for the position. I think Jack and Vicky were old friends from college." Martha cleared her throat and drew her face closer to Katy's ear, lowering her voice to a whisper. "And if rumors are true, they still are—*very* good friends."

Katy raised her eyebrows as if she were surprised by the news, even though she wasn't. In addition to witnessing first-hand the way Jack and Vicky acted together around the office, she had heard the rumors too.

"In any case," continued Martha, "Bruckman's not blind. So given the potential conflict of interest, he chose you to sub in my place."

Katy didn't respond to that last comment. Instead, she looked at her empty glass and scanned the room. "Where is that waiter? I need another drink." That's when she spotted Jack and Vicky squeezed face-to-face in the middle of the crowded hall. At that very moment, Jack happened to glance up and noticed Katy looking at him. With a painted-on smile, he lifted his hand and gave her a short wave. Then Vicky looked up in her direction, but there was no smile, just a stone cold look.

Katy immediately turned her face back toward Martha and continued the conversation. "So what do you think about the takeover, or merger, or whatever is going to happen to the station?"

"I guess we'll have to wait and see," said Martha.

Just then, Katy spotted a waiter carrying a drink tray and flagged him down. She replaced her empty champagne flute with a glass of Chardonnay and took a nice long swallow.

Martha patted her on the arm and motioned for her to look over to her right. "See that tall, good-looking guy over there talking to Norm Baker from our parent company?"

Katy twisted her neck around slowly in an effort to be discreet. "Which one?"

"The one in the blue pin-striped suit with the gold silk handkerchief in his breast pocket." Martha sounded like she was drooling.

"Oh yeah, I see him."

"That's Jason Miller. He's the news director for WJPTV in Johnstown. I wouldn't mind merging with him if you know what I mean."

"Martha!" Katy exclaimed, giving her a shocked look, and shared a good, hearty laugh, although the only man on her mind was Mike.

By ten o'clock, Katy had had her fill of small talk for the evening and decided to get her coat and leave. Besides, she had promised Darla she'd be home no later than eleven. *Thank God, it's Friday*, she thought. She was looking forward to spending the whole weekend with Mike, as this would be the last she'd see of him until after Christmas.

Chapter Forty-Five

"Mommy, Mommy, the doorbell's ringing, Mike's here!" yelled Lilly, running into her mother's bedroom.

Katy looked at her clock, then slipped on her robe and shuffled over to the front door with Lilly behind her, bouncing with enthusiasm.

"I know I'm early," said Mike, "but I couldn't wait to get the weekend started."

"I just need a cup of coffee to get me going," she said, dragging her feet toward the kitchen. She did not want to spoil the mood by telling him she had barely gotten any sleep because of another nightmare.

"Why don't you go get dressed, and I'll make the coffee?" said Mike.

"I'll try to hurry," she said, but by the time she and Lilly were ready to go, it was almost ten o'clock.

"So, who's ready to go out into the woods and cut down a Christmas tree?!" he shouted, rubbing his hands together exuberantly.

"Yay, meeeee!" yelled Lilly, with unrestrained excitement.

"It's pretty cold out there, so make sure you bundle up."

Lilly ran into her room and then ran back out with her red helmet over her wool hat.

"I don't think you'll be needing your fire helmet," laughed Mike.

"But what if a tree falls on me?"

"Don't worry, I've cut trees down before. I'll make sure it doesn't fall anywhere near you."

"Maybe I'll bring it, just in case."

It had been snowing off and on all week, but today was exceptionally crisp and clear. The three of them were walking out the door when Mike grabbed the helmet from Lilly's head and placed it on the snowman she and her mom had built two days prior. "There, now he's better equipped to watch over your house while we're gone." As they drove off, Lilly watched it fade away with a simper of appeasement on her face.

Mike took them to a Christmas tree farm, where they trudged around in circles through ankle-deep snow until they found the perfect tree. The girls stood off to the side and watched as Mike raised his axe with his muscular arms. With just a few manly swipes, the magnificent fir fell to the ground in a deliberate, accepting motion, as if it knew its time had come. Together they dragged the tree back to the truck, and Katy and Lilly helped Mike load it onto the bed of his pick-up.

Once home, Mike positioned the tree in front of the big picture window in the living room and strung up the lights while Katy made dinner. By the end of the meal, they were pretty exhausted, except for Lilly, who was still overflowing with energy and eager to finish decorating the tree.

"How 'bout we decorate the tree tomorrow?" said Katy. "We'll make popcorn to string around the tree, and then you can help me bake Christmas cookies that we can hang as ornaments."

Lilly's eyes lit up. "Can we make gingerbread men?"

"Yes. And stars, and bells, and little Christmas trees, and—"

Lilly was screeching with delight and began running circles around the couch where her mom and Mike were sitting. When she finally settled down, Katy got her ready for bed and was tucking her in when Mike came in to kiss her goodnight.

"Can you read me a bedtime story, Mike?"

"Sure, what would you like me to read?"

Lilly yanked off her blanket and ran over to her bookcase, where she pulled out a thin paperback booklet. "I want you to read this one."

"Of course, *The Night Before Christmas*."

As Mike sat down on the edge of her bed and began to

CHAPTER THIRTEEN 231

read, Katy couldn't help but think to herself, *How did I get so lucky?*

Sunday flew by with a flurry of activities that included baking cookies and decorating the tree, and before Katy knew it, the weekend was slowly coming to an end. It was a perfect evening. The night was completely still, and the sky was radiant with stars. Lilly had fallen asleep the minute her head hit the pillow, and Katy and Mike had just cozied up on the couch, warming themselves with the incandescent glow of the artificial fireplace and a bottle of Merlot.

They were almost finished with their second glass of wine when Mike stood up and walked over to the coat closet. She was afraid he might be getting ready to leave. She did not want the evening to end. Instead, he unzipped the inner pocket of his jacket and pulled something out. He walked back over to the couch, holding a small black velvet box in his hand, and then he got down on one knee.

"Since I won't be with you on Christmas Day, I wanted to give this to you now."

He opened up the box, and Katy cupped her hands over her gaping mouth. "Oh my God, Mike! It's the ring from Maude's antique shop—the pink Morganite!"

"Yeah," he blushed. "I'm sorry you had to wait so long for it. When I went back there looking for it, I was afraid it might have been sold. Maude said it must have been waiting for the right person to come along." He took Katy's finger and placed the ring on it. "The right person did come along—you."

Chapter Forty-Six

Monday morning came, and Katy floated into work, flashing her engagement ring around proudly. She barely had time to settle into her chair before Jack casually strolled by, making a couple of backward steps toward Katy's desk. "Soooo, how was your weekend?"

"A-w-e-s-o-m-e," responded Katy.

"Great party Friday, aye?"

"It was all right, I guess. I'm not much for office parties."

"Well, you seemed to be pretty good at making friends."

Katy gave him an underhanded look. "What do you mean?"

"I think you know what I mean. You had the mayor drooling, and I don't know what kind of spell you have on Bruckman, but you know Vicky was being groomed for that anchor job from day one. You might consider stepping aside to avoid exposing yourself to an embarrassing situation."

"What exactly are you getting at, Jack?"

"You know very well what I'm getting at. I didn't land my anchor job on my looks alone. I started out as a street reporter, like you. And just like you, I know how to get access to the inside story."

Katy held her tongue as she waited for him to get to the point.

"I know you've been seeing a shrink for years. Now, how would that look in the public eye if that were to come out, that their new anchor is a psycho?"

That did it. She had reached her tipping point. "A psycho! Are you threatening me? Because if you are, two can play at this game, Jack. We all know you're married, even though you never wear a wedding ring. And the fact that you have been having an interoffice affair with Vicky is no surprise to anyone, least of all Mr. Bruckman. So if you think you can blackmail me, think again because it *will* backfire, *trust me*."

Jack was rendered pale and speechless. He turned to leave but spun back around to sputter out one final thing. "Oh, by the way, nice ring."

Katy was so upset from her discourse with Jack that she decided to leave work early. Christmas was just a few days away, and she hadn't seen Evelyn for a while, so she thought it would be a nice gesture to bring her a plate of Christmas cookies she and Lilly had baked over the weekend. She stopped home and arranged a colorful variety of the frosted ornaments on a plate. She covered the plate with Saran wrap, secured it with red and green ribbon, and topped it off with a festive bow. Then she threw on her coat and hurried out the door.

The freeways had been cleared, but the back roads were still blanketed with a good two inches of powder. As she neared the driveway leading to the mansion, she noticed fresh car tracks in the snow. She also noticed fresh footprints while trudging up the unshoveled steps to the front door. Maybe Ruby was out running errands. She decided to try knocking anyway. There was a slim chance that Evelyn might answer the door.

After shivering on the front porch for a good fifteen minutes, Katy tried knocking one more time. Her hands were numb from the icy brass knockers against her gloveless skin, and she was just about to turn around and head to the car when Ruby finally came to the door.

"Why hello, Miss Katy, what brings ya here?"

Katy quickly spun back around. "Hello, Ruby. I was hoping to see Evelyn. I just wanted to bring her a little something," she said, lifting the plate up for her to see.

"I'm sorry, but Miss Brewer had a car pick her up early this mornin'."

Katy's mouth dropped open. "Oh?" she said, dumbfounded. She was under the impression that Evelyn never left the house. "Where did she go?"

"I can't tell ya exactly, but I can tell ya that every year she goes on sabbatical to get away from the trials of winter and to renew her spirit. When she returns, she's like a new person."

This was news to Katy's ears. Evelyn had never made any mention of this to her before. "When will she be back?"

"Not till the snow's a melted and the bulbs be comin' inta' bloom."

Katy was silent for a moment, wanting to know more but not wanting to pry where she clearly wasn't privy. "I'm sorry I missed her. So, are you going to be here all alone, Ruby?"

"Me? Goodness, no! I have ta make sure everything is locked up and secure, then I'll be headin' up to Reddin' tomorrow to stay with me daughter and her family."

"Well, um, I'd better get going. Uh, here, why don't you take this?" Katy extended the decorative platter over to Ruby. "They're just cookies—my daughter and I made them."

"Why, thank ya, dear, they look lovely! I'll take them to Reddin' to share them with me relations."

"Goodbye then," Katy said hesitantly, not sure if she should give Ruby a hug.

"Well, ya 'ave a Merry Christmas then, and thank ya for the cookies," said Ruby, giving a hearty wave before shutting the door in Katy's face.

"You too. Um...see you in the spring—I guess," Katy said to no one.

Chapter Forty-Seven

The first day of the new year was going to be spent at the news station. Katy was a little nervous but eager to take on her temporary role as early evening anchor. She hadn't even reached her desk when her boss stopped her in the hallway.

"'Morning, Kate."

"Good morning, Mr. Bruckman. How was—?"

Before she could finish her sentence, he interrupted her and handed her a small stack of papers. "I want you to familiarize yourself with the news stories you'll be reading, and let me know if you have any questions. We may have to adjust the script in case we get any late-breaking news."

Katy couldn't contain her inner laughter. *Late-breaking news — as if!*

She had sat down to review her draft when Jack walked by. "Hi Katy," he said in an unusually friendly manner as if nothing ever happened.

I wonder if Bruckman spoke to him.

She decided to play along. "Hi, Jack."

"How were your holidays?" he asked.

"Fine, how were yours?"

"Let's just say I've made a few New Year's resolutions."

Katy looked at his left hand. Imagine that! He was wearing his wedding ring.

"So, are you ready for your first 'prime time live'?"

"Ready or not, here I come," said Katy, trying to screen her anxiety.

"Just relax, and you'll be fine."

Jack and Katy sat down at the anchor desk and were

getting ready to go on air when Bruckman walked over to her. "Are you ready?"

"Yes sir, I'm ready," she answered in her most confident voice.

The cameras were pointed and ready to go. Katy adjusted her suit jacket.

"Five, four, three, two, one...and we're live."

"Hi, I'm Jack Travor."

"And I'm Katy Barton, filling in for Martha Goodrich, who is on maternity leave."

"And welcome to PTTV early evening news at five," led Jack.

Katy started out a little shaky, taking advantage of each commercial break by swallowing large amounts of water and rolling her shoulders frontward and backward.

At the end of the broadcast, they signed off with, "Thank you for tuning in. This is Jack Travor...."

"And this is Katy Barton...."

Katy gave a big sigh of relief and looked over at Jack.

"You were great," he said. "You'll be a pro before you know it."

"Thanks," said Katy, gathering up her papers. She felt pretty proud of herself. *I did it – and with no major flubs!*

There was no way to avoid walking past Vicky's cubicle as Katy headed back to her desk, and she was hoping she wouldn't have to come face-to-face with "the woman scorned." She hadn't seen her all day, so hopefully, she was out on assignment. *That's strange*, she thought to herself, glancing over her dividing wall. Vicky's computer was off, and her desk looked barren. There were no papers in her in-box, and all her personal effects were gone, including her pictures and her purple potted orchid.

When Katy got back to her own workspace to gather up her things, Mr. Bruckman peered over the flimsy partition. "Good work today, by the way."

"Thanks, Mr. Bruckman. I know I was a little nervous, but I'm sure I'll be better tomorrow."

Bruckman smiled wittingly, then turned to walk away.

Katy pursed her lips for a moment. "By the way, I haven't seen Vicky today. Is she taking an extended holiday leave?"

Mr. Bruckman shifted his head in Katy's direction just for a second before moving on. "Nope, she gave me her notice a week ago."

Katy's lack of sleep did little to impede her determination to shine in Martha's chair. She still had to get up early to take Lilly to school, but since she didn't go on air until five, she was able to go back home and rest for a few hours before going in to work. Thankfully, Mike and her father shared the task of picking Lilly up. The weeks flew by, and before she knew it, Martha was back in the anchor's seat, and everything was back to the way it was before.

~*~

It had been a particularly frigid winter, but March's arrival melted the snow, and the tulip bulbs had forcefully begun to erupt their way through the thawing ground.

It was early on a Saturday afternoon, and Katy had just dropped Lilly off at Meghan's house for a play date. She was dying to stop by the mansion but didn't know if Evelyn had returned from her "sabbatical." Since Lilly didn't have to be picked up for a few hours, Katy thought this would be a good opportunity to go to the library. In the last few months, she hadn't made time because she was too preoccupied with her new co-anchoring gig. She had wanted to go ever since that last unsettling conversation with Evelyn and that last session with Dr. Fleming, where he had revealed pertinent teachings of *The Tibetan Book of the Dead*. Whether she believed in reincarnation or not, she wanted to do a little research of her own into the matter. Who knows, maybe she might come across some clue as to where Evelyn had gone.

When she arrived at the library, there was a young lady behind the desk. The senior librarian who usually ran the library wasn't there today. Katy asked the young girl if she had *The Tibetan Book of the Dead*, and was not surprised to hear that she had never heard of it. "Would you like me to see if I can get it from the main branch in Pittsburgh?" she asked. "No thank you," said Katy, "but maybe you can show me where I might find some books on reincarnation."

The girl looked puzzled. "Well, we do have some books on different religions, like Buddhism. They believe in reincarnation, right?"

"Yes, they do," Katy answered, with a mocking smile and a slight twinge of superiority in her tone.

"This way," said the girl, not returning the smile.

After spending a good deal of time searching through the shelves, Katy stumbled upon several books on the subject of reincarnation. There were two in particular, by author Alexandra David-Neel, that caught her eye: *Immortality and Reincarnation: Wisdom from the Forbidden Journey* and *Magic and Mystery in Tibet*. She also found two of the books Dr. Fleming had suggested she read: Dr. Ian Stevenson's *Children Who Remember Previous Lives*, and Tom Shroder's *Old Souls: The Scientific Search for Proof of Past Lives*. While perusing the books, she became so engrossed that before she knew it, it was time to pick Lilly up, so she walked over to the front desk and checked out all four of the books. *That should keep me busy for a while.*

Katy stepped into Sue's front room to find that all the couch and chair pillows had been removed and were stacked up against each other on the floor with blankets draped over them. Lilly heard her mom come in and peeked out from behind one of the blankets. "Can I stay longer, Mommy, please? We just built a fort."

"I can see that," answered Katy, giving Sue a sympathetic look.

"Let them play a while longer," insisted Sue.

"How can you not be tearing your hair out by now?" asked Katy.

"Oh, it doesn't bother me. I have a maid who comes in twice a week. She can deal with it."

Katy knew Sue was divorced and worked part-time at the art gallery, but couldn't imagine how that would be enough to afford her a maid two times a week.

"Come on in for a while. What's your hurry? Is there somewhere you have to be?"

"No," answered Katy, following her over to the kitchen table.

"Can I get you a Coke or a Sprite or something?"

"A Diet Coke would be great if you have it."

Sue walked over to the refrigerator, and Lilly ran up to her mom, waving a large pink envelope in the air. "Look, Mommy, it's an invitation to Meghan's birthday party—and it's gonna be a sleepover!"

"A sleepover birthday party, how fun!"

"It's not for two weeks," clarified Sue, pouring the soda into a glass and handing it to Katy.

"What day?"

"Friday, April 12th."

"That's a day before my birthday," said Katy.

"Actually, Meghan's birthday is on the 11th, but that's a Thursday, and since it's going to be a sleepover, I had to do it either on Friday or Saturday."

"Meghan said there's gonna be party games and prizes and pizza and cake!" interrupted Lilly.

"My mom might let us make another fort and sleep in it," said Meghan.

Katy looked over at Sue. "Are you sure you can handle a houseful of five and six-year-old girls overnight?"

"I think I can. If not, I'll be giving you a call," laughed Sue.

"On another note," began Katy, "I can't thank you enough for all you've done for me with respect to the Brewer mansion. The amount of signatures you were able to collect at the Halloween soiree was amazing."

"Well, we did have a great turnout."

"And the artist your gallery employed to do the billboard did a beautiful job! I hope I can meet your boss, Mr. Reeves, one day, so I can personally thank him for his generous donation."

"He's out of the country a lot, always searching for new talent, but I'm sure you'll get to meet him real soon."

CHAPTER FORTY-EIGHT

Katy went back to the Morganville Library to return her books, unduly weighted from the fantastical material she had ingested. As she was about to enter the building through the glass-paneled doorway, she observed a woman with an arm full of books on her way out. "Here, let me get that for you," she said, holding the door open. That's when she realized this wasn't just any woman, it was Mrs. Flaherty.

"You're back!" shrieked Katy.

"Why yes, yes I am," replied Mrs. Flaherty.

"Is Miss Brewer back, too?"

"Oh, she's been back for a week now. That's why I'm here — to replenish her infinite thirst for knowledge."

"Do you think she'd mind if I stopped by to see her?"

"I don't presume so, now that she's had time to settle back inta' her old routine."

Katy couldn't imagine what "routine" Evelyn could possibly be settling back into but chose to gleam over the statement. "Please let her know I'll be by to visit on Wednesday if that's okay." As curious as Katy was to find out where Evelyn had been, she didn't want to appear over-eager.

"Indeed I will," responded Mrs. Flaherty. "Indeed I will. Have a nice day now."

~*~

Katy took one last swig from her fourth cup of coffee before leaving the office on Wednesday. She arrived at the mansion filled with anticipation, only to be left standing in the foyer. "Miss Brewer will be right with ya," said Mrs. Flaherty, exiting the room. Katy took a quick look around while she was standing there. Everything looked the same—the blue and white vase on the intricately carved table, the family portraits on the wall—not that she expected otherwise. She turned her focus back on Evelyn's portrait and became transfixed by the eyes. The more she looked at it, the more it felt as though she were looking into a mirror. Suddenly, she was distracted by the faint sound of music. It seemed to be coming from the parlor. It was that tune again—the one she had heard when she envisioned a younger Evelyn humming in the garden and the same one she had heard Evelyn humming at her desk the first time she met her.

The music suddenly stopped, and Evelyn entered the room. "I thought you'd have come sooner."

"Well, uh, I was very busy. That song I just heard, it's so familiar."

"I'm sure you've heard it before. You just heard the original from 1933, sung by Tamara. Other artists have recorded it throughout the years, but Tamara's version is still my favorite."

Katy followed Evelyn into the parlor and glanced over at the antique phonograph to observe its needle raised above the small 78 RPM disc.

As usual, Evelyn made her way to her flowered chaise and sat down. "I understand you've been co-anchoring the news recently."

How did she know that? Katy wondered, walking over to sit in the armchair next to her. "Yes, well, only for two months while the regular anchor, Martha Goodrich, was on maternity leave. Now I'm back 'on the beat,' so to speak," Katy laughed, rather nervously. "So what about you, Evelyn. Where have *you* been all these months?" She waited for a response with bated breath.

"Since my father's death, I've sought reprieve from Pennsylvania's unforgiving winters by returning to the land of my religious awakening. There, I find solace and renewed spiritual nourishment through meditation and prayer—and it's warm," Evelyn added with a chuckle.

Katy thought about the books she'd just read by the author, Alexandra David-Neel, whose travels led her to China, India, and Tibet. Evelyn must have been referring to India or Tibet.

"Do you believe in prayer, Kate?"

"What?"

"Do you believe in the power of prayer?"

"Um, I used to. I mean, I was brought up Episcopalian, but I haven't been to church in a long time."

"And why is that?"

"Having experienced losses of my own, I guess I just became disillusioned with religion in general."

"You know, Kate, the benefit of prayer is in the asking."

Katy nodded half-heartedly.

"When you open yourself up to meditative prayer, you gain access to the living force that can direct the outcome of your desires. You have the power to *control* your destiny, but only with clear thought and perseverance. In the words of the Great Buddha: 'all that we are is a result of what we have thought.'"

Just then, Mrs. Flaherty brought out a pot of hot steaming tea and two teacups.

"So it appears you and Ruby keep running into each other at the Morganville Library," posed Evelyn, taking it upon herself to fill both cups.

"Thank you," said Katy, letting out a curt chortle. "Yes, we do."

"And what were you *researching* this time?"

"Well, ever since you told me about *The Tibetan Book of the Dead* and all that other stuff, I've wanted to do a little research into reincarnation myself. Unfortunately, they didn't have a copy of the *Book of the Dead*—"

Evelyn interrupted. "They wouldn't. Most of the books I need, Ruby has to have transferred from the main library in Pittsburgh."

Katy continued. "However, I did find two books by the author, Alexandra David-Neel. Maybe you've heard of them: *Magic and Mystery in Tibet* and *Immortality and Reincarnation: Wisdom from the Forbidden Journey?*"

"Madame Alexandra David-Neel. Why yes, of course, I've heard of her. She is believed to be the first Western woman ever to visit the holy city of Lhasa, the center of Tibetan Buddhism.

Madame David-Neel was also involved in a study group associated with the Theosophical Society of Madame Blavatsky."

"Who is that?"

"Helena Petrovna Blavatsky," Evelyn began, accentuating the name, "was a Russian spiritualist, occultist, and spirit medium. She was one of the most extraordinary and controversial figures of the 19th century. She cofounded the Theosophical Society, located in Adyar, South India."

"What exactly is a Theo-soph-ical Society?"

"They are a major advocate of occult philosophy." Evelyn took a drink from her teacup, then continued. "Her most important work was published in 1888. It was entitled, *The Secret Doctrine: the Synthesis of Science, Religion and Philosophy*. The tomes, which were in two volumes, were an overview of theosophical teachings and occult ideas claiming to reconcile ancient Eastern wisdom with modern science. They addressed such matters as the continuity of life and death, the purpose of existence, good and evil, consciousness and substance, sexuality, karma, evolution and human planetary transformation."

"I don't imagine I'd find that at the Morganville Library," Katy noted sarcastically.

"No, you will not. I own both tomes if you ever feel inclined to borrow them. But keep in mind, they are labyrinthinely complex, and one must be wholly open to the theories they promulgate in order to fully appreciate their conceptualizations."

"I think I'll pass," said Katy. "I got enough enlightenment from Madame David-Neel's book: *Magic and Mystery*. It's pretty 'out-there,' if you know what I mean. She talks about Tibetan folklore and their mystical theories and psychic training practices—"

Before Katy could finish, Evelyn broke in. "Like *siddhis*: the spiritual, paranormal, or otherwise magical capabilities obtained through rigorous spiritual practices, such as yoga and meditation."

"You mean, like meditative prayer?" asked Katy.

"Yes, and that powerful formation of thought can generate magical formations called *tulpas*."

"I remember reading that," said Katy, leaking out a giggle. "It's like a mental visualization to create a mind-made body."

"Precisely. Once the *tulpa* is endowed with enough vitality to be capable of playing the part of a real being, it tends to free itself from its maker's control."

Katy shook her head back and forth. "I'm sorry, but I find this all a tad bit preposterous. You don't really believe that stuff, do you?"

"I do more than believe it, my dear, I *live* it," replied Evelyn, quite calmly. "You have to keep yourself open to *all* possibilities."

Katy took another sip of tea and thought this would be a good time to change the subject. "So, how's your memoir coming?"

"Why, it's almost done. Would you like to read it after I've finished it?"

"Only if it's not too 'labyrinthinely complex,'" joked Katy.

"Don't worry, my dear, it will all become crystal clear."

Something about the way Evelyn said that gave Katy an uneasy feeling. She gulped down the last of her tea and looked up at the clock on the fireplace mantel across the room. "I really have to get going. I'll see myself out. Oh, and thank you for the tea."

Katy was almost to her car when she got the sudden urge to turn around. She noticed that the curtain in the bay window was partially drawn, and off to the side was Evelyn's pallid face with her eyes fixed upon her. A cold shiver ran up and down her spine. *I don't think I'll be coming back here for a while.*

CHAPTER FORTY-NINE

Lilly and the babysitter were on the couch playing the board game Guess Who? when Mike arrived to pick Katy up for their date. "I win!" shouted Lilly, jumping up and down with her hands in the air.

"Not again!" moaned Darla, pretending to be upset.

"I'm not sure what time we'll be back, and tomorrow is a school day, so please have Lilly in bed by eight thirty," instructed Katy, while Mike helped her on with her coat.

"So where are you guys going?" asked Darla.

Katy looked at Mike. "I don't know — where are we going, Mike?"

"We're going into the city to have dinner, but we haven't decided where."

"If there's a problem, Darla, you know my cell phone number is on the fridge next to my dad's."

As usual, Mike held the door open for Katy as she stepped into the car. "So, what are you in the mood for?"

"I don't know. I'm thinking I could really go for some pasta."

"Then I've got just the place. There's this nice little Italian restaurant called Aldo's. It's been around for ages. It looks like a hole in the wall, but the food is really good. I know the owners, Aldo and Francesca. She gets up every day at the crack of dawn and rolls out the pasta by hand. It's amazing. You'll love it."

"Do they have checkered table cloths?"

"Yes, and tiny vases with plastic daisies in them."

"Then I'm in!" laughed Katy.

The quaint little eatery was exactly as Mike had described

it. They walked in, and their senses were immediately inundated with an aromatic wave of garlic, onions, and fresh tomatoes, proffering a preview of what their taste buds had in store. As soon as they were seated, Mike ordered a bottle of Italian wine while Katy studied the menu. She was already salivating.

"Everything sounds so good, I can't decide."

"Well, I'm definitely getting the lasagna," said Mike, taking a sip from his water glass. Katy took a deep breath and then exhaled. "I saw Evelyn today."

Mike raised his eyebrows. "I thought you said she was on sabbatical."

"I ran into Ruby, her housekeeper, at the library again a few days ago, and she told me she was back. I was dying to know where she'd been, so I went to see her."

"So where was she?"

"She didn't say exactly, but I think it might have been India or Tibet. She said she goes there every year to meditate. She suggested I try it. Then she went on about some Russian occultist who wrote this secret doctrine."

"Sounds like she's trying to convert you."

Katy let out a nervous laugh. "I think she is."

In that moment, they were interrupted by the waitress, who brought over two thick wine glasses and a bottle of Chianti encased in dried palm leaves. She poured the wine into Mike's glass first for a pre-emptive taste. After a swirl and a quick sniff, he belted out, "*Magnifico!*" in his best Italian accent.

"So, are you two ready to order?" asked the waitress.

Mike motioned to Kate with his eyes for her to order first.

"I think I'll have the pasta...a...la...carbonara," she garbled out.

"And I'll have the lasagna — with extra sauce."

As the waitress left to fill their orders, Katy unfolded her red linen napkin and placed it on her lap. "I don't think I'll be going back to visit Miss Brewer anytime soon. She's starting to creep me out."

Mike studied her face as if to see if she meant it. "That's probably for the best. Let's just forget about her and enjoy the evening." He lifted his glass for a toast. "To an evening meant only for us."

To the tune of *O` Sole Mio*, followed by a playlist of piped-in sonatas, the two of them devoured their meal and polished off the whole bottle of wine. Mike patted his belly and looked over at his date, who was wiping the saucy residue from her lips with her napkin. "The night is young. I know this lively piano bar just a few blocks away. A nice brisk walk will do us good, and it'll help us burn off some of these calories."

"Sounds great!" said Katy. "I love to sing."

With remnants of winter still lingering in the nighttime air, Katy, who was always cold, had to squeeze her collar tightly to ward off the unsheltered current tapering through the narrow walkways.

Like Aldo's, the bar was located on a one-way street, sandwiched in between dark brick storefronts that had managed to dodge urban modernization. Much of the bar's frontage was taken up by a wood-framed window, stenciled with white fleur-de-lis and green shamrocks, that subtly camouflaged the interior. In the center of the window, printed prominently in orange, green, and white letters, was the name of the venue: McMurphy's Pub, established in 1888.

Mike and Katy stood outside for a while, peering through the unobstructed portions of the glass, trying to decide if they wanted to go in. The sound of raucous singing reverberated through the flimsy pane and detonated to a thunderous blast each time someone opened the door. Mike looked over at Kate, "It looks pretty crowded. Do you still want to go in? You did say you love to sing."

"Sure," she answered, never having been intimidated by a crowd.

As soon as they stepped foot in the pub, Katy felt an overwhelming sense of déjà vu, even though she couldn't recall ever having been there before. A dozen or so drunken patrons were seated in a half-circle around the piano with their shrill voices singing, of all things, that Kenny Rogers song, "Ruby, Don't Take Your Love to Town," their drunken cries blaring,

"For God's sake, turn around!"

Mike stretched his neck up, trying to locate a place to sit, while Katy stood frozen, as the pock-marked floorboards rumbled from the guttural thumping of feet, and she was overtaken by a another vision or a hallucination, or something else.

The room became enshrouded in a smoky haze, infused with the strong smell of tobacco, and she was suddenly transported to a different era. Women wearing calf-length skirts and Mary Jane shoes were sitting at the bar with their legs crossed, all laughing in merriment while sipping cocktails and puffing on thin dark cigarettes. A group of men wearing pleated, loose-fitting trousers held up by suspenders were circled around them, gripping their beers in a boisterous display of manhood.

Katy's gaze turned to the piano in the center of the room, where one woman dressed like a flapper shined luminously apart from all the others. Her arms and torso leaned over the side of the piano while her deep-set eyes stared longingly at the piano player as she sang. Her throaty voice droned over the resonating keys, fading out all the other noise in the room. "Smoke gets in your eyes...."

All of a sudden, the music, the noise, and the laughter grew louder and louder and throbbed in Katy's brain like a shooting cannon. She pressed her hands over her ears in an attempt to drown it out. The room began to spin, and all eyes turned on her as if she were spinning herself. She couldn't take it anymore. She was about to let out a scream when a strange look came over her face, and she moved both hands to her stomach and doubled over, gasping for air.

Mike was reaching for her arm to lead her to a table across the room when he realized something was terribly wrong. "Katy!" he yelled out, grabbing her and holding her upright. "What's the matter?"

"I have to get out of here—now!"

Kate kept silent all the way home. She couldn't get that song out of her head. Its melancholy melody continued to pound in her brain—"Smoke gets in your eyes...."

CHAPTER FIFTY

The brilliant swell of the rising sun did little to coax Katy out of bed, but it did provide her with an excuse to be wearing her sunglasses when she walked into work. Her eyes were still bloodshot from the smoke-filled bar the night before and exacerbated by the 2:38 a.m. wake-up call from the ever-burning embers in her subconscious mind.

She was staring blankly at her computer screen while it took its sweet old time to boot up when she heard a knock on her divider. Apparently, Mr. Bruckman had been standing there for several minutes watching her over the partition before deciding to snap her out of her coma.

"What's going on with you, Kate? You look like death warmed over. I thought you took care of your insomnia."

"I was out late last night."

"Well, maybe you shouldn't be out so late on a work night."

"Sorry, boss. I usually don't—"

"I need you here *mentally* as well as physically, ready to go if we happen to have a breaking news story. Which granted, doesn't happen very often in Morganville, but we've got one today."

"What is it?" asked Katy, straightening her posture.

"There was a theft at the Good Shepherd Episcopal Church, and I need you to go down there right away. I've already let Dan know, and he's getting his equipment ready now."

"That's it?" bemoaned Katy, with an obvious lack of enthusiasm.

"That's it," replied Mr. Bruckman, slightly agitated. "Now

get going!"

Katy rode along with Dan on the way to the church. As he pulled his van into the parking lot, her face took on an undertone of melancholy. She was humbled by the unpretentious house of worship standing before her. It really hadn't changed much since the last time she had been there. It had the same arched wooden doors and the same raised steeple. The only difference was that the white plaster siding had turned to an ashen shade of grey.

"I grew up going to this church every Sunday with my parents when I was a little girl."

"Oh really," replied Dan, barely feigning interest.

"I wonder if the same rector is still here."

"Well, you're about to find out."

Katy couldn't help but bow her head instinctively when she stepped through the eight-foot doors. A man of the ministry, wearing a white clerical collar over a black shirt with short sleeves, was kneeling in front of the alter. When he heard her come in, he made the sign of the cross and stood up. As he turned to walk toward her, she recognized him immediately. His steps padded so lightly along the scuffed aisle, it was as though he were walking on water. He looked a lot older than she remembered. His black hair had gone completely grey, exposing a bald circle on top.

"Reverend Sykes, hello! I don't know if you remember me, but I'm Katy Barton. I'm going to be doing your live interview today."

"Why Katy," he said exuberantly, extending a hearty, double-fisted handshake. "It's good to see you again. It's been a long time."

"Yeah, my mother's funeral," she answered, her voice dropping with heaviness.

"Yes...yes." Reverend Sykes lowered his head, shaking it from side-to-side.

Katy felt like she needed to provide an explanation as to why she hadn't been to church in so long, so she started out to say, "You know Reverend, I was away at school for a long time —" But before she could continue, he cut her off.

"I see you're a famous personality now, on the news and all."

Katy shrugged modestly. Then she noticed Officer Jenkins from the Morganville Sheriff's Department come through the door. Next to him was a petite, stocky woman, probably in her fifties, with a masculine haircut and graying black hair, wearing a black sweater over a knee-length black skirt. Katy wasn't sure if the dark clothes were being worn out of respect for the church or if they were meant to create a slimming effect. In any case, it turned out that she was the rector's secretary, Dottie.

When Katy looked at her watch, she realized she wouldn't have time to prep them. It was time to get the broadcast underway, so she announced to her cameraman that they were ready to go.

"Five...four...three...two...," counted Dan, "and we're live."

"Hi, this is Katy Barton with PTTV reporting. I'm standing here in front of the Good Shepherd Episcopal Church in Morganville with Reverend David Sykes—"

"Uh, you can call me Father Dave," interrupted the rector, grabbing the mic and moving it toward his mouth.

Katy steered the mic back toward her lips. "Uh...Father Dave, his secretary, Dottie Smith, and Deputy Officer Will Jenkins from the Morganville Sheriff's Department. Would you like to tell me what happened, Father, um, Dave?" she announced, repositioning the mic back over to him.

Father Dave cleared his throat. "Yes, well, it seems that somebody stole the weekend collection."

"You mean this past weekend?" Katy asked, surprised. "Did you just discover it?"

Dottie pulled the mic away from Father Dave's face and put it in front of her mouth. "Yes," she began. "Usually, I bring it to the Morganville bank after I count it all up on Monday afternoon, but I was visiting my daughter in the hospital—her name is Angie—actually, that's short for Angela. She just gave birth to a baby girl! She named her Dorothy (smiling smugly)—after me. It was their first girl. After two boys, they had been trying for a girl for some time, so—"

Katy had to cut in. "So when did you notice it was gone—the money?"

"Well, you know how caring and compassionate Father Dave is. He said I could have a few days off to visit my daughter, Angie—"

Katy's patience was running thin. "Can you get to the point, Mrs. Smith?"

Dottie, looking a little befuddled, continued. "ANYWAY, I came back to the church on Wednesday morning with the full intention of taking it to the bank first thing. And it was gone!"

Katy pulled the mic back over to her mouth, "What *exactly* was gone?"

"The lockbox, the whole lockbox!" said Dottie. "I keep it in my desk drawer, on the left-hand side, and I keep the key to the lockbox hidden in a secret spot in my office. I can't tell you where, though, because then everyone would know. You understand."

"Yes, I understand. So how much money *exactly* was in this lockbox?"

"Well, I don't know exactly because I hadn't yet had the chance to count it, what with it being gone and all."

Katy's frustration was becoming more and more visible. "So how much do you *think* was in there, Mrs. Smith?"

Dottie and Father Dave both turned to look at each other with uncertainty when the reverend decided to speak up. "We usually gather anywhere from $500 to $800 a week, depending on who shows up. Some people can afford to give more than others—that's not to say that the smallest donation wouldn't do."

"And the weather," butted in Dottie. "You'd be surprised how many fewer people go to church when it rains!"

Katy wanted to roll her eyes all the way to the back of her head but turned the mic over to Officer Jenkins instead. "So when were you notified of the situation, Officer Jenkins?"

"Not till yesterday afternoon, when I was called over to the church to make a report."

Dottie butted in again, moving her face as close to the mic as possible. "Father and I spent all afternoon looking for it, thinking it might show up—maybe it had gotten misplaced or something."

Katy moved the microphone back up to her lips and turned to the camera, desperate to get the interview wrapped up. "Okay, well, if anyone out there has any knowledge as to where the missing lockbox might be, or if you have any knowledge as to who might have taken it, you can leave an anonymous tip by calling the Morganville Sheriff's Department at the number on your screen."

Just as Katy was about to sign off, Father Dave grabbed the microphone out of her hands and began to speak directly into the camera. "Whoever did this, whatever your reason, *God will forgive you*. Maybe you needed the money, or maybe you're just a misguided youth. Either way, I pray that you search your soul and find it in your heart to return the money. There will be no questions asked. You can remain anonymous by dropping the money off in the rectory mailbox at any time. And I speak on behalf of all the parishioners of The Good Shepherd Episcopal Church, if you *truly* are in need, if you've lost your job or you're very ill and cannot afford to pay your medical bills, we will do everything we can to help you get back on your feet, even if it means taking up a special collection for you and your family. Remember: Ask, and it shall be given."

Katy once again took over the mic. "Thank you, Father Dave, for all your goodness." Then she looked straight into the camera and reminded the audience once more. "'Ask, and it shall be given.' This is Katy Barton, PTTV, reporting from The Good Shepherd Episcopal Church in Morganville."

Katy and Dan were packing their gear when she whispered in his ear, "That was torture!"

Dan had to hold his stomach when he erupted into a rolling belly laugh but had to stop short when Father Dave snuck up behind Katy. "I hope to see you in church again, Katy—only next time, without a camera and microphone."

Katy instantly felt her face flush. "I don't know, Reverend. Honestly, I think I've lost faith."

Reverend Sykes looked at her with his weary, deep-set eyes, as though he were extracting whatever demons were lurking in her soul. "You may think you've lost it, Katy, but you can always find it again. You just need to search for it. Remember: Seek and ye shall find."

The reverend's words stuck in her head all the way home. *Maybe hypnosis is not the answer — maybe God is the answer.* That evening, before she laid down to sleep, she picked up the phone from her nightstand and, with utmost conviction, firmly pressed those ever-familiar numbers on the keypad.

"Mike, if you're not working this weekend, would you mind accompanying me and Lilly to church on Sunday?"

CHAPTER FIFTY-ONE

"Wake up, sleepyhead," said Katy, gently swaying her daughter back and forth on the bed.

Before Lilly even opened her eyes, a big smile overtook her face. "You woke up before me!"

"Yes, I did. Do you know why?"

"Why?"

"Because we're going to do something special today."

"What? What?" Lilly shot up with excitement and started jumping up and down on the bed. "Are we going to the fair?"

"No."

"Are we going to the cemetery?"

Katy wrinkled her forehead. "No."

"Tell me!" she shouted, still jumping.

"God, I wish I could bottle up your energy. We're going to church!"

Lilly abruptly stopped jumping. "Church? What's that?"

Katy's mouth dropped. She suddenly felt like the worst mother in the world. After an informal christening in New York, with only her dad and her aunt and uncle being present as godparents, she never again brought her daughter into a church. She raised her head to the ceiling and whispered, "Please forgive me, Lord."

Mike never looked more handsome than when he showed up at her door in a tailored navy blue suit and tie. The three of them embodied the perfect family as they walked, hand-in-hand, up the steps of The Good Shepherd Episcopal Church.

Reverend David Sykes was standing in the entryway and immediately greeted them with a warm smile. "Welcome back,

Katy."

His sermon could not have been more appropriate. He chose to speak on rebirth.

"The Episcopal Church welcomes you, regardless of race, ethnicity, age, income, or the number of times you've been born. You might ask yourself, what does that mean? Being 'born again' can happen more than once. How many times have you gone through a spiritual crisis and come out of it somewhat changed? In a sense, you were reborn. So why must water be involved? Water is a sign that rebirth happens constantly. The spirit cannot enter the kingdom of God without water...."

Reverend Sykes kept redirecting his eyes toward Katy as she weighed every word that came out of his mouth with heavy contemplation. She looked down at Lilly's sweet angelic face and squeezed her hand tightly. She thought about how lucky she and her daughter were to have survived that horrific accident.

She remembered how hard it was raining on that perilous night. Could it be that the rain was a sign of her imminent rebirth? After all, it was as if an angel had been sent from heaven to save her from Mark's burning vehicle.

Then she turned her gaze upon Mike, who was seated on the other side of Lilly. She studied his solemn profile as he listened attentively to Reverend Sykes's sermon. He looked so stoic, like an archangel, ready to heed the call of duty at a moment's notice.

Then, all of a sudden, it hit her like a spiritual awakening. How could she have been so blind?

~*~

After the service, Mike suggested they stop at the Boar's Head Diner for breakfast. They were all settled into their booth, and Lilly was busy coloring on her special placemat with the crayons provided by the waitress.

Mike surveyed the room. "I think this is the same booth we sat in on our very first date."

"I think you're right," responded Katy, taking a quick glance around.

"Yep, this is where it all started."

Katy just looked at him. "Is it, Mike?"

He stopped to think for a minute and let out a short laugh. "Okay, the moment I saw you at the Flamingo Trailer Park, that's when I knew."

"Knew what?"

"That you were the one."

"Oh really? And how did you know?"

Katy could see him concentrating in the direction of her neckline where her pendant used to hang.

There was a pause. "I don't know, Kate, it's something I can't explain. When I saw you, it felt like I'd been waiting for you all my life."

Katy looked down at her daughter, who was immersed in her coloring. Then she took a long hard look at Mike. "It was you, wasn't it?"

"What do you mean?"

"It was you who saved me from Mark's burning vehicle that rainy night six years ago."

Mike lowered his eyes, hesitating to answer, while Katy focused on his expression, unblinking.

"Yes...it was me. When I first saw you at the trailer park, I wasn't sure if you were the same girl, but then I saw the pendant around your neck—that's when I knew."

"So, the day we ran into each other in the library—was that a coincidence, or had you been following me?"

Mike looked down and didn't answer.

"Why didn't you tell me? A relationship should be built on trust. How could you keep it from me for so long?"

"I don't know. I guess I was afraid of losing you again."

"*Again*? What do you mean *again*?" Katy covered her eyes with the palms of her hands and shook her head in frustration. "I'm sorry, Mike. You may be sure that *I'm* the one, but I'm not so sure that *you're* the one anymore." She stood up and slid her Morganite engagement ring off her finger. Then she dropped it down on the table in front of him. "Come on, Lilly," she said. "We have to go."

CHAPTER FIFTY-TWO

Father Sykes's sermon may have led Katy to the truth, but it did not save her from her inner demons. Once again, she was jarred awake by the same unsettling nightmare, and needless to say, she had a hard time getting back to sleep. Lucky for her, it was Friday, and since it had been a slow news week, she had decided to take the day off. Unfortunately, she still had to get up and take Lilly to school. First, she went into the kitchen to make a pot of coffee, then she went into Lilly's room to wake her up, but she wasn't there. Today was the day of Meghan's birthday sleep-over, and Lilly had been so excited, she couldn't sleep either. She had been waiting for this day ever since she got that pink Cinderella invitation. Katy found her standing on her little stool in the bathroom, already brushing her teeth. Since she had extra time this morning, she thought it would be nice to braid her daughter's hair for the party. She couldn't remember the last time she braided her hair on a school day because she was always in a hurry. This particular morning, however, Lilly was the one who was in a hurry.

"I can't braid your hair if you don't hold still, Lilly!"

"Come on, Mom, we have to go!" groaned Lilly.

"Did you put your pj's in your backpack?"

"Yes," Lilly answered assuredly.

"What about your toothbrush?"

"Yesssss."

"And don't forget the present!" yelled Katy, rushing toward the door.

"I've got it!" bellowed Lilly, with her shoulders hunched over and the box in her hands, taking extended strides as if the present weighed fifty pounds. Once they were in the car, Lilly couldn't stop talking about the birthday party. "Meghan said her mom has lots of party games planned, and we're gonna have popcorn and watch *The Wizard of Oz.*"

Katy glanced up at her daughter in the rearview mirror with raised eyebrows.

She pulled up in front of the school and jumped out of the car to unbuckle Lilly's seat belt. "Don't forget, I'm *not* picking you up after school. You're going home with Meghan and her mom. I'll pick you up tomorrow morning."

"I KNOW, I KNOW," droned Lilly.

"Wait," yelled Katy, reaching back into the car, "you forgot the present!" Lilly rushed back over to grab it out of her mother's hands. "Now give your mother a smooch."

Lilly stretched her head up for a kiss.

"Love you!" said Katy.

"Love you too, Mom," yelled back Lilly, scrambling off toward the school entrance.

Katy was looking forward to going home and crawling back into bed. She had promised Sue she would help her set up for the party, but she didn't have to be there until noon, so she'd have a little time for some shut-eye beforehand. She got home, kicked off her shoes, and snuggled back under the covers, but as she lay there, all she could think about was Mike and how he had kept the truth from her. The vision of the silhouette of a man in a black Stetson hat carrying her from the car crash lingered in her mind, followed by that song: *Smoke Gets in Your Eyes*. It played over and over in her head, pounding relentlessly into her skull until it became unbearable. She finally let out a scream and covered her head with her pillow to try and vanquish it from her brain. That's when the telephone rang, momentarily rescuing her from her harrying thoughts.

"Hi Katy, it's me, Janice. I tried calling you at work, and they told me you had the day off."

"It's been a slow work week. Besides, I just needed a day off, you know what I mean?"

"Actually, I don't—it never slows down at the DOT. So

what are you doing later?"

"I promised Sue Blakeford I'd go over there this afternoon to help her with the decorations for her daughter's birthday party."

"Well, that's not going to take all day, is it? I mean, what are you doing later tonight?"

"Oh, nothing. Lilly is going to be at the birthday sleepover, and I was just going to take it easy."

"Is the boyfriend working?"

Katy wasn't quite ready to divulge everything to Janice as of yet. "Uh, yeah."

"Great! Me and some friends are going into the city and meeting up at the Crazy Eights Bar around nine. Since you obviously have nothing better to do, you have to join us."

"I don't know...," Katy replied in an uncertain tone.

"Come on, this is the perfect opportunity! How often are you without a kid and without a boyfriend in one evening?"

Katy thought about it for a moment. It would probably do her good to get out of the house and get Mike off her mind. But what if she had another hallucination like she did at McMurphy's Pub? *I can't stop living because of some stupid hallucinations.* "You know, Janice, you're absolutely right. I'll be there at nine!"

Katy wasn't supposed to be at Sue's until noon, but since she couldn't sleep and needed the distraction, she was out of the house before eleven. Sue opened the door with a surprised look on her face. "I didn't expect you for another hour," she said, turning her head to look behind her shoulder.

"I hoped you wouldn't mind. I haven't seen you in a while, so I figured we could catch up."

"Um...sure, come on in," said Sue, with a hint of hesitation in her voice.

When Katy walked in, she noticed a man through an open door leading to the kitchen, adjusting his tie.

"If you'll excuse me," said Sue. She walked into the kitchen and whispered a few words into the man's ear before they came back out together. "Katy, I'd like you to meet Tom Reeves."

Katy tried not to appear too shocked, although it was

pretty evident what was going on. Not that it mattered, nor was it any of her business—Sue was divorced, after all. He looked quite a bit older than Sue, although his trim, pepper grey hair and beard gave him a very distinguished look. He was tall and slender like Sue and carried himself as would any refined English museum curator.

"I've been looking forward to meeting you," said Katy, extending her hand out to the gentleman. "I've wanted for some time to thank you personally for your generous donation and everything you've done on behalf of the Brewer estate."

"The pleasure is all mine," said Mr. Reeves. "A chance at preserving art in any form is a worthwhile cause. I'm sorry I can't stay, but I have a plane to catch." He bent over to kiss the back of Katy's hand. "Until we meet again."

Katy felt herself turn a few shades of rose as he grabbed his suit jacket and valise and started for the door. Sue excused herself again and followed him out, leaving the front door partially open. Katy stood up to shut it and observed the two of them a few car lengths up the street standing next to his Mercedes. She continued to watch while Sue cupped her hands around his neck, initiating a prolonged kiss. He turned to open his car door, and Sue, smoothing her hair into place, started making her way back to the house. At that point, Katy quickly shut the door and sat down on the couch.

When Sue walked in, Katy wasn't sure what to say. "I'm impressed. He's quite the gentleman and much handsomer than I pictured him to be."

Sue cracked a lofty smile. "Let me show you the cake. It was delivered from the bakery this morning."

Katy followed Sue into the kitchen to see the most elaborate birthday cake she had ever seen, complete with a Cinderella carriage, meticulously handcrafted out of icing, on top. "Wow, that's amazing," she exclaimed. But she didn't really want to talk about the cake. She wanted to deflate the elephant in the room. "So, how long have you been working at the art gallery?"

"Since my divorce," answered Sue.

"If you don't mind my asking, how long have you been

divorced?"

"I kicked him out a year after Meghan was born. He had been cheating on me the whole time I was pregnant with her."

Katy lowered her eyes, feeling like she may have misstepped her boundary. "That sounds rough."

"Emotionally, it was, but financially—well, let's just say Meghan's dad is a doctor and makes enough money for us *and* his new family. I got a part-time job at the gallery just to get me out of the house."

"How did you end up at the gallery?"

"My husband, Ron, and Tom had been friends for years, but I first met Tom when he was hosting a fundraiser at his gallery. I was pregnant at the time. That's when Ron bought me that painting." Sue pointed to an enormous canvas hanging on the living room wall. "I won it in the divorce settlement, even though I hate it. He only bought it to make up for the fact that he was having an affair. I'd get rid of it if it weren't so damned expensive." Katy looked at the picture. It was nothing more than a blend of the most unlikely colors streaked over a silver background. *How much could it possibly cost?* she thought. *Even Lilly could have painted that.*

"So Tom Reeves delivered the painting to me personally, while Ron was at work. We got to talking, and that's when he offered me the position. I've been with the gallery ever since. I can't complain. I like the job, and Tom takes good care of me."

"How does Meghan's dad feel about it?"

"I don't care how he feels about it," replied Sue, with lagging hostility in her voice.

"Will he be at the birthday party?"

"No, but he sent me a nice check to cover it—just another installment on his guilt. Anyway, enough about him. Are you doing anything special for *your* birthday?"

"My mom died the day after my 21st birthday, so ever since, it's been hard for me to celebrate. My dad and his 'lady friend' want to take me and Lilly out for a nice, quiet dinner. I made him promise he wouldn't have a cake brought out for me, especially not one with candles on it."

The conversation took on a livelier beat when they began hanging the decorations and filling balloons from the rented helium tank. Katy thought this would be a good time to bring up something that had been bothering her since that morning. "Lilly mentioned the girls were going to be watching *The Wizard of Oz*. I've never let her watch it before because I don't know about you, but that movie scared the heck out of me when I was a little kid. That wicked witch and those flying monkeys!"

Sue let out a chortle. "Don't worry. Meghan has seen it before and loves it. She was the one who insisted they all watch it on her birthday."

Since Sue had been so forthright with her personal life, Katy felt comfortable enough to bring up another matter that was concerning her. "Are Meghan's grandparents still alive?"

"My dad passed before she was born. My mom is still alive, but she's been in a nursing home for three years now. I don't even bring Meghan to visit her anymore. She has dementia and barely recognizes me, let alone her granddaughter."

"That's too bad," expressed Katy, then steered the conversation in the direction she was heading for. "Has Meghan ever, um, told you she's seen her grandpa?"

"What? No, I told you, he died before she was born."

"I mean, like...his spirit," Katy elaborated.

"His spirit!" Sue blurted out with laughter. "I hope not. He'd tell her she was a spoiled little brat! Why? Has Lilly ever seen any ghosts?"

Katy now felt stupid for bringing it up. "Oh, I don't know. Maybe she was just pretending, but she told me she saw her deceased grandmother."

Sue sensed her friend's embarrassment, so she lightened the matter with a joke. "I'm sorry, but Lilly's grandma was not invited to the party, so if she shows up, I'm going to have to kindly ask her to leave. Unless, of course, she shows up with a present. Then I'll let her stay for cake and ice cream."

Katy appreciated her friend's candor and laughed along, albeit nervously.

CHAPTER FIFTY-THREE

I wonder if this is too much black, thought Katy, scrutinizing the short black dress over her dark stockings and charcoal pumps. *Oh well*, she thought, glancing at her watch, *it's too late to change now*. She adjusted her skirt and took one last look at herself in the full-length mirror before grabbing her new handbag. It was larger than what she was used to carrying, but it was black and matched her dress. Finally, she walked over to the coat closet and pulled out her black, fleece-lined jacket. March hadn't exactly gone out like a lamb. The bone-chilling dampness of the past months had carried well into early April's nights.

By the time she reached the city, the sky had become overcast and misty, amplifying the neon signs and bright city lights with iridescent halos. Katy's stomach started to growl. It dawned on her that she hadn't eaten anything all day, except for a handful of peanuts and M & M's while she was at Sue's helping set up for the party. She reached into her open purse on the seat, hoping to find some mints, but was forced to make a sudden brake for a red light, knocking her purse and some of its belongings onto the floor.

By the time she arrived at the bar, Janice was already there, waving her down from her bar stool.

"I saved you a seat," shouted Janice, trying to override the raucousness of the packed room.

"Thanks!" Katy yelled back. "It's so crowded in here!"

"It's always like this on Friday nights because they have a DJ *and* a live band. So, how've you been? I haven't seen you in a while."

"In need of a break," said Katy, just as the DJ started to

crank out the tunes.

"What? I can barely hear you over the music!"

"I said, I needed a break!"

"You and Mike are breaking up?"

Katy detected an undertone of optimism in Janice's voice. "Yeah...I don't know."

"I thought he was perfect," Janice implied, with a smart-alecky slant.

"Yeah, well, things aren't always what they seem," said Katy.

"What'll you have, ladies?" interrupted the bartender, laying out a couple of cocktail napkins in front of them and a ceramic bowl filled with peanuts.

"Hey, it just occurred to me. Isn't today your birthday?"

"No, actually, it's tomorrow."

"Then I'm buying," asserted Janice, in her usual boisterous tone.

"No, you don't have to—"

"Don't worry, I'll let you get the next one." Janice looked over at the bartender. "We'll have two shots of tequila followed by two Buds."

"Make mine a Lite," said Katy, grabbing a handful of peanuts from the bowl and tossing them into her mouth.

The bartender poured two shots. "I'll be right back with your chasers."

Janice held up her shot glass. "Cheers to the newly single birthday girl!"

"Cheers," repeated Katy, raising her glass unenthusiastically and depleting it quickly.

"So, what about that lawyer I referred you to—John Doherty. He's good, right?"

"He's great," said Katy.

"That whole Brewer business has just fallen into place, hasn't it? I'm glad I was able to get the ball rolling for you."

"Uh, yeah," mused Katy. *Is she really trying to take credit for this?*

At that point, the bartender showed up with their beers

and poured them into mugs, with Janice immediately lifting hers. "To John Doherty!"

"To John Doherty," echoed Katy, taking a large swig.

"Too bad he's married," said Janice.

"What about the bartender? said Katy, casually checking him out. "He's good looking, and he's not wearing a wedding ring."

"Yeah, I dated a bartender once—didn't work. They keep too many weird hours."

"Yeah," resounded Katy, with Mike's face coming to mind.

"Besides," continued Janice, "they're always surrounded by drunk chicks willing to give it up for a couple of beers."

Just then, Janice noticed some of her other friends walking into the bar, so she jumped up to wave them over. "You remember Amber and Glen from high school, don't you?"

"Yeah, of course, I do," said Katy, standing up to give each of them a hug.

"And this is their friend, ummm...what was your name again?" Janice asked, crinkling her nose.

"Sam," replied the thin, shaggy-haired male.

"Hi Sam," smiled Katy.

As the disc jockey wound down his playlist, the band members came out on stage to set up their equipment. That gave Katy and her friends a little time to converse without competing with the loud music.

"Another round of beers!" harkened Janice, motioning to the bartender to come back around. "Oh, and by the way," pointing to Katy, "she's buying."

"Actually, make mine a Chardonnay—with a twist," inserted Katy.

When the bartender returned with their drinks, the band was about to hit the stage for their first song. Janice excused herself and meandered over to the ladies' room while Sam, who appeared to be on the prowl, disappeared into the crowd.

Glen spotted an empty table across from the bar and motioned his arm for Amber and Katy to join him. Amber had barely sat down when she blurted out, "Oh my God, I love this song! Do you mind saving our seats, Katy, while we go up to dance?"

"Sure," said Katy, squeezing the lemon twist into her Chardonnay. As she sat there sipping on her wine and swaying to the music, she could feel herself becoming a little light-headed.

Three songs later, Janice finally came back from the ladies' room. "There you are!" she called out. "I've been wandering around looking for you guys. I didn't know you got a table."

"We got lucky. Someone left early."

"By the way, did you get up on stage to sing with the band while I was in the bathroom?"

"No," Katy said curiously.

"Are you sure? Because the female lead singer looks *just* like you! Is there something you're not telling me? Do you have a twin or something?"

"Uh, no," replied Katy, standing up from her chair, trying to catch a glimpse of this singer. "I can't see her. There are too many people in here. You're probably exaggerating anyway."

"I'm not exaggerating—I had to look twice!" insisted Janice

"I'll check it out when I go to the ladies' room," reckoned Katy.

After a couple more songs, the band went on break, and Sam reappeared, looking at Katy. "Hey, I didn't know you were in the band," he said, point-blankly.

"What are you talking about?"

"I just saw you up on stage."

"I'm not in the band!" blasted Katy, beginning to get annoyed with the situation.

"Come on," he insisted. "She looks just like you!"

"It's true, I love to sing, but I swear I'm not in the band! I'll prove it to you." She stood up, surveying the crowd, trying to locate the band members, who had left the stage and had now disbursed into the crowd.

"Maybe it's your doppelganger?" snorted Janice.

"I hope not," said Katy. "I've read that one sees his or her doppelganger just before they're about to die." She looked at her watch. "Oh my gosh, it's after midnight. I have to get going. I need to pick Lilly up in the morning!"

"What time do you have to pick her up?"

"Around ten."

"That's not early!"

"It is for me. I like to sleep in on Saturdays." Katy put on her jacket and gave Janice a quick hug goodbye. As she was about to leave, she noticed her oversized black purse hanging over the side of her chair and grabbed it.

"Are you sure you can drive? I'm gonna catch a cab ride home. If you stick around, we can go together and split the tab."

"I'll be fine," said Katy. "I just need some fresh air."

"Call me tomorrow," Janice yelled out as Katy was leaving. "Or I'll call you — or whatever."

"Excuse...me....excuse...me...," repeated Katy, fighting her way through the crowd to get to the front entrance. When she reached the lobby, she thought she'd call Sue to ask her if she could pick Lilly up a little later so she'd have more time to sleep in. With a house full of screaming little girls, surely she'd still be up. She rummaged through her purse, searching for her cell phone, but couldn't find it, so she decided to use the payphone in the front lobby. While she was waiting for Sue to pick up, she could hear the disc jockey, who was back on stage.

"And here's a new one from Cher, 'Do you Believe in Life After Love?' For all of you hopeless romantics out there, you've got to BELIEVE!" And the music blared.

"You've got to be kidding me," Katy murmured under her breath. Her head started spinning, and she had to lean against the payphone to keep herself from falling while she waited for Sue to answer. After several rings, the answering machine picked up, so Katy left a message that if she didn't mind, she'd be picking Lilly up around noon.

Katy staggered out of the bar, feeling like she had escaped from a hot sweltering furnace fueled by the sweat of five hundred bodies, only to step into a frozen meat locker. Shivering, she lifted her hood and clutched her jacket tightly around her neck while she stood outside the nightclub, trying to remember where she had parked. The combination of noise from the screeching traffic, the brilliant city lights, and the icy dankness of the midnight air began to initiate their sobering effects.

As she scanned the street to her right, she noticed a young woman with shoulder-length, blondish-brown hair standing directly under the flickering, neon Crazy Eights sign. She was wearing a glittery black dress and was slumped up against the bar's red brick façade, smoking a dark tapered cigarette. The woman turned her head gradually while she continued to puff on her cigarette until her focus landed on Katy. The vacuous glare of her icy blue eyes left Katy spellbound until she realized that the face she saw was identical to her own. Katy stood there motionless, trying to utter something out, but was rendered speechless.

And then Katy's jaw dropped. The young woman removed her cigarette from her mouth and broke into a sinister smile. In a slow, creeping motion, her fresh young face became distorted until it took on the image of an older woman—a much older woman. But not just any old woman. It had morphed into Evelyn's face, still framing that same sinister smile. The "old woman" dropped her cigarette butt and slowly budged herself away from the wall, crushing it into the cement with her black pump, then turned around and headed into the bar.

Katy was so struck with fear she could feel her hair stand on end. In a panic, almost tripping over her heels, she started running rampantly down the opposite side of the street, praying that she would eventually remember where she parked. She had almost hit the point of exasperation when she finally spotted her car. "Thank God!" she spewed out loud, her weighty breath condensing the frigid night air to create a vaporous veil. "I've definitely had too much to drink!"

CHAPTER FIFTY-FOUR

Katy fumbled for her keys and stumbled into her car, stuck her key into the ignition, and started up the engine, letting it idle for a while before turning on the heat. She couldn't get that horrifying image out of her mind—that sinister smile on that old woman's face. As she sat there rubbing her hands together, trying to warm them up, Evelyn's remarks on their last visit began to resurface.

"All that we are is a result of what we have thought."

"I do more than believe it. I live it."

"Don't worry, my dear, it will all become crystal clear."

The more she thought about those statements, the more obsessed she became until she was suddenly struck with the irrational urge to drive to the mansion. Maybe it was the booze talking, but Katy's inner monologue turned into a debate between her rational self and her irrational self: *I know it's late, but I have to go back to see Evelyn right now. I'll bet she's still awake—she stays up reading and writing well into the night. It's obvious she's trying to tell me something. If I don't find out what it is right now, tomorrow might be too late!*

How could she argue with herself? Her mind was already made up. She may have had a little too much to drink, but she was sober enough to know that she probably should not be behind the wheel. She picked up the thermos still sitting in her cup holder from the day before, which had about half-a-cup of coffee left in it. She took a big gulp, hoping it might help sober her up, and almost gagged. *Yuck, I hate cold coffee!* Nonetheless, she waited a few seconds before forcing herself to swallow down the rest. *Fresh air should help too*, she thought, rolling her window all the way down. She pushed the gear shift into drive and was on her way to the Brewer estate.

She cranked up the heat and kept the window down for a while, but it was so cold she had to roll it back up, exposing just a few inches. Once she had reached the edge of town, where the roads turned desolate, she slowed down to a near snail's pace, fearing that another deer might jump out in front of her. When she was halfway to the mansion, it started to drizzle. *Oh great*, she thought, turning her wipers on. The incessant drizzle soon turned into a hard, steady rain, forcing her to shut her window completely, but then the heat from the defroster began to steam up the windshield. She had to drive with her face protruding over the steering wheel, squinting to see the road through the heavy condensation. Eventually, she grabbed a napkin from underneath her thermos and began wiping the windshield. This helped a little. The problem was that she was in the middle of nowhere, with no street lamps to guide her through the dark winding road, except for the occasional headlight beams coming from the opposite direction. The good thing was that she had become adeptly familiar with the road, to the point where she could have driven it blindly, which basically was what she was doing.

So Katy ventured on, her eyes fixated on the inky rain spiraling against the windshield until the droplets exploded into intermittent flashes of Evelyn's distorted, melting face. She squeezed her eyes tightly and rattled her head back and forth, trying to get the frightening image out of her head, when suddenly, she caught a glimpse of the mansion looming on the horizon. The disturbing reflection shattered into a kaleidoscope of trajectory shards until they exploded into oblivion, and a shroud of relief fell upon her.

She proceeded along the gravel driveway, stopping just short of the front entrance, and opened her car door just long enough to stick her head out into the pouring rain. *It's so dark out here, I can't see anything!* she snarled, reaching back in to open her glove compartment. *Where's that emergency flashlight when I need it?* Blindly, she began to canvas her hand along the floor mats trying to find it and lifted her purse off the floor to set it back on the seat. That's when she discovered her cell phone had been lying under it. *So that's where you disappeared to!* She tossed it back into her open bag and continued to feel around for her flashlight. After discovering a toy, a comb, and her pack of mints, her hand came across a smooth oblong object. "Ah ha! There you are!" she yelled, pressing the on-switch with her thumb. *Thank goodness the batteries still work.*

With her flashlight defining her path, she hurried through the rain and hopped up the stairs to the front door. Using the large knockers, she knocked once...twice...three times, but there was no answer. *Ruby must be asleep*, she thought, so she tried turning the knob. The door had been left unlocked. "Yessss!" she exclaimed, with a breath of relief.

The door was very heavy, so she gave it a good, hard thrust to get it open. When she entered into the pitch-black vestibule, she could hear music coming from the parlor. It was that song again, the one by Tamara. Using her flashlight as her guide, she slowly made her way into the parlor. She could see the faint flicker of a candle whose wick was close to burning out on top of Evelyn's desk. The phonograph had reached the end of the recorded melody and had started skipping. "Smoke gets in your eyes, your eyes, your eyes, your eyes...."

As Katy carefully made her way toward the hutch where the phonograph was, she saw that sitting right next to it was a Victorian lamp. She had never actually seen it lit, so she wasn't sure if it even worked. She pulled on the small chain dangling from its side, and *Voila`!* It turned on! *I can't understand why Evelyn always uses candles when she has other lighting available to her,* thought Katy, as she lifted the needle arm above the disc and set it on its rest. She took a quick look around the room and didn't see Evelyn, so she figured she must have gone to bed. That's when Katy started having second thoughts. *What am I doing here? I should just leave. I don't even know why I came here in the first place. I must be out of my mind!*

Katy was about to turn around and head for the door when all of a sudden, she let out a high-pitched shriek.

It was in that sobering moment that she spotted Evelyn lying on the floor between the coffee table and the chaise. Her eyes were closed, and her right hand was resting over her heart. Katy ran over to her, bending over to check her wrist. She could feel a very slight pulse, so she decided to try mouth-to-mouth resuscitation. As she swept back the hair off Evelyn's face, Katy let out a small gasp. Something immediately stood out, something she hadn't noticed before. Up in the left-hand corner of Evelyn's forehead, near the hairline, was a scar about the size of a bottle cap, in the shape of an "L," in the same spot and an exact duplicate of the one on Katy's own forehead. She was taken aback for a moment, but sensing a hint of life left in Evelyn's motionless body, carried on with her resuscitation attempt. "Don't die on me, Evelyn, you can't die!" she bellowed. As she repeatedly thrust her encapsulated fist against the old woman's chest, her mind took her back to that fateful night on April 13, 1936.

A heavy wind was blowing through the window left open in the parlor. The sheer curtains were billowing wildly, high and low and back and forth, until the corner edge of one landed on the candle left smoldering on Evelyn's desk. The fire was beginning to spread, shooting upward toward the vaulted ceiling. The parlor became filled with smoke, and Katy began gagging and coughing as if she were experiencing the ordeal in real time. She was holding the front of her neck, gasping for air when gradually, her illusion dissipated, and she came back to the realization of the situation at hand.

"Hang in there, Evelyn, you're going to be okay. I'm going to call an ambulance," she shouted, wrapping her arms around the old woman's shoulders. Evelyn appeared to be making an attempt at opening her eyes, but they barely made it to a sliver. Her lips moved slightly as though she were trying to say something. Her voice was so weak, Katy had to lower her ear to Evelyn's mouth, where she was able to discern a whisper.

"No ambulance, Kate. You are my vehicle."

At this utterance, Katy's mouth dropped open. She realized it was her quest for the truth that had drawn her here tonight. She was prepared to come face-to-face with the fear that had plagued her from the time she first laid eyes on Evelyn's portrait. The words spilled out of Katy's mouth like an erupting volcano. "Am I you, Evelyn?" There was no reply. So she repeated it louder this time, gripping Evelyn's arms and shaking her. "Evelyn, am I you?!"

Evelyn's answer came through softly but pronounced. "You and I, Kate, we share the same soul after all."

"But how? Why?" Katy cried out, cradling the old woman in her arms.

Evelyn's head fell to the side, and Katy felt her wrist once more. There was no longer a pulse. In that exact moment, she was jolted by the crackling sound of thunder, followed by a streak of lightning, illuminating the whole length of the parlor. The clock on the fireplace mantel ticked loudly as its face came clearly into display.

Katy lifted her head to see that it was precisely 2:38 a.m.

CHAPTER FIFTY-FIVE

"No, no, you mustn't die," screamed Katy, shaking Evelyn's lifeless body. She stood up and looked around the room. *Ruby must be around here somewhere!* She started running from room to room, navigating her way with her flashlight, and calling out Ruby's name. She bolted up the massive staircase, which led to a long hallway of closed doors. One by one, she opened each door, revealing bedrooms where the furniture had been covered with sheets that had grayed from must. When she entered the last room on the left, she recognized it as being Evelyn's bedroom from seeing it while under hypnosis. The furniture was not covered up, but the decor was somberly plain.

It suddenly occurred to her, from witnessing the fire while under hypnosis, that the servants' quarters were somewhere downstairs, so she ran back down the stairway. She ran past the parlor and past the grand dining room. When she reached the library, she noticed that both the tiffany floor lamps had been turned on, so she decided to go in and look around. There was no sign of Ruby, but there were two books lying on the coffee table between the lamps. The limited sphere of ambient lighting from the prismatic domes shone upon the copies of *Conversations with a Spirit* and *Tapping into the Power of Love* with an aura of divination that drew shivers up Katy's spine.

Immediately she ran back into the hallway, which led her into an enormous kitchen with two doorway exits. One ushered her into the butler's pantry, and the other led her to a large dishwashing area with an arched opening that led to yet another short hallway. There were three closed doors in the hallway, and straight ahead at the end of the hall, she could see a type of mudroom accessing an outside entryway. *Good grief, it's like a maze in here. No wonder it took Ruby so long to answer the door!* She opened the first door to her right, which appeared to be another bedroom where the furniture had been covered. *These must be the servant's quarters. Maybe Ruby is in this other room sleeping,* she thought. She opened the next door to her left to find that it was indeed another bedroom. The furniture wasn't covered, nor was Ruby in there sleeping. The bed had been neatly made with no sign of anyone having used it recently. As Katy shined her flashlight around the room, she noticed there was nothing sitting out. There were no photos, no knick-knacks, or any personal items. It looked stark and barren. She pulled open the armoire, where the only things hanging were a few empty wooden hangers. She opened up the dresser drawers and found them empty as well. Finally, she pulled open the single drawer in the nightstand. It, too, was bare, except for one small shiny object in the back corner of the drawer. She shone her flashlight on it to see what it was—a key.

She walked out of the bedroom to open the third door in the hallway—the one on the left. When she did, it led her down several stairs to yet another door. She tried opening that, but it was locked. It dawned on her that the key in the nightstand might open it. Katy ran back into the bedroom to get it. She was right.

She carefully inserted it into the keyhole, first turning it to the right, then to the left, until it unlocked. Slowly and cautiously, she pulled the door open, a little bit frightened of what she might find. The room was completely dark except for the faint light from two candles appearing to be at their wick's end, on a credenza at the opposite end of the room. In the very center was a round table with one chair on either side, facing each other. The wood-planked floors seemed to creak more obtrusively in this isolated space as she stepped closer toward the table. She pointed her flashlight to the middle of the table, where a square wooden board lay. It was engraved with two rows of alphabet letters with a moving planchette in the middle. At the top were the words "yes" and "no." The planchette itself was in the shape of a heart and was pointing to the word "goodbye."

There was no doubt in Katy's mind what this was—an

Ouija board. She had used one once at a friend's sweet sixteen party. It was meant to have been all in fun, but she remembered getting freaked out when it spelled out an ominous warning and pointed directly at her.

Katy quickly redirected her flashlight toward the credenza against the wall. Above it hung a large crucifix with a lifelike replica of the savior with blood-stained tears streaming down his cheeks. Sitting on the credenza were the two candles, barely smoldering, and between them stood a large picture frame partially concealed beneath a dark veil. Gradually, Katy lifted the veil and shined her flashlight upon it. What was revealed was a black-and-white photo of a man in a black Stetson hat. But it wasn't Marcus's face, the face she had seen while she was under a hypnotic trance. No, it was *Mike's* face in the picture—her ex-fiancé! And lying at the base of the frame was Katy's pendant—the one Mark had given her—the one she thought she had lost!

Katy let out a shriek and turned and ran up the steps as fast as she could, her heart pounding furiously until she found her way back to the parlor where Evelyn's body lay. She wanted to run out of the house, to get away from there, to go back home, but her moral sense of obligation got the best of her. She looked around the room and saw the phone on Evelyn's desk. She hurried over to it and tried dialing, hoping it would work, but the line was dead. *Of course, it doesn't work*, she huffed, slamming down the receiver. Then she remembered her cell phone in her purse. *Darn it, I left my purse in the car!* As Katy made a mad dash out the front door, she found that the rain had not let up. In fact, it was raining harder. When she got back into the house, she immediately called for an ambulance.

Her boss needed to be informed of Evelyn's death, but she really didn't want to wake him in the middle of the night. He usually went into the station early on Saturday mornings for a few hours, so she opted to leave a message on his office line instead.

Katy paced the floor nervously while she waited for the ambulance to arrive, the photo of Mike's face lingering in her frontal lobe. She stared at Evelyn's dormant body stretched out on the rug as if she expected her to rise at any moment. It didn't surprise her that the old woman was dressed all in black as if she had been planning her own funeral. And then, something caught Katy's eye. There was something protruding out from under Evelyn's dress. She hadn't noticed it before, probably because it was the same color as her dress. She walked over to get a closer look. It was the black, leather-bound journal that Evelyn kept her daily writing in. It was her memoir. She felt as though it was too soon to be intruding into Evelyn's past and hesitated for a moment before picking it up. But her curiosity got the better of her, and she opened it up to the first page.

Evelyn had actually titled it: *Reflections of a Past and Future Life. That's an odd title*, she thought, turning to the second page. Her mouth fell open, and her eyes bulged from their sockets when she read, "I dedicate this book to my beloved daughter, Lilly."

Katy began to read further. "I was born Evelyn Katherine Brewer on April 13, 1917." Katy set the notebook down to yell, "What the F...ck! She was born on the same month and day as me!" Then she continued, flipping through several pages at a time.

"On December 16, 1923, I lost my mother, my best friend, to pneumonia, from complications from the flu. How could a child as me at the tender age of six even begin to comprehend the meaning of death? My dear father did his best to keep my fragile emotions in check. Without his strength and the unrelenting love of my dear, sweet Tandy, I would not have been able to go on."

The words cut through Katy's heart like a knife, and her eyes began to tear up. These were the same feelings she had felt when her own mother died. Quickly, she flipped through another handful of pages.

"I first met Marcus at the vulnerable age of sixteen, when his father, who was my father's business partner, came over to drop off some financial papers. When the two of them retired into the library to discuss business matters, I was left to keep the young Mr. Shilby entertained. As nervous as I was, I did my best to play the piano and sing for him. His unwavering fascination for me, and his undeniably good looks, left me feeling weak in the knees. He and his father ended up joining us for dinner, and by the time dessert was over, I had fallen head over heels. He filled the empty void that resulted from my mother's loss. The day he asked me to marry him was the happiest day of my life."

Kate continued thumbing through the pages until she had arrived at the final chapter — CHAPTER 13 — which read,

"As I'm lying in the hospital devastated from the news of my fiancé's death, the doctor has revealed to me that I am with child. Lilly has filled the emptiness I suffered at the loss of my one and only true love, Marcus."

Katy took a long hard gulp. *The doctor told her she had lost the baby in the fire — I saw it while I was under hypnosis!*

Then, she turned to the final sentence on the last page.

"By the powers that come from the light within, I shall embrace the new life that has been bestowed upon me in the springtime of my rebirth, when we have all been reunited once more."

In that instant, the paramedics, as well as a policeman, arrived, and Katy quickly tucked the book into her handbag. When she had finally finished speaking to the ambulance attendants and made a written report to the police, her mind and body were wracked to the point of collapse. Completely sober now, she got into her car and drove home, still trembling from what she'd read.

By the time she pulled up to her townhouse, the clouds had dissipated, and an orange splinter of sun was peeking up through the horizon. She parked the car in the driveway, and just as she was about to shut her car door, she heard a soft mewing sound. Katy looked down and could not believe her eyes. Below her stood a scruffy little black ball of fur with scintillating copper eyes, languidly gazing up at her.

"Oh Tandy, I can't believe it's you after all this time!" She picked him up and squeezed him tight, as the tears she had been holding in until now broke loose into a streaming waterfall.

With Tandy in her arms, she unlocked the front door and walked over to the refrigerator to pour him a bowl of milk. Then she opened up a can of tuna, scooped it into a bowl, and set it on the floor next to his milk bowl. "I'm sorry, Tandy, I've got to get some rest now," she told him, dropping her coat to the floor. She made her way to the bedroom, and the minute her head hit the pillow, she plunged into a deep sleep.

Chapter Fifty-Six

The annoying sound of the telephone blaring woke Katy up. In her sleepy haze, she had forgotten to set her alarm clock. It was almost noon — it had to be either Sue or Mr. Bruckman.

"Hello," she answered, her eyes struggling to open.

"Hello, Kate." It was Bruckman. "I got your message, and I've already been on the phone with the coroner's office. I know you've probably had a rough night and were supposed to have the day off — being it's your birthday and all — but I need you to come into the office and get a story ready for the evening broadcast. You'll also need to provide an article for the weekend edition of the *Morganville Herald*."

"Okay, but I have to go pick my daughter up first and bring her to my dad's."

"All right, just get here as soon as you can."

Katy got up to make a pot of coffee while Tandy followed, meowing at her feet. She looked at the two empty bowls on the floor and poured him a little more milk. "Sorry, Tandy, this will have to do for now. I'll stop by the store after work and buy you some real cat food," she said, scratching the back of his little neck.

But before she did anything else, she needed to make a call. She knew Dr. Fleming's office would be closed on Saturday, so she was prepared to leave a message with his answering service, explaining that it was imperative she see him as soon as possible. To her relief, they called her back right away, and she was able to get an appointment for Monday afternoon. The next thing she had to do was call Sue to let her know she was on her way to pick up Lilly.

"I'm sorry I'm running late. Did you get my message?"

"I did, and it's fine."

"I hope the party went well and there were no problems."

"It turned out great. The girls had a wonderful time—except for one minor little thing."

"Oh, what's that?"

"By the time all the girls had finally fallen asleep on the living room floor, Lilly woke up in the middle of the night from a bad dream."

"Oh no," said Katy.

"It's okay. I stayed up with her until she fell back asleep."

"I'll be there as soon as I can. Can you just make sure Lilly has everything in her backpack? I have to bring her to my dad's right afterward because I have to go into work for a few hours."

"Why don't you just leave her here until you get off work? I'll be here all day."

"Are you sure?"

"Not a problem."

"You're a gem. I owe you," said Katy. "Oh, and tell Lilly I have a surprise for her when she gets home. Maybe that'll help her forget about her bad dream."

Katy hung up the phone and remembered she and Lilly were supposed to go out to dinner with her dad and Johanna that evening to celebrate her birthday. She obviously wasn't feeling up to it and didn't know what time she'd be getting off work, so she called him up to ask if he wouldn't mind going out tomorrow instead.

As usual, her father was more than accommodating. "Absolutely, Katy Bear. If you don't feel well, I'll just change the reservations to Sunday."

Katy arrived at the news station and immediately began working on the feature for the evening broadcast regarding the demise of the sole heir to the Brewer mansion. When she was finished with that, she wrote a short article for the Sunday *Herald*, then walked over to Mr. Bruckman's office and dropped it on his desk. "Here it is, ready for your review."

"I'm sure it's fine, Kate. You don't have to stick around. Why don't you get back home and get some sleep? I'll take care of the rest."

"Thank you, Mr. Bruckman."

"Oh, Kate?"

"Yes, Mr. Bruckman?"

"Thanks for coming in. I know this whole ordeal has been hard for you, but there *is* some good news."

"What's that?" she asked, thinking she could use some good news right now.

"Remember the story you did on the Morganville Animal Shelter and how it was going to be shut down if they couldn't get the proper funding?"

"Yeah."

"The shelter has been saved. Two days ago, they received a donation in the amount of $500,000 dollars from an anonymous donor."

Katy couldn't believe her ears. "That *is* good news."

"I expect you to follow up on that on Monday," he added.

"Of course."

"Oh, and by the way, Happy Birthday."

~*~

By the time Katy showed up at Sue's doorstep, Lilly had her backpack all packed up and was ready to go. Katy bent down and gave her daughter a kiss. "Did you have fun?"

"Yeah," yelled Lilly, echoed by Meghan, who was standing right next to her.

"You can tell me all about it on the way home."

"Mrs. Blakeford said you had a surprise for me! What is it?"

"You'll have to wait and see, or it won't be a surprise."

After Lilly talked almost non-stop all the way home about how much fun she had at the party and all the presents Meghan got, Katy finally got a chance to interject a few words of her own. "So Mrs. Blakeford told me you had a bad dream."

Lilly was hesitant to answer. "Yeah."

"Do you want to tell me about it?"

"No, not really...but okay." Gradually, Lilly proceeded with her story. "I dreamt we were living in that really big house—

you know, the one we visited that one day. And it caught on fire. It was really dark, and there was smoke all around. I was scared because I didn't know where you were. So I started running all around the house looking for you, but when I found you, you were melting! I tried to save you by pouring water on you, and that's when I woke up."

"Oh, sweetie!" cried Katy, watching the bereaved look on her daughter's face in the rearview mirror.

"I guess I screamed, 'cause Mrs. Blakeford ran into the living room and turned on the light. I was afraid to go back to sleep, so she stayed up with me until I fell back asleep."

Katy wanted to reach around and give her daughter a hug. "Oh, honey, it was just a dream." Then it dawned on her. "Wait a minute, didn't Mrs. Blakeford let you girls watch *The Wizard of Oz*?"

"Yeah."

"That's probably what caused your bad dream. At the end of the movie, doesn't the Wicked Witch of the West melt?"

Lilly looked at her mom in the mirror with a smile of encouragement.

I knew that movie would be too scary, thought Katy. But then her thoughts reverted back to the Crazy Eights Bar, where she witnessed her doppelganger's melting face. Surely there could be no correlation.

As Katy drove up to their townhome, she could already see Tandy through the sheer curtains. He was on the inside ledge of the front room window pacing back and forth, waiting for their arrival, just as he had always done in the past. This time she pulled directly into the garage to keep his return a secret since Lilly hadn't noticed him as they were pulling up. The minute they walked into the side door, Tandy raced into the kitchen and began rubbing up against Lilly's ankles, meowing with delight.

Lilly's eyes expanded to the size of saucers, and she could barely contain her giddiness. She threw down her book bag and grabbed Tandy in her arms, practically squeezing the life out of him.

"Mom, it's Tandy! Did you know he was here?" she

screamed.

"Yes, honey, that's the surprise."

"Where did you find him?"

"When I came home last night, he was right here in our driveway, just like the first time we found him."

Lilly extended a quizzical eye toward the ceiling with her index finger over her mouth. "I wonder where he's been all this time." Then she smothered him with kisses while shouting in his ear, "I'll never let you out of my sight again, Tandy!"

While Lilly was in her room reading *The Fire Cat* book to Tandy, Katy thought she'd give Sue a call. There was something weighing on her mind.

"I just wanted to thank you again for letting Lilly stay until I got off work. I was just wondering, do you remember, off-hand, what time it was when Lilly woke up from her nightmare?"

"Hmm, let me think," replied Sue. "The girls didn't fall asleep until well past midnight. I was in the bed in the next room sleeping when I heard her scream. I wanna say, about 2:30?"

CHAPTER FIFTY-SEVEN

Monday morning couldn't have come soon enough, but the first thing Katy had to do was drive over to the Morganville Animal Shelter. She arrived to find the same young lady manning the front office. The chimes rang, but the girl didn't budge.

"Hi there," Katy said loudly, hoping to prompt her to notice.

It was obvious she was in no hurry to get up. "Be right there," she answered in a monotone voice.

As Katy waited in front of the counter, she saw that Tandy's picture was still posted on the bulletin board, so she walked over to remove it from the wall. While she was doing so, the director of the shelter, Vera Gibbons, walked in from the back room.

"Why hello, Ms. Barton," she said cheerfully as she approached the counter. "What can I do for you?" Ms. Gibbons was looking at the flyer in Katy's hand. "I'm sorry, we still haven't come across a black cat with copper eyes."

"Oh, no," said Katy, starting to cough and using the flyer to cover her mouth. "Excuse me. I took the picture down because we found him. We found our little lost Tandy!"

"I'm so glad to hear that," remarked Ms. Gibbons. "He was gone for a long time. It's a wonder he survived the winter. Someone must have taken him in."

"Either that or cats really do have nine lives," joked Katy, coughing again. "Actually, I'm here to find out a little bit more about the anonymous donation you received."

Ms. Gibbons' face lit up. "Oh yes, miracles truly do exist."

"I'm preparing for a news story in that regard, so I've come to get a little more information from you, if I may."

"Of course," said Ms. Gibbons. "But, I don't think I can provide you with much. I was not here the day the donation came in." Ms. Gibbons directed her glance toward the young lady sitting at the desk. "Gina was the only one here that afternoon." Ms. Gibbons called out to her. "Gina, would you mind coming over here for a minute, please?"

Gina slowly rose from her chair and meandered over to the front counter at the speed of a sloth.

Katy removed a pen and notepad from her purse. "So Gina, when exactly did this donation come in?"

"Sometime last week, like Tuesday—or maybe it was Wednesday."

"Did it come in the mail?"

"No, some old lady brought it in."

"Did you get her name?"

"No."

"Wouldn't it be written on the receipt?"

"She said she didn't need a receipt."

For Katy, this was like pulling teeth. "Do you remember what she looked like?"

Gina let out an annoyed breath. "Okay, like this short, kinda chubby woman. She was wearing this flowery dress and a scarf tied around her head."

"Did you see her face?"

"I don't know. She was wearing big sunglasses."

"Well, what did she say?" persisted Katy.

"She was carrying this big box. She just said she had some food for the cats. I told her to put it on the stack of the other donations in the corner over there," she said, pointing across the counter.

That's when Ms. Gibbons jumped in. "I didn't open the box right away, figuring it was full of cans or dry pet food. It wasn't until a few days later that I opened it. Needless to say, I was more than shocked to find it was full of cash. I counted it all myself—$500,000 dollars, all in $100 bills!"

Gina had started meandering back to her desk when she stopped midway and turned around. "I do remember one thing—she had this annoying accent. I think it might have been Irish or something like that."

A twinkle erupted in Katy's eyes, and the corners of her mouth curved upward.

After the interview, she drove straight to the news station to get the story ready before her appointment with Dr. Fleming.

"Did you get that story from the animal shelter?" Mr. Bruckman yelled out as she passed his office.

Katy took a few steps backward until she reached his door. "Of course I did," she answered, pulling out a tissue to blow her nose.

"So, it'll be ready for the evening broadcast?"

"Sure thing, along with my article for the *Herald*."

A few hours later, she dropped the story off on his desk for his review.

"Thanks, Kate. I appreciate all your hard work."

"Do you mind if I take the rest of the day off? I'm not feeling so good."

"Sure, go ahead. You don't *look* so good."

She put her palm to her forehead. She was feeling a little flush. Maybe she was coming down with something, probably from everything that had happened Friday night—the drinking, the rain, getting home at the crack of dawn. Yep, that would do it.

Before she left, she went into the break room and popped two Tylenol tablets in her mouth. She sped to Dr. Fleming's office, blowing through every yellow light on the way, not wanting to be late for this very important appointment.

No sooner had she walked into his office than she asked if she could lie down on the couch. Besides not feeling well, there was so much to remember since she last saw him that she needed to collect her thoughts.

"Let me know when you're ready," said the doctor.

She started out by telling him about her episode at McMurphy's Pub and hearing that song that Evelyn loved, *Smoke Gets in Your Eyes*. She told him how her fiancé Mike confessed to being the man in the black Stetson hat who had saved her from Mark's burning car. Next, she described the incident at The Crazy

Eights Bar, where she saw her doppelganger's mutating face. She explained how Evelyn died in her arms at exactly 2:38 a.m. and that her last dying words were, "You and I, Kate, we share the same soul after all." She stressed the fact that she found an Ouija board and a picture of Mike with her lost pendant laying in front of it in a hidden room at the mansion. She went on to tell him about her daughter's nightmare, in which she woke up screaming "around 2:30 a.m." She also told him how Tandy reappeared in her driveway after being gone for almost eight months. Lastly, Katy went on to summarize everything she had read in Evelyn's memoir before handing the notebook over to Dr. Fleming.

The doctor's pen was moving at the speed of sound as his ears were processing each and every word. He continued writing for a good fifteen minutes afterward, which was fine for Katy since she needed to rest after that exhaustive recountal. Finally, Dr. Fleming placed his pen over his ear and walked over to the window. He pulled open the drapes and stared blindly out the window, appearing to be in deep thought.

Katy waited as long as she could for some feedback, and her hour was almost up, so she had to speak up. "Dr. Fleming, please tell me I'm not crazy and that there's a logical explanation for all of this."

The doctor turned to look at his patient. "There are no fast and easy answers," he said. "You've been through quite an ordeal, Kate, and you've given me a lot to consider. I'll need to study Evelyn's journal thoroughly. Then I'll need to review all of my recordings, as well as my notes from our previous sessions. It's going to take a while to process all this information. Your case is unique from anything I've ever encountered before. There are aspects of your situation that will require me to conduct further research. With your permission, Kate, I would like to consult with some of my colleagues from the University of Virginia's Department of Neurobehavioral Sciences and The Parapsychological Association in Edinburgh."

"Um, sure, whatever it takes. I just want to get to the bottom of this."

"It may take several weeks, but I'll be in touch to let you

know of my progress. In the meantime, why don't you get some rest? You don't look so good."

Seriously! How bad do I look? As Katy stood up to make her way to the door, Dr. Fleming buzzed his receptionist.

"Marjorie, will you please clear my calendar for the rest of the month and refer my patients to Dr. Lindsey? But first, get Gregory Claeger on the phone for me."

Katy was relieved to get all that off her chest and felt a sense of reassurance, having left Evelyn's memoir in his charge. She had hoped he could have provided her with some immediate answers, but considering everything that had happened, she should have known it could not have all been explained in just one hour.

Katy's birthday dinner had ended early, with Katy explaining that she still didn't feel well. Mr. Barton had noticed that his daughter's mind was somewhere else. He attributed it to her breakup. He knew that she and Mike had split, but she never explained why. He wasn't one to press for details, however. He knew that she would open up to him when she was ready.

That evening, Katy took two Tylenol PM tablets and walked over to her daughter's bedroom, where Tandy was already curled up next to her. "Would you like me to read you a bedtime story before I tuck you in, baby?"

"No," cried Lilly. "I want Mike to read me a story. I miss him! When is he coming back?"

Chapter Fifty-Eight

It had been over a month since Katy had last seen Dr. Fleming. He had called her just once to let her know that his "investigation" was progressing, but he never let on as to reveal any pending outcome or determination. The rainy season had ended, and the lilies were in full bloom when Katy finally received the call she had been waiting for.

She had taken the whole day off on Friday so she would have plenty of time to digest whatever the doctor might have to reveal. Lilly was going home with Meghan after school for another sleepover, with Katy promising she'd be right over if she had another bad dream.

"You can go right in," said Marjorie. "They've been waiting for you." Katy wondered who "they" were as she walked toward the door. She stepped in to find Dr. Fleming sitting behind his desk, which was barely visible from all the scattered notes and open books. Another older-looking gentleman, whose sleeves were rolled up to his elbows and whose suit jacket was hanging over the back of his chair, was sitting on the opposite side of the desk facing him.

Dr. Fleming lifted his head. "Come in, come in," he said excitedly, as he and the other gentleman both stood up. "Kate, I'd like you to meet Dr. Gregory Claeger. He is a very distinguished colleague of mine from The Parapsychological Association in Edinburgh. He is one of the most renowned experts in the field of reincarnation and has written a great many books on the subject. When I approached Dr. Claeger with the circumstances surrounding your case, he was more than eager to assist me with my research in forming a viable conclusion."

"It's a pleasure to meet you," said Katy, extending her hand.

"Believe me, the pleasure is all mine," said Dr. Claeger. "I couldn't wait to meet the young woman who has altered the very precept of reincarnation."

Katy had no idea what he meant by that.

"Have a seat," said Dr. Fleming, walking around his desk to pull out the other chair for her. The two of them were gaping at her as though she held the key to the meaning of life. "You know, Kate," Dr. Fleming started out, "from our very first session, I knew you were sleeping beneath a bodhi tree waiting to be awakened."

"What's a bodhi tree?"

"It is the tree under which Buddha acquires enlightenment."

"I must still be sleeping, so enlighten me, please."

"In the past weeks, Dr. Claeger and I have studied Miss Brewer's journal frontward and backward. We've replayed the recordings from your hypnotic sessions over and over to make sure we didn't miss anything, and we have thoroughly reviewed my notes from everything we discussed with a fine-tooth comb. As a result of our research and investigations, Dr. Claeger and I have made a cataclysmic discovery as it relates to the subject of reincarnation—a parapsychological breakthrough, if you will, that would explain the strange barrage of events in your life that have culminated to this end. To further substantiate our findings, we also consulted with numerous members of The Society for Psychical Research who have concurred with our established theory. We are as eager to tell you of our conclusions as I'm sure you are to hear them."

Get on with it already! thought Katy, who was on the edge of her chair, anxious for an explanation she could understand.

"Are you ready to hear it?"

"Yes!" resounded Katy, with bated breath.

"By the way, have you had any recurring nightmares since Evelyn Brewer's death?"

Katy thought for a moment. "No, as a matter of fact, I haven't," she answered, surprised at her own revelation.

"As I suspected," said the doctor.

Dr. Fleming stood up from his desk and began pacing around the room as he proceeded with his explanation while Dr. Claeger sat vigilantly in his chair. "Do you recall when we talked about *The Tibetan Book of the Dead,* and I explained to you how the hunger of the soul has a plan of its own in its eternal quest to achieve perfection on the highest plane?"

"Yes," answered Kate.

Dr. Fleming continued. "This might sound farfetched and maybe a little fantastical, but hear me out. Evelyn was nineteen years old when the Brewer mansion caught fire in 1936. At the time of the fire, she underwent a near-death experience. Her body—her *physical* self, or her *ego* self—was still alive, but in the deepest recesses of her subconscious mind, she was very much dead. In that moment, her soul believed it had entered *devachan.* Or, to put it more plainly, her soul was in *limbo.*

"Evelyn's soul remained in limbo all those years until 1999, when *you,* Kate, *almost died* in the car accident at the age of twenty-one. That's when her soul found the perfect opportunity to seize the life she believed she was meant to have to achieve that higher level of perfection it had been seeking. You, Kate, provided the perfect vehicle for her soul to reincarnate."

Katy's head dropped along with her jaw, straining to understand what the doctor just said. After a moment or two, she lifted her head back up. "But how could she have picked me if I wasn't dead?"

"Because, Kate, when you almost died in that car accident, your soul was prepared to accept the reincarnation. In that moment, Evelyn stopped you from entering into the bright light and intersected with your soul so that she could relive her life through you."

"But *why me?* Couldn't she have picked someone else?"

"Her soul picked you because of the many parallel life experiences you shared, such as the death of your mothers, your love of singing, your determined personalities, and so on. But most importantly, because of the death of your true loves."

Katy looked at Dr. Fleming and then at Dr. Claeger, with

disbelief in her eyes.

"And then there's the matter of your fiancé, Mike."

"I confronted him," said Katy, "and he admitted he was the stranger in the black Stetson hat who saved me from Mark's burning vehicle."

"Yes, but it goes deeper than that. You see, Mike is the reincarnation of Evelyn's fiancé, Marcus. Evelyn's manifestations prompted Marcus's soul to reincarnate into Mike so that he could later be reunited with his true love."

"But how can that be?"

"Well, how old is Mike?"

"He's twenty-eight," said Katy.

"So he was born in 1977. Marcus died in 1936, so Marcus's soul had plenty of time to reincarnate into Mike." Dr. Fleming paused for a moment to gauge Katy's reaction. There was no reaction, only frozen shock. "Just how much do you know about Mike, Kate?"

She looked up at him, startled, then dropped her head to think. "Other than the fact that he grew up in Pittsburgh and works for the fire department in Morganville, I really don't know much about him. I know that it's his dream to own a ranch...." Katy got a strange look on her face. "Evelyn told me that was Marcus's dream."

Dr. Fleming went on. "And then there is Lilly. With the help of Evelyn's manifestation, the soul of her deceased child also reincarnated when the time was right—into your surviving baby."

Katy stared blankly at the floor, then back up at Dr. Fleming. "Then, Lilly is actually Mike's baby!"

"If I may," interrupted Dr. Claeger. "In her ultimate death, Evelyn gets what she wants. She assumes the 'happily ever after' life she believes she was meant to have—that is, to be reunited with her beloved Marcus and her dear departed Lilly."

Katy hunched her torso down into her lap and buried her face into the palms of her hands. "So basically, you're telling me that Evelyn Brewer has taken over my life here on earth?"

Dr. Fleming looked contrite. "It would appear so, Kate.

Evelyn's heart and soul were imprinted in you. Your paths have intersected to become one and the same."

Katy tugged her hair with clenched fists. She didn't know if she should laugh or cry. Her eyes moved from Dr. Fleming to Dr. Claeger and back to Dr. Fleming. "I still don't get it. Whenever I met with Evelyn, she spoke as if she was aware of everything that was going on. How could she have known?"

Dr. Fleming answered. "According to what you told me, Evelyn had been doing a lot of research on reincarnation as well as the occult. She told you she had studied Animism, and then you discovered the Ouija board in that small, private room in the mansion."

"Yeah...."

"Animism incorporates the unconscious fabrication of a spirit manifestation by someone—usually a medium. A medium connects those who have gone and crossed over into the spirit world with those who are still here in the physical world and channels information from one to the other. From what you told me, I have no doubt that Ruby was more than just a housekeeper. She told you herself that she was good at 'facilitating the melodramatics.' I believe Evelyn sought out Ruby while she was in England so she could tap into those resources. I believe Ruby served as her medium, channeling Evelyn's own spirit, which was still in limbo, as well as the spirits of her beloved Marcus and dear Lilly until they were able to achieve their new state of reincarnation."

Katy sat quietly and swallowed the lump in her throat. "Do you think Mike could have known?"

"I believe that deep down, he knew, but there were things going on in his head that he wasn't fully aware of. For instance, the pendant Mark gave you was the same pendant that Marcus had given Evelyn before his death. It was Evelyn's manifestations, whether they were through meditative prayer or through occult measures, that led Mike to you. He *knew* you were the one—his long lost love, Evelyn—when he saw your pendant, even though he didn't fully understand why. That's why he pursued you so ardently."

"But how did my pendant end up in that room in Evelyn's house, in front of his picture?"

"That we don't know. It may have slipped off your neck while you were there. You don't remember the last time you had worn it?"

Katy slowly lifted her chin until her eyes met Dr. Fleming's. "It was the day I found Mike in my house cooking a surprise dinner for me and Lilly."

Nothing more was iterated until Katy was gathering up her things to leave when Dr. Claeger brought up one final observation. "It's interesting to note that Evelyn ends her memoir with Chapter 13. In bankruptcy, Chapter 13 forgives one's debts and allows them to wipe the slate clean. In Evelyn's mind, this final chapter — thirteen — was the perfect plan that would allow her to begin her life anew."

Katy was about to walk out when she turned to Dr. Fleming. "I have one more question. So how do you explain Tandy?"

"That in itself is a mystery. Perhaps cats really do have nine lives."

Chapter Thirteen
April 13, 2019
Somewhere
Just Outside of Morganville, Pennsylvania

Katy got little sleep that night. The baby was kicking again. *One more month*, she thought, gently rubbing her tummy. She lay in bed with her eyes fixed upon the sheer curtains across the room. A smile formed over her face as the sun triumphantly broke through the horizon, and an orange glow penetrated the room. She rolled out of bed and slipped on her robe, and made her way into the kitchen to make herself a cup of coffee.

As she stirred two teaspoons of instant decaf into the steaming hot water, she peered out her kitchen window. He was already out there, leading his horse, Midnight, to the watering trough. It struck her how handsome he looked in that black Stetson hat. Katy couldn't keep from chuckling. Mike had done his research. The Morgan horse was known as "the breed that chooses you." They are strong and spunky and known for their loyalty and affection. When he purchased it, he said it reminded him of her.

She sat down at the table, clutching her warm mug between her hands, appreciating everything that had happened these last thirteen years. Mike had been promoted to fire chief, he had built the ranch of his dreams, and then she found out she was pregnant again, after all these years—well, that came as a complete surprise.

Just then, Tandy strolled over and gave a little meow while he rubbed against her ankles. She bent over as best she could and gave him a little scratch on the head. "Why, thank you, Tandy, for remembering!" she said out loud. "I wish I knew how old you were, so we could celebrate your special day, too."

A while later, Mike walked into the house and leaned over to give her a kiss on the forehead. "Happy birthday, honey. You should have taken the day off so you could sleep in."

"That's okay. I couldn't sleep anyway. The baby's getting restless. She wants out."

Mike walked over to pour himself a cup of coffee, and Katy got up to give him a hug from behind, but she couldn't quite reach her arms around him because of her protruding belly.

"I had better start getting ready for work," she said, glancing out the window. The sun had already started playing peek-a-boo in and out of the clouds.

While she was busy applying her make-up, she heard the faint sound of her cell phone. She dropped the tube of mascara on the bathroom counter and waddled as fast as she could into the kitchen. *Where did I leave that phone?* There it was, on the kitchen table, buried underneath the newspaper. She picked it up to answer it just in time.

"Hi, Mom, what took you so long? I was about to hang up."

"Sorry Lilly, it took me a while to find my phone."

"The last time you left it in your purse, remember?"

"I know, but then I couldn't find my purse."

"Well, I just called to wish you a Happy Birthday!"

"Awe, thanks, honey, you remembered."

"How could I forget? Today is Friday the 13th!"

"Oh yeah, thanks for reminding me. And, of course, there's a fifty percent chance of rain in the forecast. But enough about me, how are your classes going?"

"They're going fine, Mom! Ugh, didn't you ask me the same thing just two days ago?"

"Yes," said Katy. "But this is your first year of college, and I need a day-by-day update!"

"Okay. I love my classes, and I'm glad I chose psychiatry as my major. I think I might have a predisposition for it. In fact, I've decided I'm going to pursue a master's degree — maybe even a doctoral, who knows?"

"Well, we can certainly afford it, considering the inheritance you received as the beneficiary in Evelyn Brewer's will."

"By the way, how's my little Tandy?" asked Lilly.

"He's a lot slower these days but still hanging in there."

"Well, give him a big hug for me. I miss him so much!"

"I know, but you'll see him when you come home for summer break."

"By then, I'll be a big sister. I can't wait! Whoa, look at the time! I'll have to call you back tomorrow. I've gotta go, or I'll be late for my next class. Bye, Mom, love you!"

"I love you, too, Lilly," Katy ended, with a wistful smile. *And I miss you*, she thought as she set the phone down on the table. Then she noticed the time displayed on the screen. *I'd better get moving if I want to have time to prepare for the afternoon news.*

~*~

After the morning meeting in the newsroom, Katy walked over to her anchor desk to look over her script. She normally reported the early evening news, but since it was her birthday, the afternoon anchorwoman was nice enough to switch with her so she could get home early.

Katy conducted the newscast with her usual professional charm, concluding with, "Thank you for tuning in. This is Katherine Stratton reporting from WKPTV in Pittsburgh."

As she eased out of her seat, she could feel the baby's weight bearing down. She was forced to use her hand to support her lower back as she passed the maze of cubicles and made her way down the hall. She was in a nice new office now, the kind befitting the well-known anchor personality she'd become. This building was a lot nicer than their old PTTV headquarters too, which was eventually sold and refurbished into a restaurant bar.

As she approached her office, she observed through the Plexiglas wall that her room had been decorated with balloons, and a group of coworkers was huddled inside.

"Happy Birthday!" they all yelled as she straddled through the door.

The group moved away from the desk to reveal a

beautifully decorated cake brimming with lighted candles. Katy was so overcome with hormones she almost began to cry. "Thank you so much, everybody!"

"Make a wish and blow out the candles!" shouted her assistant.

"I don't know what to wish for. I've been so blessed." She caressed the beautiful pink stone on her left finger, and lowered her head and closed her eyes. Then she took a long, deep breath and proceeded to extinguish each and every candle in one circling blow.

Everyone clapped, and her assistant had to ask, "So, what did you wish for?"

"I'll never tell," replied Katy, with a devious smile on her face. "But, I do want to say one thing. When we were bought out by CBS and merged with our sister station here at WJPTV, I wasn't sure how things would work out. But you have all become like family to me." Katy released a sad sigh. "I'm just sorry that Mr. Bruckman couldn't have been here to share it with me."

On her way home, Katy passed that familiar billboard on the side of the freeway. The one with the enlarged black and white rendering of the Brewer estate and the big, bold letters underneath that read, **VISIT THE HISTORIC BREWER MANSION TODAY! Just off Exit A-1 on the 46 Freeway.**

Gosh, I haven't been back there since the official ribbon-cutting ceremony, she thought. Her mind couldn't help but return her to that fateful night in 2006 when Evelyn passed in her arms. In a split second, Katy decided to grab the next exit off the freeway. *In honor of **our** birthday, Evelyn.*

Everything had gone just as planned. The highway project had been modified, and the exit was rerouted to avoid encroachment onto the Brewer property. The new exit was a little farther out but made driving there a lot easier. It did eventually lead her to her favorite path. It had since been paved, but it was still shrouded beneath that luscious canopy of trees, newly rejuvenated from the heavy rains experienced in the past weeks.

As Katy approached the mansion, her expression took on an inflated sense of pride when another large sign came into view. MORGAN BREWER MANSION — NATIONAL HISTORIC LANDMARK (1914).

She pulled her car into the designated lot where the vegetable garden once thrived and stepped out of the vehicle. The clouds were circling overhead, and it started to sprinkle, so she held her rain jacket up over her head as she made her way across the parking lot. She stopped to admire the resurrected flower garden, sprouting a rebirth of yellow daffodils, purple hyacinths, and white lilies.

A gardener who was stooped over some bushes doing some early pruning lifted his head. "Sorry, miss, no tours today. The house will re-open at its regular hours next month."

"I know," said Katy. "I was just looking around."

She wandered over to the swing hanging from the big oak tree in front of the house and grabbed the rope in her hand. *Good, they didn't take it down, like I asked.* Then she removed a tissue from her pocket and wiped the wet, wooden board, and carefully positioned herself on it. *I hope it'll still hold me up — I am a little bigger these days,* she giggled. Slowly she began to swing back and forth, thinking about everything that had happened since she first set foot on the property. The nightmares were gone now, and so were the visions. Her soul was finally at peace. She had embraced her fate and looked forward to the future without fear or reservation.

The baby was kicking again. She took a deep, cleansing breath, inhaling the fresh, dewy fragrance emitting from the flower garden, and patted her belly. *Well, Evey, we'd better be on our way. Your father has a special dinner planned for us.*

Carefully, Katy scooted herself off the swing and turned to take one last look at the perfectly renovated Brewer mansion. A gentle breeze blew through her hair, and she looked up at the sky. The rain had stopped, and an explosion of color in the form of a luminous rainbow arched over the mansion in magnificent splendor — proof that *everything* had been restored to its former glory.

ACKNOWLEDGEMENTS

First and foremost, I'd like to thank the High Sierra Writers of Nevada for providing the tools I needed to start me on my publishing journey, and to its members for lending their support.

I'd like to thank my publisher, Karen Fuller of World Castle Publishing, who gave me invaluable advice on what it takes to make a successful novel.

I'd further like to thank my editor, Maxine Bringenberg, whose keen insight and expertise helped me polish my manuscript to make it the best that it could be.

Finally, I'd like to thank my husband, Bill, who supported my obsession in every way, from accompanying me to writers' conferences to preparing the most awesome meals for me while I was locked away in my office for hours on end.

ABOUT THE AUTHOR

Maria Palace is a long time member of the High Sierra Writers. When she is not busy writing, she enjoys spending time with her three grown children, traveling the world, and hiking the beautiful Sierra Nevada landscape with her husband and "soul mate" of over thirty-seven years. You can find her at: mariaapalaceauthor.com.

www.ingramcontent.com/pod-product-compliance
Lightning Source LLC
Chambersburg PA
CBHW020255200626
46816CB00001BA/297